ABSOLUTION

Best Mystery-Suspense-Thriller — 2009 Premier Book Awards

"A New Orleans killer thriller." — Jan Herman, Arts Journal

"Relentless tempo . . . sharp writing." — Kirkus Discoveries

"Creole-flavored suspense, colored with musical connections which Fleet handles with particular deftness." — The Attleboro Sun Chronicle

"A crime drama that stands far above the ordinary whodunit. A wholehearted bravo!" — The Florida Times-Union

DIVA

"Great character development [and] an absolutely fascinating ending . . . a very suspenseful book!" — Feathered Quill Book Reviews

"Fleet subtitles *Diva*, her new thriller, a novel of psychological suspense. That's an understatement." — Jan Herman, *Arts Journal*

"Frank Renzi returns in a relentless hunt through ravaged, drug infested neighborhoods in search of murderous thugs and a psychotic stalker. Another nail-biting page-turner!" — K. G. Hunt

"Fleet takes us inside the head of an obsessed stalker as he lusts after his victim." — Tom Bryson, author of *Too Smart To Die*

NATALIE'S REVENGE

"The coolest detective in literature at the moment, Frank Renzi, [has] a new crime to solve. Natalie is a truly intelligent and seductive character. This is one great author!" — Feathered Quill Book Reviews

"An amazingly great read, fast paced, well written and extremely challenging to put down." — Rebecca's Reads

"Fleet's superbly drawn character, Natalie, pursues revenge for the death of her Vietnamese mother, murdered when Natalie was ten years old. Another excellent read from Susan Fleet." — Tom Bryson, author of *Too Smart To Die*

JACKPOT

A FRANK RENZI NOVEL

"Everyone's a winner in their own mind."

— anonymous

Susan Fleet

Music and Mayhem Press

Published by Music and Mayhem Press

Excerpt of *Natalie's Art*, © 2013 by Susan Fleet

ISBN-10 0984723552

ISBN-13 978-0-9847235-5-3

Cover photographs used with permission:
Illustration of slot machine showing jackpot © stockshoppe at Fotalia
Bullet Holes © andrew7726 at Fotalia

Back cover author photo by Pete Wolbrette

Printed in the United States of America

Novels by Susan Fleet

Absolution

Diva

Natalie's Revenge

Non-fiction ebooks by Susan Fleet

Women Who Dared: Trailblazing 20th Century Musicians
Violinist Maud Powell and Trumpeter Edna White

Dark Deeds: Serial killers, stalkers and domestic homicides

For R. A. L.

CHAPTER 1

Tuesday, April 25, 2000 — Chatham, MA

Florence peered out her living room window. What a dismal day. No sun, just sullen gray clouds like yesterday. And no sign of the cable company van. At 9:30 a man from the cable company had called and said they were having problems in her area. As if she didn't know.

Wavy lines filled the forty-six-inch screen of her new TV set, and static was hissing from the speakers. The man said he'd be here soon to fix it, but that was twenty minutes ago. Where was he? If he didn't hurry up, she'd miss Regis and Kathie Lee. Poor Kathie Lee. Her husband had a roving eye.

Florence and Chuck had been married forty years, and she was certain he hadn't so much as looked at another woman until the day he died.

She looked at the lumps of dirty snow on the driveway across the street. Ginny was in Florida and wouldn't be back until Memorial Day. She sure did miss Ginny. This had been a long lonely winter, terrible storms, the snow piling up in huge drifts. Ever since Chuck died, she had to hire a man to plow her driveway so she could go out for groceries and visit her son.

Her heart skipped a beat as the cable company van stopped in front of the house. Halleluiah! Maybe she'd get to watch Kathie Lee after all. A short chunky man in a blue uniform got out and came up the walk lugging a big metal toolbox. Goodness, why didn't he wear a jacket? It was chilly today.

She opened the front door, then the storm door. A gust of cold air made her shiver. "Thank goodness you're here. Regis and Kathie Lee are on at ten and I'd hate to miss them."

The man glanced at an order form on his clipboard and smiled at her.

"Don't you worry, Florence. I'll have it fixed in a jiffy. You don't mind if I call you Florence, do you? My boss says it's friendlier. We like to keep our customers happy."

What a nice young man, thick blond hair, chubby round cheeks. But beads of sweat dotted his forehead. Strange. "Your name is John. It says so on your pocket. Come in. It's cold out there."

The man went in the living room, walked past her new recliner and set the toolbox down on the carpet in front of the television set.

"What's wrong with the cable connection?" she asked.

"Just a little glitch. Don't worry, I'll fix it." He knelt beside his toolbox and gazed up at her.

His blue eyes had an odd look in them, like a cat about to pounce on a bird. Why was he looking at her like that? It made her nervous.

"Could I have a drink of water? My boss sent me out early this morning because of the problems. I already helped three customers and I'm behind schedule."

Florence hesitated. She wanted to keep an eye on him while he fixed the TV, but she didn't want to be rude. "Goodness, here I am thinking you've got such nice rosy cheeks and you've been hard at work all morning. Wait a minute and I'll get you a glass of water."

She went in the kitchen and stood at the sink. She didn't like being alone in the house with a stranger. Gary was worried about her. He said people might try to take advantage of her. Two days ago the ADT man was here, but he couldn't install the security system until next week. Maybe she should call Gary and tell him a repairman was here. But what good would that do? Her son was miles away in a rehab facility. Her darling boy had come home from the Gulf War with both legs amputated above the knee.

Now Gary was hooked on drugs. Her throat thickened and tears filled her eyes. Half the time when she went to see him he hadn't even shaved. Overcome with sadness, she bit back a sob. Freckles still dotted Gary's cheeks, but now his face was gaunt. It seemed like only yesterday that her smiling six-year-old had gazed up at her with his gap-toothed grin after he ate one of her chocolate chip cookies, put his skinny arms around her and said: "You're the best mom in the whole world!"

With a heavy sigh, she turned on the cold water. Lord knows she couldn't change what happened to Gary. She'd give the repairman his glass of water and get him out of the house. That odd look in his eyes made her uncomfortable. But she was probably worrying over nothing.

Still, her hand trembled as she filled the glass with water.

———

Now that the old biddy had left the room he felt better. On his way to the door he'd put on a big smile. The smile was important. Reassuring. Before he rang the bell he'd made sure his name showed on the flap of his pocket. Then he'd delivered his bullshit lines to Florence. She let him in right away, but she'd been watching him like a hawk ever since.

2

He hated that. His mother watched him too, whenever she could.

He glanced around the room. Florence had money, but she had shitty taste. Her blue pantsuit was hideous. But she'd used her winnings to buy a sleek leather recliner and a big flat-screen TV. He assumed the beat-up sofa with the ugly blue-striped upholstery was headed for the dump.

So was Florence. His lucky winner.

He heard water running in the kitchen and opened his toolbox. Inside were the tools he needed to fix the cable connection. And the other items he brought along for his lucky winners. He took out a yellow plastic bag, spread open the drawstring cord and hid the bag behind the TV.

Footsteps sounded in the hall. His heart thrummed in anticipation. He mopped his sweaty face with his shirtsleeve. His uniform shirt stuck to his back, damp with sweat.

The old biddy came back and handed him a glass of water and gave him a prissy smile, a smile that disappeared when she saw the latex gloves on his hands. He gulped some water, made his eyes go wide with innocence and beamed her a big smile. "I've got eczema. My hands bleed sometimes. I wouldn't want to mess up your carpet."

"Oh. Well, that's thoughtful of you. It's brand new and so is the television set. I wish my husband were here to enjoy it with me. He passed on three years ago."

"Pretty exciting hitting the jackpot, huh? Lucky you."

She bit her lip, frowning at him now, a stooped old woman with wispy white hair tinged yellow. Why didn't she go to the hairdresser? She had plenty of money. He set the empty water glass on the table beside the recliner. "I'm about done, but I need you to help me finish."

"You do? Why?"

"I need you to unplug the TV and plug it in again when I tell you."

Her frown deepened. "I don't know . . . It's hard for me to bend over. I've got arthritis."

He gazed at her silently. Made his eyes go cold. *Do as I say, you old biddy.*

The flesh on her cheeks quivered and her shoulders slumped. He loved it when they realized he had the power. She was old and weak. He was young and strong. Alone together in an isolated house. Exquisite. A shiver racked him and he felt himself grow hard.

With a heavy sigh, she went to the electrical outlet on the wall. To steady herself, she held onto the table that held the TV set, got down on her knees and bent over the plug. Intent on her task, she didn't hear him creep up behind her. Wisps of yellow-white hair curled over the collar of her blouse, and he could smell her perfume, a disgusting lilac scent.

He plunged the plastic bag over her head, pushed her facedown on the floor and yanked the cord tight around her neck. She screamed, but the bag muffled the sound.

She put up a struggle, thrashing violently. It took him by surprise. Before he could react, she rolled onto her back and lashed out at him, flailing her arms blindly. Her forearm slammed against his ear and sent pain shooting through his head.

Enraged, he punched her face. Even through the plastic bag, he felt her nose crunch.

She let out a muffled squawk and thrashed her legs, kicking at him.

How dare she fight him? He couldn't hold her down! He pulled his toolbox closer, grabbed a heavy wrench and slammed it down on her head.

Her body went still. Moments later blood seeped out of a rip in the plastic bag. Disgusting.

He yanked the drawstring tighter.

Still she fought him, groping at the bag with both hands and moaning.

How dare she fight him! Enraged, he yelled, "Stop fighting me!"

With a mighty heave, he rolled her onto her stomach, pinned her arms behind her back and sat on her. She made grunting sounds and kicked her feet, thump-thump-thump, against the carpet.

Blood soaked the carpet beneath her head. He pulled the cord tighter, trying not to look at the blood. He couldn't stand the sight of blood. He studied the wavy lines on the TV screen instead, counting the seconds.

Her struggles grew weaker. He pulled the drawstring tighter, savoring the power he had over her, feeling the ache build in his groin.

At last she lay still.

Aglow with triumph, he rose to his feet, unzipped his fly and stroked himself. His breathing grew ragged as the power swelled and intensified. The power and the glory.

He shuddered as the spasm coursed through him. A glorious release.

But there was no time to savor the moment.

He rolled her onto her back. Blood had seeped into the carpet in a widening stain. The sight of it sickened him. But she'd brought it on herself, fighting him, making his head hurt.

From his toolbox he took out the nip bottle of J&B with the red letters and the red cap. His autograph.

In her desperate attempt to breathe, her mouth had sucked a deep hollow in the bag. Just like the others.

He shoved the J&B nip into the hollow.

"I guess you weren't so lucky after all, right, Florence?"

Now it was time to tidy up.

It took him less than a minute to reset the cable connection. He checked the television screen. The picture was fine, Regis and Kathy Lee joking about something.

4

JACKPOT

Florence was lying face up on the floor with the yellow plastic bag over her head. He folded her arms over her chest and noticed the bracelet on her wrist, tiny oval scarabs in a gold setting.

Beautiful. She'd want him to have it, he was sure.

He undid the clasp, removed the bracelet and shoved it in his pocket.

His eyes swept the room. The water glass!

He put the glass in his toolbox and grabbed his clipboard.

Everything was perfect. He blew Florence a kiss and left.

Tonight he would look for his next lucky winner.

CHAPTER 2

Wednesday, April 26, 2000 — Milton, MA

At 4:50 a.m. his cell phone went off like an air-raid alarm. Dead bodies seldom turned up at convenient times. He grabbed his cell phone off the bedside table and punched on to silence it.

"Yo, Frank. Rise and shine, baby. Got a gang hit in your territory." Detective Rafe Hawkins worked the Boston PD Narcotics Unit. He also served on a taskforce that targeted gangs. Rafe's favorite saying: *Drugs and guns go together like ham and eggs.* Homicide Detective Frank Renzi tended to agree.

Conscious of his wife stirring in the other bed, Frank got up and went in the bathroom and shut the door. "What's up? Where are you?"

"Uniform patrolling Mass Ave found a banger in the gutter, one shot to the head, called me a half-hour ago. I'm at the scene, three blocks up from Boston Med Center."

"Gimme fifteen and I'm there." He splashed cold water on his face and gazed into the mirror over the sink. Surrounded by puffy skin, dark bloodshot eyes stared back at him. He'd been in his basement office until one a.m. poring over three new cases. When he got in bed, he couldn't sleep, ugly crime scene photos dancing through his head like stills from a horror movie.

He combed his fingers through his dark hair. No gray hairs yet, but he was only thirty-seven. If he didn't start getting some sleep, he'd look like Methuselah. Dark stubble covered his cheeks and jaw, but he'd worry about that later. He brushed his teeth and crept into the bedroom. In the twin bed on the left, Evelyn was sound asleep, her auburn hair spread over the pillow.

He put on his navy running suit, strapped on his Sig Sauer and left the house. The dusky light of dawn was creeping over his neighborhood in Milton. Two minutes later he got on the Southeast Expressway, the thirteen-mile divided highway that people south of Boston used to get into the city. Wondering which gangbanger caught a bullet this time, he took the Mass Ave

6

exit and sat at a red light beside the sprawling Boston Medical Center complex. He yawned, wishing he'd stopped for a cup of coffee.

The light turned green and he swung onto Mass Ave. Three blocks up, he parked behind a Boston PD cruiser, got out and flashed his badge at a BPD officer directing snarled traffic, sleepy-eyed folks headed for work clocking the sheet-covered body in the gutter.

Elegant redbrick townhouses with bay windows lined this part of Mass Ave. Someone had tied yellow crime scene tape to a wrought-iron fence in front of one townhouse and fastened it to a telephone pole fifteen yards away. On the sidewalk numbered pieces of folded cardboard marked evidence. A dozen distraught women stood behind the tape in bathrobes and slippers, older black women, talking in low voices.

A hulking six-foot-four wide-body with ebony skin and large dark eyes trotted up to him. Trash-talking Rafe Hawkins played center on the District 4 hoop team, a fearsome sight below a basketball hoop. Now he wore a gray running suit and a grim-faced expression. "We got a few shell casings, not much else."

Frank tilted his head at the onlookers. "Any wits?"

"Nobody talks when cops are around. Too many eyes watching. Might get some later."

They ducked under the yellow tape and Rafe pulled back the covering on the body. A young black male, clean-shaven but for the soul patch under his bottom lip. He wore baggy sweatpants, a green hoodie and expensive sneakers. Blood pooled under his head, a ragged wound visible on one side of his face. In death he appeared young and defenseless. Another wasted life, Frank thought. Too many kids involved with gangs these days. When he caught the killer, another life would go in the toilet.

"Heavy firepower," Frank said. "Was he carrying?"

"Had a Glock-nine in his hand. We bagged and tagged it. Won't know if he got off a shot till they test his hands for residue."

"I don't recognize him. Who is he?"

"DeVon Jones, age twenty-three, busted for dealing, served most of a five-year stint at the House of Correction, released three weeks ago. We keep tabs on 'em, so I got an email. He runs with the Ashmont Hill gang in Dorchester. Bad move, coming here alone. Not his territory."

Frank scanned the crowd and saw a little black kid, nine or ten maybe, peeping around two older black women. The kid made eye contact, then turned and ran north on Mass Ave toward Symphony Hall.

He nudged Rafe's arm. "The kid knows something."

They ran after him, the kid scampering away like a frightened rabbit, skinny arms pumping. One block later he grabbed a wrought-iron fencepost and swung himself around a corner. He wasn't big but he was fast.

They reached the side street in time to see him dart into an alley. Most days Frank did a five-mile run, but Rafe had longer legs and outpaced him. Five feet from the alley, they stopped.

"Looks young," Rafe said, "but he could be packing."

True, and more gunslingers could be waiting in the alley. After eighteen years with Boston PD, Frank had two basic rules. Never let down your guard. Always assume the worst. He'd never forget his gut-churning fear when he responded to a homicide call—a Haitian woman with her throat slashed—and her husband attacked him with a machete.

Another time two fleeing bank robbers emptied semi-automatics at him, slugs buzzing by his ear like deadly mosquitoes. Just last month a former mental patient with an AK-47 had taken a hostage in a South End tenement and held off an army of police officers for three hours.

The memories flashed through his mind in a nanosecond, made his mouth go dry.

They drew their service weapons and approached the alley.

An adrenaline buzz jumped his heart rate. What awaited them around the corner? An innocent kid or a posse of gunslingers?

Rafe sprinted to the opposite side of the opening. No shots.

Frank gave a nod. Weapons raised, they sprang into the alley. The stink of rotted garbage from two overflowing dumpsters hit his nostrils. Still no shots, but the gunslingers might be watching inside an apartment, taking aim from a window.

His heart pounded like a machine gun. He looked skyward, eyes darting from one five-story building to the other. Metal fire escapes zigzagged down the sides of both buildings. No one on the fire escapes. A pair of jeans and two polo shirts flapped on a clothesline outside a third-floor window.

Sound from a radio or a TV drifted through an open window on the left. But no gunfire. Five-story buildings on both sides. Five floors of windows, dozens of vantage points. He glanced at Rafe. Rafe was eyeballing the windows, his dark-skinned face set in fierce concentration.

They marched down the alley. Two heart-pounding minutes later they reached the other end. No gunfire. No gunslingers. No sign of the kid.

Rafe lowered his Glock, looked at him and shrugged. "The little bugger got away."

"You think he lives here?"

"No telling." Rafe checked his watch and gave him a sardonic grin. "Now we got the excitement over with, want to grab breakfast? Come back in an hour, we can talk to the folks that live here."

Frank holstered his Sig Sauer. "Sounds like a plan."

Ten minutes later they were sitting in a booth at Waffles and Wings, a soul food diner on the lower end of Mass Ave, sipping the steaming black coffee the waitress had brought them without asking. They came there often and she knew them by sight. The odor of frying bacon and sausage permeated the air as harried waitresses delivered breakfast to hungry patrons.

Other than a few white and Asian workers from Boston City Hospital, most were African-American. To their left, several diners perched on stools along a yellow Formica counter. A bell dinged as the chef slapped two plates onto the shelf behind the counter.

"How's my favorite horseback rider?" Rafe said, eyeing him over the rim of his coffee mug.

His daughter Maureen rode at a stable in Milton and Rafe had attended several horseshows there. Unlike Frank's house, the stable was in a ritzy section of Milton, and Rafe's ebony skin stood out in the sea of white faces. Not that it bothered Rafe. Few things did. At twenty-nine, he was living the good life, owned a three-decker in Dorchester where he lived with his chic fashion-designer wife and their two cute-as-a-button kids.

"Mo's doing great," he said, "made the Dean's list her first semester."

"Uh-huh. Probably made the hit list, too, fine-looking girl like that. What I hear there's plenty of horny pre-med students at Johns Hopkins."

The waitress, an older black woman with wiry arms and a world-weary air, delivered their breakfast: waffles and sausage for Frank; a three-egg omelet, sausage and grits for Rafe.

"I gave her my birth-control lecture when I drove her down to Baltimore to get her settled in."

Rafe paused with a forkful of omelet halfway to his mouth. "You? Not Evelyn?"

He poured maple syrup on his waffle, wishing he'd kept his mouth shut. At last he said, "Be serious. Evelyn thinks birth control is evil. You know how it is with Catholics. Every sperm is sacred."

Rafe flashed a sly grin and started humming: "Every Sperm Is Sacred" from the Monty Python film, *The Meaning of Life.*

"I got her a credit card, had the bills sent to me. I told her if I didn't see a pharmacy charge for the pills every month, I'd cancel the card."

"And? So?" Rafe asked, methodically slicing his sausage into bite-sized portions.

"So she's taking them. She hasn't mentioned any boyfriends, but at least she's protected." He grinned. "Wait till *your* daughter's a teenager. Ten years from now you'll be beating them off with a stick."

"You got that right. So, uh, how's Evelyn doing?"

He didn't want to talk about Evelyn. Since he'd joined the District 4 hoop team ten years ago, he and Rafe had become close personal friends, but most of the confidences they shared about their personal lives came from Rafe, not him.

"Not so hot now that Maureen's gone. She used to take Evelyn shopping, you know, for clothes and whatever doodads women buy at the mall. Now she just mopes around the house."

"Hey, take her to a movie."

"She won't go to movies. Too many people. Too many germs."

Rafe stopped chewing and stared at him. "Too many germs. Far out. Somebody better investigate that, find out where all those germs are."

"Hey, dummy, the germs are on the too-many people."

A cackling laugh from Rafe. To the Beatles tune "Lonely People," Rafe sang in a low voice, "Ohhh, look at all those germs and people." Drummed a riff on the table with his fingers.

They cracked up, and several heads turned to see what they were laughing about. But talking about Evelyn's hang-ups was one thing. Living with them was another.

"I suggested a part-time job, figured it might distract her, but she said it would interfere with church. She goes to early Mass every day."

"You got a tough row to hoe, buddy." Gazing at him over his coffee cup. "Hope you got something going on the side."

He ate a bite of sausage, took his time chewing. Rafe played a mean bass in a jazz combo. Much of their friendship revolved around their passion for jazz and basketball, activities that allowed them to forget the ugliness of the mean streets they policed every day. Rafe also had a mistress, a white woman he'd met at the steady jazz gig he played in Newport, his hometown.

Frank had met her once. But no one knew about Gina, not even Rafe, and he intended to keep it that way.

"What I've got is three dead lottery winners, all of them in New England."

Rafe cocked an eyebrow. "Lottery winners? What's up with that?"

Relieved to escape any more discussion about his personal life, he said, "Remember the FBI agent I told you about? The guy I met at Quantico? He's convinced it's a serial killer and asked me to help."

"Told you that course would load you up with more work. Like you don't have enough already."

True. He thought about the black kid, the fear he'd seen in the boy's eyes. He wanted to know why the kid was so scared, but the odds of finding him were slim. Too many cases, too little time.

"I don't mind. Ross is a good guy, and it never hurts to have a connection at the Bureau. He sent me the three case files." The files that had kept him awake last night. Three elderly women murdered in their homes. If Ross was right, the killer was probably stalking his next victim right now.

Frank pushed his plate aside. "You set?"

Rafe grabbed the check. "I am. You set for the big game? We gonna whup those District 6 losers or what?" When it came to basketball, trash-talking Rafe had a killer-attitude.

Amused, Frank said, "Beat 'em by twenty for sure."

But as they left the diner his mood darkened. He needed to change his clothes, but he didn't want to go home and face Evelyn. *"Where were you, Frank? I woke up and you were gone and you didn't even leave me a note!"*

Screw that. He kept some spare clothes in his office at the District 4 station. A quick shave, a change of clothes, and he'd go back to the Mass Ave murder scene and talk to some residents. Any kind of luck, someone might know who the little black kid was.

After lunch he'd dig into the files FBI Special Agent Ross Dunn had sent him. The Jackpot Killer files.

CHAPTER 3

Suffolk Downs, East Boston

"Ladieeees and gentlemen! The fifth race post parade is about to begin!"

Booming over the clubhouse loudspeaker, the announcement brought a familiar thrill of excitement. Nigel Heath looked down at the horses, dappled in sunlight, jockeys in bright-colored silks coaxing their mounts to show off for the gamblers at the rail. The tote board flashed: Post time: twelve minutes.

"I thought this morning's rehearsal went well," Vicky said, beaming at him. "I love the Gershwin, especially the *Rhapsody in Blue.*"

He smiled at her, his beloved Vicky, super-talented and gorgeous, liquid brown eyes, sensuous lips, and smooth olive skin, set off to perfection by her gold-print dress.

"I chose it for the clarinet solo and you played it spot on." He caressed her forearm and murmured, "Seductive and sexy, like you."

She ran her tongue over her lips suggestively and grinned.

He glanced around Legends Bar and Grill. No Pops musicians at Suffolk Downs on a Wednesday, just hard-core gamblers. If the BSO bigwigs found out about their affair, his shot at the Pops conducting job was over. Conductors weren't supposed to get romantically involved with the players.

"I wish you were in Boston more often," she said. "Maybe you'll get the Pops gig."

"A middle-aged Brit with a bald spot? No chance, luv. They want a matinee idol like that flashy bloke that's conducting next week. Give him a screen test, he'll be the next teen heartthrob."

He checked the tote board. Post time: ten minutes. His pulse quickened. He'd studied the racing form this morning. The six-horse in this race was the only nag worth betting on.

"But you're a better conductor, Nigel. The players love you, and you're great with the audience. Must be that British charm."

Touched by her loyalty, loath to admit how badly he wanted the job, he said, "Doesn't charm the BSO bigwigs. They think I'm a Hollywood hack because I conduct film scores. And the Vegas gigs don't help."

"You must be on the short list. What does your agent say?"

"Hale's a smooth operator, but he's not ICM. They manage the superstars. Hale deals the jack-of-all-trade blokes like me. I'd better call him. Just past noon in L.A., he's not swimming in the martini-pool yet."

Vicky's eyes grew somber. "You're not going to bet, are you?"

"Not me. Quit that months ago."

"I saw you checking the tote board. Maybe we shouldn't come here."

"Go on, luv, it's good fun." He rose to his feet and took out a pack of Winstons. "I need a cigarette. Bloody stupid you can't smoke in here. I'll pop outside for a butt, call Hale on my mobile, be back in no time." Vicky rarely smoked, after a romp in bed, perhaps, or when she was anxious about something.

"Tell him to get you the Pops gig!" she called after him.

Her words echoed in his mind as he left the restaurant, but landing the Pops gig wouldn't solve his current crisis. He rushed downstairs, thinking of all the wagers he'd put on horses over the years. But this was different. Intent on reaching the betting booths, he pushed through a swinging door and bumped into a slim woman in a stylish red dress.

"I beg your pardon," he said. "How clumsy of me!"

She eyed his blue shirt and tailored slacks. Apparently he passed muster. Her frown melted and she flashed a saucy grin. "What's that accent? British?"

"Dead right." He smiled and saw a flicker of interest in her eyes. God knows what women saw in him. He was no Robert Redford, but he'd discovered long ago that his smile made women melt. No time for flirting now, though. Goldilocks was waiting. He nodded pleasantly and walked away.

Goldilocks was the four-year-old filly he'd spotted in the racing form. The morning line had her at three to one, but the tote board was showing *nine* to one. It was clearly an overlay, much higher odds than would normally be expected. The morning line was only the handicapper's prediction, nothing sacred about it, but odds like this were hard to resist.

"Five minutes to post time," the announcer said, urging people to place their bets.

The fifth race was a mile and an eighth. According to the racing form, Goldilocks had made strong stretch runs in her three previous races, and her jockey was tops. The favorite was a big gray. Gray was his lucky color, but the gray was in position four. Goldilocks was in slot six, his lucky number.

Through a large plate-glass window he watched Goldilocks prance down the track. She looked ready to run. He checked the board. Bloody hell! Now the odds on Goldilocks were *twelve* to one! The bettors were backing the favorite, which didn't have a chance, in his opinion.

13

Flushed with excitement, he went to the hundred-dollar window where the high rollers did business. After Hale threatened to pull the plug on the Vegas gigs, he'd promised to stop gambling. He'd made the same promise to his ex-wife, but bloody hell, she was the cause of his current difficulty. Joanna wanted five grand by the end of the month, had threatened to haul him into court if she didn't get it.

Panic hit him like a fist. He didn't have it, behind on all his credit cards, paying off more loans than he could count. He joined the queue at the hundred-dollar window behind two men in flashy suits. Maybe he'd split his bet between Goldilocks and the favorite. That way he couldn't lose.

Four minutes to post time. The queue moved forward, and the man ahead of him began placing his bet.

Guilt crept into his heart like a poisonous fog. Vicky thought he'd quit gambling. He'd fallen in love with her the first time he conducted Pops two years ago. He was forty-one, eight years older than Vicky, but that didn't seem to matter. He'd told her about his previous problems, though not the size of his debts, and she had convinced him to stop. Vicky thought gambling was stupid. He hated to let her down.

Three minutes to post time. The man in front of him left the window and Nigel stepped forward.

"What'll it be?" the clerk said.

"Fifth race. Three thousand to win on the six-horse."

The clerk's eyes darted to the bills Nigel put down, then to his face. "Yes, sir. Fifth race, three thousand to win on number six." The man counted his money, punched the computer and handed him the ticket.

He left the window with the sickening feeling he'd done something stupid. But it was out of his hands now. A burning sensation seared his chest as he raced upstairs to the restaurant.

Vicky was staring at the track, nibbling her thumbnail. He kissed her cheek and slid into his seat.

She beamed him a radiant smile. It made his heart ache. Raven-black hair curled in ringlets around her face, and round black-rimmed glasses framed her velvety-brown eyes.

"I got us a hot-fudge sundae," she said. "With mocha ice cream. But I only ordered one. We can split it. If I don't take off ten pounds—"

"You're gorgeous the way you are, luv. Who wants a skinny little string bean?" Nothing wrong with Vicky's appetite, but he loved women with healthy appetites.

"What did Hale say?"

"Same old California-speak. He just booked me a gig in Cincinnati. That's the good news."

"And?"

14

"My ex-wife is badgering him. Badgering me, actually. I'm a bit behind on alimony, and her career's on the skids. Joanna's forty-six. Hollywood's not keen on older actresses."

Vicky reached over and stroked his hand. "If you're really short, I can lend you—"

"Not a chance, luv, wouldn't hear of it."

The announcer's agitated voice came over the loudspeakers: "They're in the gate!"

"Let's watch the race," he said. "Should be a good one."

His palms dampened with sweat. *Come on, Goldilocks, win one for Nigel.*

The favorite broke in front, followed by a cluster of four horses. Goldilocks was on the outside, running easily, clear of the pack. So far so good.

"This ice cream is delicious," Vicky said.

Her words barely registered. He focused on Goldilocks. Going into the first turn she stumbled. His heart leapt into his throat. Bloody hell, if she tossed her jockey, he was done for.

But no, she recovered. Now she was off and running again.

"Have a bite, Nigel."

He stared at the chocolate sauce and the mountain of whipped cream. Just looking at it made him queasy, but he managed a smile. "I'll have the cherry."

Holding the stem, Vicky fed him the cherry. He sucked it into his mouth and concentrated on the race. Bloody hell! Goldilocks was running third, four lengths off the pace. But she was a sprinter. The jockey was probably saving her for the stretch run.

"Nigel," Vicky said quietly.

"Mmmm," he said, unable to tear his eyes off Goldilocks. The crowd roared as the horses rounded the final turn. Coming into the stretch, Goldilocks passed the two-horse. His heart pounded. Goldilocks was in second at the eighth pole with two hundred yards to go. But the favorite was two lengths ahead. Why didn't the stupid sod of a jockey whip her?

"Nigel, this is delicious. You should try some."

He held his breath as Goldilocks moved up on the leader. The jockey was whipping her now. About time. And it worked! She was gaining on the favorite. *Come on, Goldilocks, you can do it!*

The crowd went wild as Goldilocks and the gray horse raced neck and neck to the finish line. They crossed it together, so close he couldn't tell who won. Exhausted, he sank back in his chair and wiped his sweaty palms on his trousers. A photo finish. Fractions of an inch would decide his fate.

A monumental dread swept over him.

"Nigel, what's wrong? Your face is all sweaty. You didn't bet, did you?"

He forced a smile. "Of course not."

A roar went up from the crowd. He didn't dare check the board.

What if Goldilocks lost?

Terrified of the answer, he forced himself to look.

Bloody hell, the gray horse was the winner!

Numbed by the disaster that had just befallen him, he slumped in his chair. Now the three-thousand-dollar advance from his credit card was gone, and Joanna wanted another five. He wanted to smash his head against the wall. He'd gone back on his word and lied to Vicky. He'd lost control and acted stupid.

He vowed never to bet on another horse as long as he lived.

"Look at that gray horse in the winner's circle," Vicky said, pointing down at the track. "Isn't he beautiful?"

———

Seated at his desk with a telephone clamped to his ear, Frank watched a screen-saver airplane swoop across his computer monitor. A low hum purred from a ceiling vent, sending recycled air through his office. The voice on the phone droned on: ". . . no reason to kill her. My kids are devastated."

Loath to interrupt, he swiveled his chair and studied a brass plaque on the wall. Anything to avoid the ugly crime scene photographs on his desk.

The plaque cited Detective Franklin Sullivan Renzi for his work with underprivileged children. When he wasn't busy hunting killers, he coached a middle-school basketball team in Mattapan.

Now, two thick murder books sat on his desk.

A third case file lay open in front of him. Five minutes ago he'd called the victim's son. He stifled a yawn. It had been a long day but he didn't feel like going home, didn't want to deal with more problems there.

A muscle worked in his jaw as the son's voice, full of anguish and rage, said, "They keep asking for Grammy. Why can't you catch the bastard?"

"George, I'm very sorry about your mother—" And listened to another litany of sorrows.

He studied a snapshot on his desk, a photo of him with his arms around two boys, his rangy six-foot-one frame dwarfing them. The twins played on the basketball team he coached. Their proud mom had taken the picture and sent him a copy. Dad was AWOL, like a lot of black fathers these days. Too bad he wasn't coaching them now. That was a lot easier than listening to the grief-stricken son of a dead lottery winner.

"Her necklace is missing."

Instantly alert, Frank picked up his pen and jotted a note. Last year his boss had sent him to the FBI Academy to take a course on serial killers. The behavioral analysis instructor said serial killers often took trophies, a souvenir they used to relive their crimes later. The most depraved killers took body parts. Some took underwear, panties or bras. Others took jewelry.

"You're sure?"

"Of course I'm sure. It was a birthday gift. She wore it when we went out for dinner. I took her picture."

"A picture? Great! Can you send it to me?"

George agreed to Fed-Ex the photo, and Frank promised to call if he had any news.

Sickened by the brutal murders, he rubbed his eyes. Ross Dunn, the FBI agent he'd met at Quantico, had asked him to act as liaison on the case. Three murders in Vermont, Connecticut and, most recently, a town west of Boston. Three Caucasian females, the youngest fifty-nine, the oldest sixty-seven. Two were widows, one had never married, all lived alone.

The telling detail: before the murders all three had collected lottery prizes ranging from one million to six million dollars. In each case, cash and credit cards were readily accessible but not stolen. George's mother was the first. A sixty-three-year-old widow, Lillian Bernard had lived in Vermont. George, her only son, lived in California.

He opened his desk drawer and took out a pack of Merit Lights. Five months ago he'd pretty much quit smoking, but George had gotten to him, his voice shaking with grief and outrage. Frank didn't blame him. His own mother had died three months ago, and he was dealing with his own grief.

George's kids missed their grandmother. His daughter Maureen was in college, but she missed her grandmother, too. He clenched his jaw, recalling the final days when he visited his mother, a shadow of her vibrant self, wasted by the cancer that ravaged her. He missed her, missed confiding in her, telling her things he would never reveal to his father. Or his wife.

He left his office and rode the elevator downstairs. The District 4 lobby was noisy: police-radio chatter and the belligerent voice of a man mouthing off at the officer who'd collared him. Later it would be worse. District 4 covered the South End, Back Bay and the Fenway, a wide area with a dozen colleges and 27,000 residents. And after dark the thugs came out to play.

He went outside and lit up, his first cigarette in two weeks. The first drag gave him a head rush. Clouds hung low in the dusky sky. He hunched his shoulders against the chilly wind, listened to horns honking, drivers jockeying for position in rush-hour traffic. In the distance, a siren squawked, the distinctive whoop of an ambulance headed for Boston City Hospital a few blocks away.

He should call Evelyn and tell her he'd be late, but he didn't feel like it. He didn't want to go home. His marriage had been on life-support for years, held together by his daughter. Now it was dead, a dry husk with the juice sucked out of it. A pang of regret hit him. Eighteen years ago he couldn't wait to go home and play with his daughter.

Now when he pulled into his driveway, he felt only dread, the essential question being: How would he get through another night with Evelyn?

When he really wanted to be with Gina.

Was she home, he wondered, or still at work? He decided to call her, but when he took out his cell, it began to ring. He punched on. "Renzi."

"Frank, you home?" The distinctive bass voice of Lieutenant Harrison Flynn, his supervisor.

"No, outside the D-4, getting some fresh air." *I'm in no hurry to go home these days.*

"I just got a call from the State Police. We got another dead lottery winner down on Cape Cod."

"Damn! I just got off the phone with the first victim's son. Where was this one?"

"Chatham. Postman rang her bell around noon, got no response and called police."

"Thanks for the heads-up, Hank. I'm on it."

He flipped the cigarette in the gutter, returned to his office and studied the photographs on his desk. George's mother sprawled on the floor, her head encased in a yellow plastic bag. The close-up of her face after they removed the bag was heartbreaking: a look of horror, eyes shut tight, her mouth open in a silent scream. He was glad George hadn't seen it.

First Lillian, then another, and another. Now there were four.

He was no gambler, but he'd bet money the Jackpot Killer was already trolling for his next victim.

A palpable feeling of outrage jumped his heart rate.

"You sick bastard," he muttered. "I'm going to get you."

CHAPTER 4

Thursday, April 26 — Chatham

"Whoever did it was sick," Sergeant Cooper said. "Florence was a wonderful person, a great lady."

An older man with gray hair and a weathered face, the Chatham police chief was outraged. Frank didn't blame him. Earlier, a State Police detective had showed him the crime scene photos: Florence lying on the floor, her head encased in a yellow plastic bag. He couldn't begin to imagine her panic, her desperate struggle to breathe. A close-up showed a nip bottle of J&B in the hollow her mouth had made in the bag.

The Jackpot Killer's signature, letting them know he'd killed again.

But this time there was blood. Frank tried to picture it: Florence fighting for her life, the killer slamming her head with something, crushing her skull.

A sickening image. *An evil deed by an evil man.*

The FBI instructor had warned them not to get emotionally involved. Easier said than done.

"She didn't deserve to be murdered, that's for sure. Does she have relatives around here?"

"Her husband died a few years ago. She's got a son, but I gather he's been a problem."

"What kind of problem?"

"Gary joined the Army, got sent overseas during the Gulf War back in 1990. From what I understand, his vehicle hit an IED. Two of his buddies died and Gary lost both legs. Sad. Twenty-eight-year old guy comes home with no legs. Then his wife left him, turned him bitter, I guess. He lived with his parents for a while. Florence and Chuck built a wheelchair ramp so he could get in and out of the house. But Gary started drinking and got into drugs. Chuck got tired of it and threw him out."

"Where's Gary now?"

19

"In a rehab facility up in Plymouth. Florence used to visit him every week. I had to do the notification. Gary started swearing and cursing. I guess he'll inherit the money. Hard to say if that'll help or hurt."

"Straighten up and fly right, or use it to buy drugs?"

"Wouldn't want to bet, either way," Cooper said.

"The front door was unlocked?"

"Yep. The postman said he had a package for her, rang the bell and got no answer. He saw Florence's car in the driveway and got worried, thought maybe she had a heart attack, so he tried the door and it was unlocked. He went in and saw her. What with the blood and all, he figured she was dead. So he backed out the door and called the station from his mail van."

"Does Gary have a key?"

"I don't know. I found the house keys in Florence's purse, used them to lock up. The thing is, a lot of older folks around town go south for the winter. I think Florence was the only one on her street that didn't. The woman that lives in the house across the street goes to Florida every year."

Located on the lower elbow of Cape Cod, Chatham currently had 6,625 residents, more in the summer probably, but winters were bleak on the Cape, no surfing, no swimming, no outdoor concerts, just ice and snow and freezing weather. On his way to the station, Frank had seen a few maple trees with tiny green buds. They seemed out of place, with patches of dirty snow below them, leftovers of the winter storms.

"It's a damn shame," Cooper said. "Florence was a sweet lady. I'd see her at the grocery store most every week and chat with her."

"Is that where she bought the lottery ticket?"

"No, at a gas station in the center of town. The *Cape Cod Times* did a feature article when she collected the prize. You think the guy did this before?"

"Could be." He didn't want to start any rumors. "I need to talk to Gary." Florence's son, a man with his own problems. A man who stood to inherit millions if he was the beneficiary of Florence's will.

Cooper grimaced. "I don't envy you. He's already bitter. This might put him over the edge."

———

The dark-haired young woman behind the reception desk at the Plymouth Rehabilitation Center greeted him with a smile. "How can I help you today?"

"I'd like to talk to Gary Mason."

Her smile faded, replaced by a frown. "This might not be a good time."

"Detective Frank Renzi, Boston PD." He flashed his photo-ID. "I need to talk to him."

"Oh. Well, in that case, he's in Room 28." She pointed to a hallway. "Down there."

He wove his way through a maze of corridors. The facility was bright and airy, sunlight streaming through skylights in the ceiling, the white walls lined with cheery posters that exhorted "You can do it!"

He stopped at Room 28 and tapped on the door.

An angry voice filtered through the door. "What? I'm busy!"

"Frank Renzi, Boston Police Department. I'd like to talk to you."

Silence. After a long minute, the door opened. Seated in a wheelchair, Gary Mason glowered at him. "Boston PD, huh. Why should I talk to you?"

"I'm investigating your mother's murder."

Mason gazed at him, expressionless, finally said, "Okay. Come on in."

Frank stepped into a room clearly designed to accommodate someone in a wheelchair. A tiled floor, a large bed, a low chest of drawers and a small desk. A wide door led to a bathroom. Three photos stood on the bureau, a mini-family history: gap-toothed Gary in a Little League uniform; Gary in a cap and gown at his high school graduation; Gary in his Army uniform, before he went off to war. And came home with no legs.

Gary Mason rolled his wheelchair to the desk. Beyond it, doublewide windows overlooked green shrubbery and a well-kept lawn. A telephone, a notepad and pen, and a glass of water sat on the desk.

"I was on the phone with the funeral director," Gary said. "Making the arrangements." His agate blue eyes were full of fury. A dark beard covered much of his face, and his long dark-brown hair was pulled into a ponytail similar to those worn by Vietnam War vets. A sleeveless T-shirt revealed muscular arms. Cut-off jeans exposed what remained of his legs, which had been amputated above the knee.

"I'm sorry for your loss," Frank said.

"Yeah?" A curt laugh. "Which one. My legs? Or my mother."

"Both. But I'm here about your mother. I want to catch her killer, and I'm hoping you can help me."

The agate-blue eyes flickered momentarily, then resumed their flat level gaze. "I'd like to catch the fucker, too. How come you're on the case? Too hot for the Chatham cops to handle?"

Gary clearly had no use for cops. "You mind if I sit down?"

"Sure. Pull up a chair. I'd offer you a beer, but the assholes that run this place won't let me have any."

"Right about now, I could use a beer." He dragged a blond-wood chair with a padded seat over to the desk and gestured at Gary's legs. "How'd it happen? War injury?"

Clearly not expecting the question, Gary studied him for several seconds. "Yeah. A fucking war injury in a war nobody gives a shit about."

"Which war was that?"

21

"The Gulf War. Fucking IED blew up my Jeep, killed two of my buddies."

"And changed your life forever."

"You got that right. They ship me home, slap me into rehab. Like they're gonna fix me up and life's gonna be great." His thin lips curled inside the dark beard. "They got these cheerleader slogans, you know? But at the end of the day they go home and live normal lives. What the fuck do they know?"

"What about a wheelchair van with adaptive controls? I've seen that work out for a few guys."

Gary laughed, a short biting sound. "Adaptive controls? You know what I get for rehab? Adaptive gardening. Adaptive golf. Like I give a flying fuck about shit like that. How about adaptive sex? Teach me how to get in bed with some chick and bang her." Challenging him with his eyes.

Frank let it go, waited a beat and said, "Your mother won the lottery a couple of weeks ago."

The angry glower disappeared, replaced by a pensive look. "Yeah," Gary said softly. "I told her to be careful. I told her there'd be people that would try to take advantage of her."

"Your mother might not be the first person he killed. Your mother's the fourth lottery winner in New England that got murdered."

"Fuck! Are you serious?"

"Yes. Last year Boston PD sent me to Quantico to take an FBI course on serial killers. That's why I'm on the case." In addition to all the other murders he had to solve, but Gary didn't care about that.

"I told her to put in a security system. The ADT guy was there last week, but my mother said he couldn't install the system until the end of this week. Friday, she said. Jesus. If she'd had a panic button she might still be alive."

But Frank knew a panic button wouldn't have saved her. "There was no sign of a break-in, so we think she let the killer in. Any idea why she'd do that? Or who it might have been?"

Lost in thought, Gary stroked his mustache.

Frank studied his bulging biceps, tried to picture him as the killer, wheel up the ramp, open the door and say, "Hi, Mom, I'm home." But he didn't drive. How would he get there? One of his drug supplier buddies?

A loud thump startled them. Gary half-turned in his chair to look at the window behind him and said, "A bird. Happens all the time. They keep the glass so clean the birds can't see it." He heaved a sigh. "Look, I'll be straight with you. Mom and I had a few problems, so she didn't confide in me much. I got no clue who she might let in. My father died three years ago. Maybe she was lonely. Maybe she met somebody at those stupid Bingo games she goes to twice a week. Hell, it could have been anybody."

"No, not just anybody. Why would she open the door to a stranger?"

"Beats me." Gary's shoulders slumped, a dejected posture of defeat. "She was all excited when she won, drove up here and told me before she even claimed the prize. She was gonna buy me a motorized wheelchair and a handicapped van so I could drive." His mouth twisted and he turned away.

Frank waited for him to compose himself.

Moment's later Gary looked at him, his eyes hard. "The funeral's Saturday morning, that's all I can tell you."

He held out his card. "I'm very sorry about your mother, Gary. If you think of anything, even if it's not important, call me anytime, day or night."

He left the facility, picturing the heartbreaking close-up of Florence's face, her horrified expression. Most days he loved his job, but some days it got to him. Yesterday, a young black man dead in a gutter and a scared little kid who might know who shot him. Today, a murdered sixty-two-year-old woman and her embittered son in a wheelchair with no legs.

Sometimes he wished he'd followed his youthful passion to become a jazz trumpet player. He'd make a lot less money, but at least he'd be able to sleep at night.

———

7:10 p.m. — Braintree

"Another day, another murder," Frank said, raising his wineglass in a mock-toast.

Perched on the barstool beside him, Gina grinned and clinked her glass against his. "Hey, that's what keeps us in business, right? You solve 'em, I write about 'em."

"I could do with a few less." All he wanted right now was to chill out with a glass of wine, engage in some verbal foreplay with Gina and take her to bed. His lover of nine years, a five-foot-four dynamo, smart as a whip, a great sense of humor and enthusiasm to the max, in bed and out.

South Shore Seafood was slammed, but they'd managed to find two seats at the bar. It wasn't their usual haunt, but by the time he wrote up his notes on the Chatham murder it was late so they decided to meet here. Close to the highway in Braintree, the popular seafood restaurant was ten miles from Frank's house in Milton, fifteen miles from Gina's house in Westwood.

Best of all, once rush hour was over, it was only a short ride to Gina's beach house, the place they used for their trysts.

"What's the scoop on the gang hit?" Gina said. "I caught it on the scanner driving in to work yesterday."

"Same old story. Dorchester 'banger goes outside his territory and gets popped. Man, I've got too many cases already and that serial killer I told you about did another one in Chatham."

"Wow. Another lottery winner?"

"Yeah. Older woman, sixty-two, lived alone, same MO. I spent the morning in Chatham. Then I went to Plymouth and talked to her son. He's in a rehab facility."

Gina sipped her wine and twirled a lock of dark hair around her finger. "Drugs?"

"Worse. He's a disabled Gulf War vet, lost both legs, got into booze and drugs. Sad story." He slugged down some wine. "What's up with you? Is Ryan coming home tomorrow night?"

"No, Saturday morning. He's in Austin, rescuing some dot-com company." Gina gave him a droll smile. "Not that I'm complaining. He said he'd be there for two months, maybe three."

Gina's husband worked for a financial firm similar to Bain Capital. Forty-five weeks of the year he flew around the country taking over bankrupt companies, firing people to shore up the bottom line. Frank didn't ask what happened on the weekends. He didn't want to know.

Gina's eyes widened. An instant later a woman's voice said, "Hi Frank. I thought it was you."

When he turned, Myra Genest was standing by his elbow, smiling at him, a sharp face, beady eyes, fresh red lipstick on her mouth. The mouth that never stopped talking. His heart jolted and his mind went into crisis mode.

He'd met Gina in the parking lot. Separate cars. No kisses, no hugs, no signs of intimacy as they walked to the restaurant. *Damn it to hell!* He should have scanned the crowd to see if there was anyone they knew.

Now Myra was looking pointedly at Gina. He nudged Gina's foot. "This is Myra, a friend of my wife." Purposely omitting Myra's last name. "Myra, say hello to Gina."

"Hi, Gina," Myra said, homing in on her like a hawk on a chicken. "Gee, your face looks familiar. I feel like I've seen it somewhere."

"I cover the crime beat for the *Boston Herald,*" Gina said, maintaining a business-like expression. "I'm interviewing Detective Renzi about a murder."

"Oh," Myra said, pointedly looking at their wineglasses. "Nice to meet you. My husband's pulling the car up to the door for me. Nice to see you, Frank. Be sure and tell Evelyn I said hello." She turned and left.

"Fuck," he muttered.

A stricken look appeared on Gina's face. "Sorry, Franco. I didn't know what to say. Damn. All these years and we've never run into anybody we know."

"Yeah. Just our luck it was Motormouth Myra, the Gossip Queen."

"You think she'll tell Evelyn?"

"Are you kidding? Now that Mo's gone, all Evelyn does is watch TV and talk to her women friends. She goes to Mass every day, comes home and watches Regis and Kathy Lee, who, in case you don't know, is dealing with a philandering husband. Evelyn gives me the gory details every night at dinner."

"Nothing better to talk about, huh?"

"You don't think she wants to hear about the scary bad men that kill people, do you? Or talk about the Celtics. No. After she finishes gossiping with her girlfriends about Kathy Lee and her bad-boy husband, she tunes in the religious channel."

Gina widened her eyes. "Not *The Young and the Restless?*"

As intended, it made him laugh. "That'd be rich, watch a bunch of sexy chicks bed-hopping like crazy. Living in sin. What bullshit." He signaled for the tab and drained his wineglass. "Let's get out of here."

In the parking lot, he eyeballed every vehicle, fearing he'd recognize one, and walked Gina to her bright red Mazda 323. The one with the extra antenna so that she could monitor the police channel. The one with the *Boston Herald* bumper sticker. Damn.

"Go ahead to the beach house. I'll follow you."

And make sure no one else is following you.

Gina squeezed his hand and gave him a tentative smile. "We'll be okay, Franco."

"Sure," he said, unwilling to ruin the mood.

But if Myra checked the *Herald*, figured out Gina's last name and told Evelyn, the shit would hit the fan.

For him, and for Gina, if Ryan got wind of it.

CHAPTER 5

Saturday, April 29

Nigel stood in the wings of the Symphony Hall stage listening to the Pops musicians tune. The last few minutes were always pure hell. He'd played his first recital when he was six, but even now, hundreds of performances later, panic still seized him before a solo performance.

Thirty-five years of dread. His fingers felt like frozen sausages. Years ago at piano competitions he'd taken to soaking them in hot water before he went onstage. Otherwise his fingers locked up, unable to negotiate the treacherous leaps in the concertos.

The Pops format split the concert into thirds, with two intermissions for people in the balconies to have a go at the bar. Waitresses delivered drinks to listeners seated at tables on the floor. To open the concert he'd chosen Rimsky Korsakov's *Russian Easter Overture*. The score was on the music stand, but he never used one. He knew the piece cold, saw every note in his mind's eye. Bloody useful, that. Within eight bars he knew the orchestra was in good form. When he cued the trombone player for his solo, it was spot on. The other brass players shuffled their feet. Musicians' applause. At the end of the piece, he'd given him a solo bow.

The Pops musicians played with spirit and verve, responding to his slightest gesture, strings, winds, brass and percussion blended as one. How marvelous it would be to lead them all the time. TV specials. Record contracts. Fabulous money. Best of all, he could live in Boston with Vicky.

But it wouldn't happen, no matter what Vicky said. Where would he be in ten years, fifty-one and still a guest conductor? Lord knows why. His credentials were impeccable. Royal College of Music. Conducting studies with Colin Davis. Arranging and conducting the film scores hurt, of course, and so did the Las Vegas gigs, but bloody hell, he had to work somewhere, didn't he?

He massaged his icy fingers. Now he had to play the Gershwin. *Rhapsody in Blue*. Vicky's solo opened the piece, gorgeous Vicky and her sultry clarinet

26

sound. But then it would be his turn. His heart bolted like a horse escaping a fire. Play the piano solo and conduct from the keyboard.

Double duty, double trouble. Eighteen minutes of hell. No hiding, no bollixed notes. Everyone in the hall knew the *Rhapsody in Blue*.

The stage manager tapped his arm. "They're ready for you, Maestro."

A moment of panic seized him, but he forced a cheerful smile and strode onstage. Threading his way down a narrow path between the musicians, he ascended the podium to thunderous applause. He bowed to the audience, sat down at the Steinway and turned to the musicians.

One hundred pairs of eyes regarded him.

He looked at Vicky. Their eyes met, but her expression didn't change. On stage they were all business. She raised her clarinet and lapped the reed with her tongue, focused on the music, ready for her solo. He gave a nod and she began the seductive trill. Snaked through the ever-rising scale. Executed the glissando flawlessly and played the bluesy theme.

Her dark, sultry sound soared through the hall. His heart burst with pride. Bloody marvelous! He knew the hours of practice it took to perform at that level. Not only did Vicky have discipline and determination, she was fearless and confident as well, always in control.

Everything he was not.

After the bluesy trumpet solo, he brought in the orchestra. A wall of sound swept over him, a visceral jolt that filled him with joy. He made his entrance, muscle-memory took over, and his troubles fell away. His financial worries. His idiotic bet on Goldilocks. His despair when she lost. At the end of a solo passage, he glanced at Vicky. The clarinets had a rest and she was swabbing moisture out of her clarinet.

Duke Ellington had titled his autobiography, *Music Is My Mistress*. Vicky was his mistress and he loved her dearly, but music was his salvation, a soothing balm when his life crumbled to ashes. Incessant creditors. A vindictive ex-wife. Bad luck at the race track . . .

He plunged into the next solo passage, fingers flashing over the keys, reveling in the sound of the orchestra. Nothing fazed these musicians.

Bloody hell, he wanted this job!

At the end of the piece the audience brought him back for two bows, clapping and whistling, the musicians shuffling their feet. He bowed deeply and gave Vicky a solo bow.

On impulse he decided to play an encore. The worst part was over. Why not enjoy himself? Chatting up the audience was always fun. He did it all the time in Vegas. He went to the microphone and the audience quieted.

"Thank you so much. You are terribly kind and you shall have your reward." He beamed a smile at the well-dressed patrons seated at tables below the stage and another to those in the balconies. "Gershwin composed many brilliant pieces. One of my favorites is *I Got Rhythm*."

Amid more applause, he went to the Steinway. Thanks to the jazz gigs he used to play in Hollywood, the piece was right up his alley. His fingers flew over the keys, effortlessly playing the intricate variations. He improvised a jazz chorus, putting his own stamp on the Gershwin tune. God this was fun!

He finished to another burst of applause. Even the musicians were clapping. He nodded to the players, then bowed to the audience. *Take that, you bloody BSO bigwigs.* If they saw how he charmed the audience, maybe they'd hire him to do it permanently.

Then *his* name would be on the marquee outside Symphony Hall.

"Nigel Heath, Boston Pops Conductor."

————

Westwood — 9:25 p.m.

"Hey Gina, what happened to my shirts?" Ryan yelled from their second-floor bedroom.

"Hold on, I'll be up in a minute." She finished loading the dishwasher, dumped in detergent and slammed the door shut. At noon she'd picked him up at Logan, and he'd been bitching at her ever since. *The yard looks like a weed garden. What'll the neighbors think?* As if she gave a shit. He was the one who'd insisted on buying an expensive house in a snobby neighborhood.

She topped off her wineglass from the bottle of Shiraz she'd bought. Another bone of contention. Ryan never drank alcohol, and he didn't want her drinking any either. She took a big swallow and glanced at the clock, wondering what Franco was doing. Almost 9:30. Was he watching a movie on TV with his uptight wife?

Her thoughts flitted to the sharp-faced woman who'd ambushed them in the bar. Franco was afraid she'd tell his wife. But why worry about something that probably wouldn't happen? She had enough problems dealing with Ryan, gone all week and he comes home with a suitcase full of dirty clothes. She'd spent the afternoon in the laundry room, washing, drying and folding them.

All quiet upstairs. Ryan was packing for his trip back to Austin on Monday. She leaned against the marble countertop and sipped her wine, gazing at the stainless-steel refrigerator, dishwasher and stove. Her designer kitchen. Designed for a woman who wanted to stay home and cook all day.

Ryan thought it was great. He thought her life should revolve around his weekend visits.

Ten years into the marriage she couldn't remember why she'd married him. Seemed like a good idea at the time? Whatever. In the beginning he doted on her, buying her expensive presents. But six months into the marriage the bloom left the rose. No more presents when Ryan came home from trips, just critical comments: *You better go on a diet, Gina, you're getting fat.* And kinky sexual demands. *Do this, do that.*

But she didn't want to do this or that.

She gulped some wine and tried not to think about what might happen later in bed. Two weeks after her first wedding anniversary, she'd met Franco. His intense dark eyes made her melt, and his bawdy sense of humor equaled hers. Simpatico from the start, they always had plenty to talk about, and the sex was great, even the first time. Franco didn't roll over and fall asleep afterwards. She smiled, recalling that first night when she ran a finger over the scar on his chin and asked how he got it.

"Did something stupid when I was six," he'd said. "The kid next door dared me to ride down a big hill on my new bike no-hands. So I did. Split my chin open when my bike hit the curb and threw me over the handlebars. My mother had to take me to the emergency room."

She loved the story, especially his bashful confession. "It hurt like hell, but that wasn't the worst part. The blood freaked me out. I thought I was gonna bleed to death." Then he'd grinned and said, "So I choose a profession where I look at blood and gore almost every day. The weird thing is I can handle that, but even now if I cut myself shaving, part of me still freaks out."

She sipped her wine, imagining a newsflash on TV: *American Airlines plane crashes in Texas*. And instantly felt guilty.

She didn't want Ryan dead, she just wanted him out of her life. Maybe she'd leave him. She didn't make big money like Ryan, but she didn't need a house with a designer kitchen and a Jacuzzi in a bathroom bigger than most people's bedrooms.

"Gina! I can't take these shirts to Austin. They're wrinkled!" Louder now and insistent.

"So take them in the laundry room and iron them," she muttered.

But as she mounted the stairs her stomach got that familiar tight-queasy feeling. Their bedroom had mirrors on two walls and a king-sized bed. Last year Ryan had bought a big-screen TV and made her watch porn videos with him in bed.

When she entered the room, he looked at her accusingly.

"Gina, I told you not to use Prentiss Cleaners. Look at this." He held up a white dress shirt. Telltale wrinkles showed where it had been folded.

"Hey, you've got plenty of money. Why don't you just buy new ones and throw the dirty ones away?"

Momentarily speechless, he glowered at her, six-three and muscular as a boxer from his daily workouts. Ryan stayed at expensive hotels with indoor swimming pools and gym facilities. Most women considered him attractive, carefully styled dark hair, curly locks falling over his forehead. Lately he'd begun to obsess about losing his hair. In fact, his hairline *was* receding. His features were ordinary. His wide-set blue eyes were his most attractive feature, when he wasn't glaring at her.

"Most wives want their husbands to look good when they go to work."

"Ryan, give it a rest. You've got ten designer suits in the walk-in closet, *Armani* suits that cost an arm and a leg for God's sake. Who sees the shirts? They're under the suit."

"Sometimes I like to take my jacket off. I'm not sitting in a board meeting with high-powered executives looking like a tramp in a wrinkled shirt." He turned on the persuasive smile he used to cajole clients. "Come on, Gina, be a dear and touch them up for me."

A haze of anger fuzzed her vision. "No. I picked you up at the airport, worked my ass off doing your laundry, cooked you a nice dinner and cleaned it up. I'm tired. I want to relax."

"Fine," he snapped. "I'll buy new ones. If you ditched that stupid job at the *Herald*, you'd have more energy on the weekend. You think you're some kind of hot-shot journalist like that chick on *Murphy Brown*."

"It's not a stupid job." *Franco loves it. He calls me his Ace Reporter.*

"You wouldn't be living in a nice house in Westwood if I wasn't paying the mortgage."

"I'm a good journalist. How do you think I got a job writing for a big newspaper in one of the hottest media markets in the country?"

"Yeah, and it pays shit."

The phone on the bedside table rang. Relieved by the interruption, she took the call and heard a familiar voice say, "Hey Gina, wait till you hear my news!"

Gina grinned. Orchid, her kooky roommate at Boston University, was still her best friend.

"Hey, Orchid, what's going on?" she said, and saw Ryan frown.

"A national outfit that runs craft shows called me. They want me to do an exhibit at a big show in Phoenix. I am psyched! They already bought some of my designer pottery."

"Wow! Congratulations! This will really put you in the big time." Ryan rolled his eyes at her. She turned her back to him. "How are sales going at the studio?"

"*Comme si, comme ca.*" Orchid tossed French phrases around like a native, which in fact she was. Her mother had been living in Saint-Tropez on the French Riviera when Orchid was born.

"Gina," Ryan said loudly, "get rid of your weirdo friend. We need to talk."

"Uh-oh," Orchid said, "who's that? Mr. Important home from the business wars, wanting attention?"

"Yes. Can I call you tomorrow?"

"Sure, but not before noon. I'm going out tonight and tie one on to celebrate. Wanna come?"

"I'd love to, but—"

"Don't speak. Mr. Important is listening. Call me tomorrow," Orchid said, and clicked off.

She replaced the receiver and said to Ryan, "You know, I don't sit around all week while you're doing your big important business deals. I have friends."

"Orchid's no friend. She's a bad influence on you."

"What's that supposed to mean?"

His face turned as dark as a thundercloud. "What I said. She puts on airs like she's some artsy-fartsy artist, but she's going nowhere because she's got no talent."

"What do you know about talent? All you do is manipulate numbers on a spreadsheet."

His eyes narrowed and his lips thinned, that dangerous look she knew so well. He took a step toward her, fists clenched. Her heart pounded and she backed away. Sometimes the intensity of his fury scared her. Damned if she'd let him know it, though. If he touched her, she'd scratch his eyes out.

"Is that what you think I do?" he yelled. "Push numbers around? Try explaining to twenty people why you need to lay them off so they don't wind up sabotaging the company—"

"Jesus! You fire people and expect them to like it? Six weeks later you walk away and forget them."

"Hey, my obligation is to the stockholders." He came closer and sniffed. "You've been drinking. Don't deny it, I can smell it on your breath. You smell like a cheap barroom whore."

Her fingers tingled, icy with fear. *And you're a dry drunk, just like your father.*

"Ryan, I'm tired. I'm going to go lie down in the TV room and watch a movie and fall asleep." *No kinky sex tonight, bubba.*

His eyes morphed into blue steel, as cold and hard as the stainless-steel appliances in their kitchen. "Things better be different tomorrow, Gina. You're my wife. You better start acting like it."

CHAPTER 6

Sunday, April 30

Vicky heard Nigel shut off the shower and peered nearsightedly at the clock radio beside her bed. Almost noon. Feeling delightfully decadent and not the least bit guilty, she snuggled into her pillow with a contented sigh. Nigel was a wonderful lover.

After last night's concert she'd come straight home to her North End apartment, glowing from the compliments she'd gotten for her solo. Nigel had made his obligatory stop at his hotel and hadn't arrived until midnight. As her busybody Italian landlady no doubt noticed. The nosy old bat sat by the window in her first-floor apartment every night, checking up on her.

She sat up as Nigel entered the room, slim and trim, a white bath towel wrapped around his waist. He said conducting kept him fit. Damp curlicues of ginger-brown hair swirled over his chest. He didn't look forty-one, she decided, even if he did have a bald spot on top.

He took her face in his hands and kissed her. "That was a lovely farewell nudge this morning."

She giggled. "Nudge? Is that the Brit word for it?"

His face lit up in a smile, displaying even, white teeth. He'd had the front ones capped when he was living in Hollywood with his wife, ex-wife now.

"No, but it suits us." He took his suitcase out of her closet and set it atop the rumpled bed. "Okay to leave my suitcase here till next Sunday? Baggage claim is a bloody nuisance."

"Sure," she said, smiling mischievously. "Then you'll be sure to hurry back and see me."

"No doubt about that, luv. The *Rhapsody* is a great showpiece for you. Your solo was superb."

"Think it'll land me the second clarinet chair with the BSO?"

"Should do. You deserve it."

32

"But three hundred clarinet players will show up for the audition. What if they pick somebody else?"

"I thought you liked freelancing."

"Nigel, I'm thirty-three. I'm sick of living in the North End and paying rent. I want to buy a condo."

"And I'm sick of traveling. This Iowa gig Hale booked is absurd. Rehearse all week, do four performances of *Music Man* and fly back for next Sunday's Pops concert."

"Why did you take it?"

He opened his suitcase, frowning, then flashed her a grin. "It's not *Music Man* I'm worried about, it's the bloody Gershwin. Conducting *Rhapsody in Blue* and *Concerto in F* from the keyboard is no cake walk."

"No kidding. I don't know how you do it."

He shrugged. "I've done it before, but not in Boston. That's why they hired me. Why pony up big bucks for a soloist when they can pay me ten percent more and get a soloist *and* a conductor."

"Have you conducted *Music Man* before?"

"No, but Hale sent me the score. Piece of cake. But I hate these bloody road trips. If I got the Pops job, I'd be in Boston with you." He shrugged. "Time will tell. Should know in a couple of weeks."

He took a stack of clean underwear and socks out of the suitcase. "I'll sling these in my suit bag, but I need something to take them to the hotel."

"Use that." She pointed to a shopping bag with a Lord & Taylor logo beside her bureau. "Can you start the coffee while I take a quick shower?"

He kissed her forehead. "Will do."

She got in the shower, luxuriating in the steamy spray. The building was old and sometimes when other people took showers, the water pressure in her second-floor apartment slowed to a trickle. But not now.

When she emerged, ringlets of damp, dark hair curled around her face. She put on her glasses and stepped on the scales: 140 pounds. She wished she were tall and slim like her sister, but she had inherited her father's stocky build. Nigel didn't seem to mind though.

She put on a bathrobe and went out to the kitchen, a tiny alcove with a stove, refrigerator and a sink. The only counter space, a Formica-topped breakfast bar, separated the alcove from the living room. Dressed in gray-tweed slacks and a blue shirt, Nigel stood at the stove pouring coffee into two mugs. The first time he stayed over, she had offered him tea for breakfast. Didn't all Englishmen drink tea? But he'd said, "Never touch the stuff. Just coffee, the stronger the better."

She opened the refrigerator. "Want some eggs? I could make an omelet."

"No time, luv. Got to check out of the hotel and go to the airport." He fished in his pocket. "Blast! I'm out of cigarettes."

"You can get some at the store on the corner. Want me to drive you to the hotel?"

"I'll take a cab. Wouldn't want anybody to see us. Besides, you've got a gig this afternoon."

She glanced at the clock. "That reminds me. I better tape my show."

"Right-o. Can't miss Wanda the workout woman, can we?"

Teasing her. He knew she watched Wanda's Workouts every Sunday. If she had a gig, she taped it and watched it later. She went in the living room, stuck a disc in the DVD and set the timer.

On the way back to the kitchen, she noticed a crumpled scrap of paper on the floor. When she picked it up, her heart sank.

Faint red letters at the top said: SUFFOLK DOWNS.

She went in the kitchen and waved the ticket at Nigel. "What's this?"

He plucked it from her fingers and put it in his pocket, avoiding her eyes.

"You said you didn't bet on that race."

"That's an old ticket, probably been in my pocket for months."

She almost asked to see the date on the ticket, but she didn't want him to think she didn't trust him.

He kissed her, picked up the Lord & Taylor bag and went to the door. "I'll call you from Iowa. Wish me luck with *Music Man*."

"Okay. But don't you dare go to any race tracks out in Iowa!"

"You can count on *that*, luv."

———

He dashed down the front steps. Intent on buying cigarettes, he didn't notice the elderly woman seated by the first-floor window watching him hurry down the street. He stopped outside Marie's Variety and studied the array of lottery slips taped to the door.

A sign block printed on them in red crayon said: **NO MEGABUCKS winner last night!!! WEDNESDAY prize . . . $12 MILLION!!!**

Wouldn't *that* be a lark, he thought as he opened the door. The store was dark and cramped, with iron bars over the grimy windows. Two aisles of groceries led to a cooler for milk, juice and soft drinks. A stack of Sunday newspapers sat on the floor beside the counter. Behind it, an elderly woman with gray hair perched on a wooden stool.

"Two packs of Winstons please," he said, eyeing the betting slips on the counter as she rang up the cigarettes. "Big Megabucks prize this week?"

"No winner for two months. Everybody gonna buy tickets now." Her brown eyes regarded him steadily.

He put a twenty-dollar bill on the counter. "P'rhaps I'll try my luck."

"Quick picks?"

"Whatever works."

She punched the computer and he waited impatiently as twenty tickets spewed out the top. She handed him the slips. "Time somebody hit the jackpot. Maybe it will be you."

"Right-o," he said. "Wish me luck."

Outside the shop he stopped to cram the tickets in his pocket. An errant slip fluttered to the sidewalk. Caught by a faint breeze, it blew into the gutter. He dashed over and grabbed it before it could fly off down the street. Just his luck to leave the winner on a street corner. He shoved the slip into his pocket, mulling over the woman's comment.

No one had won the Megabucks for two months. A winner was due.

Twelve million bean. Wouldn't *that* solve his money problems!

Bloody hell! Why hadn't he bought more tickets?

When he reached North Station, a lone cab stood at the curb. A dark-skinned man in a fuchsia shirt sat behind the wheel, eyes closed. Nigel leaned down to the open window. "Hallo there! Anybody home?"

The driver woke with a start and opened his eyes. "Where to?"

"The Back Bay Inn on Huntington, but I've got a few errands to run. Make it worth your while."

"No problem, mon," the driver said in a lilting West Indian accent.

"I need to pop into the station first. Start the meter. Only be a minute."

He found an ATM, punched in a three-hundred-dollar withdrawal and waited anxiously, praying his credit card would give it to him. To his relief, twenty-dollar bills poured into the slot. He put them in his billfold, dashed back to the cab, jumped in and said, "Any grocery shops 'round here?"

"Be some over on Charles Street."

"Good show." He sank back in his seat as they drove up Cambridge Street, went over Beacon Hill and turned onto Charles. The cabby stopped at a red light and pointed at a store on the far corner. "That one okay?"

He saw a sign in the window for lottery tickets. "Perfect."

But there was a line at the register. By the time he reached the counter, several people were behind him. He didn't dare ask for two hundred tickets. It would take forever for the machine to spit them out. He got fifty quick-picks, went out and told the cabby he hadn't found what he needed. They made three more stops: another corner store, a Store-24 and a 7-Eleven. Now he had two hundred tickets. Should he buy more? No. He had to pay the cabbie, and he'd need cash when he got to Iowa, no telling if his maxed-out credit card would give him more. He told the cabbie he had what he needed.

On the way to his hotel they passed Symphony Hall. He eyed the current Pops conductor's photograph on posters. Who would the next conductor be? Nigel Heath? Or that young flashy bloke?

Would his luck ever change? God knows what he'd do if it didn't.

Two hundred lottery tickets. He knew the odds were against him, but bloody hell, someone had to win, didn't they?

Sandwich, MA

He wheeled his mother up the handicapped ramp along the front of the Seaside Diner. A breeze fluttered the red canvas awning that shielded the windows from the afternoon sun.

The Sandwich police chief came out the door and held it open for them. "Afternoon, Mrs. Kay. Beautiful day, isn't it?"

His mother smoothed her wavy blonde hair, simpering at him. "Every Sunday is beautiful! It's the Lord's day."

Stringy cords stood out in her forearms as she maneuvered the wheelchair inside. It was almost 2:00 so the dinner rush was over. The booths near the door were occupied, but they never sat in that section. His mother said it was too noisy. He pushed her past eight chrome counter stools with padded red seats. Another Sandwich cop sat on one, eating blueberry pie and ice cream. Two stools down an old-timer townie was eating his solitary Sunday dinner, a fried clam plate with French fries and cole slaw.

The odor of fried fish permeated the diner. There was meat on the menu, but most people came to the Seaside Diner for its fish dinners, clam cakes and clam chowder. Conscious of curious stares from other diners, he pushed his mother toward her favorite table at the far end. Her wheelchair bumped a chair, and two teenagers looked up from their apple pie and ice cream, smirking at him. The pimply-faced one whispered to his buddy, then moved his chair to let them by. The little shit.

A rail-thin waitress came out of the kitchen with a full tray and delivered fish dinners to a table of four. Her carrot-red hair was cropped in a crew cut, and looped earrings dangled from her ears. She waved and called to them, "Hi Mrs. Kay! Hi Billy! I'll be right over with coffee!"

He settled his mother into her usual spot in the corner, facing out so she could see the other diners. She loved watching people. Especially him. He took the chair facing the window. He didn't want to look at her during dinner. He did that enough at home. From here he could keep an eye on the cop at the counter. All the Sandwich cops ate here. The Seaside Diner was a local hangout. The tourists stayed at Sandwich's historic bed-and-breakfast inns and ate at restaurants overlooking the ocean or the Cape Cod Canal.

Arlene arrived with their coffee and a basket of dinner rolls.

"Gee, Mrs. Kay, your hair looks pretty today. How do you get those waves to fall so nice?"

"I found a hairdresser that comes to the house." She patted her dyed-blonde hair. "Billy's tired when he gets home from work. I don't like to ask him to take me."

"I don't mind, Mom. It's no trouble."

36

"Well, it looks real nice." Arlene tilted her head, and her hoop earrings swayed back and forth. "What'll it be today? Wanna hear the specials?"

"That won't be necessary. I'll have the usual," his mother said.

Arlene nodded, scribbling on a pad. "How about you, Billy?"

"I don't know. What's good today?"

"The meatloaf special's your best bet. Home-made, fresh green beans, glazed carrots, mashed potatoes and gravy."

"Sounds great. I'll have that."

She nudged his shoulder. "But y'know what the *really* best bet is? Megabucks tickets. No winner last night. They say Wednesday's prize might hit twelve million. I sure could use some of that."

He glanced at his mother. Her lips tightened, but she liked Arlene so maybe she wouldn't lecture her about gambling. He hid his hands under the table and picked at a scab. His eczema had flared up yesterday.

His mother took a sip of coffee and set her cup down. "This coffee is too hot."

"Put some cream in it, Mom."

"Too much fat." Her thin lips pursed. "I'll wait till it cools."

He took a roll and noticed a drop of blood on his thumb. He wiped it on a napkin and bit into the roll. His stomach rumbled with hunger. Every Sunday they went through the same routine: up at 7:00, get dressed and drive for an hour to the Pentecostal Word of God Church near Brockton.

Fifteen years ago his mother had found God.

The service lasted two hours; then they drove back to Sandwich. In the summer it was brutal, traffic backed up for miles, tourists fighting to get over the Sagamore Bridge onto Cape Cod. His mother wouldn't eat Sunday dinner anywhere else, but that was fine with him. He liked the Seaside Diner.

He especially liked watching the cops. He glanced at the counter. The cop was gone. Sometimes he came in by himself at night and sat near the detectives. Sometimes they talked about the cases they were working on. Maybe he'd come in tomorrow and find out what they knew about Florence.

He finished the roll and reached for another one.

"Don't eat so much bread before dinner, Billy. It will spoil your appetite."

He put the roll back, put his hands in his lap and scratched. Today's sermon was about gambling, probably because of the Megabucks prize. The preacher had a loud voice. It scared him, just like his father scared him when he was little. The preacher ranted on and on about the sin of gambling. He knew why. If people spent all their money on gambling, they wouldn't have any to give to the church. The offering was important. Then came the healing ceremony—his mother's favorite—the laying on of hands. After that people got up and spoke in tongues. Creepy. He got the shivers listening to them.

"Look at those girls, Billy." His mother pointed at two teenage girls at a nearby table. "It's shameful the way girls dress these days. Those tops look like undershirts!"

"Tank tops, Mom. All the kids wear them."

"Well, it's disgraceful."

Then Arlene arrived with their dinners. "There you go, Mrs. Kay. Roast beef special. I got you an end cut. I know you like it well done." Her hoop earrings swayed as she set his meatloaf dinner in front of him.

His mother eyed his plate and frowned. "Billy got more vegetables."

"We got a hungry fella here, Mrs. Kay. He's just a little guy, but he still needs his nourishment!"

He flushed and ducked his head. He hated it when people called him little. He couldn't help it if he was short. He forked mashed potatoes into his mouth and swallowed.

"Don't eat so fast, Billy. It's bad for your digestion." His mother scraped gravy off her roast beef and cut the meat into tiny morsels. She put one in her mouth and chewed. Her mouth moved in short rapid strokes. It reminded him of the rabbit at the pet store, nibbling on a chunk of carrot.

"Preacher Everdon is absolutely right. Gambling is evil. It's the ruination of people like Arlene. She's had a hard life, poor thing. No husband and four boys to support. But *her* mother helps out. Not like mine, after your father died." She put a green bean in her mouth and chewed. *Click, click, click.*

She put down her fork. "Look at that woman! She must weigh two hundred pounds and she's eating pie and ice cream. It's not healthy to be so fat."

He dipped some meatloaf in the gravy. If she said anything about the gravy, he'd throw the plate in her face. Well, no, he wouldn't. But he'd like to.

Arlene came back, sipping a mug of coffee. "How's the meatloaf, Billy?"

"Wonderful," he said, smiling up at her. "You're the best waitress on Cape Cod."

"Aww, you're so sweet, Billy."

"Sit down, Arlene," his mother said. "You must be tired."

"Thanks." She perched on the captain's chair opposite his mother and ran a hand over her carrot-red hair. "Sundays are always busy. I've been here since seven and this is my first break."

"You're a hard worker," his mother said. "The Lord will reward you."

"Maybe, but I'm gonna buy me some Megabucks tickets in case He don't. My boys need new sneakers."

"Don't waste your money. You'll never win. Billy played the lottery after the library fired him—"

"They didn't fire me, Mom. It's only a layoff. I'll get the job back."

"Maybe." His mother smirked at Arlene. "Billy comes home one night and says he hit the jackpot and hands me the ticket like it's a big prize! Big deal. We only won two hundred dollars."

He put his hands in his lap and scratched. "It got us the van," he muttered.

"It did not! I got us the van. That nice reporter came to interview me and I told her you lost your job at the library." His mother lowered her voice and said to Arlene, "We almost lost the house, you know."

He dug at the scab on his thumb. *Too bad we didn't lose you.*

"I sure do admire you, Mrs. Kay. Being in a wheelchair don't stop you from getting what you want!"

"Almost twenty years, with the help of the Lord. But it's hard. And poor Billy with his headaches. Billy! Look at your hand! It's bleeding. I *told* you not to scratch like that!"

He dropped his fork and it clattered onto his plate. The girls in tank tops looked over, staring at him.

Arlene stood up. "Want some pie, Billy? We've got key lime today."

"No," his mother said, "we've got errands to do."

He smiled at Arlene. "I'm taking Mom to Morrow's to get some of those special chocolates they make."

"You're a wonderful son to treat your mom so good. I hope my boys grow up to be just like you."

"It's just an excuse, Arlene. Then he'll go to the pet store next door and buy food for his goldfish. His *girls*!"

His hands grew still beneath the table. "I might buy a new one today."

"What are you going to call this one?" His mother shook her head and said to Arlene, "I don't know where he gets these silly names. Lulu. Tessa. Florence."

"Well," Arlene said, edging away from the table. "You folks have a nice day. See you next Sunday."

CHAPTER 7

Tuesday, May 2

When Frank got back to his office after lunch his boss, Detective Lieutenant Harrison "Hank" Flynn, stood outside the door, sipping from a container of Dunkin' Donuts coffee. Usually if Frank ran into him in the hall, Hank would toss him a friendly *Hey, how's it going?* Not today.

Today, he said, "Hey, Frank, got a minute?"

"Sure, come on in." Frank unlocked the door, waved Hank into his office and sat down at his desk.

Hank took the visitor chair beside it and set his coffee container on the desk. "You hiding out from your wife? Evelyn called me yesterday, wanted to know where you were."

Blindsided, he thought about Evelyn's brusque *Good morning* when he got home from his five-mile run this morning. Was she checking up on him?

"I was testifying in court. The Johnson murder case finally went to trial."

"Uh-huh." Hank took a sip of coffee. "How'd it go?"

"Okay. No surprises from the defense team. The guy should go down for it. Hell, we got the gun, got two wits to testify that actually showed up."

"Good." Hank waited a beat, then said, "Evelyn called me at 6:30 last night, said she called you here, then called your cell phone and you didn't answer."

Definitely checking up on him. "You know, when I first joined Boston PD, Evelyn said having a police officer husband made her feel safe. But the first time someone shot at me . . . remember that bank robbery in the South End?"

"I do. The Tierney brothers held up a Citi Bank three blocks from here, a teller hit the silent alarm and two squads showed up."

"Right. Mine was one of them. I get out and they start shooting." He fingered the scar on his chin, remembering the jolt of fear when he pulled his service weapon. "Nobody got shot, and we captured them, but when I got home that night and told Evelyn what happened, she freaked out and started crying." Aware that he was dissembling like a suspect avoiding questions, he said, "Did that ever happen with Meredith?"

Hank ran a hand over his hair, dark brown flecked with gray. "No. Not that Meredith wanted to hear about the shit that goes down on the job, but she said she'd rather hear if from me than see it on the news."

"Not Evelyn. She won't watch the news, doesn't want to hear about it from me, either. So I went out with one of my buddies. We had a beer and a burger and hashed over some cases."

Making it sound like he'd been out with a cop friend, not Gina. After his long day in court he wanted to relax and talk to someone who'd make him laugh, someone who wouldn't freak out if he said the F-word. Talking to Gina was way better than talking to a guy, the hint of sexual attraction lurking below the surface.

"I told Evelyn but maybe she forgot." *Fat chance. Evelyn forgot nothing. Especially the bad things.*

"How's it going with the Jackpot Killer case?"

Hank was the one who'd urged Boston PD to send him to Quantico for the serial killer course last year. Because all three Jackpot murders were in New England, FBI Agent Ross Dunn had asked him to act as liaison on the case, his first time, and he didn't want to screw up. Hank had okayed it. He was hot on the case, too.

"Yesterday I checked VICAP, the FBI database, for cases with similar MO's. Two years ago a Rhode Island lottery winner got murdered. The local police didn't enter it in the database until last week. That's probably why Ross wasn't aware of it."

"Some police departments don't have the personnel or the time to do it. Same MO?"

"Yes. An older woman, Caucasian, asphyxiated with a plastic bag, and a J&B nip, which seems to be the Jackpot Killer's signature. No sign of forced entry. No witnesses, no leads."

"Men hit the lottery, too. I wonder why he picks women?" Hank said.

"Older women. Maybe he figures they're easier to overpower."

"Maybe he hates his mother. Plenty of weirdoes out there do."

"Maybe he hates his wife."

Hank's eyes widened. Frank knew what he was thinking: Freudian slip by Frank Renzi, who hates his wife. Hank was fifteen years older than Frank, fifteen years more experience on the job and a bullshit detector to go with it.

"Or his mother-in-law," Frank quickly added. "On Sunday I spent an excruciating two hours with mine."

"Tough?" Hank said.

"Yes, and I'm not talking about the pot roast. Evelyn's mother is ultra-conservative, and as she gets older . . ." He shrugged. "Maybe the killer's mother hit the lottery and wouldn't share it with him."

"The Chatham victim had a son, right? Did you talk to him?"

"I did. Cross him off the suspect list. He's in a wheelchair, got both legs blown off in the Gulf War. He's got no way to get around. Somebody would have had to drive him."

"How did the killer get in?"

"Your guess is as good as mine. Ross Dunn says this Jackpot Killer is what FBI profilers call an organized killer. He plans his moves. Maybe he poses as a deliveryman."

"Flowers maybe?" Hank said. "We had a serial rapist once that got into women's hotel rooms that way. Knocks on the door, she looks through the peephole, sees roses in his hand, lets him in and he jumps her."

"Or it could have been UPS or FedEx. Florence didn't have many neighbors. The Chatham police chief said no one reported seeing any unusual vehicles. The State Police are running the investigation. The lead detective showed me the crime scene photographs. I asked him to keep the J&B nip quiet, but who knows?"

Hank shrugged. "The State cops pretty much do things their way. So the killer looks harmless enough for these women to let him in. Caucasian?"

"Almost certainly. Chatham's a small town. A black guy would stand out. The Rhode Island victim has a daughter that lives nearby. I want to talk to her, but I'm on call tomorrow for the murder trial, in case the defense lawyer calls me back. I caught that gang hit last week, and I've got other cases, too."

Hank glanced at his watch. "And I've got a meeting in ten minutes. What's your take on the Jackpot Killer? Your overall impression."

"I hate to say it, but it's like a lot of these serial killers. The FBI profilers would say he's a white male in his late twenties, early thirties . . ."

"Not married, lives alone?" Seven years ago Hank had taken the same FBI serial killer course.

"I'm not sure. All the murders were daytime kills, the ones we know about anyway. There could be more. So far, none on the weekend. Maybe he's got a job. Maybe he lives with someone, can't get away on the weekends."

"Okay, Frank. Keep me posted." Hank rose from his chair and gave him a pointed look. "Might be good if you kept in touch with Evelyn, too." He turned and left the office.

Frank slumped in his chair, ruminating over his workload, juggling two hot-potato cases, the Jackpot murders and the Mass Ave gang hit. Okay, maybe the gang hit wasn't a hot potato, but for some reason he'd fallen for the skinny little kid with the big brown eyes and the frightened look on his face. The kid might have witnessed the hit. Damn, he hated to see these black kids get involved with gangs.

And what about the biggest hot potato? If Motormouth Myra told Evelyn she'd seen him with Gina, he was in serious trouble. Myra would say they were drinking wine at a bar, too cozy to be working, and Evelyn would believe her. But Evelyn had to know he was getting sex somewhere. He sure as hell wasn't getting any at home.

As long as no one else knew, Evelyn could ignore it, but if Myra blabbed about Gina, Evelyn would have to do something or lose face. If she didn't, Motormouth Myra would tell all their friends that Evelyn's husband was unfaithful.

Forget the joy of sex. In Evelyn's world the joy of gossip reigned.

————

Grinnell, Iowa

Nigel gazed out the window of the pickup truck at the boring Iowa landscape, flat endless cornfields, not a tree or a house or billboard in sight. Grinnell was fifty miles east of Des Moines, might as well be the bloody end of the earth. He dug out a handkerchief and blew his nose. Get on an airplane healthy, breathe the recycled air, people coughing and sneezing, get off the plane with the mother of all colds.

He cast a sidelong glance at his driver, the man in the buckskin cowboy hat, blue jeans and cowboy boots. He was the local bank president, but he owned a five-acre farm and raised hogs on the side. For fun, he said. The hog-farmer-banker fancied himself a music buff, had offered to chauffeur him around for the week. Their conversation had ended miles ago. Nigel was too annoyed to chat him up. He fumbled in his pocket for a cigarette, then put it back. The banker thought smoking was the eighth deadly sin.

They passed signs of civilization: a gas station with a yellow Shell sign and a red Coke dispenser out front. About time. They'd be at the hotel soon. The banker turned on the radio. A whiny voice backed by twangy guitars wailed about his lost love. Nigel gritted his teeth. The next time Hale booked him a gig like this, he'd tell him to wank off. Five thousand, plus expenses for the whole bloody week. Hale took twenty percent so deduct a thousand, and taxes took a big chunk. Bloody Christ, it didn't add up to ten cents a note! In his wildest imagination he couldn't have conjured a worse week.

He lit a cigarette and took a deep lung-searing drag.

The banker looked over. "Could you open your window? Smoke really bothers me."

And country music really bothers me. Aloud he said, "Sorry, but there's no smoking in the theater. At least I can smoke at the hotel."

"Yup. One of the last holdouts. The whole township's about to go smoke-free." The banker tipped back his cowboy hat. "How'd the dress rehearsal go today?"

"Oh, jolly good," he said in his best British accent. Let the man feel important, hobnobbing with an international star. He puffed his cigarette morosely, willing the Budget Inn to appear.

The cheap hotel was just off an interstate highway exit, part of his expense package: a room and two meals a day. The first night at dinner he'd asked for the wine list. The waitress said they didn't have one and would he like a glass of the house red? It tasted like vinegar.

He smiled, recalling Vicky's merry laugh when he told her about it. Late last night he'd phoned her, dying to talk, aching to hear her voice. He missed her badly, couldn't wait to get back to Boston on Sunday.

If he won twelve million dollars, he'd never have to take a gig like this again. *The Music Man.* Jake Forester was Professor Harold Hill. Hopeless. The aging actor could spit out his lines: "Ya got trouble, yes, my friends, ya got trouble right here in River City."

Too bad he couldn't sing three notes without wandering off pitch.

The truck jolted to a stop below the canopy of the Budget Inn. "What time shall I pick you up tomorrow?" the banker asked.

"No need," he said. Damned if he'd take another ride with this relentlessly-healthy hog farmer. "Jake's picking me up so we can practice his solos. Thanks and cheerio." He climbed out of the truck, marched into the hotel lobby, took out his cell phone and called his agent.

"Bloody Christ, Hale! I've got a *hog* farmer driving me around in a pickup truck. A bleeding health nut! And the male lead's hopeless. *Seventy-Six-Trombones* went okay. Any schoolboy can sing that. But *Marion-the-Librarian* totally flummoxed the bloke. Today at rehearsal he entered a fifth too high and *kept going*, sang the whole bloody piece in the wrong key!"

"You'll shape him up, Nigel. You always do."

He rubbed his bleary eyes. "Any news on the Pops job?"

"Nothing yet."

"Okay," Nigel said wearily. "Ring you tomorrow."

———

Milton

Frazzled by the rush-hour traffic on the expressway, Frank pulled into his driveway at 6:35. His house was a modest two-story Cape on a tree-lined side street with similar homes. A far cry from the McMansions along Route 28 beside the golf course and the ritzy Victorians near Milton Academy.

He went in the side door and dropped his keys on the kitchen counter. Evelyn was putting their salads on the table. "Hi hon, sorry I'm late. Expressway traffic was tied up because of an accident."

Evelyn looked at him and frowned. "Highway driving is so dangerous. I don't know how people do it. They take their life in their hands whenever they get on it."

He said nothing, unwilling to discuss the terrible things that might befall a person if they obsessed about every tiny detail of their lives. He opened the refrigerator, took out a Sam Adams, popped the cap and took a long swallow.

"Want a beer?" he asked. Just to see what she'd say.

When she got pregnant, Evelyn had stopped drinking alcohol, a ban that continued while she was nursing. Even after Maureen was drinking out of a cup, Evelyn wouldn't touch a drop. No more alcohol. And no more sex. At first, he'd been mesmerized by his gorgeous baby girl, but after a while . . .

"Frank, you know I don't drink beer. Go ahead and sit down. The macaroni and cheese has been done for a half-hour. I kept it warm in the oven."

This was Tuesday. Was it a saint's day? Evelyn usually made mac and cheese on Fridays. The Church had ended the meat ban years ago, but Evelyn and her ultra-Catholic parents thought that was one more step on the road to perdition. Every Friday Evelyn prepared a meatless meal: mac and cheese or vegetarian pizza. He didn't mind. Evelyn was a good cook, and her mac and cheese was delicious. In the grand scheme of things, not eating meat wasn't his biggest beef with the Catholic Church. Not even close.

She took an oval casserole dish out of the oven, set it on a trivet in the center of the table and sat down across from him, her slender figure hidden under a loose-fitting housedress. God forbid anyone should think there might be breasts underneath. He hadn't actually seen them for a long time. Years. Even longer since he'd touched them.

She handed him a serving spoon and smiled. "You must be hungry after your long day."

The smile softened her face. Next month she'd turn forty, but she was still attractive, gorgeous green eyes, smooth ivory skin except for the deep lines around her perpetually down-turned mouth.

"Where did you eat dinner last night?" she said, gazing at him, not touching her dinner.

As if she cared where he ate. What she wanted to know: *Where were you last night and who were you with?*

Grateful for the heads-up Hank had given him, he said, "Had a beer and a burger with one of my buddies." In fact he'd eaten a roast beef sub in his car on his way to Gina's beach house.

He helped himself to a scoop of macaroni and cheese, poured dressing on his salad and took a bite.

"It was nice out today so I weeded the flower beds. How was your day?"

"Same as usual. Busy." He tried to think of something that didn't involve words that made Evelyn fearful. Murder. Guns. Dead bodies. Bloody victims. The usual items that filled his day.

She smoothed her auburn hair, hanging lank and listless down to her shoulders. "Christine called and cancelled my hair appointment today. We rescheduled for Saturday at 2:00. Can you drive me?"

"Evelyn, we bought you a car so you could get around when I'm not here." Saying *we* so as not to upset her. His money had bought the car. He was still making payments on it.

"But I hate driving on Saturday. There's so much traffic in Milton Square."

Tough. He wasn't going to start chauffeuring her around. "Take a cab then, or get one of your friends to drive you." *Damn! Why did he say that? Not Myra, no, no, no.* But it was too late now, the words were out. He got busy on his dinner, eating fast, bad for his acid stomach, but he couldn't help it.

Evelyn picked at her salad, ate a plump cherry tomato, then a slice of green pepper.

The room was silent, quiet enough to hear an ant crawl on the floor. Damn, he missed Maureen, missed her happy chatter about her classes and her next horseback riding meet . . .

"I feel bad for Kathy Lee. It's just awful, what she's going through with that husband of hers. He's running around with some floozy."

He set down his fork, felt acid sizzle his gut. "Evelyn, believe it or not, I'm not interested in Kathy Lee's problems. I can remember when news programs reported the important events of the day, not gossip."

Evelyn shot him an indignant look. "Maybe you don't care about Kathy Lee, but I do. I watch her every morning. It's almost like she's part of the family."

He wanted to tell her to get a job and do something productive with her life instead of going to Mass every day and saying the rosary with the preacher on TV and gossiping with her friends and whatever else she did to fill her aimless hours. But if he spoke the words churning through his mind it would only make things worse.

What the hell had happened to them? How did it all fall apart?

He felt a sharp pang of regret, recalling the fun times when they'd started dating twenty years ago. Back then Evelyn was gorgeous, long auburn hair, her curvy body slim and trim. Smart, too. She'd graduated near the top of her high school class.

But when he looked across the table, he saw no trace of the girl he'd fallen in love with, the girl who thought he was exciting and loved dancing with him. The mother of the child he adored. Maybe if they'd had sex before they got married, things would have been different. But sex before marriage was verboten for Catholics. And even if they had and he'd found out how uptight she was about sex, then what? If they hadn't gotten married, there would be no Maureen, the light of his life.

Almost as if she were reading his mind, Evelyn said, "I got a beautiful card from Maureen in today's mail. She's doing really well in school."

"Yeah, she told me. She's a smart girl."

Evelyn stared at him, a stricken look on her face. "She called you?"

"No. Sent me an email." Another no-no for Evelyn. She and her parents thought the Internet was evil, because some religious broadcaster on TV said there were a million porn sites on it.

He carried his dishes to the sink, rinsed them, put them in the dishwasher and popped three Tums to sooth his acid stomach. Maybe he was getting an ulcer. Or maybe he was getting paranoid like Evelyn.

"Jeopardy's on at 7:30," she said. "Want to watch it with me?"

Hell no. I'm in enough jeopardy already. "Sorry, I've got paperwork to do. I'll be up later." Any kind of luck, by then she'd be asleep in bed. He couldn't stand the goofy sitcoms she watched.

"Okay. I might turn in early. I was awake before sunup this morning."

He went down to the basement, inhaling the odor of fuel oil that powered the furnace. Their house was built on a slope, and the basement had a walkout door to the backyard. Years earlier he'd fixed up a small room for Maureen to use when she invited friends for sleepovers. Evelyn wouldn't let them use the playroom on the first floor. Four boisterous eleven-year-olds might keep her awake in their bedroom on the second floor. Now that Maureen was in college, he was using the room as an office.

And, he had to admit, as an escape from Evelyn.

His laptop sat on a small desk with a swivel chair. He fired it up, got on the Internet and went to the website he'd bookmarked, a site that listed lottery prizes. Tomorrow night there was a Mass Megabucks drawing, the prize estimated to be as much as twelve million dollars.

He leaned back in his chair. Did the Jackpot Killer watch the prizes?

Was that how he chose his prey?

For all he knew, the Jackpot Killer might be using this very website to troll for his next victim.

CHAPTER 8

Wednesday, May 3 — Sandwich

He entered quietly through the front door and paused, listening. No sound from the television set. Where was she? He went in the living room and shut the blinds so people walking by couldn't see inside.

"Mom," he called, "I'm home."

"I'm in the kitchen, Billy. Go wash up. Dinner's ready."

He walked down the hall to the bathroom, went in and shut the door. The room stank of bleach. The health aide must have cleaned it after she gave his mother a bath. His mother depended on the home-care workers, but he didn't like strangers in the house when he wasn't home. He took off his shirt and sniffed his underarms. Disgusting. He smelled like a ditch-digger.

Ten days ago it was cold and raw, today it felt like July, temperatures in the eighties. He'd done twenty cable hookups today and not one house with air conditioning.

The hamper was overflowing with dirty clothes. He'd better go to the laundromat tonight. He hated doing laundry, but it got him out of the house. Afterwards, he'd go to the Seaside Diner and sit at the counter with the cops.

He soaped his underarms and put on a clean T-shirt, wondering what his mother had fixed for dinner. He hadn't eaten much lunch. He left the bathroom and entered the kitchen. Even with the windows open it was stifling. She was in her wheelchair in front of the sink where the linoleum was worn down to the bare wood. He bent down and gave her a dutiful peck on the cheek. Beads of sweat dotted her nose and forehead.

"How was your day, Mom?"

"The girl from the health service was new. I had a terrible time washing up." She wheeled over to the card table and set paper napkins by their plates. "I tried a new recipe today. Nobody can say I don't cook for my family." She picked up a serving spoon. "Did you shut the light off in the bathroom?"

48

"Yes, Mom."

"Are you sure? I got up this morning and it was on. We can't afford to waste electricity, you know. Go check and make sure."

He got up and went around the corner to the bathroom. The light was off. When he returned to the kitchen, a glutinous gray mound filled his plate. "What's the new recipe?"

"Tuna casserole. I got it off a Campbell's mushroom soup can. I put green peas and black olives in it."

He studied the black specks in the slop on his plate. Probably the olives. The grayish-green things must be the peas. His mother looked at him expectantly. Her portion was smaller, and she had carrot sticks and celery stalks on her plate. His mother liked her rabbit food. He took a bite and rolled it around his mouth. It felt slimy.

What was it? Overcooked spaghetti, salty, with a fishy taste.

"Do you like it?" she said, watching him, not touching hers.

He smiled and nodded. "It's good, Mom. Real good. But you shouldn't have gone to so much trouble on such a hot day."

"The recipe makes a lot, enough for two meals."

"That's nice." He set his fork down. "But I won't be home for dinner tomorrow."

His mother stopped chewing and frowned. "Why not? Where are you going?"

"Up to the library in Quincy. They might have an opening."

"Why don't you call first and see? That's the smart thing to do. Why waste gas?"

"It's better to go in person so I can leave my resume. If I get another library job—"

"For more money, I hope. We can barely afford this house. You should get down on your knees and pray for a job that pays better. With the help of the Lord, maybe you'll find one." She took a bite of carrot and chewed. "Your father may have had his faults, but he was a good provider. Silas was salesman of the month, plenty of times."

He put his hands in his lap and picked the scab on his thumb, remembering the sour whisky-stink when his father got in his face and yelled: *Sissy! Why can't you be a big boy like John?*

Big brother John.

He went to the refrigerator and took out a carton of milk. Anything to wash down the slop. He shook the carton. "Is this all the milk?"

"Yes. I used most of it in the casserole."

He poured what was left into a glass and picked up the package of hot-dog rolls on the counter.

"Don't open those, Billy. They're for tomorrow."

He put them back, sat down at the table and felt a prickle of excitement.

His mother was wearing Florence's bracelet! He stared at it, picturing Florence with the yellow plastic bag over her head. He wondered how his mother would look if—

"What did you do today?" Gazing at him with her pale-blue watery eyes.

I ate an ice cream for lunch and read one of my movie magazines. Judy was on the cover. Beautiful Judy with her sad eyes and crooked smile. The article said she missed her father. Her dead father.

"Billy!"

His head jerked up with a start. His mother was glaring at him. "I asked you what you did today."

"Oh. Nothing much. The usual."

Her lips tightened. "What does that mean? Tell me what you did."

"A bunch of installations." He forced down a bite of casserole and smiled at her. "Then I came home to you. My boss is such a pain. He called a meeting because some shirts are missing. He thinks somebody stole them."

"Thou shalt not covet thy neighbor's goods. That's what Preacher Martin said on TV today. I think that's from Luke. Or is it Corinthians?"

His mother quoted scripture, but she never read the Bible. She never read anything. All she did was watch the Christian Cable Network all day. He eyed the mound of casserole on her plate. "Are you done?"

She heaved a sigh. "Yes. I don't work up much of an appetite in this wheelchair . . ."

He took her plate to the counter, scraped the slop in the garbage and set the plate in the sink, watching her out of the corner of his eye.

The scarab bracelet on her wrist gleamed.

"I better go feed my girls. I have to go out and do laundry tonight."

"Make sure you shut the bathroom light off this time. I know you left it on last night, Billy. Did you get up in the night to use the bathroom?"

He edged toward the door. "No, Mom."

"I worry about you, sleeping downstairs. You should have put in a toilet when you built that room. Remember how you used to have accidents when you were little?"

His cheeks flamed with embarrassment. He ducked out the door without answering.

———

Nigel drained the last of the scotch and set the glass aside. His eyes were gritty from staring at the numbers, his neck had a crick in it, and his nose was clogged again. He swiveled the high-backed chair and surveyed his hotel room. The desk and chair were passable, but he hadn't gotten much sleep in the lumpy double bed. Cigarette butts filled the ashtray beside the stack of losing Megabucks tickets on the desk.

Bloody hell, he'd been at this for an hour with nothing to show for it.

One stack of tickets left. Ten more chances to win. Or lose.

He plucked a tissue from the box on the desk and blew his nose.

Whatever had made him think he'd be lucky enough to win twelve million bean? Here he was leading a third-rate cast in a one-horse town with a hog-raising banker for a chauffeur. The other day Vicky had asked why he'd taken the job. She didn't know about the packet of bills in his suitcase, or the size of his debts. Why did he take it? Because his schedule was open and he desperately needed money.

Nothing but bad news from Hale, too. Hale thought someone else would get the Pops gig.

He sank back in the chair and massaged his neck. He was over the hill. Washed up. Finished.

He took the top ticket off the last remaining pile and compared the numbers. None matched.

Bollocks! This was useless. He'd wasted two hundred dollars, money he could ill afford, on these lottery tickets. He rubbed his bleary eyes and took the next ticket off the pile.

When the first three numbers matched he could hardly believe it. His mouth went dry. Was it possible?

His heart thumped his chest and sweat dampened his palms. He set the ticket on the desk. For almost a minute he sat there, paralyzed, afraid to check the last three digits.

Why get his hopes up? This was another loser, like the rest of them.

He set the ticket below the winning numbers he'd copied off the Internet website and compared the six numbers, one by one.

They all matched!

A rush of euphoria hit him. He sagged back in the chair, laughing helplessly. Tears oozed from his eyes and ran down his cheeks. By God that old woman in the store was right. A winner was due and it was him!

He felt like screaming. Light the fireworks! Sound the trumpets!

Unable to sit still, he jumped up and paced the room. Now he could pay off his debts. Compared to twelve million, they didn't amount to a hill of beans. He'd pay them off and have millions left over.

A giddy laugh bubbled up in his throat. He'd buy a big house on the ocean. Bloody hell, he'd buy two, one on each coast!

He had to call Vicky and tell her! But she'd probably be angry with him for gambling. He'd have to tell her sooner or later, but he'd better think things through first.

Maybe he'd call Hale. No, bad idea. When it came to money, Hale was a shark. He might even try to take some of the winnings.

Should he call Joanna? He owed her five thousand dollars in alimony, and she was threatening legal action. But he couldn't face talking to her now.

He went in the bathroom and looked in the mirror. His eyes were bloodshot, and his nose looked like Rudolph the Red-Nosed Reindeer.

But so what? He was a winner. He couldn't tell anyone, but he could bloody well go down to the pub and celebrate.

He put on a clean shirt and checked the ticket again.

Every number matched. His money problems were over!

———

Still seething after his mother's humiliating taunt, reminding him he used to wet his pants sometimes when he was little, he unlocked the door to his basement room, first the deadbolt, then the lock in the doorknob. When he went inside, the fluorescent light above the fish tank gave off a dim glow.

He turned on the overhead light. His shoes were lined up in a row beside his bed, and his magazines lay on the desk, just as he'd left them. Satisfied no one had been in his room, he massaged the dull ache above his ear. After the accident the doctors had said the pain would go away, but it hadn't.

Mouth-mother pain in his head. Hearing her voice right before the accident: *Silas, you're going too fast!!*

Now his father was dead, but his mother wasn't.

The ache near his ear kept throbbing, but he ignored it and studied the nametags pasted to the fish tank. Now there were seven. But Number 7 had no name. He scattered food on the water and seven orange goldfish darted to it, but Judy hung back. Judy was different.

Judy and her beautiful calico-spotted fins.

Mysterious. Lonely. They were so much alike.

He watched his girls gobble the food, their eager mouths moving: Lulu and Tessa and Lilly. His groin ached, just thinking about them, remembering his excitement. Then came Betty and Rosie and Florence. Each one more thrilling than the last. Now he had a new girl.

"Jooody," he crooned. "My new girl needs a name."

He powered up his computer. Maybe he'd read his journals. Which one? Lulu, his Powerball princess? He touched his crotch, remembering. No. Not yet. He had to fix his resume so he could take it to the Quincy Library. He opened the file and studied it. The BS in Library Science was bullshit, of course. BS. Bull Shit. He'd taken only one course. The Film Classics professor gave him an F, but he didn't care. He had fallen in love with Judy. Beautiful, talented Judy Garland. Little, abused Judy. Judy was so brave. Her mother fed her diet pills to keep her thin. She wanted to please her parents, but the drugs and the diets finally killed her.

When he was little he wanted to please his parents too, but . . .

He scrolled past the bogus college degree. He hadn't bothered to list the electronics courses he'd taken after high school. Libraries didn't care about that. The college degree got him the job at the Bourne Library.

How he loved working there! He'd read every book and magazine he could find about Judy. When the head librarian fired him, he wanted to kill her, but she was bigger than he was, muscular, with a long horsy face. One day she caught him in the ladies restroom hiding in a stall. He loved listening to the sounds women made. Horse-face had been outraged, had told him he was sick. Right to his face.

He updated the resume and clicked print. He rarely printed things out. Never his journals. Never the lottery lists. He logged onto the Internet and went to the website that listed the lottery prizes. Powerball was at the top: twenty-six million! No winner.

But the Mass Megabucks prize was gone. His heart fluttered.

He surfed to the Mass State Lottery website.

Yes! Tonight's Megabucks drawing had a winner.

Twelve million dollars. One winning ticket.

Now all he had to do was wait and see who claimed the prize.

———

The Budget Inn pub was long and narrow and dimly lit. Fake plants with dusty green leaves lined the wall opposite the bar. Other than two men in business suits watching TV at the far end of the bar, the pub was deserted. Nigel slipped onto a stool beside the service area where plastic bins held olives and cherries and slices of lemon and lime.

A lanky bartender with a bushy brown mustache set a napkin in front of him. His arms were tanned and muscular, and he wore thick glasses. "Like a drink, sir?"

"Right-o. D'you have any single-malt scotch?"

"Single-malt? Let's see." The barman shoved his glasses against his nose and squinted at the bottles behind the bar. "Glenlivet okay?"

"Yes. I'll have a double, on the rocks." He lit a cigarette and checked his watch. 9:30. 10:30 in Boston. He wondered what Vicky was doing. Probably finishing up tonight's Pops concert.

When the barman brought his drink, Nigel raised his glass. "Join me, why don't you? On me."

"Can't. I'm working," the man said, and pushed his glasses against the bridge of his nose.

"Pity. Pub masters in London would rather have a pint than a tip. Nice custom, that."

The man gave him a dubious look and moved down the bar to chat up the businessmen.

He scooped some peanuts from a dish on the bar. They tasted stale. He washed them down with some Glenlivet. How would he get through the next three days without going mad? Bloody Christ, he'd won twelve million bean and he couldn't tell anybody!

The bartender returned to the service area, took off his glasses and polished them with a napkin.

Nigel tapped his glass for a refill. "D'you know anything about lottery payoffs?"

"Why? Did you hit the lottery?" the man asked, and put on his glasses.

"Not bloody likely. No, a friend of mine did. I just wondered how they pay off."

A knowing grin appeared on the man's face. "Your friend owe you money?" He added ice to a fresh glass, poured Glenlivet over it and set the glass in front of Nigel. "Nothing but trouble, you ask me. I knew a guy hit the lottery once. Uncle Sam takes a big chunk up front."

He gulped some scotch. Blast! He'd forgotten about the IRS. He already owed them a bundle.

"His ex-wife got most of the rest."

Aghast, he stared at the man.

"Yup. Took him to court and got all but a million of it. If I won a million bucks, I'd buy me a farm."

Nigel nodded morosely. Another hog farmer.

"The reporters hounded him for weeks. Poor guy got no peace. Everybody wanted a piece of the pie, his family, his friends." The bartender moved down the bar, polishing the dark wood.

He sat there, stunned. The bloke was right. Joanna was already threatening to take him to court. If she found out he'd won twelve million bucks, she'd be after it like a cat lapping cream, and so would Hale. Not only that, the reporters would be after him like hounds at a fox hunt.

They'd spread it 'round all the papers and the telly. He could see the headline now: BOSTON POPS GUEST CONDUCTOR HITS THE JACKPOT!

What if they found out about his gambling? And his debts?

The scandal rags would have a field day.

Bloody hell, it would be a disaster. He'd *never* get the Pops job!

A black cloud of despair descended upon him.

CHAPTER 9

Thursday, May 4 — 6:35 a.m. — Milton

Frank loped past an elementary school, almost finished with his five-mile run. In two hours kids would be outside, zipping down slides or climbing the jungle gyms. Now the sun was just starting to peep through the trees behind the school. He loved running at dawn, feet pounding, arms pumping. The repetitive movements put him into a Zen-like zone, boosting his endorphins.

A great way to start the day. Clear your mind and focus on the work ahead. Drive to Rhode Island and interview the daughter of the murdered lottery winner he'd found.

He paused at an intersection, running in place until the traffic light changed. Sometimes when he couldn't sleep, he went out and ran in the dark, jogging past elegant Victorians with carriage houses. Plenty of those in Milton, not to mention the million-dollar mansions near the golf course, their owners tucked in bed, protected by elaborate security systems in case any thugs from nearby Mattapan, a predominantly black, working-class town, invaded their ritzy neighborhood.

A large van pulled into the four-pump gas station on the corner. The driver got out and lugged bundles of the *Boston Globe* and the *Herald* into the store. Frank had only been inside once. It was a mini-gambling parlor, Keno players perched on stools, eyes fixed on monitors, older men mostly, the clerk selling scratch tickets from two dozen rolls on the wall behind the register.

When the light changed, he trotted across the street and put on a burst of speed, running flat out the last half-mile to his house. Winded but exhilarated, he unlocked the side door. Evelyn insisted that he lock the house before he did his run. "What if a burglar broke in while you're gone?"

What if the house blew up? What if a meteor fell from the sky and hit Milton? He smiled at her nonsensical fears but quickly sobered.

What if Myra told her about Gina? But why tempt fate? He banished the thought and entered the kitchen. No coffee brewing, no sign of Evelyn.

Strange. She was always up by now. He put a filter in the coffeemaker, spooned in coffee, filled the pot with water and dumped it in the machine. He pushed the Start button and heard footsteps behind him.

Evelyn entered the kitchen, wearing a charcoal gray skirt, a high-necked green blouse, and a grim expression. "I talked to a lawyer yesterday, Frank. Adultery is grounds for divorce."

No *good morning*, no *hello*, just *adultery is grounds for divorce*.

Like he was some tom-cat screwing around. He wasn't. He'd been as faithful to Gina for the past nine years as he'd been to Janine the previous ten. But he couldn't very well say this to Evelyn. His temperature was up after the run, and for an instant he felt lightheaded. He mopped sweat off his face with a kitchen towel and mustered his thoughts, biting back the angry words on the tip of his tongue.

"What's his name? The lawyer."

"*Her* name. Annette Mitchell. I told her about Gina."

Another gut-punch, but he said nothing. *Anything you say can and will be used against you in a court of law.*

He took a Sam Adams out of the refrigerator, popped the cap and took a long swig. Nothing like a cold one before breakfast. Nothing like a divorce threat to make your mind go a hundred miles per hour.

"Told her what about Gina?"

"That you were having an affair with her. Don't deny it. All those nights you don't come home for dinner? Do you think I'm stupid?"

He didn't think she was stupid, but for twenty years she'd been content to look the other way. Until Myra the Gossip Queen told her she'd seen him with Gina.

"Why didn't you talk to me before you talked to the lawyer?" He took another swig of beer.

"Why? So you could make up excuses?" Standing ramrod stiff beside the sink, quivering with outrage.

He clamped his teeth together to keep from speaking the words raging in his mind. *What do you think I've been doing the last twenty years, jerking off in the shower? If I'd known you wanted to be a nun, I'd have found a more willing bed partner.*

He held the beer bottle to his forehead. It felt cool against his skin. He had to be cool, had to tamp down the fury boiling into his throat. He still cared about her. She was the mother of his child. It wasn't her fault. Part of it was her Catholic upbringing, and after Maureen was born, Evelyn suffered from post-partum depression. Her doctor had put her on Prozac. Maybe if things had been different . . .

But they weren't. After a year without sex, he'd found someone else, Janine for ten years, then Gina. He'd gone out of his way to be discreet, never meeting them anyplace Evelyn or any of their friends frequented.

Or so he'd thought. What did Myra say, he wondered, tell Evelyn to do something or she'd look like a fool?

Dreading the answer, he said, "What about Maureen? Did you tell her?"

Evelyn gave him her tight, pinched look. "Please have your things out of the house by Sunday night. My lawyer will be in touch with you."

———

Central Falls, RI — 11:00 a.m.

"He killed other women?" Donna Calvicchio said in a high-pitched voice, outrage evident in her large brown eyes. "Before he killed Mom?"

Frank shifted in his chair, hearing her unspoken question: *Why didn't you stop him?* "Yes. Since he murdered your mother two years ago, he's killed four other lottery winners. I didn't discover your mother's case until this week."

They were seated at her kitchen table in a modest ranch house in Central Falls, Rhode Island, a working-class city near the Massachusetts border. The kitchen was small but tidy. He detected the faint odor of anisette, a familiar aroma in many Italian households. It smelled like his grandmother's kitchen.

Donna brushed long, dark hair behind her ears and shook her head. "Unbelievable."

"I know this is upsetting. But anything you can tell me might help us find the killer."

Anything you say can and will be used against you in a court of law. Like a broken record, the ominous words had played in his mind as he drove to Donna's house, unable to concentrate, flummoxed by Evelyn's accusations.

Adultery is grounds for divorce. What would Maureen think?

Out of the house by Sunday. Where the hell would he live?

He forced himself to concentrate on Donna, sitting there lost in thought. On the phone she'd said she was fighting a nasty custody battle with her about-to-be ex-husband. Just what he needed, another marriage on the rocks, another reminder of how fragile a marriage could be.

"You know," she said with a wistful smile, "I talked to Mom the day she was murdered."

"When? What time?"

FBI Agent Ross Dunn had sent him the autopsy report and the crime scene photos: a gray-haired woman dead on the floor, asphyxiated by a plastic bag. But no J&B nip. Was Tessa Calvicchio the Jackpot Killer's first victim? Maybe he hadn't yet developed his killer persona, started adding the J&B signature later.

"In the morning," Donna said. "Around nine, I think."

"Did she say she was expecting someone?"

"Not that I recall. She said her TV was messed up, but mostly we talked about my kids. I've got two, a boy and a girl." Her eyes filled with tears. "They're in school now, but back then they could be a handful."

"Yeah? You got pictures?" He said it hoping to cheer her up and it did.

She actually smiled. "Of course." She went in the living room and returned with two school portraits, a handsome dark-haired boy and a little girl with dark eyes, banana curls and a cute smile.

"Gorgeous kids," he said. "They look like you."

"Mom loved them, and they adored her." Donna's lips quivered and her eyes welled with tears.

"Was anything missing when you settled the estate?"

"I don't think so. My brothers left it to me to go through Mom's things. We sold the house last year." Donna sighed. "That was hard. We grew up in that house. Dad died five years ago, so Mom was alone." Her dark eyes hardened. "And some son-of-a-bitch killed her."

"Where'd she buy the lottery ticket?"

"At the corner store. Every Sunday she'd buy the newspaper and drop ten bucks on lottery tickets. I used to tease her about it. You'll never win, I said. But then she did." Donna's lips tightened. "But she didn't get to enjoy it, because some bastard killed her! Why did he do it? He didn't get the money."

"It's hard to say why serial killers do what they do." Donna flinched when he said *serial killer*. "When you went through your Mom's things, did you notice if anything was missing?"

Donna frowned. "You know, there was one thing. Dad gave her a pearl necklace for their thirtieth anniversary. Not that it was worth much. Dad was a fireman. He didn't make a lot of money."

"Could you describe it?"

"Just a single strand of pearls. Not a long strand, not a choker . . ." She shrugged.

"A string of pearls," he said, naming the Glenn Miller tune. But she didn't get it, just nodded. "I don't suppose you'd have a picture of it, maybe taken on their anniversary?"

"I might. Let me go check. I've got a photo album."

Adultery is grounds for divorce. I told her about Gina.

Would this day ever end? It was only 11:15 and it felt like he'd been up for twenty-four hours. His body felt like he'd done a triathlon: a stiff neck, tight muscles, his stomach sour with acid.

Donna came back, smiling now, and handed him a snapshot. "That's Mom and Dad."

He studied the photo. A typical Italian couple, they reminded him of his paternal grandparents: short and stocky, dark eyes, the man smiling broadly, the woman shyly gazing at her husband. Around her neck was a single strand of pearls. "Can I borrow this? I'll get it right back to you after I make a copy."

"Why?"

"We think he takes things from the victims, jewelry in a couple of cases."

"The necklace wasn't worth much."

"That's not why he takes it." He didn't tell her what the weirdo did with their trophies, jerking off over them, reliving their sexual fantasies and the sexual arousal they got from killing their victims.

"If it helps find the killer, I'm happy for you to take it."

"I'll get it back to you soon. Thanks for speaking with me, Donna. I know it's been two years, but I'm sure it's hard to talk about."

Her lips trembled. She nodded, unable to speak.

"Did you and your brothers inherit the lottery money?"

"Yes," she snapped, "and it brought nothing but trouble. Peter's wife went through his share like a dose of salts, Eddie gambled his away at the racetrack, and my about-to-be-ex-husband wants half of mine. The bastard. People think hitting the jackpot is great, but sometimes it causes more problems than it's worth."

———

He crossed the state line into Massachusetts and got off in Attleboro. Other than the beer this morning—his oh-so-nutritious breakfast—he hadn't eaten. He still wasn't hungry, but he needed a caffeine hit. He stopped at a Dunkin' Donuts for an iced coffee and drank it in his car. His head throbbed with a dull ache. No food. Not much sleep. Too much tension. That kind of headache.

Now he had to tell Gina. When he called her on his cell, she picked up right away. Assuming she was at work and other people were around, he gave his customary greeting. "Hey, whaddaya know?"

"Hey, not too much, but I'm working on it." Letting him know she was in her cubicle at the *Herald*.

"Can you step outside and call my cell? I've got some news for you."

"That sounds excellent. Give me two minutes."

He punched off, sipped his coffee and held the icy container against his forehead. It didn't clear his head any. His cell rang and he punched on, heard Gina say, "Hey, Franco, what's up?"

"Nothing good. Myra, the woman that saw us at the bar, told Evelyn. I came in from my run this morning and Evelyn dropped a bomb on me. She's got a lawyer and she's filing for a divorce."

"Jesus! Are you serious?"

"Yes, and it gets worse. She said, and I quote, *adultery is grounds for divorce.* She told her lawyer about you. Gina, she said. I don't know if she's got your last name, but she might. Because of the *Herald* gig, you know?"

"Fuck."

"Yeah. More like fucked. Both of us." He raked his fingers through his hair. "If her lawyer figures out your last name, you know, from the *Herald* gig, she can find out if you're married. This could get messy."

Silence on the other end. "Well, we'll just have to deal with it, I guess."

"And we will. Dig this. Evelyn wants me out of the house by Sunday."

"What??"

"Yeah. What a pisser. I'm paying the mortgage and I have to get out."

"You can use the beach house. My brothers never use it until Fourth of July at the earliest. Al lives in New Jersey and his kids are in school till the end of June, and George teaches until—"

"No. Think about it, Gina. The utilities are in your name, right? The phone? The electricity? The cable TV?"

"Yes, but—"

"All her lawyer needs to do is run a search, find those accounts and sic a private investigator on you. He sees me there, takes a picture and bam, they've got evidence."

"Okay. But where will you live?"

"I don't know. To tell the truth, I haven't thought about it. I'm worried about Maureen."

"Jesus. She told Maureen?"

"I don't know. I asked her, but she didn't answer me."

"Franco, this is awful. I'm so sorry. I never thought this would happen."

"Neither did I." He barked a sardonic laugh. "Neither do the crooks that get caught."

"But we're not crooks, we're just two people who love each other, stuck in bad situations."

He couldn't argue with that, but plenty of people could. And would.

"Maybe you could stay with Orchid," Gina said. "She's got a loft in the South End."

He'd met Orchid once, a string-bean with purple hair. Gina's best friend. Orchid knew they were having an affair, but he didn't want to bunk with Orchid. Not that he didn't trust her, but the more people that knew . . .

"Mum's the word, okay?" he said. "I need to do some thinking. Figure out some things." Figure out what to do now that his life was in the toilet.

"Can we at least have a drink tonight and talk about it?" Gina said, her tone wistful.

His throat thickened. For a moment he couldn't speak. Man, this was like a boulder dropped into a pond, the ever-widening ripples affecting everyone, shredding their emotions, his included.

"Sure," he said, his voice husky. "But someplace north of Boston. From now on we need to make sure no one sees us."

Already he felt like a criminal.

CHAPTER 10

Friday May 5

Squinting against the glare of sun, he cruised the Mass Ave area near Boston Med Center. After his morning run, he hadn't bothered with coffee, didn't bother talking to Evelyn either, just took a shower, got in his Mazda Protégé and drove to work, questions dive-bombing his mind.

Should he talk to a lawyer? He knew plenty of prosecutors and defense lawyers, but they didn't handle divorces. Why should he leave his own house? On the other hand, staying might be worse. Already he hated the tension, tiptoeing around, avoiding Evelyn's accusing looks.

When he got to his office, he'd checked his messages, none of them urgent, so he went out to Dunkin' Donuts and bought coffee and a blueberry muffin. Then he'd decided to hunt for the black kid he'd spotted at the Mass Ave murder scene. Anything to avoid brooding over his marital woes.

He drove past the alley where he and Rafe had chased the kid. No sign of him now. All the pedestrians he saw were adults. This was probably a wild goose chase. At 9:30, the kid should be in school. But some kids cut school on balmy days like this, itching for classes to be over. He turned a corner, drifted down a side street and eyeballed people sitting on their front stoop, enjoying the balmy weather, sipping coffee, reading newspapers.

But no skinny little black kid.

At the next intersection he turned left and saw a kid running down the sidewalk with a basketball. He knew that stride! The boy was dressed for the mild weather, shorts, a ragged T-shirt and sneakers. Frank drove by him, turned left at the next corner, parked beside a fire hydrant and got out.

Seconds later the kid whipped around the corner and spotted him.

"Don't run, or this time I'll grab you."

The kid froze, a deer in the headlights, huge brown eyes, dark skin, and rail-thin, five-foot-three, might have weighed eighty-five pounds soaking wet, arms as skinny as drinking straws.

"Detective Renzi, Boston PD. We need to talk." He opened the passenger side door. "Get in the car."

The kid hesitated, eyes wary. Frank showed him his ID badge. "Get in and we'll take a ride. I'll bring you back, drop you off right here."

Pouting, the boy slid onto the front seat, clutching his basketball.

Frank got in and did a U-turn. "Where we going?" A soft voice, the kid not looking at him, staring straight ahead, hugging the ball to his chest.

"Not far. You shoot hoop?"

No answer. He kept going on Mass Ave, took a right four blocks later and stopped at a basketball court. "You shoot hoop?" he said again.

The kid nodded slowly.

"Let's see you shoot then." Hoping the kid wouldn't run, he got out and walked onto the deserted court, relaxed when the kid followed him. Frank asked him for the ball, dribbled to the free-throw line and took a shot. It clanged off the rim and bounced away. The kid chased it, put up a shot, made it and ran after the ball, his stick-legs working like pistons. He put up another shot and missed, rebounded the ball and threw Frank a perfect bounce pass.

For the next half hour they took turns shooting, the kid running him ragged, full of energy.

Frank mopped sweat off his face. "Man, I need a break. Let's go sit for a minute."

Reluctantly, the kid followed him to the sideline and they perched on a cement slab. "You're good," Frank said. "Keep up your shooting, develop your passing skills, you'll make a good point guard. Who's your favorite? Rondo?" Assuming it would be the Boston Celtics point guard.

The kid ducked his head, staring at the ground. "Nah. Kobe's better."

He clutched his chest in mock horror. "You root for the *Lakers?*"

The kid half-smiled, a tiny acknowledgement of his acting skills, said nothing.

"You play hoop in school?"

A shake of the head. No.

"How come you're not in school today?"

The kid went still, his face tense.

"Look, I'm not the truant officer. I don't even know your name, and even if I did, I'm not gonna report you. Now that we shot some hoop, how about we swap names. I'm Frank Renzi. What's your name?"

"Jamal." Barely above a whisper.

No last name. Frank decided to let it go, for now. "Okay, Jamal. I won't report you this time, but you need to go to school. You're smart enough to know that. Who takes care of you, your mom?"

A quick headshake. He didn't ask about the kid's father. If Mom wasn't taking care of him, the father probably wasn't either. That left Grandma.

"You live with your grandma?"

A slow nod.

"What's her name?"

The kid looked at him, eyes wary. "You gonna tell her I skipped school?"

"Okay, Jamal, here's the deal. Promise me you'll go to school every day next week, and I won't tell her you skipped today. What's your grandma's name?"

"Wilkes." Digging his sneaker into the dirt. "Josephine Wilkes."

"I don't know about you, Jamal, but I'm thirsty. There's a Friendly's ice cream shop a couple blocks away. Let's go get a milkshake. Then I'll drop you off where I picked you up, like I promised."

Ten minutes later they were in a booth at Friendly's. The waitress, an attractive young black woman with pearly-white teeth and a welcoming smile, brought them glasses of ice water and menus, and left.

Jamal didn't touch the menu, just sucked up water through his straw.

"You hungry, Jamal?"

Jamal's huge brown eyes met his, no expression on his face.

"How 'bout we get cheeseburgers and milkshakes? You pick the flavor."

Jamal gave a tiny nod. Frank signaled the waitress who came right over.

"We'll both have a cheeseburger with fries, and a milkshake. Coffee milkshake for me. What flavor you want, Jamal?"

"Chocolate," Jamal said softly, hesitated, then said, "please."

After the waitress left, Frank did an extended monologue on his favorite basketball players, Celtics greats Bill Russell, Dennis Johnson, threw in Larry Bird to see what the kid would do.

"And Magic Johnson," Jamal muttered.

Frank grinned. "You know your basketball history, for sure. Who taught you that?"

"Cousin Tyreke," he said, and froze, a stricken expression on his face.

Pretending not to notice, Frank said, "You live with Tyreke?"

Jamal's big brown eyes filled with tears. He clamped his lips together and shook his head.

Then the waitress arrived, set down plates with cheeseburgers and piping hot French fries, then the milkshakes, coffee for Frank, chocolate for Jamal.

"Anything else I can get for you?" she asked, smiling at Jamal whose eyes were focused on his cheeseburger.

"Just the check when you get a chance," Frank said.

She tore off a slip, set it on the table and told them to have a nice day.

Jamal devoured his cheeseburger and fries in record time. Frank didn't. His stomach was too jumpy. He cut his cheeseburger in half, took two bites,

63

ate a few French fries and set his plate aside. Jamal stared at the other half of his cheeseburger, seemed like the kid hadn't eaten a square meal in weeks.

"Want the other half? Go ahead. Why let it go to waste? Besides, I think you beat me at hoops."

When Jamal finished the burger, Frank paid the tab and they went out and got in his car. "How old are you, Jamal?"

"Ten," Jamal muttered, not looking at him.

"You running with a gang?"

The boy shook his head, still not looking at him. "No. Gramma would kill me."

Relieved, Frank said, "Gramma's right. Kids get mixed up with gangs, bad things happen."

Jamal nodded, mumbled, "That's what Gramma says."

"Okay, Jamal. Here's the deal. You go to school every day from now on and I won't tell your grandmother you skipped school today. I'm gonna check. What school you go to?"

"Alma Lewis Middle School."

He held out his hand. Jamal hesitated, then shook it.

"I coach a middle-school basketball team in Mattapan sometimes," Frank said. "How about I pick you up at Grandma's on Sunday morning and we shoot some more hoop?"

Jamal looked at him, frowning now. "Be better if I meet you at that playground."

His anxious expression made Frank's heart ache. The kid didn't want a cop coming to his apartment, too many eyes watching. "Okay. Meet you at the playground at eleven. Maybe this time I'll beat you."

Jamal's lips twitched, almost a smile. "Don't count on it."

———

Sandwich, MA

He couldn't wait to finish dinner. He shoveled down his mother's tasteless slop, answered her incessant questions and raced downstairs to his room. His shoes were lined up beside his bed: blue Nikes next to his spare work boots next to the black loafers he wore to church on Sundays. Perfect.

He powered up his computer, got on the Internet and checked the *Boston Globe* website. An article in the Metro section said no one had claimed the twelve-million-dollar Megabucks prize.

The back of his hand felt like a thousand bugs were crawling over it. He scratched furiously, digging at the skin with his nails. Drops of blood beaded around the scab. Disgusting. He grabbed a towel off the shelf above his bed, wiped off the blood and turned back to the computer screen.

Today's article was longer than yesterday's. The winning ticket had been sold at Marie's Variety, a small store in Boston's North End. People in the neighborhood were thrilled. Two men with Italian-sounding names said they figured the winner was Italian, one of their pals, maybe, the ones they played bocce with in Paul Revere Park.

He didn't care if the winner was Italian as long as it was a little old lady with cable. He logged off the Net, clicked on the file that contained his journals and opened the one labeled Lulu.

His Powerball princess. Twenty-six million dollars.

Lulu. His first lucky winner.

He opened the article he'd retrieved from the Poughkeepsie *Journal* website two years ago, the day Lulu claimed the prize. Her picture was on the front page. Her name was Louisa, but he liked Lulu better. An article below her picture said the American Library Association was hosting a workshop on Women in Popular Culture that weekend. One session was on movie icons, and there, topping the list, was Judy Garland! Beautiful Judy, showing him how it could be done.

After that, it was easy. He got Lulu's address and telephone number from the cable company and told his mother he had to go to a conference. She didn't like it, but he told her it might help him get another library job. He took two vacation days and drove to Poughkeepsie. At the movie seminar he sat in the back, enthralled, listening to them talk about Judy. Icon to millions, they said. Beautiful, talented Judy, fighting the demons within her. After the seminar, he finished his preparations. The next day he went to Lulu.

Lulu was easy. Gullible, like his mother.

She even looked like his mother, pale and thin with scrawny arms.

The next day her murder had made the front page of the *Poughkeepsie Journal*.

A familiar ache stirred in his groin.

He rubbed himself through his pants, felt himself grow hard.

Make sure the door is locked, said a nagging voice in his mind.

He went to the door, secured the deadbolt and stood by his bed, feeling the excitement grow. Until the nagging voice said, *They're watching you.*

His girls, with their little beady eyes.

He draped a towel over the fish tank and shut off the light. Now he was safe. The room was quiet. Dark. He opened his fly and stroked himself, remembering how Lulu had struggled, fighting him.

But she couldn't stop him. He had the power and she had none.

His breathing grew ragged. He pumped harder and harder, seeking the glorious release.

Did you turn off the light in the bathroom, Billy?

His mother's voice, humiliating him.

He kept stroking, harder and harder until the muscles in his arm ached. But it was no use. He couldn't come. He zipped his fly, turned on the light, pulled the towel off the fish tank and watched Judy.

Beautiful, talented Judy. He would never hurt Judy. He watched his other girls swim through the water, flitting this way and that. Tessa and Lulu and Rosie and Florence. And his No-Name girl.

His hands clenched spasmodically. Someone had a Megabucks ticket worth twelve million dollars!

What were they waiting for? Why didn't they claim the prize?

He plunged his hand into the tank and captured Lulu, his Powerball princess. Her fins flailed against his hand, but he squeezed her tight.

Finally, the fluttering stopped. When he dropped Lulu in the tank, she floated on her side on top of the water.

———

Frank finished his chicken marsala dinner and signaled the waitress for another beer, his third. He'd considered eating at Doyle's in Jamaica Plain, but too many cops hung out there. He didn't want to run into anyone he knew. Besides, Nanina's in Dorchester served great Italian food.

The waitress brought him another Heineken draft and removed his plate. He was the lone person at the bar, a Formica-topped slab opposite the entrance with six barstools. Customers sat here to wait for take-out orders or a table in the dining room, but no one was waiting now. It was almost eleven.

He glanced at the TV in the corner above the bar. Golf. Boring.

He wished he could talk to Gina, but Ryan might be home. Last night he and Gina had met at a restaurant ten miles north of Boston, both of them down in the dumps but putting on a cheerful front, avoiding serious topics, like where he'd live after he moved out of his house on Sunday.

Two days from now.

Maybe he'd call Jack Warner. Jack worked homicide, too. Jack would probably put him up in his spare bedroom. But then he'd have to explain why Evelyn threw him out. Jack had been utterly devoted to his wife of thirty years until she died last year. He wouldn't understand.

But Rafe would, and Rafe owned a three decker. Maybe he'd call Rafe and ask if he had a vacant apartment. *Yo, Rafe, can you spare a bed for a philandering husband thrown out by his ultra-Catholic wife?*

Imagining Rafe's cackling laugh and his wise-ass reply: *Best not to get caught if you screw around.*

But he didn't feel like talking to Rafe either, didn't feel like explaining the crap he'd put up with for twenty years. When it came right down to it, he was a loner at heart. That's what his mother had said right before she died. "Frank, you're a loner like your father."

66

His father. What would Judge Salvatore Renzi say when he found out Evelyn had filed for divorce? Nothing good, that's for sure. A flame of embarrassment shot up his neck onto his cheeks.

What would he say? How could he explain? Tension gripped his gut in a vise, a tight sensation that wouldn't quit, a constant companion since Evelyn dropped the divorce bomb.

His father, an appellate court judge, had deep-rooted beliefs about marriage. Judge Salvatore Renzi believed that marriage was for life, for richer or poorer, in sickness and in health, till death us do part.

At the divorce hearing, Evelyn's lawyer would say Frank was having an affair. How would he explain *that* to his father? He slugged down half of his beer, unable to imagine it, much less figure out what he'd say.

A news jingle sounded on the television set and the vivid graphics of a newscast flashed on the screen. The lead story involved a hit and run in Cambridge. The second story gave him chills. Wednesday night's Megabucks drawing had produced one winner. The prize? Twelve million dollars.

Did the Jackpot Killer know, Frank wondered. If not, he soon would.

A prize that big would spawn a feeding frenzy, flashbulbs and cameras galore, every reporter in town sticking a microphone in the winner's face, asking what they planned to do with the money.

He drained his beer and set the mug on the bar. He hoped the winner wasn't an elderly woman that lived alone.

If it was, she might never get to enjoy her winnings.

CHAPTER 11

Sunday, May 7

When Frank pulled up to the basketball court at 11:00, Jamal was already there, even gave him a smile. Now it was almost noon, the kid still racing around the court. He watched him dribble toward the hoop, a fierce look of concentration on his face. He did a little stutter-step, took a shot with his left hand and missed.

Frank tried to remember if he'd had that much energy when he was ten. He should be home packing, but he couldn't face it. Shooting hoop with Jamal was more fun. His house was no palace but it was home, comfortable and familiar. Tonight he had to move out.

When Jamal tossed him the ball, he said, "You're wearing me out, Jamal. Let's take a break. Where do you get all your energy?"

The kid shrugged and followed him to the cement slab on the sideline.

"You got big hands. Put it there." He held up his right hand like he was going to do a high-five.

Jamal set his palm against his, the boy's dark skin a stark contrast to his olive skin. "Your hand's not as big as mine, but you got long fingers. That's great for playing basketball. What hand do you write with?"

"My right hand. Sometimes."

"And other times?"

"With my left."

"Far out. You're ambidextrous." Jamal gave him a blank stare, so he said, "That's when you can use either hand to do things."

"My teacher don't like it, though. She makes me use my right hand to write with."

"Okay. But basketball's different. Being able to shoot with both hands is an asset. You took a shot with your left and missed, but that's okay. Keep practicing. You'll get better."

68

Jamal picked up the ball and bounced it with his left hand, ready to go play some more.

"And study hard at school. You know why?"

"So I learn stuff."

"Right. You're smart but you need to learn how to take tests so you can get into college. Some college scout sees you play on your high school team, pass and shoot with both hands, you might get a scholarship."

Jamal stopped bouncing the ball, all attention now.

"To play pro ball, you gotta go to college. You're not Kevin Garnett you know, big guy with big hands and great defensive skills, gets drafted right out of high school."

"Uh-huh."

"Gotta go to college like . . . ?" Waiting for him to say, Magic Johnson.

"Like Shaq." The kid surprising him again.

Frank wondered who put him onto Shaq. His cousin Tyreke? Maybe not. Jamal probably listened to Shaq's rap music albums, might even have seen him in *Kazaam*. When the movie came out in 1996, the critics panned it, but back then Jamal was six years old. See Shaq up there on the big screen? Instant adoration.

He rose from the cement slab. "You hungry? Want to go get a burger?"

"Yeah, but . . ." Jamal scuffled his sneaker in the dirt.

"But what?"

"My gramma said I hadda be home by 12:30 so I can get cleaned up. We going to her mama's house for dinner."

"Okay. I don't want to make you and Gramma late for dinner. What's her mama's name?" Plot out the family tree, maybe he'd locate Tyreke in another branch of the family.

"Gramma Robinson."

"We better get going then. Want to stop for a shake so you can drink it on the way?" Bribing the kid now, Jamal skipping along beside him, bouncing the ball left-handed.

He stopped at Friendly's, bought a chocolate shake for Jamal, a black coffee for himself, and got back in the car. He caught a red light at the corner of Melnea Cass Boulevard and Mass Ave, a major choke-point on weekdays, not bad on a Sunday. He glanced at Jamal, happily drinking his milkshake.

His cell rang. He checked the ID. Maureen. This could be bad news.

He punched on and said, "Hi, that you, Mo?"

"Yes, and I'm very upset."

Worse than bad. The light changed and he swung left onto Mass Ave.

"I talked to Mom and she said you're getting a divorce!"

"Let me call you back. I'm in traffic right now." *And a ten-year-old kid is listening to every word I say.*

"She said you've got a girlfriend. Is that true?"

69

"Mo, I know you're upset, but I can't talk while I'm in traffic. Let me call you back."

"Okay, fine." His daughter ended the call.

He glanced at Jamal, drinking his chocolate shake, not looking at him.

How did his life get so complicated? Problems swarming at him like angry hornets.

————

Vicky curled up on the loveseat in her living room with a chocolate donut and the *Boston Phoenix*. An article about Nigel in the Arts Section had a picture of him conducting a Pops rehearsal. Nigel would be pleased. Ten minutes ago he'd called from the airport to say he'd be here soon. Absorbed in the article, she nibbled on the donut. The telephone on the end table rang.

When she answered, her father's voice boomed in her ear. But they'd barely begun to talk when her door buzzer sounded.

"Hold on a second, Dad. Someone's at the door."

She went to the kitchen, pressed a button on the intercom beside the door. "That you, Nigel?"

"Right-o, luv."

She buzzed him in, opened the door and heard the downstairs door slam. By the time she got back to the phone, Nigel had entered the living room, smiling broadly. She motioned him to be quiet and picked up the telephone: "Gotta go, Dad. I've got company. I'll call you back later." To his inevitable question, she replied: "Just a friend."

Nigel raised an eyebrow. "Problem with your father?"

"No, Dad calls me almost every Sunday. He's my biggest fan."

"Count your blessings. All mine ever did was tell me to practice more."

"Sounds like my mother. She keeps telling me I should get married like my sister."

"House in the suburbs and six kids?" Nigel said, giving her a bear hug.

"Wow! I guess you're happy to see me."

"You have no idea!" He gave her a long lingering kiss. "Missed you."

"I missed you, too. How'd *Music Man* go?"

"Bloody awful! The lead singer couldn't carry a tune in a steamer trunk. How was your week?"

"Great, actually. I've got a surprise for you."

He perched on a stool at the breakfast bar and lit a cigarette. His eyes were bloodshot. He looked tired, she thought, but ever so sexy in his blue Oxford shirt. The sleeves were rolled up and ginger-brown hair curled over his forearms. "Hungry?" she said. "I've got leftover chicken."

"No time, luv. Got to check into the hotel before I go to the hall. Could do with a coffee though."

She poured two mugs of coffee, brought them to the breakfast bar and sat beside him.

"What's *your* surprise?" Nigel said.

"I went condo shopping and found a gorgeous unit on Gainsboro Street near Symphony Hall. Actually I found two, but the other one had a major drawback."

"What's that?" He blew on his steaming coffee and took a careful sip.

"A woman got murdered there."

"Bloody hell, you don't say!" He put down the mug and stared at her.

"Back in the sixties the Boston Strangler was killing women all over town. One of them lived in the condo on Symphony Road. I don't think I'd want to live there."

"Can't blame you for that. What's the other one like?"

"It's gorgeous, a big bay window in the living room, two bedrooms, an updated kitchen and a bathroom with a shower." She sighed. "It's expensive, though. I'm not sure I can afford it."

Nigel started to laugh. She looked at him, puzzled. "What's funny?"

"I've got a surprise for you, too." He pulled a dog-eared *USA Today* out of his suit bag and set it on the counter. Then he took a lottery slip out of his wallet and set it beside the newspaper. "No need to fret about paying for a condo, Vicky. Our money worries are over. I hit the lottery! Check it out."

She did. All six numbers matched. Her heart began to race.

"Nigel! Is this *real*?"

"Bloody hard to believe, isn't it?"

"Wow! The Megabucks?"

"Twelve million dollars," he said, his face wreathed in a huge smile.

"But I thought you weren't gambling anymore. Nigel, you promised."

"I only bought one ticket. What's the harm? Now we've got plenty of money!"

She stared at him. "We? *You've* got plenty of money."

He took her face in his hands and kissed her. "Us, Vicky. You and me. But I've got a favor to ask." He puffed his cigarette and blew a cloud of smoke. "I need you to claim the prize. Then we'll split it, fifty-fifty."

"Me? No way! Face all those cameras and reporters? Why do you need me to do it?"

His expression changed, eyes serious, no more smile. "If I claim the prize, it will be all over the news. When Joanna finds out I won twelve million bucks, she'll have her lawyer haul me into court and take me for every cent she can get. Lord only knows how much. And Hale will take a chunk, too."

"Why should they? You're not married to Joanna anymore, and Hale isn't your relative, he's your agent. It doesn't seem fair. You're the one who bought the winning ticket."

"Might not be fair, but they'll both want a big chunk of the money, no doubt about it. And then there's the Pops gig. The publicity would be a bloody disaster, might kill my chances."

She shook her head dubiously. "I don't know, Nigel. This is crazy. I need to think about it."

Crestfallen, he put out his cigarette. "I shouldn't have brought it up before the concert. Got to keep our heads straight for the Gershwin. I'd best be going." He put the ticket in his wallet.

"Wait. There's a great article about you in the *Phoenix*. Don't you want to see it?"

"Not now. After the concert. I've got *another* surprise for you."

"Oh yeah?" She nuzzled his neck. "Is it a *big* surprise?"

He smiled broadly. "*Very* big."

She laughed. "Wow. I can't believe it, Nigel. Winning the Megabucks?"

"Our secret, luv. We'll do a bang-up concert, champagne afterwards to celebrate and . . . you'll see."

———

Frank finished packing his clothes in the large suitcase he used when he went on long trips. No telling how long *this* trip would be, maybe a week, maybe forever. He tossed in a few of his favorite CDs, zipped it shut and looked at the orange glow of the setting sun outside the bedroom window.

His bedroom, damn it. Hell if he knew where he'd sleep tonight, but it wouldn't be here. Evelyn was downstairs, waiting for him to leave. Maybe he could talk her out of it. The other day he'd seen anger in her eyes, but pain and uncertainty, too. But he didn't want to argue with her.

He cared for Evelyn, but he cared more about Gina. When he talked to Gina, he didn't feel like rats were chewing his stomach.

He went to the closet, pulled a rolled-up sleeping bag off the top shelf and slung it over his shoulder. Worse came to worse he'd sleep on the floor of his office. He towed the suitcase to the stairs and muscled it down to the living room. Every lamp was on and the curtains were drawn. He shut off one lamp, heard Evelyn call from the kitchen, "Don't turn off the lights, Frank. It's getting dark."

And after dark the scary bogeymen come out.

Seated at the kitchen table, she ignored him, pages of the *Boston Sunday Globe* Living Section spread over the table. When he dropped the sleeping bag on the floor, she looked up. "What's that?"

"My sleeping bag. Maybe I'll sleep under the Expressway with the rest of the homeless people."

She said nothing, gazing at him, her eyes full of resentment. He knew that look.

Fueled by the head of steam he'd worked up while he was packing, he said, "I can't afford an apartment. I'm paying the mortgage and the utility bills on this house, making payments on the car I bought for you."

Evelyn shot him an angry look, got up and leaned against the counter, arms folded over her chest.

"Why did you tell Maureen I had a girlfriend?" he said, still devastated by the phone conversation they'd had after he dropped off Jamal. Maureen in tears, saying "How could you, Dad?" Breaking his heart.

"Well, it's true, isn't it?"

"You want truth? You're the one who filed for divorce, Evelyn. There's no need to go into the details with our daughter, telling her things she doesn't need to know."

"You should have thought about that before."

"DON'T LECTURE ME!"

She reeled back as if he'd hit her, her expression stricken.

He took a deep breath, puffed his cheeks and blew air. He'd never hit a woman in his life, never yelled at one either, except for a few times on the job. But telling Maureen about Gina was a low blow, a deliberate act intended to harm their relationship. What if he'd said: *It's not my fault your mother turned into a nun after we got married.* He wouldn't, of course.

Maureen might be a freshman in college, but he had no intention of discussing the problems he and Evelyn had, in bed or out. Not now, not ever.

"Will you be okay, staying here by yourself?"

"I'll be fine," she said tersely. "Just go."

He slung the sleeping bag over his shoulder and towed his suitcase out of the house.

CHAPTER 12

Gina set aside the article she was trying to read and checked her watch. 9:35. Where the hell was Ryan? Now that she'd made her decision she wanted to tell him and get it over with. She tried to imagine his reaction. He'd be contrite and try to sweet-talk her. Bullshit. He'd be furious.

Earlier, she'd cooked his favorite meal, Fettuccini Alfredo, but he just gulped it down and left. Three of his buddies had invited him to play golf at their exclusive club in Milton. Tee-time was 3:00. It pissed her off. If he'd told her last night, she wouldn't have bothered cooking.

Franco lived in Milton, not that Ryan would run into him.

Franco hated golf.

But nobody played golf in the dark. They were probably talking business in the club house, Ryan nursing a bottle of near-beer, while his buddies belted down cocktails.

Ryan never drank alcohol, something she didn't know when they met.

One Thanksgiving her two brothers had dragged her to the high school football game, the big rivalry between East Boston and Southie. At halftime she bought a coffee at the hotdog stand. Ryan was next in line and bumped her arm, spilling her coffee. He apologized and asked if she'd been a cheerleader for Eastie, she was pretty enough. Not a cheerleader, she said, editor of the school newspaper, co-editor of the yearbook. He said he'd played fullback for Southie, ogling her boobs.

A portent of things to come. If only she'd known.

Looming over her, six-three and built like a boxer, he asked for a date, acting like he'd be shocked if she turned him down. Six months later, she invited him home to meet her folks. Ryan declined a glass of wine, saying he never drank alcohol. Her father raised an eyebrow and her brothers exchanged looks. Having a glass of wine with dinner was normal in the Bevilaqua household.

Her mother thought Ryan was great, a handsome young man with a college degree. But Ryan's father was an alcoholic.

"His name's perfect," Ryan had said when he'd told her, his eyes cold, his mouth set in an angry line. "Tom Collins, get it?"

A few years ago she'd told Franco that Ryan didn't drink, not even wine with dinner. Franco's take? "Sounds like a dry-drunk. Doesn't touch a drop, thinks about it every minute of every day."

Franco didn't know the half of it.

She heard Ryan's Porsche rumble into the driveway. Her hands dampened with sweat and her mouth went dry.

A minute later he strolled into the living room. "Sorry I'm late, but one of the guys gave me a lead on this belly-up company in Delaware."

Damn. If Ryan was hot on a business deal he'd be distracted, and she wanted his full attention. Maybe she wouldn't tell him.

Grousing as usual, he said, "I got stuck in traffic on the way to the golf course. Big accident on Route 128. I was late. The guys were waiting for me." He sat beside her on the couch, put his arm around her and stroked her hair, as if she were his pet. "You said you wanted to talk to me about something."

The moment of truth. Her heart fluttered, a ragged tattoo beating her chest. She took a deep breath and set her wine glass on the coffee table. "I've been doing some thinking."

Eyeing her nearly-empty wineglass, he said, "About what?"

"About us."

He gazed at her, an icy stare, his eyes cold. "Yeah? You been talking to Orchid? Your pal with the purple hair, so full of angst she's gotta talk to some highbrow Cambridge shrink twice a week."

"Maybe you should see one," she snapped, "and figure out why you're so touchy about my friends."

"Hey, that's my blue-collar roots, first one in my family to go to college, and a cheap state school at that. You went to a big-name university. I don't know why you waste your time writing touchy-feely articles for shit money. You should do television news. You're ten times better looking than Jane Pauley and way sexier."

A dull ache throbbed behind her eyes. The only time Ryan ever complimented her was during an argument, a bone he threw to distract her.

"How many times do I have to tell you? I'm not interested in doing television." She tried to remember if she'd hidden any cigarettes in the kitchen. She rarely smoked, but sometimes in a crisis, a nicotine hit calmed her nerves. She picked up her wineglass and drained it.

Ryan snapped his fingers. "Let's play shrink. Did you tell Mama Bevilaqua about your first kiss?"

She glared at him. Forget discussing serious issues with Ryan. All he did was parry them with jokes or idiotic comments. She started to get up, but Ryan grabbed her arm and pulled her closer.

"Come on, tell me. You know I love you." He stroked her cheek. "Big brown eyes, luscious lips, boobs bigger than Pamela Anderson. Man, you were *hot* last night!"

She clenched her teeth. His love-making revolted her, calling her names—cunt, bitch, whore—to get himself off. She pulled away and retrieved her empty wineglass. Why didn't she just tell him?

A lump formed in her throat and tears misted her eyes. Because Ryan had a temper and if anyone crossed him . . .

"Let's watch the ten o'clock news." He grabbed the clicker and turned on the television.

She stared at him, incredulous. "Damn it, Ryan, we need to talk."

"We can talk during the commercials."

The news jingle blared, then a three-story tease: a hit-and-run in Cambridge, a drug bust on Cape Cod, a Megabucks winner. Oblivious to her, Ryan gazed at the screen. She took her wineglass in the kitchen and filled it to the brim. Ryan didn't give a damn about her. All he cared about was impressing his boss at the oh-so-prestigious financial firm he worked for and making big bucks. She searched the drawers for a stray cigarette. Didn't find one. In the living room, the newscast droned on.

She went back and perched on the sofa. Ryan gestured at the screen. "This guy couldn't report his way out of a paper bag. Interviews some cop about a drug bust and all he gets is a two-second sound bite."

As Ryan continued his derogatory comments, she sipped her wine. Before the commercial break, another tease ran about a big lottery win. When the commercial came on, Ryan hit the mute button and turned to her.

"What did you want to talk to me about?"

"Another time, Ryan."

"Come on, babe. Don't tease me." He took a lock of her hair and twirled it around his finger.

She pushed his hand away. "You're the one that wanted to watch the news."

"Hey, you're the news junkie, always looking for stories to write for that cheap tabloid."

Baiting her. Ryan wanted to argue. Sometimes she thought he did it to get himself sexually excited. Well, he'd better not try that tonight. Tomorrow, he'd be in Texas.

The news came back on and the anchorwoman, clearly excited, said Wednesday's Megabucks drawing had produced one winner, but no one had come forward to claim the prize. The winning ticket, purchased at Marie's Variety in Boston's North End, was worth a cool twelve million dollars.

Who was the winner, Gina wondered. The winning ticket had been sold in the North End, an Italian enclave she knew well. Her grandparents had lived there. Suddenly telling Ryan she wanted a trial separation didn't seem that important.

"Maybe I'll interview the winner and do a series on gambling."

Ryan turned on her, his face a mask of anger. "Jesus! All you think about is that stupid job. I'm gone all week, come home and I gotta beg you for sex. I'm the one that makes the bucks to pay for this house. You care more about your job than you do about me."

That's right, Ryan. I care about Franco. Franco loves me and he's twice the man that you are.

"Who gives a shit about this house? It's cold and sterile, just like you."

"What did you say?" He rose from the couch and stood over her, fists clenched.

She should never have said that. Sterile was a touchy subject with Ryan. Lately he kept saying, "All these years we've been married, how come you're not pregnant? Must be your fault, Gina. I've got plenty of lead in my pencil."

He flicked his fist at her face, like a boxer jabbing at an opponent.

She flinched and pulled away from him.

"Why can't you ditch that stupid job, have a baby and stay home like a normal woman?"

A haze of anger clouded her vision. "Fuck you, Ryan. Go sleep with your goddam checkbook!"

His face turned crimson. She knew what that meant.

Her heart slammed her chest. She ran in the kitchen, grabbed her car keys and took out her cell phone, her hands shaking.

He came after her, fists clenched, snarling, "Ditch the keys, Gina. We're going to bed."

Heart pounding, she waved her cell phone at him. "Ryan, last year when you hit me, I told you never again or I'd call 9-1-1 and get the cops over here. I don't think your boss will like that." Her boss wouldn't either, but she was too terrified to worry about it.

Ryan stood there, glaring at her. "You're a pig, Gina. A fat pig. Who'd want to sleep with you?"

She opened the back door and left, her eyes brimming with tears.

———

Nigel asked the Back Bay Inn desk clerk to order a taxi and rushed up to his room. With frantic haste, he took off his tux, put on slacks and a polo shirt, and grabbed the bottle of champagne. When he reached the lobby, a cab was waiting. Ten minutes later he arrived at Vicky's apartment. He tipped the driver extravagantly and went to the door. When he rang the bell, the curtain on a first-floor window parted slightly.

Vicky's voice came over the intercom: "Nigel?"

"Right-o, luv." The buzzer sounded. He opened the door and dashed upstairs. Vicky stood in the doorway in a mauve top and black stretch pants. Ringlets of dark curly hair framed her smiling face. She looked gorgeous. He stepped inside, shut the door and hugged her.

"What a great concert," she said. "Two solo bows for the *Rhapsody*!"

"And one for you, for your marvelous clarinet solo." He held out the champagne. "Time to celebrate."

Vicky took fluted glasses from a cupboard and set them on the counter. He popped the cork, poured the foaming champagne, and they went in the living room. Vicky's music stand stood in the corner, and stacks of music filled the bookcase beside it. A table lamp cast a soft glow over the room.

Perfect. But his heart was pounding, ten times worse than when he went onstage to play a solo. They sat on the loveseat. He put his arm around her and raised his glass. "Here's to us, Vicky."

Her eyes sparkled. They clinked glasses and sipped champagne. He set his glass on the coffee table and fumbled in his pocket. His palms dampened with sweat. What if she said no?

He took out a small white box, tied with a delicate pink ribbon. "Time for my other surprise."

Her velvety-brown eyes widened behind her glasses.

"I bought it in Iowa. Not as nice as I'd hoped, but if you don't like it, we'll get you another. Open it."

She untied the ribbon and opened the box. Her mouth formed a large round O.

"You're the greatest girl in the world, Vicky. Let's get married. No more sneaking around." He took her hand and kissed it. "I love you, Vicky. More than you know."

Her eyes misted. "Oh, Nigel."

He let out the breath he'd been holding. "It's a yes then? Please say yes."

"Yes!" She threw her arms around him. "Yes, yes, yes!"

His heart soared. "Try it on! See if it fits." He poured more champagne as she slid the ring onto her finger. The diamond sparkled. She held out her hand, admiring it, face aglow. "Oh, Nigel. It's beautiful."

"I'm so pleased you like it." That was true. He loved her madly and he wanted to marry her, but now came the tricky part. "We need to figure out what to do about the Megabucks ticket."

Her smile faded.

He took her face in his hands. "Vicky, there's something I need to tell you. Remember those, ah, those debts I told you about, back when I was gambling? I wanted to be honest, not start off on the wrong foot so to speak." She nodded, gazing at him. "I didn't ask you to marry me before, because, well, the debts are a bit steep. I wanted to clear them up so we could have a proper start. But winning the Megabucks solves that."

She nodded slowly and looked down at the ring on her finger.

"The problem is, if I claim the prize . . . "

"You want me to do it," she said quietly.

He took her hands and stroked her fingers, felt the thorny callous on her thumb from years of clarinet playing. "We'll split it fifty-fifty. I mean it! Separate bank accounts, half for you, half for me."

"But—"

"After the publicity dies down, we'll announce the engagement and you can wear the ring and—"

"Not till then?"

"What's a couple of weeks? After we cash the check, I'll buy you a nicer one."

She sighed. "I don't know."

"Think of the money. Twelve million dollars!"

Vicky rolled her lips together and shook her head. "It's not the money, Nigel. I just—"

"You can buy any condo you want. You could do a solo recording."

That brought a smile to her face. Encouraged he said, "We'll do one together, clarinet and piano!"

Her eyes lit up. "Really? Promise?"

"Absolutely. It'll be smashing. When the critics hear it, your career will take off like a bloody missile." He took the winning ticket out of his wallet. "Look, I didn't even sign it." He turned it over and showed her.

"Twelve million dollars, Vicky." He took out a pen. "Sign it and half of it's yours."

She took the pen. "Honest?"

"I want you to have it, luv."

She gazed at him silently for several seconds. An agonizing eternity.

At last, she scribbled her name on the ticket. He stared at her signature.

Victoria Stavropoulos. He loved the name. Victoria was a winner!

Exultant, he raised his glass. "Here's to us, Vicky. You and me, forever!"

CHAPTER 13

Wednesday, May 10

Vicky wandered aimlessly through her apartment. She couldn't decide what to do. It was driving her crazy. Sunday night after Nigel proposed, they'd made love and stayed up till the wee hours of the morning, drinking champagne and fantasizing about how to spend the money. As a result, they overslept. Nigel had an early flight to Las Vegas so he didn't even have time for coffee. "I won't even *look* at a slot machine," he'd promised as he dashed out the door.

Now it was Wednesday, almost time for the noon news. Not that she planned to watch it. The blank screen of her television set was a mocking reminder: Every newscast led with a story about the big Megabucks prize no one had claimed and speculation about the winner.

She went to her music stand. The clarinet part for the Brahms *A-minor Trio* was on it. Next week she was playing it on a chamber music program. But practicing wouldn't solve her problem. Earlier, halfway through the piece, her mind had flitted to the Megabucks ticket, and her fingers refused to cooperate, stumbling over notes she'd played perfectly a million times.

The sweet aroma of chocolate drew her to the kitchen. Brownies were baking in the oven. Beside the stove her Pillsbury Doughboy cookie jar sat on the counter. She lifted the lid, took out the Megabucks ticket and studied her signature. The ticket was hers now. Nigel would fly back to Boston next Monday. She'd promised to claim the prize before he returned.

A chill made her shiver, the hot-cold sensation she sometimes got before a big performance. She put the ticket back in the cookie jar.

What would she tell her parents? Her father would be thrilled. He owned a successful accounting firm in Cleveland. He wasn't a musician, but he sang in a community chorus. One of her earliest memories was listening to his melodious voice when he sat her on his lap and sang to her.

The oven buzzer went off. She took out the pan of brownies and set it on a rack to cool. Her mouth watered. Sweets were her biggest weakness, thwarting her constant attempts to diet. But today she needed comfort food. She pulled off a tiny corner and popped it in her mouth. The morsel melted on her tongue. Perfect, with a little help from Betty Crocker.

Her sister would have made them from scratch. Ophelia was tall and slender and blonde, like Mom. Ophelia had a husband, two kids and a house in the suburbs. She had no interest in a career, content to stay home and cook gourmet meals. Ophelia was a fantastic cook.

Like Mom. In January when Vicky had visited her parents, she'd gained five pounds, feasting on stuffed grape leaves, Chicken Souvlaki and Eggplant Moussaka. Mom wasn't Greek, but she cooked to please her husband. She seldom asked about Vicky's love life or her career.

Ophelia was her pride and joy. Her domesticated daughter.

Vicky took out a knife, cut the brownies into squares and dug out a corner piece with a spatula. If only she could confide in someone and tell them her misgivings about claiming the prize. But who? Not her parents and certainly not Ophelia. No. Her only confidante was Nigel.

Should she claim the prize today? She bit into the brownie. Savoring the warm chocolate, she went in the living room and looked out the window. Dark clouds filled the sky. Two stories below her, raindrops splattered the windshields of passing cars. Maybe she should call the lottery office and find out how to claim the prize. She sat on the loveseat and stared at the phone on the end table. As if by magic, the phone rang.

Her heart surged. Was it Nigel? She let it ring. Unwilling to pay extra for Caller-ID, she screened her calls with her answering machine. She waited tensely through her outgoing message. *Please let it be Nigel.*

A man's voice came through the speaker: "Hello, I'm calling on behalf of the Boston Ballet to ask if you'd care to make a donation."

"Just what I need," Vicky muttered, "people asking for money."

When the machine clicked off, she called the Massachusetts State Lottery office and got a recorded message. To claim a prize worth more than fifty thousand dollars, winners had to go to the Lottery office in Braintree, twelve miles south of Boston.

She went in the kitchen and cut another brownie. Her gig book lay on the breakfast bar. She opened it and checked her schedule: Pops concerts Thursday, Friday and Saturday night. But not tonight. Maybe she should get it over with and go now. Recalling Nigel's excitement, she smiled. He was so sweet. He didn't care if she was five-foot-three and weighed 140 pounds. She held her hand under the light above the breakfast bar. The diamond glittered, sending sparkles across the counter. At least she could wear it at home.

Soon their engagement would be official. Then she'd never take it off.

They hadn't decided where to get married, or when. The sooner the better, Nigel said. His parents were dead and he had no close relatives, so whatever she wanted was fine with him. Bermuda might be nice. She pictured them beside a swimming pool, sipping exotic drinks festooned with little umbrellas and toothpicks with candied fruit. It would be romantic, and they'd have plenty of money, enough to fly her whole family there for the wedding.

She returned to the window. What a gloomy day. She didn't feel like driving to Braintree. Maybe she'd wait until Nigel got back.

But what good would that do? He wouldn't come with her. He was afraid some reporter might recognize him. She had to go alone.

She returned to the kitchen and gazed at the pan of brownies.

She couldn't decide.

Should she go today?

She cut another brownie.

———

At nine on a Wednesday night Lonny's Tavern in Dorchester was noisy, working-class guys relaxing with a cool one after work. Or avoiding their spouses, Frank thought. Rafe's three-decker was two blocks away, and they were sitting at the bar, rehashing the game, Rafe saying now, "You seemed distracted, let that pathetic excuse for a point guard blow by you for a layup."

"Got a few things on my mind," he said, and stifled a yawn.

"You tired?"

"That, too."

Rafe drank some beer, his narrow face darkly handsome, the lights over the bar glancing off his angular cheekbones. "Told you we'd whup those District 16 losers, ran their sorry-ass center ragged with my tomahawk slams, blocked his shots at the other end."

Amused, Frank stifled a smile. They'd only won by four points, but Rafe was always pumped after a win and tended to exaggerate.

"You know any 'bangers named Tyreke?"

"Not ringing any bells." Rafe set his beer mug on the bar. "Why?"

"A few days ago I caught up with the kid we chased after the Mass Ave hit, took him for a ride."

Rafe looked at him, deadpan. "What *kind* of ride?"

Frank grinned. "Not that kind. Took him to shoot some hoop. Jamal Wilkes, age ten, lives with his grandmother, Josephine Wilkes, age forty-one. The city directory lists them as residents of an apartment near Mass Ave, also lists Jamilla Wilkes, age twenty-five, Jamal's mother, I presume, currently bunking at the women's prison in Framingham. Nothing about his father."

"Too many kids in bad situations like that," Rafe said. "How'd you get Tyreke's name?"

"Jamal let it slip, seemed upset afterwards. Well, more like terrified."

"You think Tyreke's the shooter?"

"I don't know. I didn't want to lean on Jamal too much at first, took him out for a burger, coaxed him into another shoot-around on Sunday morning. That time I got his great-grandma's name, last name Robinson, no first name. Can you check your gangbanger rolodex, see if you find a Tyreke Robinson or Tyreke Wilkes?"

"Sure," Rafe said. "What's your take on Jamal?"

"Good kid. Ten years old, not running with a gang, or so he said. Said Grandma'd kill him if he did. I don't know anything about Tyreke. He's not listed at that address, but maybe he bunks with Jamal's grandma sometimes."

"Exerting a negative influence on Jamal."

"Exactly, and it's a shame. The kid is smart. I caught him cutting school, told him he better not do that if he wanted to go to college."

Rafe's eyes widened. "College? You think?"

"If he gets a basketball scholarship. He's small for his age, but he's got talent, good shooter, knows how to handle the ball. But he's got no one to make him tow the line. Grandma works at Boston Med Center, probably too tired when she gets home from work to ride herd on him." He waited a beat and said, "How about you go talk to her? You being a brother, you might get some info out of her."

Rafe eyed him over the rim of his beer mug. "I know where you're headed, Renzi, get me involved with the cute little black kid that stole your heart."

"He didn't steal my heart." Frank grinned. "Okay, he did. But I can't take him under my wing, not on a regular basis anyway. I've got too much on my plate right now."

"Whass'up, Renzi? Look like you haven't slept in a week, bags under your sexy bedroom eyes." Rafe cackled a laugh. "Your girlfriend running you ragged?"

Stunned, Frank looked at him. "What girlfriend?"

Rafe poked his chest with one of his foot-long fingers. "You got the look of a man with serious shit on his mind. Why don't you spill it, man? You don't trust me?"

It was tempting. He could talk to Gina, but right now he needed to talk to a guy, and he couldn't talk to Hank Flynn. Hank was his boss. "Evelyn wants me out of the house by Sunday."

Rafe looked at him, eyes serious. "There's a shocker. How come?"

"How'd you know I've got a girlfriend? Did someone tell you?"

"No. I just figured, you know, all the problems with Evelyn, you got somebody on the side."

He signaled the bartender for another round. "I do. But it's not something I talk about."

"That's cool. You know I got something going. Only reason I told you, we been friends for what, nine, ten years? I figure you won't blow the whistle on me."

"I won't, but someone blew the whistle on me." The bartender set their beers on the bar. Frank grabbed one and took a big gulp. In the corner, raucous laughter sounded, a group of guys at a table watching the big-screen television on the wall, a sit-com wrapping up.

"One of Evelyn's girlfriends saw me and Gina in a bar and told Evelyn."

"Damn! That sucks."

"Yeah. So Evelyn talked to a lawyer and now she's filing for divorce." He couldn't bring himself to tell Rafe she'd told Maureen about Gina. "Laid it on me last Thursday, said she wanted me out by Sunday."

"You can stay at my place, sleep on the couch."

He waved his hand. "I'd be in the way. You got any vacant apartments?"

"No, but I'll ask around, see if anybody I know has one." Rafe put a huge hand on his shoulder and squeezed. "Any way I can help, just say the word, man."

"Thanks. Believe it or not, just talking about it makes me feel better."

"Yeah, I can see you're dying to get up and dance."

He glanced at the TV, saw a breaking news headline: **Boston Pops musician claims Megabucks prize!**

He nudged Rafe and jerked his head at the TV. "We got a Megabucks winner."

"Twelve million bucks," Rafe said. "Man, I could use some of that."

Me, too, now that I'm homeless, Frank thought, watching the TV screen.

A young woman with curly dark hair, her dark eyes enormous behind round-rimmed glasses, held up a huge check—the one Lottery officials used for show, not the real one—and smiled tentatively at the cameras. Reporters surged forward, shouting questions. Frank studied her reaction.

A Pops musician, the headline had said, but she didn't seem too comfortable in the spotlight. A young woman who'd just won twelve million bucks. *Young* being the key word. Maybe she'd be okay. If her luck held, maybe the Jackpot Killer would wait for an older winner.

———

Braintree

Gina lurked behind the mob of reporters in the Lottery Office, elated but anxious. Yesterday when she'd pitched her idea for a gambling series to her editor, he had okayed it. But interviewing a big winner was key. Now, after days of speculation, the Megabucks winner was here to claim her prize.

Victoria Stavropoulos. An interesting winner, a clarinetist with the Boston Pops. The instant she appeared, the reporters pressed forward, crowding around the stage. All of them wanted an interview, but Gina figured they didn't have her chutzpah. Or determination.

Last year when her Spotlight Report on gangs won an award, her boss had given her a raise. If her gambling series increased circulation, she'd ask for a bigger one. Then she wouldn't have to fend off Ryan's constant sexual demands and worry about his violent temper. She could kiss Ryan goodbye.

She focused on the winner: twelve million bucks, eight million and change after they withheld taxes. Victoria was short, maybe five-four, and a bit plump, dressed in brown stretch pants and a loose-fitting gold top that set off her olive complexion and dark hair. Her face was gorgeous, a pert nose and huge dark eyes, reflecting her Greek heritage perhaps, gazing at the media mob from behind round-rimmed glasses.

The lottery officials handed her the huge photo-op check and dozens of flashbulbs went off. Victoria looked longingly at the door. Figuring she'd make a break for it, Gina went outside. Other reporters stampeded after her.

When Victoria pushed through the door, dozens of flashbulbs popped. If she'd kept walking, she might have escaped, but she hesitated, actually backed up, as though she might run back into the lottery office.

"Victoria!" someone shouted, "how does it feel to be a millionaire?"

"How do you plan to spend the money?"

"Are you going to quit your job with the Pops?"

As the questions bombarded her, a look of desperation spread over the woman's face.

Gina squirmed to the front of the crowd and yelled her name. "Vicky!"

When Vicky looked over, she yelled, "Gina Bevilaqua. We had an appointment, remember? My car's over there." Pointing to her red Mazda, parked in front of the Lottery Office entrance, nose out and ready to go.

Vicky's eyes registered surprise, then hope, and wariness.

"I heard you play the Gershwin *Rhapsody* last week," Gina said. "You're better than Benny Goodman!"

The woman's expression softened, but she didn't smile.

Gina extended her hand. "Come on, let's get out of here."

Clearly upset, Vicky stared at the microphones and cameras. Ignoring jibes from fellow reporters, Gina grabbed her hand and pulled her through the crowd, Vicky running to keep up as the reporters scurried after them.

When they reached her Mazda, she opened the driver's door and pushed Vicky inside. Vicky slid over and Gina jumped behind the wheel. Intent on escaping, she cranked the engine, zoomed to the exit and paused at a stop sign, eyeing the rearview to see if any cars were on her tail. Not yet.

She turned left and accelerated. A block later she stopped at a red light. The intersection was clear so she banged a right and kept going.

"I think we lost them," she said.

"That's a relief."

"I'm Gina Bevilaqua, in case you didn't get the name."

"I know. I read all your columns. I'm Vicky Stavropoulos." She looked at Gina, her dark eyes solemn. "But I guess you know that already. Sorry. I'm not used to this."

"Don't worry, you'll be last week's news in no time."

"I hope so," Vicky said in a soft voice, clenching her hands in her lap.

"Want a drink? I know a quiet little place where nobody will bother us."

"What about my car? It's parked at the Lottery Office."

"No worries. I'll drive you back here when we finish. By then, everyone will be gone."

Vicky heaved a sigh and looked over, her expression guarded. "Okay. A drink might be good."

Not exactly a ringing endorsement. Good grief, the woman had just collected a check worth millions. Didn't she want to celebrate? Gina decided not to mention it yet. She made small talk about the weather and the Red Sox until they arrived at Mama Leona's, her usual choice when she needed a secluded spot to talk to a reluctant interviewee or have a drink with Franco.

Gina asked for a booth in the back. The small square dining room had no windows. Stubby candles in glass globes flickered on each table, giving off a dim glow. Few were occupied at this hour, and no one paid any attention as they followed the hostess past vacant booths with red-and-white-checkered tablecloths. They settled into the booth in the back corner near the restrooms.

"The food is great here," Gina said. "You like Italian?"

Vicky took a pack of Winstons out of her purse and set it on the table. "I'm not hungry. Just a drink is fine."

"Okay. Sure you don't want an appetizer? The fried eggplant sticks are fantastic. I'll buy."

Vicky's lips curled in a faint smile, hinting at how beautiful she'd look if she were relaxed and happy. "No, thanks. I should buy you a drink. I guess I can afford it."

That broke the ice. They chatted about the temptations of Greek and Italian food—delicious but calorie-laden—until a stocky waitress in slacks and a white blouse came over. "Hi, Gina, how's it going?"

"Great, Donna. How about you?"

"SOS. Same old songs." Donna thumbed her order pad. "You folks ready to order?"

"I'd like a strawberry daiquiri," Vicky said.

"Make that two," Gina said, inwardly groaning. She hated sweet drinks, but hey, this was girlfriend bonding time. Drink whatever your new best-friend-lottery-winner orders.

Donna nodded. "Be right back with your drinks."

Vicky fired up a cigarette and blew a cloud of smoke, glancing around as though she feared a mob of reporters might walk in the door any minute.

"Doesn't that hurt your wind?" Gina said.

Vicky shrugged. "I don't inhale."

"Like Clinton."

"Yeah, right," Vicky said, and they both laughed.

Donna arrived with their strawberry daiquiris, tall curved glasses with bendable straws and big red strawberry halves impaled on the rim. Vicky took two big gulps. It seemed to relax her.

"That article you did on autistic children was great," Vicky said.

"Thanks. It won an award. Now I'm doing a series on gambling, and you're my big winner."

Vicky shrank back, staring at her, a stricken look on her face.

"Vicky, I'm not taking notes and I'm not wearing a wire." She grinned and opened her suit jacket. "See? No wires, no tape recorder. Anything you say right now is off the record."

"You won't write about what I say?"

"Not unless you tell me I can. Fair enough?"

Vicky sucked up more daiquiri. "Okay, I guess."

"How'd you happen to buy the Megabucks ticket?"

She fiddled with her cigarette, tapping it in the ashtray. "Just, uh, you know, spur of the moment."

"Just bopped down to that store in the North End and bought it, huh?"

"Well, I live near there."

Gina nodded. She'd already located Vicky's address. Her phone number wasn't listed, but Gina could get it easily enough. To play in the Boston Pops you had to belong to the Boston Musicians Union, and she knew a few musicians who could get her Vicky's number.

"Ever play the lottery before?"

"Now and then. I only bought one ticket."

"Pretty lucky, buy one ticket and hit the jackpot. You know what the odds are on that happening?" Vicky shook her head, and Gina grinned. "Neither do I, but trust me, they're astronomical. Your folks must be excited. Do they live around here?"

"No. In Cleveland."

She waited, but Vicky remained silent, fiddling with her napkin. She tried to think of something to loosen her up. Well, duh, how about music?

"I saw a great article about the British guy that conducted Pops last week. What's his name, Nigel Heath?"

Vicky's eyes widened. She moved her hand to flick ash off her cigarette and bumped her daiquiri. The glass tipped, and a strawberry-red puddle overspread the red-and-white checked tablecloth. Vicky pulled paper napkins out of a metal container and mopped at the liquid.

Why the panicky reaction, Gina wondered. "What do you think of him? As a conductor, I mean."

Vicky fussed with the soggy napkin. Her face had a strained look about it. "Well, he's, um, a really good musician. I hope he gets the Pops job." She frowned. "But don't quote me."

"Why not? You're entitled to your opinion."

"I have to use the ladies room." Vicky grabbed her purse and left.

Left Gina thinking: What's up with Nigel and Vicky, a hot romance?

That would light up the wow-meter.

A minute later Vicky emerged from the restrooms, her face pale as she slid into the booth. "Gina, I'm not feeling well. Would you mind taking me back to my car so I can go home?"

Damn, she shouldn't have asked about the conductor. She had a knack for reading people, or so she'd been told. Vicky's panicky reaction to Nigel Heath's name was way over the top, and she intended to find out why.

But not tonight apparently. Which meant she had to convince Vicky to talk to her again.

"No problem," Gina said, and signaled Donna for the check.

"Let me get it," Vicky said.

But Gina already had her wallet out. She paid cash and they left.

When they got in the car, Vicky slumped in her seat, hands clenched in her lap, eyes downcast. "I'm sorry. I appreciate you getting me away from that mob and all, but this is just so . . . overwhelming."

"No problem, Vicky. I understand. But I'd really like to interview you for my series. You know, get your reaction to the big win and how you might spend the money. How about it?"

But Vicky said nothing, arms clenched against her chest.

"It would make a great story. Star clarinet player gets lucky and her career takes off. We could talk about music, where you went to school, your experiences playing with the Pops."

Vicky remained silent, staring out the windshield.

"Okay, how about if I call you tomorrow when you're feeling better?"

"No, not tomorrow," Vicky said. "Next week maybe."

"Promise?"

Vicky nodded. "Next week will be much better."

CHAPTER 14

Friday, May 12 — Plymouth, MA

He slipped into the Nationwide Cable Company office and shut the door. The sun was coming up, but the blinds were closed and the office was dark. Quiet. The office didn't open until eight, plenty of time to get the information he needed and get out.

Finally, his lucky winner had claimed her prize. He'd seen her do it on TV last night. His mother had insisted that he watch the news with her. For once in his life he was glad.

Now all he had to do was get her address and telephone number.

Simple. If she had cable. He scratched his thumb.

If she didn't have cable, he had a problem. But he'd soon find out.

He dialed an 800 number. It rang six times before someone picked up.

"Hi," he said, "this is John from central billing? I need an address and phone number on a Boston customer. Our computer files are messed up."

The woman didn't hassle him, just asked for the customer's name in a bored voice.

"Victoria Stavropoulos," he said, and spelled it so there'd be no mistake.

A faint sound startled him. His heart jolted.

Had one of the clerks come in early?

His eyes darted to the door.

No. It must have been the air conditioner whirring cool air around the room. Even so his uniform shirt clung to his back, damp with sweat.

He clenched the phone, willing the woman to hurry. Seconds later she spoke in his ear. He wrote down the information and hung up.

Fantastic. Victoria had cable.

Now he had a name for his new girl and her name was perfect.

Victoria. Victory.

———

Las Vegas — 3:30 p.m.

Nigel left the men's room and went around the corner to a line of ten phone boxes. Men stood at two of them. Seeking privacy, he took the one at the far end. He pulled a handful of change from his pocket, dropped in some coins and dialed. As the phone buzzed in his ear, he glanced down the hall. The early show was over, and people had returned to the gaming room, pulling slots or hovering over roulette wheels or blackjack tables.

Oddly, he felt no desire to join them. Why should he? He'd bought two hundred lottery tickets and hit the jackpot. He'd never need to gamble again.

Vicky's phone message came on. He waited for the beep and said, "Hi luv, are you there? It's Nigel."

She picked up immediately. "Nigel!"

"How're you keeping?"

"Awful! You wouldn't believe the reporters outside Symphony Hall after yesterday's rehearsal!" Her voice rose in a plaintive wail. "I had to ask an oboe player to drive me home. Not only that, my phone's ringing off the hook, and the phone company can't get me an unlisted number till next week!"

"Hang in there, luv, I'll be back on Monday. Did you decide about the wedding?"

"Bermuda might be nice. Sunny and warm and no reporters!"

"Superb!" he said, enjoying her enthusiasm. God, he loved this woman. He couldn't wait to see her.

"We'll invite my family and a few friends."

"Whatever you say, Vicky. We'll set the date when I get back."

"I wish you were here right now."

"Me too, but I'll be back Monday morning. Only a couple of days."

"I'm counting the hours." A pause. "No slot machines, right?"

"Not a one! No more gambling for me, Vicky. I'm the luckiest man alive. Can't wait to see you."

Please deposit sixty-five cents or your call will be terminated, said a mechanical voice.

Vicky giggled. "How romantic."

"Blast! I'm out of coins. Forgot my mobile in the room. Call you tonight. Keep well, Vicky. I love you."

"Love you, too. See you Monday."

His spirits soared. Soon he'd be back in Boston. He'd already made an appointment with a financial planner. Earlier he'd talked to Hale, but he hadn't mentioned the lottery prize. Plenty of time for that after he and Vicky worked out the financial agreement and set a wedding date. No worries about money. They'd have a bang-up wedding in Bermuda.

Warm and wonderful. Just like Vicky.

Hale had said the BSO managers still hadn't chosen the next Pops conductor. A week ago that would have put him in a funk, but now it seemed unimportant. He wanted the job, sure, but even if he didn't get it, he and Vicky would be together, and his money problems would be over.

———

Swampscott, MA — 7:30 p.m.

"Rough week, Franco?"

He flexed his shoulders to ease the tension. "A long week, for sure. Any kind of luck, I won't get called to work a double homicide over the weekend."

Gina looked stunning tonight, a burgundy velour top accentuating her curves. If they were at her beach house, he'd jump her and lose himself in sensual oblivion. But they were miles away, in an out-of-the-way lounge north of Boston. Because he was paranoid and didn't want anyone to see them.

He touched her forearm, caressing her skin. "How about you?"

"You look tired. Have you figured out where you're going to live?"

"Not yet. Not until I see how things shake out."

He still didn't think Evelyn would go through with the divorce. Let her stay in the house alone a few nights, she'd have one of her panic attacks, change her mind and tell him to come home.

"I might be moving too," Gina said.

That grabbed him by the short hairs. Man, he couldn't take many more surprises. "Where to? California?"

Her eyes widened. "Are you crazy? Why would I move to California?"

"I don't know. I figured maybe you got a job at the *LA Times*."

"Yeah, and you're gonna join the LAPD."

"So? Where are you going?"

"I need to get away from Ryan for a while. My beach house, maybe."

He studied her expression as she fished cashews out of a dish of mixed nuts on the bar. Gina could put on a poker face when she wanted to. No revelations there.

"Why?"

"I've got my reasons."

He drank some beer, thinking *What reasons?* Thinking about Janine, his previous lover, and their painful breakup.

Gina munched the cashews, drank some wine and said, "I'm sick of doing his laundry and cooking for him all weekend while he goes golfing with his buddies. I work all week, too." She gave him a look. "And I can only fake so many migraines, you know? Gee honey, I've got a headache."

Trust Gina to come up with a droll *bon mot*. He never asked about what she and her husband did on weekends. Truth be told, he didn't want to know, didn't want to think about it.

"If Ryan finds out about you and me, he'll be furious," she said.

"Damn. How did everything get so complicated?"

"I don't know. Smooth sailing for nine years and then that woman sees us in the bar. I don't want to be around if Ryan finds out about it."

His detective-antenna went up, getting bad vibes now. "Why? Would he hurt you?" He couldn't stand men who beat on women. It made him sick.

She gulped some wine, avoiding his eyes. "He's got a temper, that's for sure."

The bad vibes got worse. "Did he ever hit you?"

"Franco, I don't want to talk about problems all night. Listen to this." She grinned and her dark eyes got that sparkly look, the way they did when she was excited about something. "I talked to that lottery winner."

Bada-bing. Another bombshell. "The Megabucks winner? When?"

"Wednesday night after she collected the check. On Tuesday I talked to my editor, pitched my idea for a series of articles on gambling. You know, all the problems it causes. Anyway, he okayed it. The minute the Lottery Office put out word that the winner was going to pick up the check, I was on it."

"Huh. I watched it on the news with Rafe, the center on the District 4 hoop team. We had a game that night, stopped at a bar afterwards for a beer. The Boston Pops clarinet player, right? How'd you get her to talk to you? She seemed overwhelmed."

"Overwhelmed doesn't begin to describe it. More like panic, flashbulbs going off, reporters shouting questions, sticking microphones in her face." Gina flashed a smile. "So your ace reporter rescued her. Much to the chagrin of my fellow newshounds, I put her in my car and spirited her away. I took her to Mama Leone's for a drink."

"Did you warn her about the Jackpot Killer?"

Gina looked at him. "You know, I didn't even think about that."

"Well, if you talk to her again, make sure you tell her."

"I will. But she'll probably be okay. I think she's got a boyfriend."

"Yeah? Where was he when she collected the check?"

"I don't know." Gina sipped her wine. "I think he might be a musician."

"Does he live with her?"

"Good question. Next time we talk, I'll ask her. Once she got over the fact that I was a reporter, we got along okay. It seemed like she needed to talk to someone. Her parents live in Cleveland. I got the feeling she hadn't told them about winning the lottery. She was anxious to get home, but she agreed to talk to me next week. First thing Monday morning, I'll give her a call."

CHAPTER 15

Monday, May 15

Vicky hung up the phone and went back to the breakfast bar to finish her coffee. Thank God for the answering machine. Tomorrow she'd have a new number, an unpublished one, but for now all she could do was screen her calls. The initial deluge had dwindled, but even today, five days after she'd claimed the prize, her phone had rung four times and it was only 8:30.

First Nigel had called from Logan Airport to tell her he'd set up an appointment with a financial planner for this afternoon. When she hung up, the phone rang again. A reporter left a message requesting an interview. Why couldn't they leave her alone? Two minutes later Gina Bevilaqua, the *Herald* reporter who'd rescued her at the lottery office, called. She almost picked up. She'd promised to talk to her. But she had too much to do today. She'd call Gina tomorrow.

The last call was from the cable company about a problem with the cable connection. She never watched TV in the morning, but he told her to check. Sure enough, when she turned on her television set the screen was full of wavy horizontal lines. He said he'd have to fix her cable box.

Fine, but she wasn't going to hang around waiting for him. As soon as Nigel got here, she was taking him to a rehearsal for her chamber music concert. Unable to sit still, she checked to see if the music was in her clarinet case. It was. She made sure her best reeds were in the case. They were.

Everything was going to be fine. Nigel would be here soon.

She couldn't wait to see him. After her rehearsal they would meet with the financial planner and sign the agreement to split the money. Then she'd call and tell her parents about Nigel and their wedding plans. That brought a smile to her face. Dad would be ecstatic. No telling about Mom. Yesterday, she'd called to wish her a happy Mother's Day. Her mother said Ophelia had baked her a cake, going on about the luscious white frosting and the pink and yellow rosebud decorations. Big deal. Then she'd talked to Dad.

It had taken all her willpower not to tell him about the lottery prize.

She held her left hand under the light above the breakfast bar. The diamond ring glittered, sending sparkles of light dancing over the counter.

The door buzzer sounded and her heart surged. At this hour the Sumner Tunnel was usually jammed, but maybe Nigel had beaten the morning rush.

She went to the intercom beside her door and pressed a button.

"Who is it?"

"Cable company, ma'am," said a soft voice.

Disappointed, she buzzed him in. Just what she needed. Some repairman messing with her cable connection. She didn't have time to watch television. Her life had turned upside down.

But Nigel would be here soon. Everything would be fine.

———

The taxi crept forward a few feet and stopped. Nigel glanced out the window. Four lanes of bumper-to-bumper traffic inching along like a giant tapeworm toward the Sumner Tunnel. The tollbooths weren't even in sight. At this rate it would take forever to get to Vicky's.

He smiled, recalling how happy she sounded when he'd called from the airport. He couldn't wait to put his arms around her and smother her with kisses, which he intended to do straight away when he got there.

If he ever got there.

The cab inched forward. He studied the driver's photograph on the thick plastic partition that separated them. The name was unpronounceable, a string of consonants with no vowels between them. He tried to guess where the bloke was from. Pakistan? Turkey? Timbuktu? He gave up.

The man didn't speak English, probably didn't know his way 'round the North End, either. The streets were narrow and many of them were one-way. He'd have to rap on the partition at each intersection and point to show the bloke how to get to Vicky's flat.

The taxi rounded a curve and the tollbooths came into sight. Progress, of sorts, but some lanes were for EZ-Pass and some were cash, so four lanes of vehicles began jockeying for position. A tall man with a ponytail was weaving in and out between the cars. At first Nigel thought he was a panhandler, but then he noticed the container and cups. The bloke was selling coffee. What a splendid idea!

He rolled down the window, stuck out his hand and waved. The rotgut they'd served on the flight from Vegas tasted like dishwater. A hot cup of coffee was just what he needed.

The coffee man ambled up to the taxi and tossed his head, flipping the ponytail over his shoulder. "Morning, sir. Coffee?"

"Right-o! Love a cup."

"Cream? Milk? Sugar?"

"I'll take it black, thank you."

The man held a white Styrofoam cup under the spigot on the canister slung over his shoulder, filled the cup and held it out with a flourish. "That'll be one dollar, please."

"Here's two. Give you a hundred if you can tell me how to get us through the tunnel quicker."

The man laughed. "If I could do that, I wouldn't be selling coffee, I'd be a millionaire!" With an amiable grin, the man ambled to the car behind them.

The coffee was hot and strong, almost as good as Vicky's. He reached in his pocket, took out a flattened package of Winstons and extracted a cigarette. Blast! His last one. He'd better buy some at that shop 'round the corner from Vicky's. Marie's Variety, the lucky shop where he'd bought the Megabucks ticket. Wouldn't that old woman be surprised if she knew he was the winner!

He lit the cigarette and relaxed as the cab edged down the slope toward the toll booths. The driver rapped on the plastic partition and said something, frowning at him in the rearview mirror, waving his finger.

"What?" Nigel said. "I can't understand you."

More unintelligible words. The cabbie pointed to a sign pasted on the partition. No smoking. Bloody hell! The whole bleeding planet was anti-smoking these days. Didn't they have more important problems to solve? He rolled down the window, took a final drag and tossed out the butt.

At last, the taxi pulled up to the tollbooth. The driver paid the toll and asked for a receipt. Another delay. The toll taker punched some buttons and held out a slip of paper. The driver took it, put the cab in gear and they lurched forward into the maelstrom, six lanes of cars, taxis and trucks fighting for position to enter the two-lane tunnel.

Bloody terrifying, too terrifying to watch.

He leaned back against the seat, sipped his coffee and thought about Vicky. She was so talented, a natural-born musician. Not many people had the brains and determination to make a go of a music career, but Vicky did.

She was fearless, the most wonderful girl in the world.

Vicky wanted a Bermuda wedding, and whatever Vicky wanted was what they would do. Fly her family in from Cleveland, invite a few close friends. They'd have a splendid time, sun and fun on sandy white beaches.

The traffic flow funneled them into the Sumner Tunnel, a two-lane tube below Boston Harbor, lit by garish yellow lights.

Traffic began to move and they picked up speed.

Soon they'd be out the other end and into the North End.

Almost to Vicky's. Marvelous Vicky with her gorgeous brown eyes and her hip sense of humor.

Everything would work out as long as he and Vicky were together.

Mr. and Mrs. Nigel Heath. Sharing the Megabucks prize.

———

He knelt behind the television set. One of those big monstrosities from the '90s, it stood on a sturdy wooden chest. He pretended to adjust the connections. Inside the latex gloves his hands dampened with sweat. Behind him, four feet away, Victoria stood beside the loveseat, watching every move he made. Over a pair of jeans, she wore a navy-blue T-shirt with white letters on the front: BOSTON SYMPHONY ORCHESTRA.

He squirmed out from behind the television set. The power cord snaked to a six-plug power strip tangled with cords. These old apartment buildings never had enough outlets. The power strip was plugged into an outlet above the baseboard between the television set and a three-drawer chest that held an amplifier, a CD player, a radio-tuner, and a DVD player. Victoria had too many electronics.

The back of his hand itched like crazy. He could feel her watching him. Just like his mother. Always watching, never happy, no matter what he did.

His metal toolbox was on the floor near the television set, but his lucky winner couldn't see what was inside. After he took out the screwdriver, he'd closed the cover. Kneeling beside the television set, he looked up at her. Behind her round-rimmed glasses her eyes were large and dark.

Watching him.

When she let him inside, he'd smiled at her, but she didn't smile back, just bombarded him with questions. "What's wrong with the cable connection? How long will it take to fix it? I have to go to work."

Why was she worried about work? With all her millions she didn't have to work. She was stupid, and she was making him nervous, standing there watching him. Victoria wasn't a little old lady like the others. On the news they said she was thirty-three, three years older than he was. They were about the same height, but she looked strong. What if she fought back?

He shivered. His bladder felt ready to burst. Maybe he wouldn't do it. Maybe he'd just fix the cable connection and leave.

"How much longer will you be?" she said, glowering at him.

Anger swelled inside him. Nag, nag, nag. Just like his mother.

"I'm about done, but I need your help." He rose to his feet and pointed. "I need you to unplug the power strip from that outlet over there."

She frowned. "Why?"

It sent him into a rage. Why couldn't she just do as he said?

"I'm *trying* to hurry, Victoria."

She flinched when he said her name. That was a mistake. He conjured his bashful smile. "I've got a lot more calls to make. My boss is really on my case today. You know how bosses are."

Her expression softened. "Okay. What do I have to do?"

"Just unplug the power strip."

She didn't look happy, but she went to the outlet and knelt down on the rug. He opened his toolbox, took out the yellow plastic bag and crept up behind her. Before she could pull out the plug, he jumped on her.

She lost her balance and fell forward. Her head hit the baseboard with a thump and her glasses fell off. Before she could react, he jammed his knee into her back, plunged the plastic bag over her head and yanked the cord tight around her neck.

The telephone rang.

It startled him so much he let go of the cord.

She struggled violently, legs thrashing, fingers clawing at the bag. He grabbed her arms but she was strong, much stronger than the others.

The telephone shrilled like a siren.

His head throbbed, a mouth-mother-pain in his head.

She ripped off the bag, fighting him, bucking like a horse.

He couldn't hold her down! Grasping her head with both hands, he slammed it against the wooden baseboard.

Her body went limp. Weak with relief, he sat astride her, panting.

Again the phone rang. Then it stopped.

Her legs moved and she groaned.

What if she screamed? What if someone heard her?

He dragged the toolbox closer and picked it up. The toolbox was heavy, had to weigh twenty-five pounds at least. He slammed it down on her head, flinched at the sickening crunch.

Suddenly a voice said, "Hi luv, are you there?" A man's voice.

He almost wet his pants. Panic-stricken, he looked behind him.

Then he realized the voice came from Victoria's answering machine. "I'm at the grocery shop 'round the corner, thought I'd call and see if you needed anything. Be there in half a mo, luv."

The answering machine clicked and whirred.

His heart jolted, sent stabbing pains into his head. Someone was coming!

Victoria's arm jerked and her legs twitched spasmodically.

He raised the toolbox again and dropped it on her head.

Another sickening crunch.

She lay still. But blood seeped from her head, oozing onto the rug.

Seeing the blood almost made him vomit. He was going to wet his pants.

No, no, no! He had to get out! The man was coming.

His breath came in ragged gasps. He collected the plastic bag and the screwdriver and threw them in the toolbox. The bottle of J&B was in the top tray, but he had no time to leave it, no time to fix the screwed-up cable connection, either.

Then he noticed the sparkly diamond ring on Victoria's hand, calling out to him. Unable to resist, he worked it off her finger, put it in his pocket and hurried to the door.

The answering machine!

He ran back, took out the incoming message tape, shoved it in his pocket and returned to the door. His heart pounded, beating his chest like a hammer. Cautiously, he opened the door and saw no one in the hall. Grasping the toolbox in one hand, he raced downstairs, flung open the door and dashed down the steps.

The narrow street was deserted. His van was parked right around the corner. In two minutes he'd be gone. But then a tall man in a dark suit came around the corner at the far end of the block.

He ran across the street and crouched behind a black Toyota parked at the curb. His bladder was ready to burst. Fearing he'd wet himself, he opened his fly and relieved himself in the gutter.

The man in the suit jogged up the steps to Victoria's building and went inside. The man on the answering machine.

The man who had spoiled his victory.

———

Later he would remember that the door to the building was open. Unusual, but at the time he didn't think about it, just ran upstairs, thinking he'd surprise Vicky. When he reached the second-floor landing, the door to her flat was ajar. He tapped on the door. "Vicky? It's me, luv."

When she didn't answer, he pushed open the door and called out again. "Vicky?" Then he saw her coffee mug on the breakfast bar. She was probably in the loo.

But when he stepped inside, his heart lurched in a sickening freefall.

"Vicky!"

He dropped his duffel bag and ran to her. She lay facedown on the floor between the telly and the stereo, her head near the baseboard. Rivulets of blood covered the nape of her neck. He sank to his knees, unable to catch his breath. There was blood everywhere, on the baseboard and the rug beneath her head. Beneath his breastbone, pain shot up into his chest.

"Vicky," he whispered. "Dear God, what's happened to you?"

He rolled her over onto her back and recoiled in horror. Red foam bubbled from her lips and her eyes were vacant and staring.

"No," he moaned.

Bile spewed into his throat, a stream of burning acid. Fearing he would vomit, he swallowed hard. He couldn't lose control now. He had to get help for Vicky. He struggled to his feet, went to the telephone and dialed 911.

When a woman answered, he said, "Help! There's been a . . ."

He couldn't speak, unable to tear his eyes away from Vicky, lying on the floor, her head covered with blood. "Send help quickly. Something terrible has happened . . . a terrible accident."

"Where are you calling from, sir?"

He recited the address and said, "Send an ambulance. Hurry!"

He put down the phone and returned to Vicky.

Hoping. Praying.

Please let this be a terrible dream.

But her face was a grotesque mask. Tears welled up in his eyes.

He knelt down, gently took her head in his hands and kissed her forehead. "Vicky, what happened, luv?"

In the distance, he heard an approaching siren.

Ever so gently, he lowered her head to the floor.

His hands were smeared with blood, his fingers sticky with it. He went in the kitchen and washed his hands with soap and water. He dried his hands on a towel and buried his face in his hands. This couldn't be happening.

"Vicky," he whispered.

The siren grew louder, then wailed to a stop outside.

But he knew they were too late.

A sob tore at his throat, then another and another, his body shuddering uncontrollably, tears rolling down his cheeks.

He clenched his teeth.

The medics were here. He had to compose himself.

He wiped his eyes and went downstairs to let them in.

CHAPTER 16

When Frank got to the North End, he saw no reporters or television crews on the narrow one-way street, just police vehicles and nearby residents sitting on stoops or standing on the sidewalk. He'd half expected to see Gina. She had a police scanner but she might have missed the call. Soon reporters would be swarming the neighborhood like sharks on fish bait.

A murdered Megabucks winner? Guaranteed.

But that wasn't his biggest worry. This wasn't his territory. To view the crime scene, he'd have to make nice with the lead detective. He parked behind two squad cars with their passenger-side wheels on the sidewalk and tossed a BPD card on his dashboard. Flashing his ID at two officers posted outside a red-brick apartment building, he said, "Is Gerry Mulligan here?"

"He's upstairs," said one, jerking his thumb at the door. "Second floor, first door on the left."

Frank climbed the stairs, brooding over Victoria Stavropoulos, last week's Megabucks winner. Now she was dead. If he'd warned her about the Jackpot Killer, would she still be alive?

When he reached the second-floor landing, Detective Lieutenant Gerry Mulligan stood outside a door talking to a younger man in a dark suit, another detective Frank assumed. A glance through the open door told him the crime scene techs hadn't arrived yet, no flashbulbs popping, no voices.

He'd met Gerry once at a Boston PD function but had never worked with him. Gerry looked like a heart attack waiting to happen: mid-sixties, white hair, florid face, a big gut, and a pack of Marlboros in his shirt pocket.

"Hey, Renzi, what are you doing here? This isn't your jurisdiction."

Rumor had it that Gerry, who supervised the District A1 detectives, favored traditional police methods, had no use for new investigative techniques, and like every other homicide dick in town, he could be territorial.

Gerry nudged the younger man and said, "Detective Renzi went down to Quantico last year, took one of those super-duper FBI courses."

The man offered his hand. "Detective Palumbo, nice to meet you."

"Same here," Frank said, pumping his hand. "What's up, Gerry?"

"A woman got her head bashed in, that's what's up." Gerry looked at him expectantly, waiting for him to explain why he was here.

Gerry didn't know about the Jackpot Killer, but he knew Hank Flynn supervised the D-3 Homicide Detectives. "Hank Flynn told me to get over here ASAP, said it might be related to a case I'm working."

"Yeah? Well, this one's gonna be a clusterfuck. The media hounds will be all over it." Gerry turned to Palumbo and said, "Guard the door while I confer with my pal."

They walked down an airless hall, dust balls on the wood floor, ancient wallpaper on the walls, and stopped outside another door. "Palumbo made detective last month, so I'm showing him the ropes." Gerry jerked his head at the door. "Nobody home, I checked. Landlady says he works in the financial district. She lives downstairs, got home right after I got here. She flipped out when she saw the police cars, an elderly Italian woman." He grinned. "No offense, Frank, but I never saw such weeping and wailing."

"You never heard my Irish grandmother. No weeping and wailing, just a few choice expletives." Make like they were buddies, maybe Gerry'd let him see the crime scene.

"Yeah, well, no swears from Mrs. Napoli. She was coming home from Mass at St. Leonard's."

"So she didn't see anything."

"No. She said Victoria used to have men visit her, but she didn't see one this morning because she was in church saying her prayers. Ain't that always the way? No wits." Gerry took the box of Marlboros out of his pocket. "So, you got another case like this one? Single white female. Young?"

"Musician," he said, hoping to throw Gerry off the track.

"This one collected a big lottery check last week."

"I know." He wondered how long he'd be able to keep a lid on the Jackpot Killer. A day, maybe two. The Chatham murder hadn't made much of a splash in Boston, a brief item in the regional news, but some enterprising reporter was certain to dig it up. Then the shit would really hit the fan.

"What's the deal with your case?" Gerry asked, and fished a Marlboro out of the box.

Frank smiled. "If I told you, I'd have to kill you."

Gerry's blue eyes narrowed. Then he grinned. "Good one, Frank."

"Who found her?"

"Nigel Heath, a Brit, judging by his accent. I hear he's angling for the Pops conducting job. We go inside and I see a duffle bag on the floor inside the door. He said it was his."

"How'd he get in?"

"Said the door was open when he got here, said he called the woman from Logan. I asked where he flew in from, but right about then he lost it. Did the Brit stiff-upper-lip thing at first, but . . ." Gerry waggled his bushy white eyebrows. "Seemed like he was emotionally involved with Victoria, if you get my drift."

"I do. Where is he now?"

"I had two of my guys drive him to the station. Soon as I finish up here, I'll interview him."

He wanted in on the interview, but he'd ask about that later. "Did you find any cash? Credit cards?"

"You're thinking robbery, forget it. Her purse was on the breakfast bar. I went through it looking for ID, found her DL in her wallet and realized who she was, recognized the name from the hoopla after she collected the lottery prize. She had fifty bucks in the wallet and two credit cards."

That fit the Jackpot Killer MO. Frank filed the information away and said nothing.

"A crime of passion, pure and simple," Gerry said. "Somebody bashed her head in. I dunno if it was the Brit or not, but it looks to me like the killer was in a rage, blood all over the place."

He didn't dare ask about a plastic bag or a J&B nip. "Mind if I take a look? Let your rookie detective guard the door, you go outside and grab a smoke?"

"Okay. But put on booties and gloves. I don't want the forensic team screaming at me about disturbing the crime scene. They're on their way and so's the coroner, should be here any minute."

Two minutes later, outfitted in latex gloves and shoe-booties, Frank stepped inside Vicky's apartment and did a quick assessment, imagining how the killer might have seen it. Opposite the door, a breakfast bar separated the living room from a galley kitchen with dark-paneled cabinets.

The room was stuffy. Two windows on the wall to his left were closed, an ancient air-conditioner in one cranking out musty air. It didn't do much to cool the room or dispel the fetid odor of death: the stench of blood and body wastes. In the middle of the room a two-cushion loveseat faced an older-model television on the right-hand wall. Beside the loveseat, a telephone and an answering machine sat on an end table.

A photo-montage poster of Athens mounted on one wall caught his eye. An homage to Vicky's Greek heritage? Below it, sheet music sat on a black metal music stand. Beside the music stand a four-shelf bookcase held a clarinet case, boxes of clarinet reeds, sheet music, CDs and videocassettes.

Nothing unusual there. Victoria was a professional musician.

But she wouldn't be playing her clarinet anymore.

Now she lay on her back in front of the television set. The sight sickened him, a visceral jolt accompanied by a sharp pang of regret. Blood spatter stained the lower half of the blue-painted wall between the television set and a chest of drawers, more spatter on the white-painted baseboard. The stains were confined to one area, no evidence of a chase or an extended struggle. Did Vicky fight her killer? Was that why he beat her to death?

What a waste. He fought down his anger, got into professional mode and squatted to examine the body. A large amount of blood had pooled under her head, soaking the blue-and-gold Oriental rug. The source appeared to be a head wound, a crushing blunt trauma injury. Judging by the blood spatter, the killer had knocked her down and bludgeoned her head with a heavy object.

She was dressed in jeans and a navy-blue BSO T-shirt, no jewelry. Her eyes were closed, her mouth open as though she'd tried to scream.

No yellow plastic bag, no J&B nip, and no murder weapon, whatever it was. Something heavy enough to crush her skull.

If the Brit killed her, maybe he hid the weapon before he called 9-1-1. Frank did a hurried walk-through, but nothing in the bathroom down the hall from the kitchen, or the bedroom raised any red flags. No blood, no bloody hammer under the bed or in the closet. The crime scene techs would do a more thorough search, and he wanted to get out before they arrived.

He returned to the living room. The sight of Vicky's body brought another bolt of anger. Every murder victim deserved justice, but this one hit him harder than most. He'd never met Vicky, but he'd watched her collect her prize on television. Gina had talked to her but she hadn't thought to warn Vicky about the Jackpot killer. He should have called her himself to warn her.

He hadn't, but he'd damn well find her killer.

Means, motive and opportunity. He considered the possibilities.

Vicky was used to living in an urban area, unlikely to let a stranger into her apartment. Did she know her attacker? At this point he wasn't certain it was the Jackpot Killer. She knew Nigel Heath. Big bucks provided plenty of motive. Maybe Nigel Heath killed her. Or maybe Vicky had a lover. Maybe Mr. X was here this morning. When Nigel called, Mr. X got mad, killed Vicky and split before Nigel got here.

Last week Vicky had collected a multi-million-dollar prize. Who would inherit the money? A husband, sure, but a lover? Only if she'd specified it in her will. Frank made a mental note to check her beneficiaries.

He was pretty sure this wasn't a random break-in. A burglar would have taken the cash and credit cards. And the clarinet, for that matter. The instrument was probably worth big bucks.

What if it was the Jackpot Killer? He gets her to let him in; when Nigel calls, he panics, no time for the plastic bag. Vicky fights back. She's younger and stronger than his other victims. He flies into a rage because it's not going the way he planned and beats her head with some heavy object. There's no time to pose the body, no time to leave the J&B nip, because someone's coming, so he flees the scene.

Who killed Victoria Stavropoulos?

The Jackpot Killer? The conductor? Someone else?

Too many unanswered questions. When Gerry finished up here, he was going to interview Nigel Heath, and Frank intended to be there.

———

Two coppers took him to a police station and put him in a dreary little room with gray-painted walls. Metal bars criss-crossed the only window, and a faint odor permeated the room, as if someone had crapped their pants. A tape recorder sat in the center of a square wooden table with four straight-backed wood chairs. Exhausted, he sank onto one chair. A minute later one of the officers brought him a Styrofoam cup of hot water with a tea bag in it.

Bloody hell, he didn't need tea, he needed a bottle of Scotch. Forget the glass, he'd drink it down straight.

They left him alone, but he had the feeling they were watching him through the window in the door. He set the cup of tea on the table and pulled out a cigarette, but when he took out his Bic to light it, one of the officers poked his head in the room and said, "Sorry, sir. You can't smoke in here."

He put away the cigarette and gritted his teeth, trying to control his emotions: anger, rage and fear, but above all grief. Hideous images flooded his mind. Vicky. Dead. Horribly dead. Her vacant staring eyes.

How could someone do that to his beloved Vicky?

He massaged his temples, but it didn't relieve his pounding headache. Or the questions in his mind. What would happen now? The detectives would question him. What should he say? If he told them he and Vicky were lovers, what would they think? Bloody hell, what would the BSO bigwigs think?

And what about Hale? He wasn't the greatest agent in the world, but he booked gigs for him. Any hint of scandal, Hale might dump him. Christ, he'd never get another gig as long as he lived.

For almost an hour the vexing questions tormented him. Then the door opened and two men entered the room, the portly white-haired detective who'd questioned him in Vicky's and another man, taller and younger, with dark hair and dark eyes. Accusing eyes.

"Mr. Heath, I'm Detective Gerry Mulligan. We spoke in Victoria's apartment."

"Vicky. Is she . . . ?" Down deep he knew, but he had to ask. "She's . . . gone, isn't she."

Mulligan took off his jacket and hung it on the back of a chair. "I'm afraid so. I'm the lead detective so I'll be running the investigation. This is Homicide Detective Frank Renzi. For the record, we tape all our interviews, that okay with you?" Without waiting for an answer, Mulligan punched a button on the machine in the center of the table, announced the date and time, his own name, then Renzi's name.

"Could you state your name and address, occupation and so forth?" Mulligan said.

"Nigel Heath. I live in Hollywood actually, but I travel a lot. I'm a conductor."

"You conduct the Boston Pops?" Mulligan asked.

"Sometimes, yes. Bloody Christ! How could anyone *do* such a thing?"

"That's what we want to know. You want to call a lawyer?"

"A lawyer? Why would I need a lawyer?"

Mulligan shrugged. "Just a formality, Mr. Heath. You can call one if you want."

"No, I guess not."

"Okay," Mulligan said. "What time did you get to Vicky's apartment?"

The other man, Detective Renzi, gazed at him, expressionless, his dark eyes intent.

"I don't remember exactly. Sometime after nine. I took a cab from Logan. When I got there, her front door was open. The door to her flat was open, too. That seemed odd."

"Why?" Mulligan skewered him with his pale blue eyes. "Did you go there often?"

"Well . . . no. It just seemed odd. Most people don't leave the door to their flat open."

"What did you do then?" Renzi asked.

"I called out to her, but she didn't answer. It was . . . could I . . . do you mind if I smoke?"

"This is a non-smoking building," Mulligan said firmly.

Why was the bastard being such a stiff-neck? His clothes reeked of smoke and he had a pack of Marlboros in his shirt pocket.

"Cut him some slack, Gerry," Renzi said. "He's just had a very traumatic experience. You want a cup of coffee, Mr. Heath? A bottle of water?"

He nodded gratefully. "Water would be good, thank you. And a cigarette."

"Okay," Mulligan said to Renzi. "There's bottled water in the cooler around the corner."

Renzi left the room, came back with a bottled water and a tiny red-plastic ashtray.

"Thank you," he said. He took out a cigarette and lighted it.

Renzi nodded, but didn't smile. "What happened when you went inside Victoria's apartment?"

"I saw Vicky—" Overwhelmed by the memory of that horrible moment, he couldn't speak, couldn't breathe. His throat closed up and sharp pain squeezed his chest.

"I know this is tough," Renzi said, "but we need you to describe what you saw. Where was she exactly?"

"On the floor in the living room. Near the telly. I went over to her and—"

"Was she dressed?" Mulligan asked. "All her clothes were on?"

"Yes. Jeans and a T-shirt."

"What happened then?" Mulligan said.

"I called 9-1-1."

The detectives exchanged glances. Several seconds went by, endless seconds, the room silent as a tomb.

Finally Mulligan asked, "Did you touch her?"

"No. I couldn't believe it at first. She was . . ." Willing himself not to break down, he covered his face with his hands. If he started to cry, he'd never stop. Aware of the silence, feeling their eyes on him, he lowered his hands. "She was lying on her stomach."

"On her stomach," Renzi said. "Did you turn her over?"

The question infuriated him. "Of course I did! It was horrible! I still can't believe—"

"You just said you didn't touch her," Mulligan said. "Stop lying to us."

"I'm not lying. I just—"

"Mr. Heath," Mulligan said, "if you moved the body, it makes it harder to—"

"*Body?* It wasn't a body, it was Vicky! She was hurt! I wanted to help her!"

Mulligan glowered at him. "This is a murder investigation, Mr. Heath. Don't lie to us. Don't tell us one thing and then change your story."

Good Lord, why were they badgering him? Couldn't they see how distraught he was?

"Why did you go there?" Mulligan asked. "Was she expecting you?"

"Well . . . yes. I'd called her from the airport." He puffed his cigarette.

"What time was that?" Renzi asked, gazing at him, his dark eyes unblinking.

"Sometime after eight. Might have been quarter past. I don't know."

"What time did your plane get in?" Mulligan asked.

"Around eight."

"What airline? Where'd you fly in from?"

"United. I flew in from Vegas on an overnighter."

"Okay," Mulligan said. "So you talked to her from the airport sometime after eight, correct?"

"Yes."

"Why?"

"Well . . . to tell her I'd landed and that I was on my way to her flat."

"How did she seem?" Renzi asked. "What was her demeanor?"

"She was happy." His throat constricted. He could still hear her voice, his last conversation with his beloved Vicky. If only he'd known. If only he'd told her how much he loved her.

"Happy," Renzi said. "Could you elaborate? What did you talk about?"

"I don't . . . nothing much . . . she was glad to hear from me. We didn't talk long. But I called her again later and she didn't—"

"When was that?" Renzi said. "What time was the second call?"

"I don't know. I had the cab drop me at a shop near Vicky's flat so I could buy cigarettes. There's one on the corner. I called her again, but she didn't answer."

"Called her from where?"

"After I left the shop I called her on my mobile, but she didn't answer, so I left a message on her answer-phone."

"Okay," Mulligan said. "We'll check your cell phone records. And she was a friend of yours?"

Friend? Bloody hell, Vicky was the love of my life. But if he told them that . . .

"You might say so. I mean, I knew her, of course, from conducting the Pops."

"So you were dating her," Mulligan said, fingering the pack of Marlboros in his pocket.

"No . . . not dating her." He puffed his cigarette and drank some water. His mouth tasted like he hadn't brushed his teeth in a month.

Mulligan leaned forward and got in his face, so close he could smell cigarette smoke on his breath. "So why did you go there?"

Bloody hell, why couldn't they leave him alone and let him grieve? Why couldn't they let him go to his hotel and belt down some Scotch and figure out what he was going to do?

"I had to . . . we were planning . . ." Groping for a reason, anything but the real reason. "I had to drop off some music. We were planning to do a recording, you see, and I was dropping off the music."

"So this wasn't a romantic connection?" Mulligan said, skewering him with his implacable blue eyes.

"No." *It was the love affair of my life, you ass-wipe. I loved her and now she's dead.*

"How'd you happen to be in Boston?" Renzi said. "Are you conducting Pops this week?"

"No. I just . . . no, *next* week I'm conducting Pops."

A skeptical expression appeared on Renzi's face. "Did you know Vicky won the lottery?"

"Well, yes, as a matter of fact I did. I was thrilled for her, of course."

"She told you?" Renzi asked. "Or did you see it on TV?"

He wanted to scream, *She didn't win the lottery, I did!* But that would only make things worse.

"She told me when we spoke on the phone."

"This morning?" Renzi said, battering him with his relentless questions, setting him up with a bottle of water and a cigarette, then attacking him like a bloody wildebeest.

"What difference does it make? Some bastard killed her! Why aren't you looking for him?"

"Did you have a key to her apartment?" Renzi asked.

"No." He put out his cigarette in the ashtray.

"Did you notice if anything was missing?" Renzi asked. "Valuables, jewelry, anything like that?"

"You think someone tried to rob her?"

For the first time Renzi smiled. "Could happen. You'd be surprised how often."

"Ah, well . . . Not that I recall. No."

"Did you take anything from the apartment?" Renzi asked.

"Of course not! Why would I?"

"Did you get blood on your hands?" Mulligan asked.

His stomach heaved. Would that hideous memory ever leave him? The coppery smell, the sticky feeling on his fingers. He drank some water, took out another cigarette and lighted it. "It was horrible."

"Did you wash your hands before the EMTs got there?" Mulligan asked.

"Well . . . yes."

"Where?" Mulligan asked, as relentless as Renzi, raining questions on him like blows from a hammer. "In the kitchen? Bathroom?"

Good Lord, did they think he killed her? How could they?

"Look here, I didn't kill Vicky!"

Mulligan rose to his feet and stood beside him, looming over him like a hungry predator. "We'll probably find traces of blood in the sink. Maybe the murderer washed *his* hands, too. Where'd you wash up?"

His forehead pounded with pain. "In the kitchen. Could I use the toilet? I'm feeling a bit . . . Will this take long? I mean, how much longer . . ."

"Where are you staying?" Mulligan said. "Do you have a hotel reservation? Or were you staying with Vicky?"

"No. Not with Vicky. I usually . . . I'm staying at the Back Bay Inn."

Mulligan gave him a menacing stare. "You're not planning on leaving town are you?"

"Leaving? I don't know. I hadn't thought—"

"Well, don't. We need to talk to you tomorrow after we process the scene."

"Tomorrow?" He felt like they'd punched him in the gut. He had to go through this again tomorrow?

Mulligan smiled tightly. "Yeah. Shouldn't take long."

CHAPTER 17

Tuesday, May 16 — 11:30 a.m.

The instant he pushed through the revolving door of the Back Bay Inn, the paparazzi pounced, flashbulbs popping, screaming questions at him. He fought his way to a taxi and climbed inside. When the taxi pulled away from the curb, the pack of hyenas followed them. Blast! When they got to the station, he'd have to run the gauntlet again.

He lit a cigarette. If the cabbie said anything, he'd tell him to stuff it.

Exhausted, he leaned back against the seat. He didn't dare shut his eyes. Whenever he did, nightmarish images appeared. Vicky's blood-soaked head. Her vacant staring eyes. Her mouth open in a silent scream. Last night in his room he'd downed half a bottle of Scotch, but all it did was bring his predicament into sharper focus. The detectives were sure to find his clothes in Vicky's flat. He'd been an idiot to deny his involvement with Vicky yesterday. But the shock of finding her had clouded his judgment.

Now the enormity of her death—no, not her death, her *murder*—had sunk in. He'd thought the publicity about the lottery win would be bad, but this was a million times worse, a bloody scandal, vulgar headlines all over the news. He still hadn't talked to Hale. God knows what he'd tell him.

And what about the money? The lottery check was in a safe deposit box at Vicky's bank. After they met with the financial planner and signed the agreement, they'd planned to deposit the money into separate bank accounts, half and half. But they hadn't met with the financial expert and they never would. Vicky was dead and the check was made out to her. He hadn't decided whether to tell the coppers about that. What if they didn't believe him?

On the telly this morning, it said her family was flying in from Cleveland. They planned to hold a wake in Boston tomorrow before they took her body home. Maybe he could talk to her parents and explain about the lottery ticket.

But that wasn't his immediate problem. Now he had to talk to the cops.

The white-haired detective turned on the tape recorder, stated the date and time and said, "For the record, Mr. Heath, you don't care to have a lawyer present?"

"I don't think so. No." He massaged his hands. The interview room was hot and stuffy, worse than yesterday, but his fingers felt like frozen fish sticks. No kind words from Mulligan today, and the other one, Detective Renzi, was staring at him, expressionless. No help there, either.

"We found a suitcase full of your clothes in her bedroom," Mulligan said. "What were they doing there?"

"Well, you see, what I said yesterday . . . when I said Vicky and I were just friends ... well, we *were* friends, but we were . . . more than friends."

"You were having an affair," Renzi said.

"Why'd you lie to us?" Mulligan said.

"It was such a shock, finding her like that. I wasn't thinking straight."

"Okay," Mulligan said, "you didn't mean to kill her."

"*I didn't kill her!* We were going to get married! I gave her a diamond ring!"

Mulligan shook his head. "Yesterday you weren't thinking straight, now you tell us you and Victoria were planning to get married?"

"It's true, I swear it. We were going to announce the engagement as soon as—"

"What about the money she won in the lottery?" Renzi asked.

"But she didn't . . . do you mind if I smoke?"

"Tell us about the money." Renzi's eyes bored into him, hard and unforgiving.

"Look here, I didn't kill Vicky!"

"Why should we believe you?" Mulligan said. "Yesterday you lied to us. First you said you didn't touch the body, then you said she was lying on her stomach and you rolled her over."

"You don't understand. I loved her. Bloody hell, why don't you find the bastard that killed her?"

"I get the feeling you're jerking us around," Mulligan said. "Tell us about the money."

His heart jolted. The moment he'd been dreading. "All right, I'll *tell* you. Vicky didn't win the lottery, I did. The ticket she cashed in was *mine*."

Mulligan's eyes went wide with disbelief. He brayed a laugh, then a series of hacking coughs, his face crimson. "You had a lottery ticket worth twelve million bucks, and you expect us to believe you just *gave* it to her?"

"It's *true*, I swear it! I bought it before I went to Iowa at that shop round the corner from Vicky's flat. Ask the woman that works there. I'm sure she'll remember me."

"What were you doing in Iowa?" Renzi asked.

"Conducting a Broadway show. *The Music Man*. On Sunday I flew back to Boston to conduct a Pops concert. That's when I told Vicky. After the concert I gave her the ring."

"Told her what?" Renzi said.

"About the lottery ticket. I had her sign it so she could claim the money."

Mulligan locked eyes with him. "Why would you do that?"

"I was worried about the publicity. The bloody paparazzi. We were going to split the money—"

"Where's the ring?" Mulligan asked. "She wasn't wearing one when we found her. We're required to list any valuables found on the body and we didn't find any diamond ring."

Stunned, he stared at them. No ring?

"Check the apartment. It must be there somewhere."

"We already searched her apartment," Mulligan said. "We didn't find any diamond ring."

"Why wasn't she wearing it?" Renzi asked. "Most women get a diamond ring, they put it on right away and show it off to their friends and relatives."

His chest felt like a boa constrictor was squeezing it. He stared into space, trying to visualize Vicky's hand. But he didn't want to think about that ghastly image of Vicky. Thinking about it turned his guts to mush.

"Well, p'rhaps she wasn't wearing it. When I found her, I wasn't thinking about a ring. I wanted to help her. I wanted . . . I know this sounds silly, but I wanted it to be a horrible dream and I'd wake up and Vicky would be fine." He looked at Detective Renzi. "That's the truth. You've got to believe me."

Renzi picked up a computer printout. "Your ex-wife lives in Hollywood. Maybe she was bugging you for money. Is that what happened? You said you were thrilled when Vicky hit the Megabucks. You wanted her to collect the lottery prize money and split it with you. But she wouldn't so you killed her."

How could they think that? Tears blurred his vision. If he didn't watch out, he'd start bawling like a baby. He rose from the chair and paced the room, teeth clenched. He knew they were watching, but he didn't care. He forced himself to take deep breaths, regained control and sat down.

"You don't understand," he said quietly. "I loved Vicky with all my heart. I'd never do anything to hurt her."

"You say you called her after you left the corner store and she didn't answer, right?" Renzi said.

"Yes. From the shop where I bought the ticket. But the woman wasn't there, just a young bloke."

"What woman?"

"The woman I bought the winning lottery ticket from!"

"What did Vicky say when you called her?" Renzi asked.

"She didn't answer. I left a message on her answer-phone. I *told* you that yesterday."

Mulligan shook his head. "We didn't find any tape in the machine."

"P'rhaps it wasn't working properly."

Mulligan leaned forward and got in his face. "Mr. Heath, the incoming message tape was *missing*."

"Well, where is it?"

"Did you plan to kill her all along, or was it a spur of the moment thing?"

He shook his head, unable to speak.

"You went there and the two of you argued about the money."

"No! Look here, I've got a credit card receipt for the ring. I bought it in Iowa. I'm telling you the truth."

Mulligan gave him a dubious look. "Okay, give me the receipt and we'll check it out."

He took the credit slip out of his wallet and handed it to him. "I'll need you to make a copy before I leave it with you."

I wouldn't trust you with a receipt for a quart of milk.

"No problem," Mulligan said. "That'll do for now, Mr. Heath, but don't leave town. After we check some things, we'll need to talk to you again. Come with me while I make a copy of the receipt."

———

Frank waited in the interview room, mulling over what Nigel had said. He appeared shell-shocked, bloodshot eyes, face pale and drawn, eyes darting from Frank to Gerry, then to the tape recorder. But that might not mean anything. Witnesses to violent crimes often got nervous during police interviews. The first day was bad. The second day, after they'd processed what happened, was worse.

But the conductor had changed his story dramatically.

Frank couldn't decide whether to believe him or not. His emotional distress seemed real enough. Yesterday, after word of Vicky's murder hit the local newscasts, Gina had called and told him she thought Vicky and Nigel might be having an affair. Maybe they were.

Gerry was itching to charge Nigel with Vicky's murder, but Gerry didn't know about the Jackpot Killer.

Still, some aspects of the murder didn't match the Jackpot Killer MO. No plastic bag. No J&B nip. A young victim. Vicky was only thirty-three. The missing ring intrigued him. The Jackpot Killer had taken jewelry from several of his victims. Maybe Nigel was telling the truth. Maybe Vicky was wearing the ring and the Jackpot Killer took it off her finger.

Gerry sauntered into the room and flashed a triumphant smile.

"The guy's lying, gives us some cockamamie story about he won the lottery. I say he's guilty as hell. You?"

"I'd say he's definitely a suspect, but we need evidence. What about the murder weapon? Be good if we could find it."

"The guy is full of shit. Ask the woman at the store where I bought the ticket." Gerry shook his head. "You know how many people bought lottery tickets before last week's Megabucks drawing? Thousands. Frank, we got the guy."

"We're lucky he didn't lawyer up." *Incredibly lucky. Either that or Nigel Heath was incredibly stupid.*

"Yeah, I was a little surprised that he didn't." Gerry grinned. "Good for us, bad for him."

"Thanks for letting me sit in on the interviews. I appreciate it."

"No problem. Hank Flynn called to thank me, said he owes me one." Gerry made a gun with his forefinger. "But if you don't tell me about the case you're working that's related to this one, bada-bing."

"I will when I can," Frank muttered, lying through his teeth. Gerry would be pissed when he heard about the Jackpot Killer, and that news could hit the headlines any day.

He left the District A-4 station and returned to his office.

No sooner did he sit down at his desk than his phone beeped. When he picked up, Rafe said, "Yo, Frank, you goofing off or you got time to talk about your boy Tyreke?"

"Right now I'm rating the women in the *Sports Illustrated* calendar issue, but seeing as it's you, I'll do that later. Whaddaya got?"

"Had a chat with Jamal's grandmaw, Josephine Wilkes, after she got home from a hard day's work yesterday. Also met your budding basketball star. The little guy's polite as all getout, did his grandmaw proud, says Yes-Sir, No-Sir to the big scary policeman in his living room."

Frank grinned and settled in for the ride, Rafe getting into his rap routine, belting out street lingo.

"After we finish the opening pleasantries I tell the boy I need to talk to his grandmaw and doesn't he have homework to do in his room. Grandmaw nods, Jamal goes in his room and I get down to bidness, ask has she got a relative named Tyreke? She says No, but the look on her face tells me she's scared. So I ask Ms. Josephine, Does yo mama, Ms. Robinson, know Tyreke? Josephine says No, looks even more scared. So I say, Who's the Tyreke stays in your apartment sometimes, he your boyfriend?"

"I was wondering that myself. What'd she say?"

"She laughs, says: You kidding? Tyreke is young enough to be my son."

"You believe her?"

"I do. Don't get me wrong. Ms. Josephine was once a fine-looking lady, you know, but on the worn-out side nowadays, all tuckered out from her job and taking care of her grandson, her wayward daughter presently incarcerated at the ladies' prison in Framingham for dealing crack or whatever."

"So why's Tyreke staying there?"

"Cool it, Renzi. Lemme get to it. Don't stand there bouncing the ball, 'spect me to beat off two giants and situate myself under the hoop so you can throw me an alley-oop. So anyway, I ask Josephine could she kindly tell me Tyreke's last name. The name Tyreke Evans ring a bell?"

"Tyreke Evans? No. Who is he?"

"Related to Odell Evans, one of the shooters in the Mattapan church hit back in '92. But at the time I didn't know that, asked Josephine for the particulars, you know, like how old is Tyreke and did he break his cherry yet." A cackling laugh. "Not that I phrased it that way. In my most professional manner I inquired whether or not Tyreke Evans had ever been incarcerated and if so, where. She says—dig this, man—Tyreke is twenty-four years old, spent four of his formative years in a Georgia prison."

"For what?" Frank said, scribbling notes on a yellow legal pad.

"Got to contact the Georgia prison for that. I asked Josephine, she say she don't know. I wouldn't put money on it, but why bust the woman when I can get the info myself, plus a lot more, in a phone call?"

"So what's he doing staying at her apartment?"

"Bada-bing. That's what I said. She gives me, you know, The Look, says: Sometimes I need a favor, hafta do a favor back. Which I can dig, man, her living alone with her grandkid and all."

"Okay, but I don't like it. You think she's letting gang members use her apartment as a safe house?"

"Exactly what I asked, but she said No, she didn't want Jamal mixed up with some gang. So the good news is we got the skinny on Tyreke. Bad news is we don't know his present whereabouts."

"You think he's the shooter?"

"I ask Josephine, Did Tyreke stay here the night of Tuesday April 24? She says she don't remember. So I ask, Does she remember the young black man found two blocks from her apartment the next morning lying in the gutter, one shot to the head? That got her attention. She gives me a nod. So I say, Did Jamal see anything? She doesn't answer so I get stern, say: Did. Jamal. *See anything?* She says: No, but Jamal's a light sleeper, might have heard Tyreke leave the apartment sometime during the night."

"And saw the commotion when he went out the next morning, decided to take a look. Damn!"

"Yeah. But I can't see Jamal having to testify if we make Tyreke for the hit. Judge would never let it in, hearsay, speculation, you know the drill."

"Right. So we better find Tyreke."

Rafe chuckled. "*You* better find him. It's your case, man. I work drug enforcement."

"Just what I need, another task on my overloaded do-list."

"Aw, you poor thing. So here's the good part. I call Jamal out of his room, pretend I been quizzing Grandmaw about his school attendance and does he do his homework and whatnot, say to him: My friend Detective Renzi tells me you're a talented basketball player, how'd you like to go to a Celtics game with us? The kid's eyes light up like a Christmas tree. Then I ask Josephine if it's okay and can I have her cell phone number so I can call her when I get the tickets, heh, heh, sneaky way to get the number, in case we need to call her for something else, like a cop spots Tyreke and we need her to ID the man. Anyway, she says Yes, gives me the number, so it's all set."

"I like the idea, but where do we get the tickets?"

"Buddy of mine's got seats five rows behind the Celtics bench, we pick a game where they're playing some loser team stuck in the cellar, he'll let me have three tickets for a yard apiece."

"Man, you're gonna break my bank," Frank said, visualizing his dwindling bank balance. "I'm paying bills on a house I'm not living in, remember? Plus paying three bills a week for a motel room with no kitchen, eating all my meals out, which costs an arm and a leg."

"Aw, come on. Be fun, take the kid to a Celtics game, he'll have the time of his life."

Frank had to laugh. "Okay, Rafe. Check the schedule and let me know. I'll save my pennies, go halves with you on the tickets. See? You fell for the kid. I knew you would."

"Hey, big brown eyes and those *hands*, man. He ever grows into 'em he's gonna be big. So now we got the work and recreation settled, what's up with the dead lottery winner in the North End?"

"Wish to hell I knew. Might be the Jackpot Killer, but I'm not sure."

"What about the conductor? Saw him on the news, comes out of the station looking guilty as hell."

"Gerry Mulligan thinks so, I can tell you that."

"Mulligan, huh? Worked a case with him once, seemed like he was looking to clear it quick."

"Maybe. Like I said, I'm not convinced, either way. Thanks for the info on Tyreke."

"I'll call the Georgia prison, see what brother Tyreke's been up to. Talk to you later."

———

Sandwich

At 11:10, he went upstairs and tiptoed into the kitchen. He knew she was still up. He could hear sounds from the television in the living room. He eased the lid off the box of Morrow's Famous Chocolates on the counter.

The top layer of candy was gone, but the empty wrappers remained. His mother counted them to track her one-piece-daily allotment. And to make sure he didn't eat any. He lifted the cardboard to get at the bottom layer and the wrappers slid to one side with a crinkling sound.

The television went silent. "Billy? Is that you?"

How did she know? Sometimes he thought she had an invisible antenna that kept track of where he was. Preacher Everdon said God was watching them. He didn't believe it, but he believed his mother was watching *him*. He put the cover back on the candy box.

"Come in the living room, Billy. I want you to watch something."

He should have stayed in his room. The back of his hand itched like wildfire. He scratched it, went in the living room and stood by the wingchair in the corner. Seated in the wheelchair with her back to him, she gazed at the television screen. She had on her frayed blue bathrobe, and the ends of her blonde hair were wrapped around fat plastic rollers.

"I want you to watch a story on CNN, Billy. Some lottery winner up in Boston got murdered!"

His heart surged. Victoria was on the national news!

Now everyone would know.

"I told you gambling is bad, Billy. Gamblers are lazy. They want money, but they don't want to work for it. Well, the Lord giveth and the Lord taketh away." Her thin face pinched in a frown. "Remember that woman in Poughkeepsie two years ago? She won the lottery and she got murdered, too."

"Yes, Mom." Of course he remembered. Lucky Lulu. His first. He stifled a smile as his mother's pale blue eyes bored into him. Did she suspect? No. He'd been careful. She didn't know about Victoria, either. Yesterday he'd come home from work at the usual time.

But his date with Victoria hadn't gone the way he'd planned. The back of his hand felt like bugs were crawling over it.

"Want a piece of candy, Mom?"

"I already had my piece of candy after dinner."

Right, because the dinner you cooked was so bad even you couldn't eat it.

She turned back to the television and released the mute-button. Sound blared through the room. A car commercial. A red car speeding down a winding road. The sound and the speed sucked at his mind.

RED. DEAD. VICTORY. VICTORIA.

He sank onto the wingchair, felt the excitement grow, picturing Victoria and her diamond ring. She fought him, but he had the power. Until the man called and ruined everything—

"Look, Billy! Here it is. I told you gambling is bad. Some girl won twelve million dollars, but she paid for it in the end."

And there he was—the man in the suit, the one he'd seen at Victoria's house!—leaving a police station, surrounded by reporters. The announcer said Victoria had played for the Boston Pops.

His heart surged with excitement. Everyone knew the Boston Pops. They played for the fireworks on the Fourth of July. Now he would get the fame he deserved. Everyone would know he could KILL and KILL!

"He killed her, Billy. He was after her money. Preacher Everdon says money is the root of all evil."

His hands grew still. What did *she* know?

His mother was stupid if she thought—

"Questions have been raised," said the announcer, "about Nigel Heath's relationship with the victim. Sources close to the investigation say he has not been ruled out as a suspect."

He stared at the screen in disbelief. How could they think that man killed her? Didn't they know about the others? It wasn't fair! Abruptly, he rose from the chair and started toward the kitchen.

"Billy!" his mother said, her pale blue eyes boring into him. "Where are you going?"

"I'm going to bed, Mom. I have to go in early tomorrow."

"You went in early yesterday. I didn't even hear you leave. They can't expect you to go in early every day. Why don't you stand up to them? Your father would have."

He ran downstairs to his room, went to the fish tank and stared at the name tag pasted on the side. Victoria. Fighting him, not doing what he said. He plunged his hand into the tank. The fish scattered, fins flailing, trying to hide. But they couldn't. He grabbed Victoria and squeezed. Her eyes bulged and her mouth moved convulsively. He flung her on the floor, stomped her and stared at the ugly orange mess on the rubber-tiled floor. Disgusting.

The rest of his girls hovered near the bottom, Lulu and Tessa, Florence and Lilly, Betty and Rosie. Even Judy was hiding. But they couldn't escape.

A haze of rage blinded him. He'd kill them all!

No. He would never hurt Judy. Beautiful, talented Judy. How he loved her voice, her crooked smile, her sad brown eyes.

"The cops are stupid, Judy. They think that conductor killed Victoria."

He looked at the orange-red mess on the rubber-tile floor. Victoria.

His head throbbed with a dull ache. He wiped the sole of his shoe with a towel, got on his computer, logged onto the 'Net and clicked on the lottery page. Everybody thought that conductor killed Victoria. But he'd show them.

He'd find another lucky winner right away and this time he wouldn't be fussy. He'd show them he could kill and kill and KILL!

And no one could stop him.

CHAPTER 18

Wednesday, May 17

The calling hours for Vicky's wake were 6:00 to 9:00. Gina got to the Demopoulos Funeral Home ten minutes early. Television trucks with satellite dishes were lined up outside, identified by their colorful logos: Court TV, Fox News, CNN and the local affiliates for CBS, NBC and ABC. A line of mourners stood outside the white Greek-revival building. A police officer stood at the door, to keep the reporters out, Gina assumed.

She circled the funeral home and parked in a large blacktopped area at the rear of the building. Outside a door on the lower level, a man in a suit stood outside, smoking. "Mind if I join you?" she said.

"Not at all. There's a smoking room inside, but it's stinks of smoke." He tossed his butt on the ground and opened the door. She followed him inside. So much for police details.

She walked down a hall to a stairway, went upstairs to the foyer and entered the viewing room. Beyond rows of folding chairs, a mahogany casket stood in the front corner on the left, surrounded by banks of lilies and white roses. Even from the back she could smell the sickly sweet odor.

A large photograph stood on top of the casket: Vicky, posed with her clarinet, her dark smiling eyes clearly visible. Groups of people seated on folding chairs talked quietly as two young women spoke to the bereaved family members standing to the right of the casket: Vicky's parents and her sister, Ophelia. Gina assumed the man beside Ophelia was her husband.

Unlike Vicky, Ophelia was tall and slender, dressed in a simple black sheath, her ash-blonde hair done in a French twist, a younger version of Vicky's mother. Janet Stavropoulos was taller than her husband, and lines etched the corners of her eyes and mouth.

Vicky took after her father. Short and stocky, Constantine Stavropoulos had jet-black hair flecked with gray. His face was haggard, puffy folds under large dark eyes, framed by horn-rimmed glasses.

Gina took a seat in the back row and watched people offer their condolences to the family. Some murmured a few words; others, some in tears, hugged Vicky's parents and spoke to them at length. Then they went to the casket to pay their respects to Vicky.

In the photograph Vicky looked gorgeous, dark hair, dark eyes and a beautiful smile, holding her clarinet. Gina's eyes brimmed with tears. She'd covered a lot of murders, but the victims weren't people she knew. Last Wednesday she'd shared a drink with Vicky. If she'd warned her about the Jackpot Killer, Vicky might still be alive.

She turned to check the line in the foyer. Would Nigel Heath come to the wake? Or was he holed up in a hotel, grieving in private, avoiding the reporters and cameras? Speculation about his relationship with Vicky was rampant, fueled by gossip about their alleged affair.

No wonder Vicky's parents didn't want reporters at the wake. Her father looked utterly exhausted. A sheen of sweat glazed his forehead, and his large dark eyes, reminiscent of Vicky's, were bloodshot.

By 8:30, the line of mourners had dwindled to a trickle. Maybe Nigel wasn't coming. Gina jotted down her impressions of Vicky's family and the mourners. Fine, but she wanted to talk to Nigel. If she wrote a feature article about Vicky, she had to find out if they were having an affair.

Ten minutes later, when she had almost abandoned any hope of talking to Nigel, he entered the viewing room. His face had a deathly pallor, stark white against the dark circles under his eyes. He walked down a side aisle to the casket. Gina rose from her seat and followed him.

He stood at the casket, gazing at Vicky's photograph. "What a tragedy," Gina said. "I talked to her after she collected the lottery prize."

Startled, he turned and gripped her hands. "You knew Vicky?" His blue eyes had a haunted look, but he managed a wan smile, one that faded quickly. "Would you mind . . . could I talk to you?"

Her heart surged. Unable to believe her luck, she said, "Of course. What an ordeal this must be for you."

"It's a bloody nightmare." His face settled into a grim mask. "Now I've got to tell Vicky's parents—" He took out a cigarette, then put it back. "Is there somewhere I can smoke?"

"There's a room downstairs. Come on, I'll show you."

He clenched his jaw. "Not now. I need to speak with Vicky's parents first. Meet you downstairs."

She went down to the smoking parlor, a blue-carpeted room with plush easy chairs and crystal ashtrays on every table. Piped-in organ music played faintly, a solemn dirge. An older man in a dark suit sat in an easy chair with his arm around a violin case, seemingly lost in thought. The pungent aroma of his cigar filled the room. After a moment, he put his cigar in an ashtray, picked up his violin case and left.

Moments later, a tall blonde in a black suit entered the room. She took out a cigarette and said to Gina, "Could I borrow a light?"

Gina gave her a book of matches, and the woman lighted her cigarette, puffing nervously.

"Did you know Vicky well?" Gina asked.

"We were at New England Conservatory together. She's a fabulous musician. Was, I mean. I still can't believe she's dead." The woman's eyes brimmed with tears.

"Do you play with the Pops?"

"Once in a while. I sub on second oboe." She took out a tissue and blew her nose.

"Did you ever play for Nigel Heath?"

"Yes. He's a great conductor." The woman frowned. "On TV they said he found the body."

"Do you think he and Vicky were . . . involved?"

"Vicky never said anything to me about it, but who knows? I'd better go speak with her parents." She put out her cigarette and left.

Moments later Gina heard rapid footsteps, and Nigel burst into the room. "Thank goodness you're still here. I was afraid you'd leave. What an ordeal! Vicky's father was so broken up I couldn't bring myself to tell him—"

He fired up a Winston and took a deep drag. His eyes, red-rimmed and bloodshot, beseeched her. "How could anyone kill Vicky? Some monster beat her to death." He took jagged puffs on his cigarette. "It was horrible. Everyone thinks I killed her, but I didn't. I'd never kill anyone. Could we go somewhere and chat? I need to talk to someone that knew her."

She was dying to talk to him, but she had to figure out a way to avoid the media mob outside.

"Never mind," Nigel muttered. "I'm a bloody jinx. I'm bad luck for everyone, women especially."

No, you're not. You're my inside source for a fabulous article.

"Come with me," she said. "There's a door down the hall that opens onto the rear parking lot. Wait there while I get my car and pull it up to the door. That way we can avoid the reporters."

But avoiding reporters wasn't her only problem. What would Nigel say when he found out she wrote for the *Boston Herald?*

———

She would have taken him to Orchid's loft, but Orchid was in Santa Fe, and she didn't dare take him to a bar. Someone might recognize him. Vicky's murder was huge. Every newscast featured photos of Nigel conducting the Pops, followed by clips of him leaving the police station. She decided to take him to her beach house. During the fifteen-minute ride, Nigel slumped despondently in the passenger seat, silently chain-smoking.

She parked her red Mazda by the back door and hurried him into the kitchen. Her neighbor across the street was an elderly widow. Thelma always watched the news. No telling what she'd do if she saw a murder suspect entering the house across the street.

Gina dropped her keys on the kitchen counter. "Would you like a beer? A glass of red wine?"

"Got any Scotch? I could use a shot of courage." He managed a wan smile, but his eyes were somber.

"Sure. I'll join you." She needed a shot of courage, too. How would he react when she told him she was a reporter? Would he be angry? Disgusted?

She filled two highball glasses with ice cubes, poured in a healthy amount of Dewar's, and took him into the living room. The room was a mess, books and magazines scattered over the maple coffee table.

But Nigel didn't notice. "A piano!" he exclaimed. "How marvelous!"

He set his glass on the coffee table, went to her baby grand and riffled the keys.

"It hasn't been tuned lately," she said.

"No matter, it's just what I need." With a look of rapturous bliss, he played a series of chords and launched into a tune. Could her neighbors hear it? Probably not. The windows were closed and Nigel had a light, deft touch. She sat on the futon and sipped her scotch, listening to him play. She knew the tune: "Bewitched, Bothered and Bewildered."

A reflection of his state of mind?

He looked over, effortlessly drifting into another tune. "D'you play?"

"A little, not much. The piano belonged to my mother."

He broke off in the middle of a phrase, retrieved his glass from the coffee table, gulped some scotch, and paced the room, his expression tense.

"Nigel," she said. "Come sit down. I've got something to tell you."

He took out a Winston, lighted it and took a deep drag. "Not more bad news, I hope. I've had enough bad news this week to last a lifetime."

"Nigel, please sit down. You're making me nervous."

Instantly contrite, he said, "Sorry. That won't do. Here you've been good enough to rescue me from the news vultures." He perched on the other end of the futon. "What did you want to tell me?"

"I rescued Vicky, too." She smiled, hoping to soften the blow. "There were a lot of news vultures outside the lottery office after Vicky claimed the prize. I was one of them."

Nigel gazed at her. She could see the wheels turning in his mind. There was an awkward silence.

"It was exciting," she said hurriedly. "Running red lights to escape the other reporters, sort of like Butch Cassidy and the Sundance Kid. I took her to this little restaurant I know and bought her a drink to celebrate." She took a deep breath. "I write for the *Herald*. Vicky said she liked my articles."

Nigel gulped some scotch, gazing at her silently.

"When I heard there was a big Megabuck winner, I pitched an idea to my editor about writing a series on gambling and the problems it causes."

He flinched and muttered, "Unbelievable."

"We talked for a while, but Vicky was tired. She wanted to go home, but she promised to talk to me again. But when I called her Monday morning, she didn't answer."

"You called her Monday? What time?" Nigel's blue eyes bored into her.

"I don't know. Eight-thirty or so. Why?"

"Must have been after I spoke to her. I'd called her from the airport. If only I'd got there sooner." He gulped more scotch. "You probably think I'm daft, asking to talk to you, but I feel like a bloody leper. Everyone thinks I killed Vicky, but I didn't. You believe me, don't you?"

"Yes," she said. And she did. If ever a man was devastated by someone's death, it was Nigel.

"Thank you. You're about the only person who does."

"How long had you known Vicky?"

"Since the first time I conducted Pops. Vicky was a fabulous musician. A wonderful person." He gazed at her. His eyes were very blue and very sad. He rose and went to the window, parted the curtain and stood there for a full minute, staring into the darkness.

At last, he returned to the futon and sat down. "I loved her. We were going to be married. I didn't tell the detectives right off. Big mistake, that. They found my shirts at her flat. By now they've probably checked the phone records." He lighted another cigarette and massaged his eyes. "I must have rung Vicky a dozen times from Iowa and Las Vegas. And from my hotel."

"Why didn't you tell them?"

"I was in shock. I wasn't thinking. We'd kept it secret, you see. Bloody green-eyed business, music. People would say she slept with the conductor to get the job. What a crock! Vicky was a marvelous clarinet player. But management frowns on that sort of thing."

"What does your lawyer say?"

"Well, my solicitor in California—"

"California! Nigel, you need a lawyer here!"

"But when I spoke with him—"

"Is he a criminal lawyer?"

"But *I* didn't kill Vicky! If I hire a criminal lawyer, it *looks* bad. They already sacked me for next week's Pops concerts. Mealy-mouthed manager said it's best for all concerned." He puffed his cigarette and spewed smoke. "One whiff of scandal and the bloke runs for a hole like a mouse with a cat on its tail!"

She couldn't believe he was worried about the Pops job. Didn't he realize he was the prime suspect in Vicky's murder? "Nigel," she said, "tell me what happened. Did Vicky win the lottery?"

"No. I did, but I gave the ticket to Vicky so she could claim the prize."

"Why?"

"If I claimed it, my ex-wife would get a big chunk. Last year some bloke divorced his wife after he hit the lottery and the judge awarded her the whole lot! The publicity might have cost me the Pops job, too. We were going to split the money and get married. I gave her a diamond!"

"Did you tell the police?"

"Yes, but they don't believe me!"

"Did you tell anybody else you won?"

"No." His eyes lit up. "Wait! I talked to that bartender in Iowa. Maybe he'd remember."

"You told him you hit the lottery?"

"Not exactly. But we were talking about it." He shrugged. "You see? It's hopeless."

"What about the store where you bought the ticket? Wouldn't they remember you?"

"But I can't prove the winning ticket was mine. I didn't sign it, Vicky did. And now she's dead." His face contorted in anguish. "You've no idea how awful it was."

"Where'd you get the ring?" Gina said. "Can you prove you bought it?"

"I gave the receipt to the bloody detective, but if they check my credit, they'll find out—" He heaved a sigh. "I couldn't bear to tell Vicky's parents the ticket was mine. I'd give all the money in the world—every penny!—if it would bring Vicky back." He looked at her, his expression desolate. "It's my fault Vicky's dead."

"Nigel, you can't blame yourself. You didn't kill Vicky, but *somebody* did and we have to find out who."

"That's up to the coppers, isn't it?" He drained the last of his Dewar's. "You've been very kind, but it's late and I don't want to impose. I'd best get back to my hotel. Can I get a cab 'round here?"

"I can drive you."

"No. The paparazzi will be waiting. I don't want to put you through that. Be a dear and call me a cab. "

————

After Nigel left, she poured more scotch in her glass. Nigel was in denial, unable or unwilling to admit he had a problem. He didn't even have a lawyer. Forget the Pops job. They'd never hire him now.

Forget her gambling series, too. Vicky's murder was the big story.

Still, she had just befriended Vicky's lover. People were saying that Nigel murdered Vicky for the money. But they hadn't talked to him. They hadn't seen the anguish in his eyes or his desolate expression.

123

Yesterday Franco had told her the lead detective, Gerry Mulligan, was convinced Nigel killed Vicky, but he'd warned her not to talk about it, saying that wasn't for publication. But that was yesterday. Maybe he'd know more now. She got on her cell phone and called him.

"Hey, whaddaya know?" he said in his deep resonant voice.

"Not half as much as you," she said, smiling into the phone.

"I saw you talking to Nigel at the funeral home."

"You were there? I didn't see you."

"What did he say?"

"Hmm. How about a quid pro quo. Whaddaya got for me?"

A soft chuckle. "You come to my motel, I'll show you what I got."

"Oooh, tempting. Gimme fifteen and I'm there."

"Wait. I need to give you directions."

"I know where it is. I was there last week, remember?"

"Yeah, but that was the Dorchester Ritz. Too expensive. Now I'm at the Dorchester Palace. Take the Neponset Ave exit off the Expressway. Two blocks up on Gallivan Boulevard on the left."

"Does it have a red roof?"

"Hey, you been following me?"

Gina laughed. "Yeah, I'm getting to be quite a detective."

"When you get there, detect your way around back to Room 44."

"And then?" she said.

"Better get here quick. I'm pouring you a glass of the Dorchester Palace's finest wine."

She waited for the punch line.

Franco didn't disappoint. "Carlo Rossi Chianti."

————

Frank heard a tap on the door and looked out the peephole. Gina, looking sexy as hell, even in a black outfit. He opened the door, pulled her inside and kissed her, a long lingering kiss to make up for the fact that he hadn't seen her in a week.

When they came up for air, Gina looked around and said, "Charming decor. Like the Red Roof Inn."

He gestured at two easy chairs he'd pulled up to a low table in the corner. "Your wine is poured, madam. The Dorchester Palace only puts plastic cups in the rooms, so I went out and bought real glasses."

"What a guy," she said, laughing.

"Want ice? There's some in the cooler in the bathroom."

"No, this is fine." She took off her jacket and sat on one of the chairs.

One look at her curvy figure, he wanted to grab her and take her to bed. He restrained himself and said, "How'd you get into the funeral home? The family didn't want any reporters at the wake."

She grinned. "The ace reporter always finds a way."

He took the other easy chair and raised his wineglass. "Congratulations. What did he say?"

"Not much at the funeral parlor, but I squirreled him out the back and took him to the beach house."

He stared at her, appalled. "Jesus! Are you crazy? He's a murder suspect!"

"Franco, he didn't kill Vicky."

"How do you know? Not a good idea, Gina. The guy keeps changing his story. Gerry figures they argued about the money, Nigel went into a rage and killed her."

"But he's devastated about Vicky. He told me he bought the winning ticket, but he asked Vicky to claim the prize. They were going to split the money and get married. What makes you so sure he killed Vicky? What about the Jackpot Killer?"

He gave her a stern look. "You didn't tell Nigel about the Jackpot Killer, did you?"

"Of course not. I never talk about stuff you tell me until you say it's okay."

"Good. Because it's not okay. This is a high-profile case. Gerry wants to close it fast and take the credit. If the Jackpot Killer story hits the headlines, Gerry will go ballistic."

He sipped his wine recalling what he'd told Gerry: *This might be related to a case I'm working.* Another lie that might come back to haunt him.

He glanced at the double bed. It looked inviting and so did Gina, sexy as hell in her V-neck black jersey. But he wanted to know what Nigel said.

"What else did Nigel tell you?"

"He talked to a bartender when he was in Iowa. He didn't tell him he hit the lottery, just hinted at it. He said the bartender told him a friend of his hit the lottery and his ex-wife got most of the money."

"Did he tell you he owes his ex-wife a lot of back alimony?"

"He didn't mention that. But if you talked to him, Franco, you'd believe him. I could set up a meet, just the three of us, at my beach house. Then you'd get a better idea of who he is. You can't do that in an interview room at a police station."

"Gina, you know I can't do that. One, it's not ethical. Two, Nigel knows I'm a detective. Not to mention the fact that I can't afford to be seen there."

Gina's mouth quirked. He knew that look. She was pissed but trying not to show it.

"What about your wife?" she said. "Have you talked to her?"

"No."

"Have you talked to her lawyer?"

"No." He didn't want to discuss it. "What's up with Ryan? You still thinking about moving out?"

Gina gazed at him, somber-eyed. "It was a long weekend. Let's leave it at that. If I move out, Ryan will shut me off like a faucet. That's why I pitched the gambling series to my boss. I figured it would get me a raise, but now my big winner is dead and so is my gambling series. Vicky's murder is the hot story now, so I figured I'd write a big feature article about it. But to do that I need an exclusive interview with Nigel."

"Gina, I don't want you spending time alone with Nigel. Maybe he killed Vicky and maybe he didn't, but right now he's a murder suspect."

She set her wineglass on the table and stood. "I better go. It's late."

He rose to his feet and adopted his grim-faced policeman look. "Ms. Bevilaqua, I can't possibly allow you to get in your car and drive. You just consumed a fair amount of wine."

She looked at him, half-smiling. "Is that right, Mr. Police Detective?"

"Yes. I would be delinquent in my duty if I allowed you to get behind the wheel. There's only one solution. You'll have to sleep here tonight."

Gina grinned at him. "Well, since you put it that way . . ."

CHAPTER 19

Thursday, May 18 — 4:15 p.m.

"All the other victims were killed on weekdays," Ross Dunn said, "but the Poughkeepsie woman was murdered on a Sunday."

Holding the phone in his left hand, Frank jotted notes on the legal pad on his desk. Ten minutes ago his FBI liaison had called to tell him he'd found another Jackpot Killer victim. "Maybe he lives with someone, needs an excuse to be out of the house on the weekend."

"That's what I figure," Ross said. "His wife or a girlfriend or his parents, for all we know. Poughkeepsie isn't exactly a hotbed of activity, but Vassar hosted a conference that weekend, a two-day workshop sponsored by the Northeast Chapter of the American Library Association. A lot of women go to Vassar, so the focus was on books related to women in popular culture."

Recalling Vicky's massive head injuries, Frank said, "You think our killer's a librarian?"

"Maybe. Maybe not. The workshop was open to anyone who paid the entry fee. I got a list of the registrants, a lot of Vassar students, sixty ALA members and seven others."

"That's a lot of suspects."

"Yes, but I eliminated the Vassar students and the female attendees. That left nineteen male librarians and three miscellaneous males."

"Still," he said. "Twenty-two suspects? Can you eliminate any of them geographically? All the other victims lived in New England."

"I already did, narrowed it down to ten males between the ages of twenty-five and forty-five. I doubt that our killer has hit forty, but I erred on the side of caution. Four live in New York City. Two live in Jersey, one in Newark, the other in Hoboken." Ross paused. "His name is Sinatra."

"Well, I guess it isn't Nancy, whose boots were made for walkin'."

Ross chuckled. "No, and it isn't Frank either. His boots are no longer walking anywhere. There's also a guy in Philly, not a librarian, one of the miscellaneous signups."

"Philly's quite a hike from New England. I don't picture this guy hopping on a plane, seems like he drives to the victim's homes."

"I agree," Ross said, "but this guy's a registered sex offender, Level Two. I don't want to eliminate him without giving him a once-over. Tell me about the Chatham location. There's an airport in Hyannis, right?"

"Yes, but not many flights go there, and he'd have to rent a car." He heard Ross yawn on the other end. "You losing sleep over this, Ross?"

Ross laughed. "No, but I'm wiped out today. Had a birthday party for my twin boys this weekend."

"How old are they?" Envying him. He still hadn't talked to Maureen.

"Thirteen. Scary. In a couple of years they'll be driving. We had a good time, though. My wife's parents flew in and stayed with us." Ross chuckled. "Her father can drink me under the table, kept asking me to mix up another pitcher of Manhattans."

Frank smiled, recalling how they'd met. The night after classes ended at Quantico, he'd run into FBI Agent Ross Dunn at the airport bar. In his late thirties, Ross was married with twin sons, and he was wild about basketball. They discussed the current woes of the Boston Celtics and the Washington Wizards. Inevitably, the discussion turned to law enforcement. Frank said he worked a fair number of Boston gang hits, and Rafe, the center on the D-4 basketball team, was on a gang taskforce. At that point Ross had asked for his card, saying he liked to keep in contact with cops who had special expertise.

"Here's the deal," Ross said. "I'll check the suspects in New York, New Jersey and Philly. Can you do the other three? One lives in Connecticut. Two live in Massachusetts, but one lives near the guy in Connecticut. You could do them together, with an overnight. The other one lives on Cape Cod."

"Where? It's been a month since the Chatham victim and the State cops have no leads."

"He lives in Sandwich. What's your take on the Boston case? I'm seeing a lot of chatter about this British conductor. Twelve million bucks? Plenty of people would kill for less. You think he did it?"

"I'm not sure. If it was the Jackpot Killer, there were significant differences. The victim was young, thirty-three. No J&B nip, no plastic bag. Someone beat her to death."

"If the Jackpot Killer did it and sees the hype about the conductor—"

"He'll do another one soon." Frank checked his watch. "Let me go talk to my boss. I need to get travel clearance so I can check your three suspects."

"Great. I'll email you their names, addresses and DL photos. Tomorrow I'll do the guy in Philly, fly to New York, check out those four suspects, then head to Jersey and talk to Mr. Sinatra. First name, Anthony."

"Okay, Ross. I'll call you when I get the travel clearance." He rang off and massaged his eyes, thinking about his meeting with Vicky's father at the wake last night. A brutal conversation that remained vivid in his mind.

Constantine Stavropoulos had pointed to his necktie: tiny clarinets in diagonal rows on a bright red background. "Victoria gave this to me. She was so thoughtful. She knew how proud I was of her talent. But when I ask the police who could do this to my Victoria, they give me no answers. They just ask about boyfriends. The only boyfriend Victoria ever mentioned was the one at Oberlin. And he wasn't even a musician."

"What about your wife? Sometimes girls talk to their mothers about things like that."

"I doubt it. Janet is closer to my older daughter. Don't misunderstand, Detective Renzi. I love Ophelia very much. She has given me two beautiful grandsons, but Victoria was like the son I never had. Now I must take her home for the services and the burial." His bushy black eyebrows came together in a frown. "When I leave, the police will forget about her."

Frank didn't blame him for being angry. *What if it had been Maureen?*

"When did Vicky tell you she'd won the lottery?" he asked.

"She didn't. I don't understand why she would keep this from me. I would have been thrilled."

"Did Vicky have a will?"

Struggling to compose himself, Stavropoulos removed his glasses and pinched the bridge of his nose. "My friend Demetrius owns an insurance business. Three years ago he told me about a family whose son died in a car accident. The boy was twenty and had no will. No one wants to think about their child dying, Demetrius said, but Victoria lives in a big city with a high crime rate. The next time she came home to visit, I took her to my lawyer and she made out a will."

"Mr. Stavropoulos, I'm not going to forget your daughter. I'm going to find her killer, I promise." Whereupon Stavropoulos, his face working with emotion, had gripped his hand and thanked him profusely.

Frank tapped his pen on the legal pad. Maybe Nigel did buy the winning ticket. Maybe he asked Vicky not to tell anyone until she claimed the prize. But her father didn't care about theories. He wanted justice. Vicky hadn't told him she'd won the lottery, hadn't told him about Nigel Heath, either.

But she had a will. Had she made any changes recently?

There were plenty of lawyers in Boston. What if she'd used one to make Nigel Heath her beneficiary? Another unanswered question.

But one thing was certain. He'd promised Constantine Stavropoulos that he wouldn't forget Vicky and he'd meant it. No matter who killed her—Nigel Heath, the Jackpot Killer, or someone else—he was going to nail the bastard.

He rose from his desk and headed for Hank Flynn's office.

———

The first words out of Hank's mouth were, "How are you getting along with Gerry?"

"As well as can be expected," Frank said, taking the chair beside Hank's desk. "But I don't know how long I'll be able to fluff him off about the Jackpot Killer."

Hank tapped his pen on the desk. "What's your take on the Stavropoulos murder?"

"Gerry's convinced the conductor did it. I'm not, but the MO's different from the other Jackpot cases. She was young. Maybe it didn't go the way he planned, he got pissed and hit her with something."

"Damn shame." Hank shook his head. "She wasn't much older than my daughters. What's your take on Nigel Heath? You think they were lovers?"

"According to Nigel they were. He says he bought the winning ticket and asked her to claim the prize."

"Why would he do that?"

"That's what Gerry asked him. Nigel said he was afraid his ex-wife would take him to court and get all the money. She's an actress, lives in Hollywood."

Sidetracked by the words "ex-wife" and "take him to court," Frank thought: What would Hank say when he found out Evelyn was divorcing him? Pushing the thought aside, he said, "Nigel also said he was afraid the publicity would hurt his career."

"Sounds fishy to me. He's a Hollywood hotshot, guest conducts the Boston Pops, wants to do it on a permanent basis. Most musicians bend over backwards to grab the spotlight. How would it hurt his career?"

"Beats me. He claims he made Vicky sign the ticket. They were going to split the money."

Hank shook his head, half-smiling. "Well, if that's what really happened, I bet he's sorry now."

"Right. Unless Vicky changed the beneficiary of her will."

Hank's eyes widened. "If she did and made Nigel the beneficiary, he looks guilty as hell. Are you sure she had a will?"

"Yes. I talked to her father at the wake."

"Must have been tough."

"Brutal. He said he had his lawyer draw up a will three years ago, and Vicky signed it. I didn't ask who the beneficiaries were, but I'm pretty sure Nigel Heath wasn't one of them."

"I'd be surprised if she changed her will," Hank said. "Given all the publicity, her lawyer would have contacted the family by now. But if Nigel Heath didn't kill her, we've got another Jackpot Killer murder."

"Speaking of which, I just got off the phone with Ross Dunn. He found another victim back in 1998. Poughkeepsie, New York. Long story short, he's got ten suspects, asked me to check three of them. One lives in Connecticut, two live in Massachusetts. Dig this, one of them lives in Sandwich."

Hank let out a low whistle. "A hop skip and a jump from Chatham."

"True, but a long haul from Poughkeepsie. Ross wants me to check out the others first. One lives in Chicopee, not far from the Connecticut suspect. I could do them in two days, stay over one night."

"No problem. I'll authorize the travel. We need to catch this guy. If he murdered Vicky three weeks after the Chatham kill, he's escalating."

"And Vicky's murder was more violent than the one in Chatham, looked like a rage kill. If he sees the hype about Nigel being the prime suspect, he'll do another one soon." He felt his cell vibrate against his leg, took it out and saw a familiar number. "Hank, I gotta take this. I'll call you if I get any new information."

He left Hank's office, punched on and said, "Hey, whaddaya know?"

"Things are getting crazy," Gina said.

He passed two detectives walking along the hall, tossed them a wave and kept walking. "Whose life are we talking about, yours or mine?"

Gina chuckled. "Mine, yours and Nigel Heath's. He called me at home last night."

Frank went in his office, shut the door and sat at his desk, unable to decide if he was pissed or worried. Nigel Heath. Killer or not? Making a play for Gina, or not? "Why is Nigel Heath calling you?"

"He's got no one else to call. He's emotionally distraught. The woman he loved is dead and everyone thinks he killed her. He said you and Gerry Mulligan raked him over the coals again."

"So? He's a murder suspect."

"But I'm positive he didn't kill Vicky. Can't you talk to him? Not at the police station, somewhere else. No one will know. Please? Humor me, okay?"

A tempting idea. Get the man in a neutral setting, see what he had to say.

"I'll think about it, but it won't happen anytime soon. My FBI agent contact needs me to check out some Jackpot Killer suspects. I won't be back until Wednesday night." He checked his calendar. Thursday night he and Rafe were taking Jamal to a Celtics game. "I'm tied up Thursday, too, any kind of luck I might have drinks and dinner with my favorite woman on Friday."

Gina chuckled. "Anyone I know?"

"Yeah, Gina Lollobrigida."

"Ha! So can I set up a meeting with you and me and Nigel?"

Amused, he said, "You drive a hard bargain."

"How's this for a bargain? I'll pick up a pepperoni and cheese pizza to go with the Carlo Rossi Chianti in your room, deliver it to the Dorchester Palace tonight around seven. I'll help you pack for your trip."

He started laughing. "Sounds good to me. Be careful, I might tuck you into my suitcase."

CHAPTER 20

Friday, May 19

"We talked to that bartender," Detective Mulligan said, stone-faced, his blue eyes flinty. "The one in Iowa you told us about. He said you told him your *friend* won the lottery."

Nigel shifted in his chair. "Well, I might have said that. But when all the numbers on my ticket matched the winning numbers, I could hardly believe it. I was chatting him up, having a scotch to celebrate."

He'd been here an hour and they kept asking the same questions over and over, acting like he was some sort of demented killer, the tape recorder on the table, recording every word he said. The seat of the chair felt like a slab of granite under his butt, not a breath of air in the room, the window shut, secured by iron bars, a nasty reminder that they grilled criminals here.

"But you didn't tell him *you* won, did you," Mulligan said, flashing him a triumphant smile.

"But I *did*! I bought the Megabucks tickets! Two hundred of them!"

"Not according to the woman at Marie's Variety," Detective Renzi said.

"You talked to her? She remembered me?"

"Yeah," Mulligan said, "she remembered you. Funny accent, she said. But she told us you bought *twenty* tickets, not two hundred."

"I didn't buy the whole lot there. I had a cabbie take me 'round to some other shops."

"Where?" Renzi said. "What stores?"

"I don't remember. The bloke driving the cab took me."

"Where'd you get the cab?" Renzi asked.

"Outside North Station."

"Okay, we'll talk to the driver. What cab company was it?"

"How should I know? Why are you wasting time asking about cab companies? Why don't you find Vicky's killer?"

"What color was the cab? What did it look like?" Mulligan said, the two detectives working him like tag-team wrestlers, browbeating him.

"I don't know! The driver was a black man. As I recall he had some sort of accent, West Indian or Jamaican, something like that."

"Terrific," Mulligan said sarcastically. "That really narrows it down. You don't remember his name?"

"I take a *million* cabs! How can I remember—"

"Let's talk about the money," Mulligan said. "I checked your credit card receipt for the ring. The salesman at the store out in Iowa remembered you."

"I *told* you he would. I'm telling the *truth*. Why don't you believe me?"

"Because your story's got more holes in it than Swiss cheese. Where's the ring?"

"I don't know. The *killer* must have taken it."

"Why didn't he take her money and her credit cards?" Mulligan said. "Speaking of credit, you got some problems in that area, don't you?"

He slumped in the chair. It didn't matter what he said. Answer one question and they hit him with something worse. He shouldn't have agreed to come here. Maybe he should hire a criminal lawyer. That's what the *Herald* reporter, Gina Bevilaqua, had said after the wake. Vicky's wake.

His throat thickened. He took out a pack of Winstons and set it on the table. "Do you mind if I smoke?"

"Your ex-wife says you're behind on your alimony payments," Mulligan said. "Eight thousand dollars, currently."

Bloody hell, they'd talked to Joanna? "Could I have a cigarette?"

"Forget the cigarette." Mulligan fixed him with an ugly stare. "You're in hock up to your eyebrows, Mr. Heath, half a dozen collection companies breathing down your neck. We talked to your agent."

"You talked to *Hale?*" Needles of pain stabbed his chest. He tried to get his breath, but his diaphragm was tight as a board. If they'd talked to Joanna, no telling what horrible things she'd said about him, and now they'd talked to his agent. No wonder Hale wouldn't take his calls.

"He says you got a gambling problem," Mulligan said. "Used to hit the blackjack tables in Vegas a lot."

"Well, I used to. But not anymore."

"You just buy lottery tickets," Renzi said, implacable dark eyes boring into him. "Two hundred at a clip. Is that why you're behind on your payments? Five credit cards, and you're behind on all of them."

He massaged his throbbing temples. He felt utterly helpless, felt like the detectives were driving him toward the Cliffs of Dover, hungry sharks waiting in the sea below, ready to eat him for dinner.

"Did Vicky know you were gambling?" Renzi asked.

"I told her about the debts, yes."

"That's not what I asked. Did she know you were gambling?"

Overwhelmed with exhaustion, he tried to get his breath. Impossible. He couldn't take much more of this. He had a splitting headache and his stomach had gone sour as swill.

"Kind of ironic, her winning the lottery," Mulligan said.

Smiling at him. The arse-wipe was enjoying this. "It was *my bloody ticket* that won."

"You needed money," Mulligan said. "I can understand that. Sometimes I get behind on my bills, too. Your girlfriend hit the jackpot, you argued about the money, and you killed her."

"I didn't!"

Mulligan rose from his chair, leaned down and got in his face. "What did you hit her with?"

"I'd like to call my solicitor."

———

8:05 p.m.

"There was an item about you in yesterday's *Variety*," Hale said. "And another one in *The Hollywood Reporter*. Not good, Nigel. The cancellations are coming in left and right."

Seated at the knee-hole desk in his room, Nigel flexed his shoulders, trying to work out the kinks. "I can't control what the bloody Hollywood gossipmongers write. I didn't kill Vicky. Somebody else did."

"Maybe so," Hale said, "but it looks like you're the prime suspect in a murder case. You know how it is out here. Hollywood loves a good scandal. Remember Fatty Arbuckle?"

"That was years ago, back in the '20s."

"But people haven't forgotten it. How about Lana Turner and Johnny What's-his-face?"

"Hale, I'm short on cash. Can you send me an advance? A few hundred should do." What a joke. Hundreds? He needed thousands.

"Your ex-wife's been calling me twice a day," Hale said. "She wants money, too."

"What about the Iowa gig? Did they send you the check?"

"No."

"Well, call them! Bloody hell, the only reason I took that gig was because I needed the money. You know that."

"Okay. I'll call and ask the manager to send me the check. Gotta go, Nigel. My other line's ringing. Call your ex-wife. I didn't tell her which hotel you're staying at, but if she keeps badgering me, I might."

A click sounded in his ear, then the dial tone.

Call Joanna? He'd rather have a root canal.

He poured more Glenlivet into the water glass—straight, no ice—went to the window and parted the curtain. Twinkling stars and a thin crescent moon were visible in the dusky sky. Six floors below him, a line of television vans stood in front of the Back Bay Inn. The bastards worked in shifts 'round the clock, day and night, waiting for him to come out. So they could pounce.

The telephone was his only link to the outside world, but it brought no comfort. Hale said cancellations were coming in left and right.

What would he do for money? The air left his lungs in a whoosh, as though some giant unseen hand were crushing his chest.

The detectives had mocked him this morning. Five credit cards, Renzi said, behind on all of them.

What could he say? It was true. He barely had enough cash to buy cigarettes. He'd charged the bottle of Glenlivet to his room. Add in the charges for his meals . . . How would he pay the bill?

His solicitor wanted money, too. A lot of it. Up front, Attorney Merrill Carr had said this afternoon, seated at his fancy mahogany desk in his swanky office, autographed photos of Boston sports and entertainment legends lining the walls.

Nigel belted down some scotch and sprawled on the bed. Nights were the worst. He couldn't sleep. Nightmares plagued him, stern-eyed faces and pointing fingers, jolting him awake. He took the remote off the nightstand and turned on the telly. Maybe some mindless television show would put him to sleep. He wanted to sleep forever and never wake up.

What did he have to live for? Vicky, the love of his life, was dead.

He took a pull of scotch, set the glass on the nightstand beside the bottle of Glenlivet and channel surfed. Music burst from the speaker and the screen filled with musicians. Of all the bloody luck!

A Boston Pops concert, taped earlier in the season.

Music filled the room. The Brahms *Academic Festival Overture.* He knew what was coming. Soon the woodwinds would make their entrance. The clarinets. Vicky. The camera zoomed in on the woodwind section.

Nausea turned his guts to liquid. He couldn't bear to watch, couldn't bear not to. And there she was. His beloved Vicky, her sultry clarinet sound soaring through the speakers. His throat closed up and tears filled his eyes.

He would never see her again, never make love to her again, never hear her laugh at his silly jokes.

With a low moan, he hit the off-button and gulped some scotch.

Vicky was dead and it was his fault.

The detectives weren't even looking for the bastard that killed her. They thought *he* killed her.

What the hell was he going to do? His money was gone, his debts piling up. Forget the Pops gig, everyone was canceling now. Hale couldn't get him a gig leading a high school wind band. How would he pay the hotel bill? He couldn't even go out, had to sit in his room, order up room service and send the bellhop out to buy cigarettes. And Glenlivet. He poured another finger of scotch and drank it down.

If only he could talk to someone. Maybe he'd call Gina Bevilaqua. After Vicky's wake she'd been so thoughtful. She was the only one who listened, the only one who understood, the only one who believed him.

Everyone else thought he'd killed Vicky.

He took her card out of his wallet and studied it. Gina Bevilaqua wrote for the Boston *Herald*, one of the local rags. For all he knew, she was kissing up to him, angling for an exclusive interview. But what if she wasn't?

She hadn't said much about herself. He hadn't thought to ask if she had a family. She might be married, might even have children. Calling her on a Friday night would be inconsiderate.

Maybe he'd call her tomorrow.

Visions of Vicky swam before his eyes.

How would he live without her?

He poured more scotch into the glass.

CHAPTER 21

Sunday, May 21 — Sandwich

"There you go, Billy, pot roast special," Arlene said, setting his plate down. Beaded earrings dangled from her ears almost down to her shoulders. "Here's your roast beef, Mrs. Kay. Well done. Enjoy!"

He looked at the gravy puddling over his mother's mashed potatoes and thought: Uh-oh. Trouble ahead.

His mother's lips tightened. "Arlene, didn't I tell you no gravy? I'm sure I did."

"Oh, I'm so sorry! I put it on the order, but we're so busy today. I'll take it back."

"No, that's all right." His mother sighed, one of her long-suffering-victim sighs.

Arlene's forehead wrinkled in a frown. "Are you sure? It's no trouble."

"It's fine, Arlene." Smiling her sanctimonious smile.

Driving rain spattered the window beside their table. It was no day for the beach so the Seaside Diner was more crowded than usual. He glanced at the two cops sitting at the counter, wondering what they were talking about.

Soon they'd be talking about *him*.

He speared a piece of pot roast, dipped it in the gravy and ate it. Delicious. His mother was toying with her food. He knew she'd never eat any, not with that gravy all over it.

"Preacher Everdon gave a marvelous sermon today," she said. "Honor thy father and thy mother. He said families should look after each other."

His thumb started to itch. He forced himself to ignore it and took a roll out of the basket.

"I've always looked after you, isn't that right, Billy?"

"Yes, Mom." He buttered the roll and took a bite.

137

"I feel bad for Arlene, poor thing, losing her husband, and four boys to bring up. That's why I didn't make her take my dinner back." His mother scraped gravy off her roast beef, cut a tiny piece and chewed, her teeth clicking. "She forgot to tell them about the gravy, but I'm not going to blame her for it. Preacher Everdon says if parents teach their children the proper respect . . ."

He tuned her out and studied the pattern the raindrops made on the window, thinking about his girls.

"Billy! Are you listening to me? I said remember how your pa used to take you and John to Little League games?"

Remember? He clenched his fists. How could he forget? Pa whacking him in the head when he struck out, telling him to keep his eye on the ball, and why couldn't he be more like John. Big brother John, making fun of him when he fell and hurt his knee and started crying.

Arlene came to the table with a mug of coffee and ran a hand over her close-cropped carrot-colored hair. "Gee, it's so busy today I haven't had time to visit with you." She pulled out the chair opposite his mother and sat down. "I love your dress, Mrs. Kay. That color blue goes great with your eyes."

"Thank you, Arlene. I was just saying to Billy it's too bad his pa and his brother aren't with us. John would be thirty-five now."

Arlene nodded sympathetically, the freckles on her cheeks standing out on her pale skin like little red-orange gnats.

"John was five years older than Billy, a big strapping boy. Sometimes I wonder what he'd look like now. John took after his father. So athletic."

He hid his hands under the table and scratched.

"John was the star pitcher for his Pony League team. He'd have been a success no matter what he did, just like his Pa. Silas was a liquor salesman. We had plenty of money then." His mother shrugged. "Billy's job at the cable company barely keeps us in groceries."

But it lets me find people. Addresses. Phone numbers. His mother didn't know about that.

"Can you believe that woman up in Boston?" Arlene said. "She hits the lottery, collects twelve million bucks and a week later she gets murdered!"

"She shouldn't have been gambling. I saw her picture on television. Victoria, her name was. A cute little thing, but so chubby! There's something weird about the man who found her. That conductor. Billy, what's his name? I forgot."

He set down his fork and put his hands in his lap.

"Nigel Heath," Arlene said. "I saw him on TV once. My son Timmy plays trombone and we watched him conduct a Pops concert—"

"Mark my words, Arlene. He killed that girl!"

He scratched his hand. Stupid, stupid, stupid! His mother was an idiot.

She didn't know about his skill and the power it gave him. Neither did the cops, yet. But he'd show them.

"I was watching Geraldo Rivera last night," Arlene said. "He said there might be a serial killer on the loose." She nodded, and her beaded earrings swayed. "Murdering lottery winners. He said there were other cases, before that girl up in Boston. It's scary! One of them was in Chatham!"

"Really?" his mother said. Her pale blue eyes regarded him thoughtfully.

Why was she looking at him like that? Did she suspect? No. She was stupid. He was smarter than she was. Smarter than the cops, too, especially that cop on the news, hinting that Nigel Heath killed Victoria.

"What do you think, Billy?" Arlene said, gazing at him with an earnest expression. "You think the conductor killed that girl?"

"I don't know. Mom's probably right. She usually is."

"We should be going, Billy." His mother smirked at Arlene. "He's taking me to Morrow's so we can buy a box of their low-fat chocolates."

"Oh, Billy, you're so sweet."

"Then we're going to the pet store. Billy wants to buy a new goldfish." His mother frowned. "What did you name the last one? Wasn't it—"

"Janice," he said quickly.

"I thought you named it Vic—"

"No, Mom. Janice." He gave Arlene his sad look. "Janice died, so I have to buy a new one."

"You sure do love those goldfish," Arlene said.

He nodded. "I've already got a name for the new one."

———

Westwood

Gina pushed stalks of asparagus and broiled scallops around her plate. She had no interest in food. She wanted a cigarette, but Ryan would flip out if she smoked. When she'd talked to Nigel at her beach house after Vicky's wake, she'd given him her card, but four days later he still hadn't called. It was maddening. An exclusive interview with Nigel would be a key element in the feature article she planned to write.

"How come you're not eating?" Ryan said. "You seem distracted."

"I'm writing an article about a young jazz trumpeter. He grew up in Roxbury surrounded by gangs. Now he's playing the Living Room in New York." A total fabrication, of course, but Ryan would never know. He was a country-western fan, and he never read her articles, he just ridiculed them.

"Busy week for me, too. There's a company up in Chicago, grossing eight or ten mil a year, that's about to fold. Might be my next project. I talked to the CEO."

"Mmmm. That's nice." She stifled a yawn.

"Yeah, it went really well." He pushed back his chair and gave her one of his seductive looks. "Let's go upstairs, babe. I'm ready for some loving."

Last night she'd endured one of his disgusting love sessions. She had no intention of doing it again tonight. She carried their plates in the kitchen, put them in the sink and opened the drawer with her hidden stash of Marlboros. She took one out and lighted it.

Ryan came in the kitchen and looked at her, clearly annoyed. "What's with the smoking? You know I hate the smell."

She took a bottle of Chardonnay out of the refrigerator and poured herself a glass.

His face set in a frown. "What's up, Gina? Worried about something?"

As if he gave a shit. *You bet, Ryan. Worried about how to tell you I'm leaving.*

She rubbed her forehead. She really was getting a headache. "I've got a migraine. I need to take a nap."

His eyes narrowed and his lips thinned in a line. "Sorry, honey, I've got a headache?"

Her cell phone rang. Saved by the bell. She grabbed her cell off the counter and answered it.

"Hello, Gina? Nigel Heath here. I hope I'm not disturbing you."

"Not at all," she said, turning away so Ryan wouldn't see her jubilant expression. "How are you doing?"

"The coppers raked me over the coals again on Friday. So I took your advice, told them I wanted to call a solicitor."

"Good for you," she said.

"Gina," Ryan said, in the warning tone he used when he was angry. "I'm waiting."

She ignored him and puffed her cigarette, heard Nigel say: "Could we meet some night this week? So we could talk again?"

"That sounds excellent," she said. "Call me tomorrow around five and we'll set it up."

"Thanks ever so much," Nigel said. "Talk to you soon."

She closed her phone and put it in her purse. When she turned, Ryan was holding her wineglass. He poured the wine down the sink. "We need to talk and you need to be sober."

She puffed her cigarette, her stomach churning like a cement mixer.

"Put the cigarette out. It stinks up the house."

"Don't tell me what to do. I'm not your slave."

"Who was that on the phone?"

"None of your business."

His face turned crimson. "Gina, I'm your husband. You get a phone call eight-thirty on a Sunday night, have this cryptic conversation, and tell me it's none of my business?"

He reached for her arm, but she pulled away. "Don't touch me, Ryan. I warned you, remember?"

He ground his teeth the way he always did when he was angry, his chest rising and falling, breathing hard like he'd just finished a workout at the gym.

She put out the cigarette and picked up her purse. Her car keys were in it. If he tried anything—

In one swift motion, he grabbed her, his hands gripping her biceps, and shoved her against the wall. Then he leaned down and kissed her, forcing her lips open with his tongue, sticking it into her mouth. She wrenched her head away, but his fingers dug into her arms, holding her in place.

"Gina, I'm done begging you for sex. You're a pathetic excuse for a wife. It's time we had a baby. Then you can stay home and take care of it. I'll give you a week to quit your job."

She stared at him, incredulous. The sight of him made her skin crawl. She realized she was holding her breath. She sucked air into her lungs and tried to speak calmly. "Let go of me, Ryan. You're hurting me."

His blue eyes narrowed. "I'll hurt you a lot worse if you don't quit that stupid job at the *Herald*. When I come home from Austin next weekend, you better tell me you did." He released her arms and stood there, glaring at her.

She grabbed her purse, hurried out of the house and got in her car. Her heart thumped her ribs and her hands were shaking. Should she call Franco and tell him what happened? No. Ryan had a temper, but so did Franco, and Franco despised men who abused women.

Still, she'd never seen Ryan this angry. He was out of control. She had to find somewhere else to live. Permanently.

She got on the Expressway and headed for her beach house. She could stay there for now, but not in the winter. Her brothers had installed an electric heat pump to prevent the pipes in the kitchen and the bathroom from freezing, but the cottage was freezing in the winter, especially upstairs. During cold spells, she and Franco made love on the futon in the living room.

She'd have to rent an apartment. But she was still paying for the Mazda and apartments in Boston were expensive. One month's rent would eat her entire paycheck. She'd never admit it to Ryan, but her job at the Herald didn't pay that well. Maybe her boss would give her a raise if her feature article about Vicky and Nigel attracted a lot of readers. She had already planned it.

Start with rescuing Vicky after she claimed the lottery prize, detail their conversation at Mama Leone's, then hit the emotional core of the story: Nigel's devotion to Vicky, his grief after her murder, and his feelings of guilt.

But would a feature article warrant a big raise? Probably not.

She got off the Expressway and set out for Squantum, thoughts swirling in her mind. She was positive Nigel didn't kill Vicky, but someone had. Maybe it was the Jackpot Killer. She still felt bad about not warning Vicky.

Then it hit her. Forget a feature article, she'd write a book!

Why didn't she think of it before? Plenty of reporters wrote books about serial killers: *Helter Skelter*, about Charles Manson and his followers, Ann Rule's book about Ted Bundy. Why not a book about the Jackpot Killer?

What a story that would make! She already had an inside track. This week Franco was investigating some new suspects. He and his FBI agent colleague were closing in on the Jackpot Killer. Once they captured him, she'd be in a perfect position to write a book.

The Lottery Winner Murders. That had a nice ring to it.

She'd already done some preliminary research on gambling and the problems it caused. She'd had a brief meeting with Vicky after she collected the lottery prize, and Nigel was dying to talk to her.

After she put together a book proposal, she'd discuss it with her editor. If she signed with the right agent, she might get a big advance to write the book. The *Herald* might even run a series of excerpts.

Her euphoria fizzled like a punctured balloon.

That all sounded great, but cold hard reality was different. She didn't have an agent, didn't have a book contract, and the Jackpot Killer was still at large. She couldn't even write the book, much less pitch it to an agent.

And cold hard reality was equally certain. Ryan would never change. What was he doing now? Working off his fury at the gym? Watching a porn movie on the big-screen television in their bedroom?

She had no idea how any of this would eventually play out, but one fact was crystal clear in her mind.

No more porn videos and no more sex with Ryan.

—

CHAPTER 22

Tuesday, May 23 — Nashua, NH

He took his toolbox out of the van and studied Ruthie's dilapidated bungalow. The trim needed painting, the front steps sagged, and the railing looked like it was about to fall down. Ruthie must have been hard up for money. Until last week.

His heart fluttered anxiously and his hands itched like wildfire inside the latex gloves. He didn't know what she looked like. Her picture hadn't made the paper. Prizes under a million were no big deal these days.

The article in the Nashua paper said Ruthie was a fifty-nine-year-old widow. She worked at a nursing home, but he'd called her early this morning in case she hadn't quit her job yet. He checked his watch. 10:35. Later than he'd planned, but the traffic had been horrendous.

It was risky, sneaking out of work. After he finished, he'd better call his customers so they wouldn't contact his boss and complain that he was late.

He went up the walk and set his toolbox down by the front door. This time he'd brought a heavier wrench, in case Ruthie didn't do what he said. In case she fought back, like Victoria.

This time he'd leave his autograph so the cops would know it was him.

He got his clipboard ready and rang the bell.

A dog began to bark.

His heart jolted in a spasm of fear. A dog! Why didn't he think of that?

The yapping grew louder and he heard a voice on the other side of the door. "Squeaky! Stop that barking right now."

His hands grew sweaty inside the gloves.

The door opened and a stout gray-haired woman in navy slacks and a polka-dot blouse said, "Goodness, you got here fast. Come in."

"Thank you, Ruth." He smiled as hard as he could. "Mind if I call you Ruth? My boss says it's friendlier. We like to keep our customers happy."

"Isn't that nice!" She peered at the name on his shirt. "Come in, Billy."

But when she started to open the door, the dog snarled. He shrank back.

"Could you put the dog in another room? Dogs scare me."

"Oh, don't worry. Squeaky's very friendly. Fox terriers are all bark and no bite!" She smiled broadly, displaying yellowed dentures. An upper tooth was missing on the left side.

"Please, could you put him in another room?"

"Her. Squeaky's a girl. That's why she makes so much noise," Ruthie chortled. "But I can tell you're not a dog lover. Wait here while I put her in the kitchen. Come on, Squeaky, be a good girl. Behave yourself."

He mopped sweat off his forehead with his shirtsleeve. The dog was messing up his plan, and he had no time to waste. He glanced at the house next door. What if Ruthie's neighbors were home and saw him?

She came back and opened the door. "You can come in now. I put Squeaky in the kitchen so she can't bother you."

In the living room a lumpy brown sofa faced the television set. He set his toolbox down on the oval braided rug that covered the floor.

"I hope this won't take long," she said.

"Don't worry, Ruth. Ten minutes, tops."

"That's good. I called and told them I'd be late for work. They know I'm wild about my cable TV. Not much else to do at night when you live alone."

He stared at her. How *dare* she tell them he was coming! He opened the toolbox, took out a screwdriver and knelt down beside the television. Sweat beaded his forehead, and his hands itched like crazy.

The dog yapped furiously. He could see the stupid little mutt in the kitchen, scampering back and forth behind the low wooden gate that blocked the doorway.

"Have you worked for the cable company long?" Ruthie said.

"A couple of years. My boss is a real terrier. I mean terror."

"Oh, that's a good one!" She giggled, exposing the gap in her dentures.

He gave her his sad-look. "He's always on my case. You know how bosses are."

"Do I ever! My supervisor at the nursing home is a dragon lady."

But you've got money now. You're an idiot to keep that crummy job.

"How come you're still working?" The words came out before he could stop them. Stupid! He'd made a mistake!

Her forehead wrinkled in a frown. "I guess you heard," she said slowly. "About me winning the Lotto last week?"

"That's exciting. Why don't you quit your job?"

"I thought about it, but those old folks in the nursing home depend on me. Besides, the prize didn't amount to much. By the time they take out taxes—"

"I think you should quit your job." He rose to his feet.

The dog snarled and jumped against the gate.

"Squeaky, stop that!" Ruthie looked at him apologetically. "I don't know what's wrong with her today."

Eager to get it done, he opened his toolbox and studied the yellow plastic bag and the long-handled wrench. Ruthie had told them about the cable repair. And if her stupid dog didn't stop yapping . . .

"I need you to unplug the TV," he said.

The phone rang. It startled him and he flinched.

She looked at him uncertainly.

"Ruth," he said. "I need your help *now*. Unplug the TV."

"Well," she said, frowning, "I really should answer the phone."

Why wouldn't she do what he said?

Why couldn't everything go smoothly, the way he'd planned?

His cheeks flushed with anger. He stared at her, not smiling.

The phone kept ringing. The yap-yap-yapping dog leaped against the wooden gate.

"Oh all right," she said. "It's probably a salesman or something." She went to the electrical outlet on the wall beside the television and bent down to pull out the plug.

He reached her in one quick stride and slammed the wrench against back of her head. With a loud groan, she fell forward onto the floor.

The phone stopped ringing, but now the dog was barking worse than before, *yap-yap-yap*. The sound made his head hurt.

He sat on her back, pulled the bag over her head and tightened the drawstring. Her fingers plucked feebly at the bag. The skin on her hands was rough and chapped. He pushed her hands away and yanked the cord tight.

With a savage snarl, the dog crashed against the wooden gate, knocked it to the ground and charged, ears flat to its head, eyes barely visible behind tufts of brown fur, teeth bared.

His mouth went dry and his legs turned to jelly.

Panic stricken, he grabbed the wrench, swung hard, felt it connect. The dog yelped and scampered away. But Ruthie kept calling for help, her words muffled by the plastic bag.

Enraged, he slammed the wrench down on the yellow plastic.

The dog lunged at him, snarling viciously.

He swung the wrench and hit the dog's head. The dog fell to the floor, yelping. He hit it again. At last the dog lay still.

Rage consumed him, and pain pounded his head. Why couldn't Ruthie behave? Ruthie and her yappy dog. Ruth-less. He had to be RUTHLESS. He pounded her head with the wrench, beating the yellow plastic until a jolt of pain shot up his forearms. When he stopped, his breath came in gasps.

Smears of bright red blood covered the wrench and the latex gloves. His stomach heaved. He ran in the kitchen, found a towel beside the sink and wiped his gloved hands on the towel. Looking at blood made him sick.

He wrapped the bloody towel around the wrench and checked the time. 10:55. He was late! If he didn't call his customers, they'd complain to his boss.

And he still had to leave his autograph.

He ran back to the living room and fixed the cable connection. Then he rolled Ruthie over, folded her arms across her chest and jammed the J&B nip into the hollowed plastic in her mouth.

J&B. John and Billy. John was always first. Billy was last. Least.

You make me sick, his father had said.

He looked at the dog. Sickening. A pool of blood had formed under its head, staining the braided rug.

Ruthie and her dog had fought him, but they couldn't defeat him.

Now the cops would know he could KILL. Power surged into his groin.

His hand went to the zipper of his workpants. Then he saw the stains, blood spatters on both pant legs!

How could he go to work with blood on his pants?

It was all Ruthie's fault, Ruthie and her stupid dog. His head throbbed with a dull ache. It made him dizzy. He closed his eyes.

He had to change his pants before he went to work.

Blood. Blood. BLOOD.

The letters fell into place in his mind. BOLD. He had to be BOLD.

———

Manchester, Connecticut

It was almost noon when Frank drove into Manchester. Theoretically the trip from Boston should have taken two hours, but parts of the highway were under construction, so it took almost three. Ten miles east of Hartford, Manchester was home to fifty-five thousand residents, most with incomes higher than the national average. Homes on the main street looked expensive, large brick-front houses with attached garages and sprawling green lawns.

Anxious to get on the road, he'd skipped breakfast, had polished off a large Dunkin' Donuts coffee on his way down. Now it was almost noon and his stomach had that hollow feeling. Time for lunch. Then he'd check out his suspect at the public library. Timothy McDermott lived and worked in the same city as Betty McMillan, the fourth Jackpot Killer victim.

Frank ate a burger and some sweet potato fries at a cafe on Main Street, then walked to the library. Faint thunder sounded in the distance. Here it was sunny, but off to the east, dark clouds filled the sky.

A young female librarian was tending to patrons at the circulation desk. Thanks to the driver's license data and photo Ross Dunn had sent him, Frank figured Timothy McDermott would be easy to spot: age thirty-two, six-foot-four, blue eyes, brown hair, unsmiling in the DL photo. Frank went in the stacks near the desk and paged through a book, waiting, watching.

A minute later McDermott emerged from the elevator and carried an armful of books to the circulation desk. Tall and gaunt, he wore dark trousers and a short-sleeved shirt, arms like sticks, looked like a male version of Twiggy. Except Twiggy didn't have a pronounced limp like McDermott.

A man that tall and that thin, with an obvious limp, would not go unnoticed. If McDermott was the Jackpot Killer, he'd had an unbelievable streak of luck.

After McDermott returned to the elevator, Frank went to the desk. The librarian, a young woman with a pixie haircut, gave him a pleasant smile.

"Is the head librarian in?" Frank asked.

"Ms. Farnum? Yes, she's in her office." The woman pointed to a glassed-in cubicle in the corner with waist-high wood paneling.

Frank thanked her, went to the cubicle and tapped on the open door.

Ms. Farnum, a small, bird-like woman with gray hair, looked up and cocked her head like a sparrow. "Can I help you?"

"Detective Frank Renzi, Boston PD." He showed her his ID. "I have some questions about one of your employees. Timothy McDermott."

Ms. Farnum frowned and her hands fluttered nervously. "Goodness, is there a problem?"

To avoid towering over her, he sat on the chair beside her desk. "How long has he worked here?"

"For almost eight years. Why? Has Tim done something wrong?"

"Have you had any problems with him?"

Her frown deepened. "Problems? No. His performance reviews are excellent."

"I understand he attended a workshop in Poughkeepsie, New York, a couple of years ago."

"Yes. Tim's our popular culture expert. I rely on his advice about which books and media to acquire. Tim's a devout Christian. He says there's too much sex and violence in the movies these days. I agree."

Frank wondered if she had watched the sex orgy in *Eyes Wide Shut*. Somehow, he doubted it. "Tim is single?"

"That's correct."

"He lives alone?"

"I believe so."

"Any girlfriends?"

Her lips pursed. "Tim's a very private person. If he had a girlfriend, I very much doubt that he'd mention it to me."

"Ever see him lose his temper?"

"Tim? Lord, no. All our patrons love him." Another big frown. "What's this about?"

He gave her a sheet of paper with a list of the Jackpot murder dates. "Could you check and see if Tim was working on these dates and fax me the information?"

Ms. Farnum glanced at the dates. "Well, I can tell you he wasn't working on January 19th of this year. He had a bad car accident during that big snow storm we had, broke his leg in three places. He was out of work for five weeks. When he came back, he was on crutches."

That accounted for the limp. Nix Timothy McDermott for the murder of Jackpot victim number four.

"Thank you, Ms. Farnum. No need to mention to Mr. McDermott that we've talked."

"Everything's all right then?" she said anxiously.

"Thanks for your help, Ms. Farnum."

Disappointed, he went out and got in his car. Cross McDermott off the suspect list. One down two to go, next stop Fitchburg, Massachusetts, eighty miles away. He got out his highway map and studied the route. Barring any major traffic tie-ups, he'd be in Fitchburg around four. Rush hour.

A bad time to investigate his next suspect. He'd check into a motel, call Ross and see how he was doing with his suspects.

———

The health aide's car wasn't parked out in front when he got home. Excellent. His mother was alone. After he left Ruthie's house in Nashua, he'd used his disposable cell phone to call his customers, saying he'd been delayed by an emergency. Fortunately, none of them had called his boss to complain.

Now all he had to do was change his pants. His bloody pants. He eased open the front door, slipped inside and listened. Silence greeted him. He peeked in the living room. She wasn't in there. Where was she?

The bathroom door at the end of the hall was shut. She must be in there. If he hurried, he could change his pants and leave without her seeing him.

He crept down the hall, tiptoed past the bathroom and went downstairs to his room. He turned on the light and took off his work pants, careful not to touch any of the ugly brown spots, the disgusting blood.

In the fish tank, his girls swam languidly through the water. Including Ruthie. Ruthie, the trouble-maker. Ruthie and her obnoxious yappy dog.

He pulled on a pair of clean chinos. He'd better ditch the dirty ones. He folded them carefully to hide the blood stains, tucked them under his arm and smelled the sour, sweat-stink on his shirt. Disgusting, but he had no time to change his shirt. He had to get out before his mother saw him. He locked the door to his room, crept upstairs and paused on the top step, listening.

The bathroom door was still shut. He heard the toilet flush.

Hurrying now, he walked down the hall to the front door and reached for the doorknob.

"Billy!"

His heart fluttered wildly, like a moth at a flame. He turned and saw his mother wheeling herself down the hall, pale blue eyes fixed on his, lips pursed. "What are you doing home?"

He pasted on a smile. "Gee, Mom, your hair looks nice. Did you get it done today?"

"Doris did it yesterday." She patted the soft waves into place, then frowned. "Why aren't you at work? Why were you sneaking out without speaking to me?"

"I left my afternoon work schedule in my room. I didn't want to disturb you in the bathroom, Mom." He half-turned, angling his body so she couldn't see the bloody pants under his arm.

"What's that you're carrying?"

His head throbbed. He stared at her mouth. The mouth that was never still. The mouth that never gave him any peace.

He opened the door. "I have to go. I'm late for my next customer."

"Well, do a good job, and they'll pay you better. *That's* what you should do, Billy. Ask for a raise!"

He went out and shut the door hard, like he wanted to shut his mother's mouth.

His heart beat furiously, sending shooting pains into his head.

MOTHER making pain in his HEAD.

Mouth always moving.

Shooting words at him.

Making mouth-moving-pain in his HEAD.

Words. Stop the words.

RUTHLESS. MOTHER-LESS. HEAD-LESS.

CHAPTER 23

Tuesday, May 23 — 10:45 p.m.

"Fancy another glass of wine?" Nigel rattled the ice cubes in his glass.

"No, thanks," Gina said, "but you go ahead." She'd barely touched her Merlot, but Nigel had already downed two glasses of scotch.

"Be right back," he said, flashing her a smile as he left their table.

Gina watched him as he went to the bar. Nigel would play a major role in her book, but so far the essence of the man eluded her. After Vicky's wake he'd been eager to talk. Tonight, not so much.

An hour ago, fearing some local reporter might recognize her red Mazda, she'd parked two blocks away and walked to the Back Bay Inn. Avoiding the media mob outside the entrance, she entered through the parking garage. The hotel catered to business travelers, and at 9:30 the lounge on the first floor had been jammed. But the rooftop bar wasn't. Few people knew about it. The bar closed for the winter and re-opened in the spring, but only in fair weather. When it rained, the rooftop bar was closed

She sipped her Merlot, enjoying the fresh air. The view was spectacular, lights on the buildings in Copley Square and beyond. In the distance, she could see the lights at Fenway Park. The bar had no wait staff; a bored older man tended a short bar with no barstools.

Most important, no reporters occupied the half-dozen tables. Aside from a young couple seated at another table, she and Nigel were the only ones here, and the young lovebirds had eyes only for each other.

Tonight Nigel looked worse than he had at Vicky's wake, deathly pale, bloodshot eyes. Still, apart from the receding hairline, he was a good-looking man. She could understand why Vicky had fallen for him: a talented musician, intelligent and undeniably charming. As soon they sat down with their drinks, Nigel had asked how long she'd worked for the *Herald* and did she do any other sort of writing? He seemed genuinely interested, gazing at her with his startlingly blue eyes.

But he hadn't said much about himself. She'd already gathered the basic facts about his life and career, but she wanted the lowdown on his Hollywood years with his ex-wife, the actress, and the unexplained interval between his abandoned solo career and his days at the Royal College of Music.

She pulled out the CD she'd found at a used record store. Released on an obscure European label, it featured Nigel improvising jazz standards. His picture was on the front, seated at a piano in a London club.

When he came back with a tall glass of scotch and sat down, she set the CD on the table. "This is terrific, Nigel. Ever think of doing another one?"

He seemed pleased, smiling at her. "Where'd you find that?"

"I'm a big jazz fan. You're really good. Any other jazz players in your family? Brothers? Sisters?"

His expression grew somber. She thought British men were supposed to be stoic, stiff-upper-lip types, but Nigel's face clearly signaled his emotions.

"I'm an only child. Mum was the musician in the family. She sang opera before she married my father." He shrugged. "That was the end of that."

Gina nodded. A familiar scenario for earlier generations of talented women. They set aside their careers in order to marry and raise a family.

"Did you play jazz when you were a kid?"

"Not bloody likely. Not when my father was around, that's for sure. Just practice, practice, practice, and play the competitions."

"But you were a prodigy. Didn't you win a big competition when you were twelve?"

Nigel didn't answer. She had assumed he'd be eager to talk about his glory days, but maybe a piano prodigy's life had its drawbacks.

"That must have put a lot of pressure on you," she said.

"Right. Win the competitions, play the recitals, smile for the cameras."

She tried to imagine him as an adolescent. Talented, sensitive and what? Tortured?

"And if you don't win, it's hell?"

His eyes regarded her steadily for several moments. Finally he said, "You're a good listener, Gina. Very perceptive." He sipped his scotch. "This is off the record, okay? Can't have you writing about this."

Her heart sank. Damn! He was going to tell her something juicy, and she couldn't write about it?

She didn't say anything, but he didn't seem to notice. "When I was eighteen my father entered me in a big competition in Belgium. He said if I won, my career would take off like a shot. I did okay, breezed through the early rounds and made it to the finals. But the night before the final competition, Mum called me from London, terribly distraught."

"Why? Was she ill?"

"No. Well, not physically. But like a lot of opera singers, Mum was a bit high-strung. She said she was dying of boredom, sick of staying home to keep house for my father. He ran a local music shop, open six days a week, dawn to dark. I wasn't too sympathetic, I'm afraid. I had to play the finals the next day and I had some stiff competition."

He gulped some scotch and massaged his eyes. After a moment, he said, "The next morning, my father couldn't wake her. She'd taken some pills. He rushed her to the hospital, but they couldn't save her."

"Nigel!" she gasped. "How awful! You must have felt terrible."

"Yes, well, I try not to think about it. When my father called to tell me, I was devastated. Here Mum had called me looking for sympathy and I'd more or less blown her off. My father told me to carry on with the competition. He said that's what Mum would have wanted." Nigel belted down some scotch. "Heartless bastard. As if he knew what Mum wanted."

Observing his torment, Gina felt a certain sense of kinship. She knew the anguish death by suicide could cause, and she didn't like to think about it either. "Something similar happened to me when I was eighteen."

Nigel touched her hand. "I'm sorry to hear it. Want to talk about it?"

Did she? She'd never told anyone about Denise, not even Franco. But Nigel had bared his soul to her. Maybe she should do the same.

"I was co-editor of my high school yearbook. Denise, my co-editor, was really smart, but she was running with a tough crowd. One day we were alone in the office and she told me she was pregnant."

Gina sipped her wine, remembering the awkward scene. "I didn't know what to say. I didn't feel like it was my place to tell her what to do. When I said her parents would help her, she started crying. She said she couldn't tell them. They'd disown her, something like that. Anyway, she got up and left. Two days later, she borrowed her mother's car and drove it into a bridge abutment. They said she had to be going a hundred miles an hour."

Nigel shook his head. "And she was only eighteen? What a waste."

"I felt so guilty. I didn't know her parents, but I should have been more supportive. I felt like I should have done something, helped her somehow."

"Hindsight is always a killer," Nigel said, and gulped some scotch.

"What happened at the piano competition?"

"I fell apart, fingers froze up, it was a bloody train wreck. When I got home, I had a colossal row with my father and went off to London."

He stared into space, his expression desolate. "I haven't talked about Mum in years. She had this way about her. Even in a roomful of people, she made you feel like you were the most important person in the world." He shook his head. "Sorry to go on about it. P'rhaps we should call it a night."

Damn! She needed more. Down and dirty details. More juicy revelations.

"Okay, but can we can talk again?"

Nigel heaved a sigh. "Sure. Provided the cops don't throw me in jail."

———

Wednesday, May 24 — Fitchburg — 10:10 a.m.

Frank entered the Fitchburg library, a three-story red-brick building that had seen better days. A male librarian stood behind the circulation desk. Pitted with acne scars, his narrow ferret-face fit the DL photo Ross Dunn had sent him. John Lipton, age twenty-eight, five-foot-ten, blue eyes, brown hair. Two years ago Lipton had been charged with soliciting a prostitute but got off on a technicality.

Frank went to the desk, but the man ignored him, staring at the computer. "Mr. Lipton?"

"Yeah?" Lipton didn't look up.

"I'd like to speak with the head librarian."

"She's not in today."

"Can you give me her phone number? I need to speak to her."

Lipton's eyes met his briefly, then flicked away. "We don't give out personal information."

He flashed his ID. "Boston PD. I need her name and phone number."

Lipton flipped through a Rolodex on the counter, his expression sullen, wrote a name and phone number on a slip of paper, shoved the slip at Frank and stared at the computer screen, ignoring him.

John Lipton didn't like having a cop visit his workplace.

Anxious to wrap up the Lipton investigation, Frank left the library. Tomorrow he would drive to Sandwich and check out his last suspect.

When he called Jean Halliwell, the head librarian, she agreed to meet him at a Dunkin' Donuts near the library in ten minutes. Frank ordered an iced coffee and a blueberry muffin and grabbed a table facing the door. He was just finishing the muffin when an attractive woman in black slacks and a red blouse came in and headed his way, exuding an air of vitality and confidence.

"Detective Renzi?" she said. "Jean Halliwell. Nice to meet you."

"My pleasure. Thanks for meeting me on your day off."

"It's not every day a Boston police detective comes calling. What can I do for you?"

"How about I buy you a coffee? Then you can tell me about John Lipton."

"Oh. John." Her smile faded. "Okay, I'll have a small iced coffee."

When he returned with her coffee, she took a sip, gazing at him, her eyes somber. "John has worked at the library for three years, but I don't know him well. His work is adequate, but . . ." She sipped her coffee. "Have you spoken with him?"

This woman was sharp. Frank hoped she'd be candid. "I have."

"We're there to serve the public. John's biggest failing is dealing with patrons. He can be rather curt."

"Is he married?"

"No, but he has a girlfriend. I met her at our Christmas party last year."

His cell phone rang. He checked it and saw Ross Dunn's number. "Sorry. I need to take this." He left the table, stepped outside and answered.

"Frank," Ross said. "The Jackpot Killer got another one."

"Damn! Where?"

"Nashua, New Hampshire. The lead detective called me. He's a former FBI agent, remembered the email alert I sent to police departments around New England asking them to notify me immediately about any unexplained lottery winner deaths."

"Ross, I'm in Fitchburg checking one of our suspects. I could be in Nashua in forty-five minutes. Any way you can get him to preserve the crime scene till I get there?"

"Sure. I'll call him back and tell him you're on your way. Detective Sergeant Steven Huff."

He wrote down the detective's name and cell phone number, and went back inside.

Jean Halliwell saw his expression and said, "Looks like you got bad news."

"I did. Sorry, but I need to leave."

"Does your emergency have anything to do with John Lipton?"

He thought for a moment. Lipton was working today, but he didn't know when the Nashua woman had been murdered. "I doubt it, but could you check and see if he was working yesterday and call me?"

"No need to call," she said. "I was at the library all day yesterday and so was John Lipton."

Anxious to leave, he said, "Thanks for your help."

———

Nigel glanced at Merrill Carr, seated beside him in the taxi, examining his manicured nails as they drove to the police station. His high-powered defense attorney had on a gray pinstriped Versace suit and a red power tie. The bloke's nasal voice grated on his ears, but Merrill was the best criminal defense lawyer in Boston. Or so he'd claimed. Merrill said he specialized in high-profile cases and charged accordingly. Which no doubt paid for his expensive suit.

He was desperate for a cigarette, but the sign in the cab said: No Smoking. Bloody hell, what if the cops arrested him? Not a peep out of Merrill. Maybe he was planning his strategy.

He'd told Merrill everything. Well, not everything, not about the gambling and the debts. When he'd said, "I didn't kill Vicky, I loved her. You believe me, don't you?" Merrill had said, expressionless, "Wrong question, Nigel. It doesn't matter if I believe you. The question is, can I get you off?"

Smiling tightly, he'd said, "And I almost always get my clients off. That's what they pay me for."

Merrill wanted a five-thousand-dollar retainer, up front. He'd promised to give it to him. God knows where he'd get it. This morning he'd called Hale again to ask him to send an advance. Hale's secretary said he wasn't in.

Bullshit. He didn't believe it.

The cab pulled up to the station. The inevitable mob of newshounds and television cameras were waiting. Merrill told the cabbie to wait and to keep the meter running. Then he turned his frosty-gray eyes on Nigel and said, "Not a word out of you, unless I say so, understand?"

He nodded. Already he felt sick to his stomach and his fingers were icy claws. He needed a cigarette to settle his nerves, but the detectives probably wouldn't let him smoke, the bastards.

Merrill forged his way through the reporters, his silvery-haired head held high. "Let us through please. My client has no comment and neither do I."

Not "My client is innocent," Nigel thought, sinking into a pit of despair. Didn't anyone believe him?

Mulligan was waiting in the lobby. He didn't seem happy to see Merrill Carr. When they went in the interrogation room, Detective Renzi wasn't there. Another man with dark hair and dark eyes sat at the table. Mulligan didn't introduce him.

Nigel sank onto the chair opposite the younger detective. Merrill took the chair beside him. The moment Mulligan turned on the tape recorder, Merrill said, "This is harassment, pure and simple, Detective Mulligan. My client gave you his statement already. *Without* benefit of counsel, I might add."

"We offered to let him call a lawyer but he declined," Mulligan said. He turned to the other detective and said, "Detective Palumbo, get Mr. Heath and Attorney Carr a cup of coffee."

"Sure thing," Palumbo said. "What'll it be, Mr. Heath? Cream? Sugar?"

"Black is fine, thank you." The friendly gesture encouraged him. The last time they hadn't offered him so much as a drink of water.

"None for me," Merrill said. "Detective Mulligan, are you prepared to press charges against my client?"

"No, but we've got questions for him. This is a high-profile murder. We need to find the killer."

"Well, it wasn't me," Nigel said. "Why don't you find the bugger that—"

Merrill put a hand on his arm and squeezed. "Detective Mulligan, I fail to see what further questions you could possibly have for my client."

Mulligan coughed, a smoker's hack, Nigel thought, judging by the nicotine stains on his fingers. Damned if he'd beg the bastard to let him smoke, though. Detective Palumbo returned and set a mug of coffee in front of him. Nigel took a sip. It was so hot it burned his tongue, but at least it warmed his hands.

"We need to go over the timeline," Mulligan said. "What time did your plane get in from Las Vegas?"

He set down the mug. "My flight got in at 7:55."

"And you didn't check any bags?"

"Whether my client did or did not check baggage is irrelevant," Merrill said.

"Merrill, we need to establish what time Mr. Heath got to Victoria's apartment."

"I *told* you!" Nigel said. "I took a cab from Logan—"

"Wait for the *question*," Merrill said in his nasal voice. "If I want you to answer, I'll *tell* you."

"Mr. Heath," Mulligan said, "what time did you call Vicky from the airport?

He glanced at Merrill, who nodded. "Might have been eight-fifteen or so. I can't remember exactly."

"But it could have been *earlier*."

"Detective Mulligan, my client answered your question to the best of his *recollection*. Let's move on."

"What did you and Vicky talk about?" Mulligan said.

"That's privileged," Merrill snapped. "My client will not answer."

He looked at Merrill, but Merrill's eyes were fixed on Gerry Mulligan. He tried his coffee. It had cooled a bit, just the right temperature now. He sipped it gratefully, cupping the mug with his hands.

"You took a cab to Victoria's apartment?" Mulligan said.

"Yes. I told you that before."

Detective Palumbo spoke for the first time. "We checked every cab company that services Logan Airport, but we didn't find any cab driver that remembers taking you to the North End."

"That means nothing," Merrill snapped.

Mulligan frowned. "Yes it does. It means he could have gotten to the North End *earlier*."

"My client will not answer any further questions about how he got to the North End. He took a cab. It's not *his* responsibility to locate the driver. That's *your* job."

"What time did you call Vicky from the store?" Mulligan said.

"Around nine. The traffic was bad—"

"Nigel, just answer the *question*." Merrill glared at him, his eyes hard as granite.

"The woman in the store doesn't remember seeing you," Detective Palumbo said.

"She wasn't *there* that day. I *told* you—"

"Detective Mulligan, this is a fishing expedition, pure and simple. You have no evidence to charge my client. He's already given you a complete and accurate statement. Mr. Heath is a busy man, so—"

"Hold it!" Mulligan's face got red. "He can't leave town. He's a primary witness. I'll get a judge—"

"That won't be necessary." Merrill rose to his feet. "My client has no plans to leave Boston. I suggest you get busy and find the *real* murderer. My client did *not* kill Victoria Stavropoulos."

A surge of hope rippled through him. At last Merrill had spoken the words he longed to hear.

But Merrill said nothing as they returned to the taxi, his face grim as they fought through the mob of reporters.

When they drove off, Nigel said, "That went pretty well, didn't it?"

Merrill skewered him with a look. "Not now. Wait till we get to your hotel."

They rode in silence the rest of the way. At the Back Bay Inn Merrill forged his way through another mob of reporters and television cameras, barking, "No comment."

When they got to his room, Merrill didn't sit down. Nor did he smile.

"Nigel, I always level with my clients, so I'll give it to you straight. You're the prime suspect in the murder of Victoria Stavropoulos. Mulligan hasn't got his ducks lined up in a row yet, but when he does, he's going to charge you. My guess is, it'll be murder one."

CHAPTER 24

Frank got to the Nashua crime scene in thirty-eight minutes flat. A Nashua police cruiser stood outside the victim's house, a one-story bungalow painted pale green. The front door opened and a rugged-looking older man stepped outside.

"Detective Renzi? Steve Huff. You made good time."

"Thanks to your directions. Nice to meet you. Frank Renzi."

Huff pumped his hand and said, "Brace yourself. This one's brutal."

He put on the booties and latex gloves Huff gave him and went inside. Ignoring the stench, he surveyed the room, gathering impressions. A woman sprawled on the floor. A yellow plastic bag over her head. On the carpet under her head, a large dark bloodstain. Inside a hollow in the plastic bag, a J&B nip stood out like a red flag. The Jackpot Killer had left his calling card.

This time there was another victim. Near the woman's body, a small dog, some sort of terrier by the looks of it, lay on its side. Blood matted the fur on its head, and dark-brown bloodstains marred the carpet underneath the dog.

"Any idea how long they've been dead?" he asked Huff.

"At least twenty-four hours I'd guess. I didn't touch the woman, but I tried to move one of the dog's legs. The dog appeared to be in full rigor. Assuming they were killed at the same time, I'd say she is, too."

"Who found her?"

"We got a wellness-check call from her daughter this morning. She lives in Billerica, just over the line in Massachusetts, said she'd called her mother three times yesterday, got no answer, same thing this morning. We sent a patrol officer. He couldn't see much through the window, tried the front door and it was unlocked. It was obvious this was a homicide, so he called me."

"Looks like he hit her with something heavy."

Huff nodded, his expression grim. "I see a lot of rage here. He beat her head to a pulp."

Like Vicky, Frank thought. The Jackpot Killer was losing control.

"You're hunting a serial killer, right?" Huff said.

"Is that what Ross Dunn told you?" He didn't want to reveal too much. Ross wanted it kept quiet.

Huff shrugged. "Not in so many words, but I worked in the Bureau for twenty years. Agent Dunn sent an email asking for an immediate call about any unexplained lottery winner deaths." Huff gave him a pointed look. "I watch the news. A lottery winner was murdered in Boston. I figure that's why you're here. Agent Dunn said you were his liaison on some recent murders."

"True. This one didn't go the way he planned. Looks like the dog tried to protect her, so he killed the dog, too. How'd you know she was a lottery winner?"

Huff didn't answer, just took him in the kitchen and showed him a newspaper clipping on the table. "That's what tipped me off. I need to call the forensic team. I held off till you got here like Agent Dunn asked, but it'll take them a half-hour to get here."

"Go ahead," Frank said, scanning the news clip. Last week, Ruth Bennett, age sixty-three, had hit the NH Lotto and won forty-five thousand dollars. She worked at a nursing home, but didn't plan to quit her job. "Those folks need someone to take care of them," she'd told the reporter. "I love my job. It makes me feel good to help people." Doodled around the article were smiley faces in red ink. The sight tugged at his heart.

Huff closed his cell phone and gestured at the article. "Sad, isn't it?"

Frank nodded, thinking: *They're all sad.* A week ago, he'd been consoling Vicky's father at her wake. Now, another Jackpot Killer murder. The interval between kills was getting shorter. The bastard was escalating.

"No forced entry," Frank said. "Why do you think she let him in?"

"Could be a trade person, electrician or a plumber maybe, or some kind of delivery man." Huff grimaced. "Hate to say this, but the killer could be someone with police ID."

Frank doubted this. Of the seven Jackpot Killer victims so far, eight if he included Vicky, none of the neighbors had reported seeing a policeman or a police cruiser. "The Boston victim's head was beaten, too."

"What about the Pops conductor, the guy that found her? Judging from the news reports I see, seems like the investigation is focused on him."

"That might change when the lead detective gets wind of this one." He locked eyes with Detective Huff. "Do me and Agent Dunn a favor, okay? Keep the details of this case quiet, especially the J&B nip."

"I'll do my best, but I can't control the forensic people or the coroner. You know how it is."

"I do. Could you send the autopsy report and whatever else you get to Agent Dunn and copy it to me?"

"No problem," Huff said. "We need to catch the bastard."

"The sooner the better," Frank agreed. "Before he kills another one."

Westwood — 8:30 p.m.

Gina finished packing more clothes into her suitcase, zipped it shut and lugged it down to the kitchen. An open bottle of Shiraz stood on the counter. She poured the last of it into a wineglass. Why waste it? Ryan didn't drink, didn't smoke and didn't swear. The perfect altar boy, except when it came to sex. Never again would she watch porn videos with Ryan on the big-screen television that faced their king-sized bed.

But forget Ryan. Focus on the book.

Too edgy to sit, she paced the kitchen, thinking about Vicky and Nigel. She felt like a vulture. She'd been too focused on interviewing a big lottery winner for her gambling series to warn Vicky about the Jackpot Killer. When Vicky was murdered, Nigel became the prime suspect.

Now she was using him, too.

On the 6:00 p.m. news, she'd seen footage of him leaving the police station with his lawyer earlier today, his mouth set in a grim line. She didn't know what happened, but she was glad he'd hired a criminal defense lawyer.

She sipped her wine, thinking about what Nigel had told her last night about his mother. Even now, twenty-three years later, he appeared devastated. When a family member committed suicide, it stayed with you for a lifetime.

Her telephone rang, startling her. Who was calling at this hour? Franco never called her landline, only her cell. She checked Caller ID. An icy chill froze her in her tracks. Ryan, calling from Texas. He never called during the week. She hadn't spoken to him since Sunday night.

But better to talk to him by phone than in person.

She picked up and said, "Hello?"

"Hey, Gina, how you doing?" Ryan said jovially, acting like nothing was wrong.

"Okay. How are you?" As if she cared.

"I had a great day today, picked up a new client. But that's not why I called. I was kind of rough on you last Sunday, might have said some things I shouldn't have."

Might have? Grabbing her, shoving her against the wall and kissing her? Telling her to quit her job, have a baby and act like a real wife?

"Hello? You still there, babe?"

"I'm listening." Waiting for an apology. Not that she'd ever get one from Ryan.

"I'm coming home early on Friday so we can go away for the long weekend."

Go away for the weekend? Was he out of his mind?

Maybe he thought he'd get her pregnant. Fat chance. She'd been taking birth control pills for the past six years. Ryan would flip if he knew. God knows what he'd do if he found out she was having an affair with Franco.

"Want to go to the Cape? New York City? Your choice."

My choice would be *Take a hike, Ryan*. But she didn't dare say it.

Her cell rang. Her stomach tensed, but then she thought: *It's Franco*.

"Hold on a second, Ryan. My cell phone's ringing."

But it wasn't Franco, it was Nigel. "Hope I'm not calling at a bad time. Got time to chat for a bit?"

Pressing the landline receiver against her thigh, she said softly, "Let me call you back, Nigel. I'm talking to someone on my landline."

"Blast! Sorry to be such a bother. The detectives had another go at me today. My lawyer says I'm the prime suspect. He says they might throw me in jail any day now."

"Hold on, Nigel." She raised the landline receiver and heard Ryan yell, "Gina! Don't leave me hanging!"

She could pictured him, his mouth set in a line, his blue eyes flinty.

She spoke into her cell. "Nigel, I've got to go. Call you back in a half hour, I promise." She punched off and spoke into her landline: "Sorry, Ryan. Something about work."

"Don't lie to me," Ryan said, his tone venomous. "You were talking to Nigel Heath."

Damn. He must have heard her say Nigel's name. She took out a cigarette and lighted it. "So?"

"Seems like you and Nigel are pretty cozy these days."

"What's that supposed to mean?"

"What I said. His girlfriend's dead, so now he's got a new one. You're sleeping with him."

"I am not!"

"What's the attraction? He's a big-shot conductor? Not anymore. I saw him on the news tonight. He looked like an old man. He's washed up, Gina."

"Ryan, I'm a reporter. He's in the news. I'm working on a story."

"Forget the story. Stay away from him."

"Don't tell me who I can talk to!"

"I knew it. You're sleeping with him."

She drank some wine and puffed her cigarette. Why bother to respond? Ryan's mind was made up, and when he made up his anal-retentive mind about something, nothing would change it.

"Listen up, Gina. I already booked my return flight from Austin. When I get home Friday at four o'clock, you better be there. Think about where you'd like to go. It's a holiday weekend, so hotel reservations will be tight. If I don't hear from you by noon tomorrow—"

"Ryan, I'm not going anywhere with you this weekend."

Silence on the other end. Her heart pounded as she waited for the explosion. None came. Ryan disconnected and the dial tone droned.

Her hands trembled as she gulped some wine. She had no idea where she'd be at 4:00 on Friday, but it wouldn't be here. What would Ryan do when he came home to an empty house? She realized she didn't care. Any feelings she might have had for him had disappeared years ago.

She got on her cell and called Franco. The man she loved. The man who called her his Ace Reporter.

The man who spoke into her ear in his deep melodious voice. "Hey, I was just thinking about you."

"Miss me?" she said.

"Always."

Her eyes misted with tears and her throat closed up.

"What's up, Gina?"

"Nigel Heath just called me. He said Gerry Mulligan gave him another hard time today."

"Damn! Gerry knew I'd be out of town. What happened?"

"Nigel's lawyer thinks they're going to arrest him. Can't you talk to him? Please?"

"I'm flat out for the next two days. Another lottery winner got murdered in Nashua."

"No!" she gasped. "Was it the Jackpot Killer?"

"Looks like it, but that's not for publication, so mum's the word. Earliest I could talk to Nigel would be Friday night."

"That would be fantastic! Where and when?"

"We better go to his hotel, but make sure his lawyer isn't there."

"Okay. I'll come to the Dorchester Palace at 9:00 and we can drive in together. How does that sound?"

"Sounds great." A soft chuckle. "Then I can bring you back to my room and have my way with you."

She burst out laughing. "That's my Franco. Always the wise guy."

162

CHAPTER 25

Thursday, May 25 — Sandwich

Frank drove alongside the Cape Cod Canal from Bourne to Sandwich, enjoying the scenic view. It was a gorgeous day, sunny and mild. No traffic yet, but tomorrow it would be brutal, the start of the holiday weekend. He might have to finish investigating his third suspect next week.

This morning he had spoken to the head librarian at the Bourne Library.

A no-nonsense woman with thin lips and a long nose, she'd said: "Billy only worked here three months. I used to find him in the stacks reading movie magazines. I think he stole some of them. He's a creep. One day I caught him in the ladies' room. Well! That was it. I gave him his marching papers and good riddance!"

That was three years ago. Frank tried not to get too pumped up over it. But two years ago William Karapitulik, then twenty-eight, had registered as a librarian at the Poughkeepsie conference. Still, they needed a lot more than that to peg him as the Jackpot Killer.

At 12:15 Frank parked on a side street in Sandwich and walked back to Number 14. William Karapitulik's house. Near the ocean it was cooler, and a pleasant breeze riffled budding green leaves on maple trees along the street. Most of the houses were Victorians, fresh paint, gingerbread trim, manicured lawns. When he stopped to let a car back out of a driveway, the woman driver smiled and waved at him.

Nice neighborhood. Friendly folks. Was one of them a killer?

He slowed his pace as he passed Number 14, a small two-story cottage, blue-painted clapboards, white shutters around the windows. All the shades were drawn, looked like nobody was home. Maybe Karapitulik had found another job. He could ring the bell and find out, but he was pressed for time. He and Rafe were taking Jamal to a Celtics game tonight, and Chief Duggan was expecting him.

163

When he entered the police station, Chief Duggan was waiting by the front desk. Tall and gaunt with thinning gray hair, Duggan looked to be in his early sixties. "What can I do for you, Detective Renzi?"

Frank glanced at the officer behind the desk and said, "Could we talk in your office?"

"Sure thing, follow me."

At the end of a short hall they entered a sunlit room with two large windows, a metal desk and several file cabinets. The chief motioned him into the visitor chair, sat at his desk and looked at him expectantly.

"I'm working a murder case, and I need information on a Sandwich resident. William Karapitulik."

"Billy?" Duggan seemed surprised, almost amused. A far cry from the Bourne librarian's reaction.

"Yeah, you know him?"

"Sure. He's lived here for, oh, maybe twenty years or so. He lives with his mother."

Frank's antenna went up. Maybe he was on the right track. Other than the Poughkeepsie woman, all the victims had been murdered on weekdays during the daytime. Ross thought the killer might live with someone and couldn't manufacture an excuse to go out at night or on weekends.

"Could you give me some background on them?"

"Can't say I know them well, but Mrs. Kay . . ." Duggan shrugged. "That's what everybody calls her. Karapitulik is a mouthful. Anyway, Mrs. Kay's disabled, had a leg amputated after she was in a car accident. She uses a wheelchair to get around. Don't guess she'd be murdering anybody."

"Where was the accident? Here in Sandwich?"

"No. It happened before they moved here, someplace in Kentucky, I think she said." Duggan frowned. "You got Billy pegged as a suspect in a murder case?"

"Right now I'm checking several leads. You know how it is."

"Well, Billy's a little guy, sort of on the plump side. He's no Charles Atlas, that's for sure. Hard to picture him as a killer."

Frank had encountered that reaction before, even from law enforcement people, but over the years he'd encountered some brutal killers who looked like the boy next door. "Where does he work?"

"I don't know. Can't say I ever had a conversation with him. I could ask around and find out for you."

"Thanks Chief. That would help." Ross could get the information faster, but he wanted to keep Duggan involved. If the lead panned out, a local pair of eyes might be useful.

"His mother's a born-again Christian. Billy takes her to some Pentecostal church up near Brockton every Sunday. Afterwards they have dinner at the

Seaside Diner." Duggan stroked his jaw. "You might try talking to the waitresses at the diner. Arlene's the one usually waits on them."

"Thanks, I will. Has Billy ever been in trouble? Peeping Tom, anything like that?" Ross had already run the name through the FBI's VICAP database and got nothing, but a misdemeanor peeping-tom charge wouldn't show up.

"Not that I'm aware of, and believe me, I'd know if he got in trouble, him being a year-round resident. Summer folks and tourists, that's another story. I hear that murder in Chatham was brutal. Does this have anything to do with that case?"

Unwilling to tip his hand, Frank said, "Right now I'm working another investigation." Not a total lie. He was working a lot of cases: Vicky's murder, the Jackpot Killer, the Mass Ave gang hit and several others.

"Uh-huh," Duggan said. "Damn shame about the woman in Boston that hit the Megabucks. Collects a big prize, gets murdered a week later. You working for Boston PD, I figure you'd know something about it."

He put on his blank face. Like everyone else, Duggan watched the news, had already made the connection between the Chatham winner and Vicky. Sooner or later some sharp-eyed reporter would dig up the Nashua case, connect the dots and run with the story.

If Billy turned out to be the Jackpot Killer, he might need Duggan's help, but at this point he didn't want to tell him Billy was a suspect. It was way too soon for that. He gave Duggan his card.

"I'd rather you didn't tell anyone I was here. Could you keep an eye on Billy and call me if you notice anything unusual?"

"Sure thing. Nobody'll hear it from me," Duggan said, but his eyes had a speculative look.

"Thanks for your help, Chief. Let's keep in touch."

———

Billy balled up the wrapper and tossed it on the floor on the passenger side. A cool breeze floated through the van window. He'd parked under a shade tree behind McDonald's. Last night his mother had fixed her usual rotten dinner. He figured she'd feed him the leftovers tonight so he'd ordered a Big Mac, a large order of fries and a chocolate shake.

While he waited for his order, he'd watched CNN on the television set mounted on the wall. Nothing about a dead lottery winner, just some story about a big airline merger, United and US Airways. As if he cared.

Early this morning, he'd read the Nashua *Telegraph* online. Ruthie's picture was front and center. The Nashua cops said they had no suspects. Liars. They had to know it was him. He'd left his autograph. The article didn't mention the J&B nip, but the cops didn't always tell the reporters everything.

He picked at the eczema scab on his thumb and thought about Ruthie and her yappy little dog, remembering how badly the dog had scared him.

What if the dog had been bigger? What if it had been an attack dog? What if the dog had bitten him?

But next time he wouldn't need to worry about that. He picked up the *Soldier of Fortune* magazine on the passenger seat, folded open to an advertisement for the New Mark II. The picture was striking. He loved the description. Rugged. Reliable. That's what he needed, a rugged reliable gun.

The specifications? Steel construction, chambered for the .380 ACP cartridge. Affordably priced at $280, each pistol comes with two ten-round magazines, a field cleaning rod, and a handy padded carrying case.

Perfect. He'd already ordered one.

When he chose his next lucky winner, it wouldn't matter if she had a dog, not even if it was an attack dog. In fact, it wouldn't matter if his lucky winner was young or old, a man or a woman.

Once he had his New Mark II, he could make his lucky winner do exactly what he said.

———

Frank parked outside the Seaside Diner, a converted boxcar with rustic red siding and a flat shingled roof. Contrary to what the name indicated, the diner was nowhere near the ocean. Red canvas awnings shaded the windows along the front, and a wooden wheelchair ramp led to the door.

He went inside and sat at the counter three stools away from two older men eating pie and ice cream. They appeared to be hard of hearing, loudly debating the pennant chances of the Boston Red Sox this year.

A young dark-haired waitress in a short black skirt and a white blouse handed him a menu. "Thanks," he said, "but I'm not having lunch. Is Arlene in? I'd like to talk to her."

"Hold on." The waitress pushed open a swinging door behind the counter and yelled, "Arlene! Someone here to see you."

Moments later a skinny woman in a similar outfit, short black skirt, white blouse, came through the door. She had spiky carrot-red hair, and freckles dotted her cheeks. She appeared to be in her forties, though her dangle earrings hinted at a young-at-heart personality. She beamed him a smile.

"Hi. I'm Arlene. You wanted to talk to me?"

"Frank Renzi," he said, returning her smile. "Could we talk someplace private? Chief Duggan said you might be able to help me out with some information."

"Oh. Okay. There's a table open in the back. Want some coffee?"

"Thanks. That would be great." He waited while she poured coffee into two mugs. They sat at the table in the back corner. Arlene sipped her coffee, eyeing him over the rim.

"Chief Duggan said you wait on William Karapitulik and his mother sometimes."

She nodded and her big-hoop earrings swayed. "They come in every Sunday after church. I feel sorry for Mrs. Kay, being in a wheelchair and all. Billy's a cute little guy." She grinned. "I keep telling him some girl's gonna go for him in a big way."

"Ever hear them argue about anything?"

Her eyes widened. "Billy and his mom? Never. Billy's real polite. He's devoted to his mother, always taking her places. What's this about, anyway?"

He showed her his ID. "I'm checking some leads related to a murder case."

"Well, you can forget Billy. He'd never hurt a fly. He's a sweet little guy. He collects goldfish, buys a new one almost every month. He even gives them names."

"Such as?"

"Let's see," she said, frowning in thought. "I think he named one of them Tessa. I forget the others."

The back of his neck prickled. Tessa. The murdered lottery winner in Rhode Island.

"His mother nags him about his job sometimes, though."

Out of the mouths of waitresses. "Where does he work?"

"He works for National Cablevision. I'm not sure what he does."

Dumbstruck, he stared at her. Television. Cable connections.

If Billy was a cable technician, he could probably get into most any house with no trouble at all. Then he remembered what the daughter of the RI lottery winner had said: the day she was murdered, her mother had complained that her TV was messed up.

"But I guess the job doesn't pay very well," Arlene went on. "That's what his mother says, anyway."

He wanted to kiss her. "Thanks, Arlene, you've been a big help." He locked eyes with her and said sternly, "This is a police investigation. Please don't tell anyone that I asked about them."

"Okay," she said, eyes serious now. "I won't."

———

Boston — 7:15 p.m.

When Rafe picked him up outside the D-4 station, Jamal was in the shotgun seat. Rafe winked at him and said, "Sorry, Frank. Jamal's my co-pilot this evening. Hop in back."

Frank pushed file-folders and empty coffee containers aside, the usual police car detritus, and climbed into the back seat. "How you doing, Jamal? All set for the big game? Got your cheers ready? Go Celtics!"

Jamal turned and gave him a big smile. "Yes, sir, Mr. Frank. Go Celtics!"

"Very good," Rafe said, eyeing Frank in the rearview. "Had to explain the proper mode of address to Jamal, don't want him saying Detective Hawkins or Detective Renzi, ruin our evening, not to mention spoil things for the folks nearby, thinking there's cops sitting beside them."

He grinned. Rafe's enthusiasm was contagious. He stretched his legs and tried to relax. Forget the Jackpot Killer. Shove his looming divorce and financial problems down to the bottom of his worry pile. Get to the Garden, show Jamal a good time and have fun.

Rafe parked behind a Boston PD squad car, put a Boston PD card on the dashboard and said, "Okay, Celtics fans, let's hit it!"

With Jamal trotting beside them, they entered the Garden. Rafe gave their tickets to the man at the turnstile, and they joined the mob surging toward an escalator. When they reached the upper level, Jamal's eyes widened, drinking in the huge posters and on the concession stands. The odor of popcorn and grilled hot dogs filled the air.

Rafe said to Jamal, "Who's your favorite Celtic?"

"Paul Pierce."

"Good choice," Frank said. "Can't go wrong with the captain."

"You got that right," Rafe said. "Hold on while I get you a Paul Pierce T-shirt with Number 34 on the back." He eyed Jamal. "A medium might be a little big, but it'll shrink in the wash."

While Rafe strolled over to a man selling Celtics T-shirts out of a pushcart, Frank waited with Jamal. A steady stream of Celtics fans dressed in Celtic green—hats, T-shirts and sweatpants—passed them, chattering happily as they walked along the concourse to the doors that led to their seats.

When Rafe came back with a Paul Pierce T-shirt, Jamal's eyes lit up. "Thank you, Mr. Rafe."

"Put it on over the one you're wearing," Rafe said, "see how it fits."

Jamal pulled it over his head and tugged it down. It was way too long. The bottom fell to his crotch, but so what?

"Looks great," Frank said. "Let's go grab our seats."

"Not so fast, partner," Rafe said. "We got to think about nourishment. Can't have this young man cheering on an empty stomach. Also needs a drink to wet his throat, in case he gets hoarse from yelling. I'll get the food. You take Jamal and get the drinks. I'll have an extra-large Pepsi. What'll it be, Jamal? You want a hamburger? A pizza? A hot dog?"

"A hot dog, please," Jamal said, unable to stand still, stutter-stepping around, gazing at the people and the Celtics posters and the flashing lights.

Watching him, Frank stifled a smile. Wait till he got inside and saw the flashing lights on the JumboTron scoreboard.

"Great idea, Rafe. I'll have a burger and fries."

Ten minutes later they reached their seats. Jamal's eyes almost popped out of his head. Rafe had promised good ones, and they were, ten rows behind the Celtics bench. They sat Jamal between them and got their food organized. Jamal ignored his hot dog, sipping his Pepsi, his eyes fixed on the Celtics doing their shoot-around before the game. Frank couldn't decide what was more fun, watching the Celtics or watching Jamal watching the Celtics.

A loud buzzer went off, and the players cleared the court. The announcer introduced the Washington Wizards to a polite spatter of applause. Then the JumboTron flashed big scarlet letters: NOISE, NOISE, NOISE. The place went dark and spotlights bobbed and weaved around the arena. When it settled on the alleyway near the Celtics bench, the crowd erupted in cheers.

The announcer introduced the Celtics starters, his voice booming, culminating in a primal scream: *And now, number thirty-four, the Celtics captain, PAUL PIERCE!!*

Transfixed, Jamal stared as Pierce trotted through a tunnel of his teammates, high-fives all around, and joined the other four starters.

Rafe looked over, waggled his eyebrows, mouthed: Having fun?

He gave Rafe a thumbs-up. Better than fun. For a couple of hours at least he could forget about his problems, relax and enjoy himself.

Jamal sipped his Pepsi and let out a little burp. He glanced at Rafe and said, "Excuse me."

"*Excuse* you?" Rafe said in mock-horror. "Puny little burp like that?" He took a big gulp of Pepsi and let out an enormous belch: *Rrrrrrrrrrrrrup!*

Jamal started laughing.

"Okay, Mr. Frank," Rafe said. "Your turn."

He sucked up some Pepsi and let out the best burp he could muster, no where near the size of Rafe's monster belch, but Jamal laughed anyway.

Then it was tip-off time, so they focused on the game.

Two minutes before halftime the Celtics were up by ten, and as Rafe had predicted, Jamal was having the time of his life.

"You tired, Jamal?" Rafe said. "Want us to take you home now?"

"I'm not tired," Jamal said, eyes fixed on Paul Pierce doing his fancy spin move, cutting through two defenders and laying the ball in the hoop.

Frank looked at Rafe, who gave him a big wink. "Okay," Frank said. "But we don't want to hear you were too tired to go to school tomorrow."

"Don't worry. I'm gonna wear my Paul Pierce T-shirt to school."

It was after eleven by the time they dropped Jamal off at his grandmother's apartment. Frank waited in the car while Rafe took the boy inside. Five minutes later, Rafe came back, jumped in the car and drove off, saying, "Got some info on Tyreke Evans from my PO pal yesterday."

"Parole officer? I thought you said Tyreke didn't have a sheet up here, only in Georgia."

"Correct. My PO pal got it from one of his other offenders, you know, toss out a bribe, not have to come in and pee in a cup three times a week, cut it down to two. Like that."

Frank laughed and shook his head. "Ah, the ways of the criminal justice system and the wily men who administer it. So what's up with Tyreke?"

Rafe looked over, frowning. "Bad news. The man said Tyreke's back in town."

"Very bad news. We don't want him messing with Jamal and his grandmother."

"Exactly. So when I was upstairs just now, I took Ms. Josephine aside, said Tyreke's back and I don't want him anywhere near the boy. Had her program my cell number into her speed dial. If Tyreke shows up here, I said, or even if he just calls you, don't talk to him. Push that button and I'm here in ten minutes."

"And she said?"

"She says: Thank you for bringing happiness into my boy's life, Mr. Rafe, and don't you worry, I will push that button the minute I hear a whisper about Tyreke."

The tight knot in Frank's gut returned, twisted even tighter.

"I don't know," he said. "We might have to find Josephine and Jamal a new place to live. She pushes the button, fine, but a lot can happen in the ten minutes it takes you to get here."

CHAPTER 26

Friday, May 26

Frank went through his notes, underlining the important points with a red pen. The Bourne librarian thought Billy Karapitulik was a creep and fired him, but the Sandwich police chief, who'd known Billy for twenty years, considered him harmless. So did the waitress at the diner, but she'd added an important piece to the puzzle. Billy worked for a cable company, which might allow him to access the homes of lottery winners. The waitress said Billy had named one of his goldfish Tessa.

But none of this proved Billy was the killer.

Working Homicide could be a downer: grisly corpses, grieving families and hours of work, much of it frustrating. Taking Jamal to the Celtics game with Rafe last night had cost him a bundle, but watching the kid's excitement was worth it. He leaned back in his chair, wondering how Jamal's classmates reacted when he came to school today wearing a Paul Pierce T-shirt.

His desk phone rang and he picked up: "Detective Renzi, Homicide."

"Frank," said Ross Dunn, "our Jackpot Killer theory made the front page of the *Huffington Post*."

He groaned. "Shit."

"My sentiments exactly. We got a leak. Somebody talked about the J&B nip and the plastic bag. By tomorrow it'll be all over the news, CNN, Fox News, and all the rest."

"Well, we knew it might happen. A lot of people working the scenes, somebody blabs, over and out."

"Exactly. How's it going with your three suspects?"

"Forget the guy in Connecticut and the Fitchburg librarian, but I like the guy in Sandwich. He works for a cable company. If he screwed up the cable connections, that might be why the women let him in. Once he got off the

Cape he could hop on the Interstate and get to most of the crime scenes within an hour or two."

"Where was he on the Poughkeepsie murder date?"

"Hold on." Frank scanned his notes and located the information he'd obtained from the manager of the National Cablevision office. "He took vacation days the Friday before and the Monday after the murder."

"What about the Boston case?"

"He called in sick that morning, came to work late. I talked to the Sandwich police chief. He can't picture the guy as a killer, but he said he'd keep an eye on him. Karapitulik lives with his mother. She's disabled, uses a wheelchair. The chief said she was in a car accident somewhere in Kentucky before they moved to Sandwich twenty years or so ago. Can you dig up some information about the accident?"

"I can ask my assistant to check the police reports for any major accidents before 1980, but without a specific date and location, it might take awhile. Did you talk to the mother?"

"Not yet. I want to talk to her while he's at work, but Monday's a holiday, and Tuesday I'll be in court testifying on another case, might be there all day. I'll talk to the mother on Wednesday. How's it going on your end?"

"Man, these road trips are a killer. I talk to my boys every night on the phone, but they're upset that I won't be home for the holiday weekend."

Frank envied him. At least Ross could talk to his sons. He'd left several messages for Maureen, asking her to call him: *I know you love your mother, and she needs your support, but there are two sides to every story.* But she still hadn't called. Nineteen days. An eternity. He'd never gone this long without talking to her.

"How's it going with your suspects?" Frank asked.

"Forget the Philly librarian and forget Anthony Sinatra in Hoboken, too. He's a thirty-two-year-old librarian obsessed with Tina Turner. That's why he went to the conference in Poughkeepsie, which, as you may recall, featured, among other lovelies, Madonna, Judy Garland, and Tina Turner."

"Hey, I like Tina Turner."

"Not as much as this guy. He's got all kinds of Tina Turner memorabilia, posters, concert programs, recordings, DVDs, you name it. But I don't see him as our killer. Anthony's a big fella, must weigh three hundred pounds. A guy that big? One of the victims' neighbors would have noticed him."

"Okay, forget Anthony and the guy in Philly. What about the others?"

"The Newark librarian is looking good. He lives near the New York state line, hop on the Interstate he could be most anywhere in New England in a few hours. His boss thinks he's got a gambling problem."

"You think he's got a hard-on for lottery winners?"

"Frank, I've investigated a lot of serial killers, and I have no idea what goes on in their minds. But I can tell you this. The Newark librarian is missing, AWOL from his job, nobody's seen him for two weeks."

A sharp rap sounded on his door. Frank turned and saw a Sheriff's department deputy standing in the doorway with a clipboard and some paperwork. "Hold on, Ross. Someone's at my door."

He left his desk and approached the deputy, an older man dressed in standard deputy attire, a light blue shirt, dark blue pants. The man squinted at him and said, "Franklin Sullivan Renzi?"

He got a sinking feeling in his stomach. "Yes."

The deputy thrust a sheaf of papers at him. "Consider yourself served, Mr. Renzi. Your wife, Evelyn Renzi, has filed a Complaint for Divorce in the Norfolk County Family Court. Your lawyer can access any documents filed there. If you wish, you can file an answer to the charges at that courthouse." The deputy checked off a box on his clipboard and said, "Have a nice day."

Stunned, he stood there holding the papers. He'd been expecting it, but getting served with the legal document was a shock. Evelyn had made good on her threat. He started to thumb through the papers, then realized he'd left Ross hanging on the phone. He tossed the divorce papers on the desk, sat in his chair and picked up the receiver. "Ross, you still there?"

"I am. What's up? Not another murder, I hope."

"No. My wife just had me served with divorce papers."

After a shocked silence, Ross said, "Whoa! Did you see it coming?"

"She threatened to do it a couple weeks ago, but I figured she'd come to her senses." Figured or hoped? Denial had put him into wishful-thinking mode. In a way he was glad it was out in the open. Lying was never his first choice when it came to personal interactions, and he'd been lying to Evelyn for years, most of their married life.

But deep down, he never thought she'd go through with it.

"Maybe we should finish this conversation another time," Ross said.

"No, let's wrap it up now." He uttered a sardonic laugh. "Then I can go out and tie one on."

"Okay. I crossed one of my New York City suspects off the list. That leaves three, but given the holiday, I may not finish until Tuesday. Want to talk again Tuesday night?"

"Wednesday night would be better. By then I'll have talked to Billy's mother. The lead detective on the Boston case is convinced the Pops conductor killed Vicky, but he doesn't know about the Jackpot Killer. Well, he didn't the last time I saw him."

"He'll know all about it tomorrow. You can take that to the bank."

"Right, but the Nashua crime scene was like the Boston murder, brutal and bloody. I think the Jackpot Killer murdered Vicky Stavropoulos, which means the Pops conductor got there right after the killer left." He decided not to tell Ross that he'd be talking to Nigel tonight. And not at the police station.

"If he killed the Boston woman and did the woman in Nashua eight days later, he's escalating. Call me right away if you get anything."

"Damn it, Ross, we know he'll do another one soon, and we've got no clue who it will be."

"I hear you, but that's how it is with serial killers, especially when the victims aren't confined to a specific geographical area. Keep an eye on the big lottery winners."

"Now that the Jackpot Killer theory is out in the open, maybe women that win the lottery will be more careful about who they let into their homes."

"Let's hope so," Ross said. "Have a drink and try and relax."

Frank hung up. Relax? He couldn't imagine it. Acid was chewing a hole in his gut. Now he had to hire a divorce lawyer, and worry about what might happen if Gina's husband found out they were having an affair.

Worst of all, it was Memorial Day weekend, the first Memorial Day since his mother died. On Monday he would pick up his father so they could put flowers on her grave. Afterwards, if he had the guts, he'd tell his father about the divorce. A nightmare. He had no idea what he would say.

———

At 9:30, Frank tapped on the door of Nigel's hotel room and glanced at Gina. Now that he'd agreed to talk to Nigel she appeared happy. He tried to psyche himself up for the interview, but he was in a rotten mood. He was pissed about the divorce papers, Maureen wouldn't call him, and he was sick of living in a crummy motel room with a stained carpet and dingy wallpaper.

When Nigel opened the door, Gina said, "Hi Nigel, say hello to Frank Renzi. You met him at the station."

"Thank you for coming," Nigel said, grasping Frank's hands. "Gina said you might be able to help me."

"I can't promise anything, but let's talk." The conductor's hands were cold and clammy, slender hands with long thin fingers, a pianist's hands. Frank wondered if he ever played jazz.

The room reeked of cigarette smoke. A butt-filled ashtray stood beside a half-empty bottle of Glenlivet on a cherry-wood writing desk. Nigel gestured at two easy chairs grouped around a low table and sank onto the high-backed swivel chair near the desk. Frank studied the man. Below bloodshot blue eyes, purplish circles stood out against his pale skin, and his royal-blue blazer smelled of cigarette smoke. An anxious man, clearly troubled. Was he guilty?

Nigel rubbed his hands together, gazing at him earnestly. "All I can do is tell you what happened. Seems like that Mulligan bloke is convinced I killed Vicky, but I didn't!"

"Nigel," Gina said, "it's okay. We're on your side."

She had on a casual but eye-catching outfit, a V-necked maroon top over a pair of white culottes, short dark hair combed behind her ears. But he had to keep his eye on the ball. Gina might be on Nigel's side, but he wasn't. He needed solid evidence to prove Nigel innocent.

He glanced around the room: embossed blue-patterned wallpaper, thick carpeting, plush easy chairs, a king-sized bed and a large television set.

"Nice room," he said. *A lot nicer than mine.*

"But I feel like a prisoner, all those reporters outside. It's like a bloody death watch. I can't even go out to buy a pack of cigarettes." Nigel looked at him, a pleading look. "What can I tell you? Ask me anything you want."

"Tell me what exactly happened when you got to Vicky's apartment. Don't leave anything out. The tiniest detail could be important."

There was a silence. Somewhere outside a siren sounded in the distance.

As Nigel began to speak Frank watched him, evaluating his manner as much as his words. Nigel stayed calm until he got to the part about finding Vicky. Then he stopped and massaged his temples. "Sorry. It was awful. I'm still having nightmares."

If Nigel was lying, Frank thought, he deserved an Academy Award.

"Would you mind if I smoked?"

"Go ahead." Whatever it took to keep him talking.

When Nigel lighted a cigarette, Gina did, too. Surprised, Frank looked at her. Her eyes met his, expressionless, then shifted to Nigel.

"Did you notice a plastic bag anywhere near Vicky's body?" Frank asked.

"Plastic bag? Not that I recall. Why?"

"Think carefully. A yellow plastic bag you maybe picked up and threw in the trash?"

"No, nothing like that."

That answered one question. "Was Vicky expecting you?"

"Yes. I'd called her from the airport. I told her I'd made an appointment with a financial planner. We were going to meet with him that afternoon so he could draw up the financial agreement."

That was new. Nigel hadn't said anything about a financial planner at the police station. "Okay, Nigel. Here's the million-dollar question. Tell me the truth. Who won the lottery, you or Vicky?"

"I did. I bought the winning ticket at that shop near Vicky's flat, but when I got back from Iowa I gave it to Vicky." Nigel gazed at him, his expression bleak. "It's true, I swear it! We were going to split the money. Bloody hell, if I didn't ask her to claim the prize, she'd still be alive."

"Nigel!" Gina exclaimed. "Stop blaming yourself. Just tell Frank what happened. He's going to help you."

She looked at him and raised her chin. His ever-feisty Ace Reporter.

Unwilling to get her hopes up, Frank gave her a warning look and turned to Nigel. "You said you called Vicky twice. What happened the second time?"

"I called her mobile first, but it went to voicemail. I thought she might have shut it off, so I called her landline. But she didn't answer that either."

"Did you leave a message?"

"Yes, on her answer-phone. I said I was at the shop 'round the corner and I'd be there soon, something like that. But Detective Mulligan said the message tape wasn't in the machine. He says it's missing."

Frank visualized the machine on the table beside Vicky's loveseat. When Nigel called, maybe the Jackpot Killer was there, heard the message, realized someone was coming and panicked. Forget the plastic bag and the J&B nip. The killer beat her to death and split. But why take the message tape?

"Tell me about the ring. Was Vicky wearing it when you found her?"

Nigel heaved a sigh. "I asked her not to wear it until after she claimed the prize. Then we were going to announce our engagement. But she knew I was coming that day. Maybe she was wearing it. I can't remember."

"Did you see anyone else when you got there? In the hall, on the stairs, outside the building?"

"Not that I recall, no."

"Think carefully. It's important."

Nigel snubbed out his cigarette in the ashtray. "Not a bloody soul."

"When you walked to Vicky's apartment from the store, did any cars or vans drive by you?"

"Not that I recall, but I might not have noticed. I couldn't wait to see Vicky." His face crumpled in despair. "If only I'd gotten there sooner."

"Did Vicky have cable?"

"I believe so, yes." Nigel frowned. "You know, there was one thing. I didn't mention it before, but . . ."

"What?" Frank said, hunching forward in his chair.

"I was so distraught about Vicky." He looked at Gina. "It was horrible. I went to lift her head and she was bleeding and the blood got on my hands."

"Nigel," Frank said sharply. "What were you going to tell me?"

"After I washed my hands, I heard this hissing sound. That's when I noticed that the telly was on. But there was no picture, just wavy lines and the static. So I shut it off."

Frank stared at him, incredulous. Jesus, the smoking gun. Vicky had cable and her TV was screwed up, just like the Rhode Island lottery winner's.

"What?" Gina said, picking up on his intent expression. "Is that important?"

"It might be. Nigel, I need to make absolutely sure. Vicky's television was on when you got there?"

"Yes, but I didn't notice it, you see—"

"I understand. You were too concerned about Vicky. But after you called 9-1-1, you noticed the television was screwed up and you shut it off."

"After I washed my hands, yes. The hissing noise was driving me mad."

Frank nodded. The jigsaw puzzle was coming together. "Okay, I think that's enough for tonight."

"If it proves that Nigel's innocent," Gina said, "shouldn't you talk to his lawyer?"

"No." He gave Nigel a stern look. "Don't tell your lawyer I talked to you. I need to check some things."

Nigel eyed him anxiously. "D'you think they'll arrest me?"

Gina rose from her chair, went to Nigel and grasped his hands. "You have to think positive, Nigel. I'm sure things will work out."

"Thank you, Gina, you're such a dear." Nigel raised her hand to his lips and brushed it with a kiss.

A courtly gesture, Frank thought, nothing erotic about it.

Still, it annoyed him.

"Gina, we'd better go. It's late." When they got back to his motel, he had to tell Gina about the divorce papers. Another worry. He had no idea how she would react.

"Quite right," Nigel said and gave him a wan smile. "Thank you for coming, Detective Renzi."

———

Desperate for fresh air after Nigel's smoke-filled room, Frank lowered the car windows. After talking to Nigel, he was almost certain the Jackpot Killer murdered Vicky, but how would he prove it? If Vicky was wearing the ring, maybe the killer took it. But why take the incoming-message tape?

When they entered his motel room, Frank opened the window, still craving fresh air. A cool breeze billowed the filmy inner curtain, bringing now-familiar sounds: a car door slamming, a truck rattling past the motel, a distant siren on the Expressway.

Gina poured two glasses of Chianti and sat on the lone easy chair. "What do you think, Franco? Are they going to arrest Nigel for Vicky's murder?"

"Why are you so desperate to rescue Nigel?"

She combed locks of hair behind her ears and stared into space. "You never met Vicky, but I did. We talked after she claimed the prize, but I didn't think to warn her about the Jackpot Killer. Now the police think Nigel killed her. Tuesday night I talked to Nigel at his hotel, at the rooftop bar." She gulped some wine. "Nigel told me his mother committed suicide when he was eighteen. He was away at a piano competition and he felt terribly guilty, like he should have been there for her."

Frank didn't see the relevance, but waited, letting her play it out.

Abruptly, she got up and paced the room. When she came back and sat down, the skin around her eyes was tight. "Ryan and I had a huge fight last Sunday. I've been sleeping at the beach house. Wednesday night when I went home to get some clothes, Ryan called."

"What happened?" Judging by the look on her face, it had to be bad.

"Ryan wanted me to go away for a romantic weekend. While we were talking on the landline, Nigel called my cell. Ryan overheard me talking to him." Her lips tightened. "Ryan thinks I'm sleeping with Nigel, but I'm not."

Wait long enough, they always came out with the vital details. But he could tell she wasn't done. His always-effervescent lover looked like she was ready to cry. He took her hand, led her to the bed, sat her down and put his arms around her. "Talk to me," he said.

In a low voice, she said, "When Ryan and I started having these horrible fights, I thought it was my fault." She looked at him, her dark eyes enormous. "Because I was having an affair."

"Hey, don't beat up on yourself." Now he knew why she identified with Nigel. Guilt, the great common denominator. He felt guilty, too. His wife was divorcing him and his daughter wouldn't talk to him. "What are we supposed to do? Slog through life in an unhappy marriage until one of us dies?"

Gina's eyes glinted with tears. "I told Ryan I wasn't going anywhere with him this weekend. I can't stand to be around him anymore."

Maybe now wasn't the time to tell her about the divorce papers. Time to lighten up. "Was your father a writer?"

Gina looked at him, puzzled. "No. He worked for a construction company, operating one of those big cranes. Why?"

He shrugged. "You're a writer. I thought maybe it ran in the family."

"Yeah? Was your father a cop?"

"No. But my mother was an FBI agent."

"Get out. She was not!"

He grinned. "Right, but she was tough enough to be one."

It got a smile out of her, a smile that quickly faded. "Franco, I'm really worried about Nigel. You saw how despondent he was tonight."

Frank gave her a stern look. "I think the Jackpot Killer murdered Vicky, but you can't tell Nigel, or anyone else. I don't want it splashed over any front pages. This killer watches the news."

"How soon do you think you'll catch him?"

"I'm not sure. My FBI agent liaison has a prime suspect, too, a Newark librarian, plus three more suspects to investigate. I eliminated two of my three, but I like the last guy a lot. He lives on Cape Cod."

"Why don't you arrest him?"

"Way too soon to do that. Judges used to hand out search warrants like lollipops, but not these days. This guy fits the profile, but all I've got is hunches. He works for a cable company."

Gina's eyes lit up and she smiled. "So that's why you got excited when Nigel said Vicky's TV was messed up."

"That's one reason. My suspect lives with his mother. I want to interview her while he's at work, but Monday's Memorial Day, and Tuesday I've got to testify in court. And this afternoon I got a nasty surprise. A Sheriff's Deputy served me with divorce papers."

"Damn." Gina put her arm around him. "I'm sorry, Franco."

"Yeah. I need to find a good divorce lawyer. Evelyn's lawyer's being a bitch." He barked a curt laugh. "The grounds are adultery, which any lawyer in the state of Massachusetts will tell you is almost impossible to prove. You can't just allege that the spouse had sex with someone, you have to prove it."

"Prove it? How?"

"Pictures." He grinned at her. "Aren't you glad we never took any during our wild sex orgies?"

But she didn't crack a smile. "I still can't believe this happened because that woman saw us."

"Well, it did, but I'm not going to let it ruin our relationship."

"Don't worry, it won't. But if Ryan hears about it . . ."

"Why? Did he threaten you?" When she didn't answer, he said, "Did he hit you? Is that why you're sleeping at the beach house?"

"Ryan's got a temper, that's for sure. He wants me to quit my job and have a baby." She heaved a sigh. "He doesn't know I'm taking birth control pills, but if he finds out . . ."

"How would he find out? Stop worrying. You got too many things messing up your mind."

She hugged him. "You know what? You're right. When are you going to talk to your suspect's mother?"

"Wednesday. I want to get into the house and take a look around. To get a search warrant I need specifics."

"Like what?"

"Some serial killers take trophies. I think he took Vicky's ring."

"That would explain why it's missing! Franco, you have to arrest him. Then Gerry Mulligan will stop thinking that Nigel killed Vicky."

Amused by her enthusiasm, he said, "I'd love to arrest him, but it's not that simple."

"Where does he live, this guy you're so hot on?"

"Sandwich."

"Nice town. I've been there a few times. What's his name?"

"Why?"

"Just curious. Don't worry, I won't blab about it." Her lips twitched in a smile. "Come on, Franco, tell me his name. Maybe he's my long-lost cousin or something."

"I doubt it. Not with a name like William Karapitulik."

CHAPTER 27

—

Sunday, May 28

A sharp rap sounded on his office door. Gerry Mulligan checked his watch. 10:25. Fifteen minutes ago, he'd called a local reporter and said he had a scoop for him. It killed him to do it, but he needed a friendly reporter.

"Come in," he yelled.

The door opened and Peter Starr burst into his office. A little runt with a Hollywood-handsome face, Starr had been around for years. Gerry knew for a fact the mop of hair on his head was a toupee. His name was probably fake, too. Starr wasn't too bright, but he had a million sources and was often the first television reporter on the scene of a major crime.

"What's up?" Starr said eagerly, taking a seat in the visitor chair. "You get a break in the Megabucks winner murder?"

"What I got is this." Gerry picked up the tabloid on his desk and thrust it at Starr. "One of your rivals rousts me out of bed this morning and asks for a comment. Which is why I'm in my office on a Sunday, Memorial Day weekend no less, instead of playing with my grandson at the beach."

Eyes narrowed, Gerry watched Starr scan the front page of the *Inquirer*. Even upside-down, he could read the headline: **Serial Killer Targets Lottery Winners**. Starr flipped pages, found the story, and began to read. Gerry knew what it said because the fucking reporter had quoted it to him.

> Is a serial killer targeting lottery winners? That's what some law enforcement officials believe, following last week's murder of a Nashua, NH, lotto winner. Sources close to the investigation say four other lottery winners in New England have recently been murdered, and they believe the same person is responsible.

Starr looked up and said, "You think this is credible?"

"Who gives a fuck? The Police Commissioner's already got lottery officials crawling up his ass. Every media outlet in the country's gonna jump on this." He took out a Camel and lighted it.

"I thought smoking was prohibited in police stations," Starr said.

"Only if you get caught." Gerry fixed him with an icy stare. "Thanks to this cockamamie serial killer hogwash I gotta do a press conference tomorrow, so you better feed me the right questions."

"Okay, but what do I get in return?"

His desk phone rang. Gerry grimaced, and let it ring.

"What about Vicky Stavropoulos?" Starr said. "You think a serial killer did it?"

"No, I don't," he snapped. "But how come Detective Frank Renzi shows up at the crime scene? It's not his territory. He works District 4. He got his boss to call and ask me to let him sit in on the Nigel Heath interviews. So I extend him this courtesy, which I was not obligated to do. But does Renzi tell me he's working another lottery winner murder? No. Now I find out there's four of them. Maybe more."

His phone stopped ringing. "Fuckin' vultures," he muttered.

"You still think Nigel Heath killed Vicky Stavropoulos?"

"Damn right, I do." He snatched the tabloid and ran his finger down the article. "They found a yellow plastic bag and a nip bottle of J&B planted on some of the victims. Most of them were asphyxiated, with the plastic bag, allegedly." He dropped the tabloid on his desk. "Our case is different. Crime of passion, pure and simple. The Pops conductor beat her to death."

"But what about this serial-killer theory? You have to admit it's intriguing."

"For you, maybe, not for me." Gerry ticked off points on his fingers. "Nigel Heath's prints were all over her apartment. We found some of his clothes in her bedroom closet, and we got phone records of him calling her from all over hell and gone. Not only that, he admitted he got blood on his hands. Our crime scene techs took blood samples from her kitchen drain."

"Did they match them to Nigel Heath?"

Gerry flinched as a sharp pain stabbed his gut. "We need to get a DNA sample, but his lawyer won't allow it. Merrill Carr. Christ, that guy never met a TV camera he didn't like. He's worse than F. Lee Bailey. But we'll get it, one way or the other." He smiled tightly. "And now we've got a new witness."

"Great!" Starr exclaimed, scribbling furiously in his notepad. "Who?"

Barely able to hide his disgust, Gerry watched him. He could read the little squirt's mind. Starr figured the District A4 Chief of Detectives was under the gun. Starr figured if he asked the right questions at the press conference, Gerry Mulligan would owe him big time. The little shit.

"Who's the new witness?" Starr said again.

"Henry Polanski, financial planner." He puffed his Camel and blew smoke. "Took his own sweet time contacting us, but I guess his conscience got to him. He called me yesterday, said Nigel Heath had an appointment to see him the day of the murder, but he never showed up. Polanski was supposed to draw up a pre-nup for Nigel and his bride-to-be. Victoria Stavropoulos, winner of twelve million bucks."

"He was setting her up!" Starr exclaimed. "He wanted the money."

"You bet your ass. Motivation with a capital M. He asked her to do a pre-nup, she balked so he killed her." He skewered Starr with a look. "I don't give a shit if the feds think some weirdo is killing lottery winners. Nigel Heath murdered Victoria Stavropoulos and I'm gonna nail his ass for it."

———

Sandwich

The cop was watching him. A half hour ago the police officer had followed them into the Seaside Diner, sat at the counter and ordered coffee. Between listening to his mother's idiotic comments and checking on the cop, he could barely eat. He pushed his plate aside and scratched his hand.

Why was the cop watching him?

Arlene finished taking an order from a young couple, then came by their table and left their check.

"You folks have a nice day," she said, and turned to leave.

"Why don't you sit down, Arlene?" his mother said. "We've hardly had a chance to chat today."

"I better not. I've got work to do in the kitchen."

"Oh, sit for a minute, Arlene. You deserve a break."

"Well, okay, but just for a minute." She sat down opposite his mother, took off one of her hoop earrings and fussed with it, not looking at him. After a moment she said, "There's an article in today's *Inquirer* about that serial killer."

"What serial killer?" his mother said.

"The one I told you about. I saw it on *Rivera Live*. Geraldo said some guy is killing lottery winners. The article in the *Inquirer* said he already murdered four women, maybe more."

His heart surged. Finally, they had noticed him!

"The cops have no clue who he is!" Arlene rubbed her scrawny arms. "It gives me the creeps. The last one was in Nashua, New Hampshire!"

"When was that?" His mother looked at him, frowning.

"I'm too scared to buy a Powerball ticket," Arlene said. "If I won, he might kill me!"

He saw the cop at the counter look over. Arlene's voice could be shrill when she got excited. He smiled at her, but she avoided his eyes, fiddling with her earring again. "Go ahead and buy one, Arlene. You've got nothing to worry about."

"Don't encourage her, Billy. You know gambling is bad. How many times do I have to tell you?"

He watched her mouth move. It reminded him of Ruthie and her dog, yap-yap-yapping until he made it shut up. He wondered how his mother's mouth would look if—

"I hear the FBI is on the case," Arlene said.

He glanced at the counter. The cop was watching him. When he turned back, Arlene was watching him too, but her eyes shifted away when he looked at her. "How do you know?" he said.

"I think I heard it on *Rivera Live.*" Arlene turned to his mother and said, "Maybe the serial killer murdered that girl up in Boston."

" Don't be silly," his mother said. "The conductor did it. They were having a romance and he killed her for the money."

He clenched his fists. Stupid, stupid, stupid!!

"Come on, Billy, we have to go. You promised me you'd wash the kitchen floor today."

Arlene rose from her chair, but she didn't smile at him the way she usually did. She looked at his mother and said, "Take care of yourself, Mrs. Kay. See you next Sunday."

———

Plymouth — 3:00 p.m.

Gina opened a bottle of water and guzzled half the contents. She hadn't had a hangover in years, but she recognized the symptoms: an unquenchable thirst and a dull headache. After their Friday night meeting with Nigel, she and Franco had stayed up late. Lord knows they had plenty to talk about: his divorce, her fight with Ryan, the Jackpot Killer. But when Franco made love to her, all her worries had faded away.

Saturday morning she'd left his motel at 10:30. Franco had a basketball date with the little boy he'd taken under his wing. He had a soft spot in his heart for boys with no fathers. Unlike Ryan, who only thought about himself.

That's why she was staying in this cheap motel.

It was Memorial Day weekend. Ryan would be at their house in Westwood, and she didn't dare stay at the beach house. Ryan might go there looking for her. He didn't have a key, but still.

Last night, she'd polished off a small bottle of Merlot, ruminating over her situation. Ryan was ruthless. If he found out she was having an affair, he'd file for a divorce. Forget the house. She'd be lucky to keep the clothes on her back. But she had no control over Ryan. All she could do was stay out of

183

his way. Ryan would never change. He wanted her to quit her job and have her life revolve around him.

But she loved her job and she loved Franco. He understood her.

She trusted him and he trusted her. Sometimes Franco played the part of the gruff, steely-eyed cop, but he had always been gentle and kind with her. He was smart as a whip, a terrific detective, and a fantastic lover, not to mention funny as hell sometimes. He had even agreed to talk to Nigel.

Poor Nigel. Friday night he'd looked like a whipped dog: forlorn and dejected, mournful eyes, slumped shoulders. But afterwards, Franco seemed convinced that Nigel didn't kill Vicky, the Jackpot Killer did.

She got up and looked out the window. It was a gorgeous day, sunny and mild, a perfect beach day. Too bad she wasn't at her beach house. Some of her fondest childhood memories were the summers she'd spent in Squantum, a tiny peninsula jutting into the ocean south of Boston.

Thirty years ago when beach property was cheap, her grandparents had bought a two-story bungalow facing the ocean, a sea captain's house built in 1878. The kitchen was antiquated, but so what? Nobody cooked in the summer. The second floor had three bedrooms. She had claimed the biggest one. It faced the ocean and there was a widow's walk outside the windows. Sometimes on hot nights, she sat out there to cool off. There was always a delightful breeze. Unlike this stuffy motel room.

She went outside and sat in a molded-plastic chair in front of her room. The exterior of the two-story motel had seen better days, fading yellow paint, rusty wrought-iron railings on the second-floor walkway. Several motorcycles, campers and pickup trucks sat in the parking lot. She had intended to rent a room in Sandwich, but all the cheap motels were booked for the weekend, and she couldn't afford to pay for three nights in an expensive hotel.

So here she was in Plymouth, twenty miles away.

She fired up a cigarette and sipped her water. The key to her financial future—and freedom from Ryan—was a lucrative book deal. She figured she had a good shot at it. Due to the Boston Pops connection, Vicky's murder was big news all over the country and so was Nigel. Now that the Jackpot Killer murders had made the national news, that was hot, too.

She'd talked to Vicky, she had an inside track on the Jackpot Killer, and she was Nigel's only confidant. But to write a bestseller, she had to spice it up with intimate details. When Nigel was young, did he ride a bike, play cricket, have a teenaged crush on a girl? He'd asked her not to write about his mother's suicide, but his mother had been an opera singer. She made a mental note to ask Nigel about her career. Surely he wouldn't mind that.

Nigel's father sounded like a tyrant. Practice, practice, practice.

Could she persuade Nigel to tell her what caused their rift? And she needed some juicy details about his ex-wife. According to the information she'd found on the Internet, Joanna was a minor film actress, an older woman, but still attractive: wavy blonde hair, a pretty smile and a curvy figure.

But the main focus would be Nigel's relationship with Vicky. She'd have to tread carefully there. Nigel was still grieving, holed up in his hotel, belting down scotch and smoking like a fiend. If she wanted the inside scoop, she'd better hurry. Nigel's lawyer seemed to think Gerry Mulligan might arrest him soon and charge him with Vicky's murder. Then Nigel would be in jail, and murder suspects rarely got out on bail.

She drank some water and puffed her cigarette. Franco seemed to think the Jackpot Killer murdered Vicky, but he'd warned her not to tell Nigel, and if Franco asked her not to repeat something, she didn't. That was the deal.

But it didn't sound like Franco was going to arrest the Jackpot Killer anytime soon. He had a suspect, but when she asked why he didn't arrest him, all Franco did was talk about evidence and search warrants. He wanted to talk to the suspect's mother while he was at work.

But tomorrow was Memorial Day, and on Tuesday Franco would be in court all day testifying on a murder case. But she wouldn't.

She smiled, recalling the ploy she'd used to worm the suspect's name out of Franco. She sounded out the name: Kar-a-pitch-oo-lik.

She had no idea how to spell it. But he lived in Sandwich, and Sandwich wasn't New York City. How many people with a weird name like that would be living in a little town like Sandwich?

She went back in her room, took out her cell and dialed information.

A bored-sounding female voice said, "How may I help you?"

"I need the phone number of a Sandwich, Massachusetts, resident. I'm not sure how to spell it, but it begins with K." She sounded out the name for the woman: "*Kar-a-pitch-oo-lik.*"

"One moment please," the woman said.

Gina gripped her cell phone. *Please find the number.*

The operator came back on the line. "I checked the Sandwich residents with names that start with K-A-R. There aren't many. Do you have a first name?"

"William," Gina said, and waited anxiously.

Thirty seconds passed, an eternity.

At last the operator came back and said, "There's a William Karapitulik living at 14 Bittersweet Lane. K-A-R-A-P-I-T-U-L-I-K."

Gina scribbled down the address. "Thank you. May I have the number?"

185

CHAPTER 28

Monday, May 29 — Swampscott, MA

It was a beautiful day, bright and sunny, too nice to be at a cemetery, Frank thought, but that's what you did on Memorial Day. He stood three paces away from his father, giving him space to grieve. Lost in thought, Salvatore Renzi stared blankly at the carved granite headstone he'd bought five months ago for Mary Sullivan Renzi.

His father still had a full head of black hair but now it was speckled with gray. At seventy, he seemed as sharp as ever, but today he looked old, his face lined, thin and stooped in his dark suit.

Was that new, Frank wondered. Or hadn't he noticed?

Maybe he just never appreciated what great parents he'd had until one of them was gone. He made a resolution to spend more time with his father.

This morning he'd driven to the house in Swampscott where he'd grown up, a small two-story Cape, nothing fancy. His father had bought it in 1960, two years before Frank was born. Back then his father had been an assistant DA and didn't make much money. The firstborn son of Italian immigrants, Salvatore Renzi was the first in his family to graduate from college.

Grampa Sal owned a grocery store in the North End; Grandma Rose stayed home to raise Salvatore, Jr. and their three daughters. Frank hadn't seen his aunts in years; they were living with their husbands in California, Arizona and Florida. A child of the Depression, his father had heard his parents sing the praises of President Franklin D. Roosevelt, which was why he'd named his son Franklin. Frank's middle name, Sullivan, was a concession to Mary Sullivan Renzi's Irish heritage.

This morning, driving through Swampscott, a seacoast town fifteen miles north of Boston, he realized he missed his hometown. As a kid he loved going to the beach, gazing at the skyscrapers across the water in Boston, the ever-present lure of the city. Swampscott had a great school system and a terrific basketball coach, but when Evelyn got pregnant, she had insisted that they live in Milton near her parents. She had no interest in visiting Frank's parents. So they'd bought the house in Milton.

"I can't believe she's gone," his father said, drawing him closer. "Some days I go home and walk in the door thinking Mary will be waiting for me in the kitchen. She was a beautiful person."

"Yes, she was. I miss her a lot. I wish—" He stopped, thinking: *I wish she were here so I could tell her about the divorce.* He loved his father, a man well-respected in the legal community and a wonderful role model. But he'd always been emotionally closer to his mother. Only now did it dawn on him how often he'd relied on her to be the intermediary. Tell his mother about some problem and she would relay it to Sal.

"What?" his father said, gazing at him with his dark Sicilian eyes, eyes that intimidated crooks and lawyers alike when they entered Judge Salvatore Renzi's courtroom.

"Nothing. I was just thinking what a great mother she was. She was always there for me." He squeezed his father's shoulder. "You were too, but you didn't bake the chocolate-chip cookies."

That brought a faint smile to his father's lips.

"I miss her a lot, but not as much as you. Married, what, forty-three years?"

Fighting for control, his father nodded. "Forty-three wonderful years."

"I've got something I need to tell you. Want to go have coffee?" He hadn't wanted to deliver the news in a phone call. That seemed cowardly. But how could he tell him while they stood at his mother's grave?

"No," his father said. "What is it you need to tell me?"

He spit it out fast. "Evelyn and I are getting a divorce."

His father remained silent for a moment. Then, "I'm not surprised."

Stunned, Frank stared at him. Not surprised? That was a shocker.

"I haven't seen much of you and Evelyn lately, but . . ." His father smiled faintly. "Over the years I've developed a certain ability to read people. You two haven't looked happy for quite a while."

"Years," he said. Anything to fill the void, anything so he wouldn't have to explain.

"Your mother always said you had a way with women."

Another shocker, and an opening as big as a house. "Not a way with women. One woman in particular. For the last nine years."

"Nine years." His father puffed his cheeks. "That's a long time. Almost half your married life."

That was true enough. The last half anyway. No need to tell him about the first half.

"I won't bother asking why you didn't get a divorce. I'm sure you had your reasons. You need to talk to a divorce lawyer. I'll make some calls and get you some names. Does Maureen know?"

Pain knifed his gut, cutting him to the core.

"Yes. Evelyn told her." *Told her more than she needed to know.*

"How's she taking it?"

His throat tightened. *Mom says you've got a girlfriend. Is that true?*

"She's pretty upset. She won't talk to me. I've called her several times but she won't answer. I left messages asking her to call me back, but . . ." He stopped, unable to finish.

His father put his arm around him. "I guess Grampa Renzi better give her a call and tell her she needs to talk to you. Can't have my favorite girl in the world not talking to her dad."

Frank felt a wave of relief. If anyone could reach out to Maureen, it was his father. She was his only grandchild and he adored her. "Thanks, Dad."

But the words seemed inadequate. He wanted to say more, wanted to tell his father how much he loved him, wanted to tell him how much he enjoyed talking to him about police work and legal matters and NBA basketball games and the Boston Celtics. *So open your mouth and say it, stupid.*

"You're the best, Dad. I love you more than I can ever say. Thanks for being there when I need you."

His father smiled. "That's what fathers are for, son."

———

Gina got up at nine, ate a hearty breakfast of scrambled eggs at a nearby diner, left her motel at ten and set out for Sandwich. It only took her a half hour to get over the Sagamore Bridge onto Cape Cod, but vehicles headed in the other direction leaving the Cape were backed up for miles.

She passed a roadside billboard: WELCOME TO SANDWICH, SEASHORE RESORT FOR ALL SEASONS. Sandwich had the largest collection of Victorians on Cape Cod, the perfect excuse for her interview. Last night she'd called the number for William Karapitulik, poised to hang up if a man answered.

But after one ring, his mother answered. It had been surprisingly easy to convince her to do an interview. What Gina knew about architecture would fit in a thimble, but last night she'd used her laptop to find photographs of Sandwich's historic landmarks on the Internet.

She entered Sandwich's Historic Town Square, taking mental notes as passed the Hoxie House, a seventeenth-century saltbox, the Town Hall, built in 1734, and the First Church of Christ, easily identified by its soaring white steeple. Along the main drag beyond the square, Victorians were lined up like wedding cakes. Several times she slowed to a stop, gawking at the mansard roofs, the steep-pitched gables and the elaborately-carved wooden shutters around the multi-paned windows.

But then she thought, forget the architecture. Find William Karapitulik's house. She sipped from her container of take-out coffee, recalling the news report she'd seen this morning on television, gruesome details about the murder in Nashua that Franco had told her about. Last week someone had beaten an elderly lotto winner to death, striking her head repeatedly with a blunt object. While trying to protect her, the woman's dog, a small fox terrier, had also been beaten to death.

The Jackpot Killer was a monster.

No wonder Franco wanted to catch him.

She'd used her laptop to map the address the telephone operator had given her so it was easy enough to find.

She drifted down Bittersweet Lane and slowly drove past Number 14, a two-story cottage with blue-painted clapboards and a small front porch.

A white van was parked in the driveway beside the house.

William Karapitulik's van, Gina assumed.

An icy chill rippled through her. Was he the Jackpot Killer?

But she wasn't interviewing Mrs. Karapitulik today. This was Memorial Day, a holiday. Her appointment was at eleven tomorrow morning.

Franco's suspect wouldn't be home tomorrow, he'd be working.

———

Dorchester

Frank poured himself another glass of wine and glanced at the clock. 2:05 a.m. He'd been lying on the bed in his motel room since midnight, unable to sleep. Now that he'd read through the divorce papers, his mind was grinding away like a blender chopping nuts. How had it come to this?

When Evelyn got pregnant, he was thrilled. Evelyn seemed happy, too. Maureen arrived in February 1983. The first few months went by in a blur. Evelyn was breastfeeding so he didn't get up for the late-night or early-morning feedings, but he didn't get much sleep either.

In November he turned twenty-two. He was horny as hell, but Evelyn wasn't interested. She was too tired. She had a headache. Whatever.

The third time she rebuffed him, he asked her what was wrong. He didn't think it was normal for a couple their age to stop making love. She said her gynecologist had diagnosed her with post-partum depression. She'd been on Prozac for three months. It annoyed him that she hadn't told him before, but he didn't want to seem unsympathetic.

He decided to let her make the first move. After five months passed, he decided nothing was going to happen. Restless with energy, he walked the streets of Boston. He loved the activity, the streets alive with young couples and college kids. When that got old, he started going to movies, losing himself in fantasyland, Jennifer Beals dancing seductively in *Flashdance*, Richard Gere and Debra Winger getting it on in *An Officer and a Gentleman*.

In April 1984 he caught a burglary call one Saturday night. Saul Bergman let him into his fourth-floor condo on Marlboro Street, took him in the living room and introduced him to his wife. Janine Bergman was a knockout, wearing a fancy black dress with sequins, the low-cut neckline showing a generous amount of cleavage.

Frank figured the dress cost more than he made in a week.

Janine appeared to be in her late twenties. Saul had to be twenty-five years older. A distinguished-looking man with silvery hair, Saul had the air of confidence that accompanied significant wealth. Condos on Marlboro Street cost big bucks, and their two-bedroom unit was luxurious: plush wall-to-wall carpeting, granite countertops in the kitchen, a king-sized bed and built-in teak bookcases in both bedrooms.

They showed him the circular hole the burglar had cut in one bedroom window above the supposedly burglar-proof lock. Several items of jewelry were missing, Saul's diamond-studded cufflinks, Janine's pearl necklace and matching bracelet. "We should have left at intermission," Saul said.

"We were at a Boston Symphony concert," Janine explained, gazing at Frank with her big brown eyes.

"The Brahms violin concerto was the only thing worth hearing," Saul said, and stifled a yawn.

Janine said to Frank, "I kind of liked the Rite of Spring. Decadent."

Her expression didn't change, but he felt something pass between them.

When Janine escorted him to the door, he wrote his cell phone number on his card and said, "If you think of anything important, call me."

A tiny flicker appeared in her eyes. "Thank you, I will."

Three days later at 4:15 on a Tuesday afternoon, she called and said she had something important to tell him. When he went to her condo, she led him into the living room and gestured for him to sit on the couch. Fancy cocktail napkins were tastefully arranged on the smoked-glass coffee table.

Was she having a party? She had on a clingy mauve top and a pair of black stretch pants, toying with her long dark hair as she sat down beside him on the couch. He got a hard-on just looking at her.

But he was here on police business.

"You said you had something important to tell me?"

"Yes," she said, gazing at him with her expressive brown eyes. "Saul's in Phoenix all week."

It took him a second to get it. When he started to laugh, Janine did, too.

He gestured at the cocktail napkins. "You expecting someone?"

"Yes. Would you like a beer or would you prefer a glass of Merlot?"

And so on a Tuesday afternoon in April 1984, their affair began.

In February 1985 Maureen turned two. She was cuter than any kid had a right to be, talking up a storm. Frank was totally captivated, but equally captivated by Janine. Saul was a real estate developer and traveled a lot. When Saul was out of town, he and Janine would meet for dinner and then go to her condo. She had a gorgeous body, full breasts with dark-pink nipples, a slender waist and a gorgeous ass. But her enthusiasm was the biggest attraction. She enjoyed sex and wasn't afraid to show it.

And so it went for nine years.

He refilled his wineglass and looked at the clock. 2:40 a.m. He was still wide awake and now he had a headache to boot. The evils of sin. Wine, women and song. Janine wasn't just eye-candy, she had a brain. After graduating from Cornell, she'd met Saul at a cocktail party. Janine was twenty-one; Saul was forty-six and divorced. Six months later they were married.

One time when he asked if she felt guilty, Janine had looked at him and said: "Of course, and so do you. But if we were getting what we needed from our spouses, we wouldn't be here."

She was right. He was happy to have sex with a willing partner who was intelligent and fun to be with. Janine enjoyed their love-making as much as he did. Evelyn was perfectly happy not to have sex with anyone.

But in 1992, Saul was diagnosed with pancreatic cancer. At the age of sixty-six, he died, leaving forty-two-year-old Janine a widow. And everything changed. As it turned out, wild and adventurous Janine had a traditional side.

She wanted to be married. To Frank.

The night she laid it on him, he didn't know what to say. He genuinely cared for Janine, but her world revolved around Boston Symphony concerts, art museums and dinners at posh restaurants. His world involved bloody corpses, gun-toting killers and late-night investigations.

Worse, if he divorced Evelyn, he might lose Maureen, and that would kill him. He adored her. He loved playing Monopoly with her and taking her to horseback-riding lessons on the weekends and Celtics games in the winter.

When he told Janine he wasn't going to get a divorce, she got misty eyed, and they made love for what turned out to be their last time. It was as good as ever. Afterwards Janine said she cared for him, but she had to move on. She wanted to be married, and when Janine wanted something, she usually got it.

A month later she'd moved away and he never heard from her again. Sometimes he wondered if she ever had a child. If she did, maybe she would understand his decision. Either way, he hoped she'd found someone.

Janine was a good person. She deserved to be happy. So did Gina, but from the sound of things, her marriage was in rough shape.

Two years ago as they lay naked in bed one night, Gina had asked him if he thought they would get bored with each other. She knew about Janine. He'd told her about their affair and how it ended.

"In the movies," Gina had said, "people who have affairs eventually go back to their spouses. God forbid they should get a divorce. Hollywood sends a message: have your fling, but marriage is best for everyone involved."

But was it? Sometimes people were just incompatible.

He and Evelyn were proof of that, and he didn't think Ryan would be thrilled to find out Gina was having an affair.

His cell phone jangled. He checked the time. 3:02 a.m.

He punched on and croaked, "Hello."

"Hey, man, sorry to roust you outta bed at this hour," said Rafe. "Got some interesting news."

"That's good. Three in the morning, I'm not in the mood to chat."

"Tyreke Evans is lying on a sidewalk in Mattapan, one shot to the head."

Frank sat up and swung his legs over the side of the bed. "You there now?"

"Yup, but I'm heading home. My PO pal called me an hour ago, gave me the heads-up. When I got there, the lead detective said it looked like a Gunfight-at-the-OK-Corral-type thing. Tyreke was packing, but the other guy must have been a better shot. Here's the interesting part. Tyreke's gun is the same type as the one that killed your Mass Ave victim."

"Did you tell the lead detective?"

"I did. He said he'd see what he could do about matching the slugs."

"That'd be great, wouldn't it?"

"No shit," Rafe said. "Now we don't gotta worry 'bout moving Jamal and Ms. Josephine out of that apartment, might even close a case for you."

"Thanks, Rafe. I owe you one."

Rafe chuckled. "Indeed you do. Big time."

"Tell you what. Get three more Celtics tickets and we'll take Jamal to another game. My treat."

"Right on," Rafe said. "Talk to you later."

He shut his cell and massaged his bleary eyes. He was glad Tyreke would no longer be a threat to Jamal, and it would be great if this allowed him to close the Mass Ave murder case.

But it didn't solve his divorce problem.

CHAPTER 29

Tuesday, May 30 — Sandwich

Gina entered the historic town square and anxiously checked her watch. 11:10. She'd left the motel in Plymouth in plenty of time, but a bad accident on Route 3 had delayed her. She was late for her appointment.

Franco thought the Jackpot Killer might have taken Vicky's diamond ring. Other than that she didn't know what kind of evidence he needed for the search warrant.

Five minutes later she parked in front of the Karapitulik house, relieved that the white van wasn't parked outside. She went up the walk, admiring the gleaming white lattice-work that boxed in the porch. Someone must have spent hours painting it. She rang the bell and heard a faint chime.

A full minute passed. The Venetian blinds on the front windows were closed. She checked her watch. 11:16.

At last the door opened and a woman in a wheelchair appeared. She had a thin pinched faced, wavy blonde hair and piercing pale-blue eyes.

"Mrs. Karapitulik? I'm Gina Bevilaqua. I'm sorry I'm late."

"Oh, call me Mrs. Kay. Everyone does. I thought you weren't coming, but come in, come in. You'll have to get the door. Would you like a tour of the house? I tidied up as best I could."

The words tumbled out in a torrent. Gina heaved a sigh of relief. The woman was a talker. That might make this easier.

She stepped into a hallway with a worn runner and said, "I'd love to see the house, but could we talk a bit first?"

"Well." Mrs. Kay pursed her lips. "Come in the living room then. It's not fancy, but it's home." Her thin shoulders hunched as she wheeled into the adjacent room. "Billy always shuts the blinds. I don't know why. The girl that helps me with my bath was late today so I didn't get a chance to open them."

The wheelchair emitted a rhythmic squeak as Mrs. Kay went around opening the blinds. Sunlight streamed into the room, revealing the shabby furnishings. A brass-framed daybed with a tattered blue comforter and two throw pillows stood against one wall. Crude cross-stitching on the pillows said: JESUS SAVES. In the corner, a wingchair with frayed brown upholstery faced a television set.

Uncomfortably aware of the woman's intense gaze, Gina perched on the wingchair. She'd worn casual clothes, a white blouse and black stretch pants, but Mrs. Kay had clearly put on her best outfit, a royal-blue pantsuit. The lower half of one pant leg was tacked up above the knee. Brass buttons lined the front of the jacket, and the bottom of the sleeves were frayed. A plain gold wedding band adorned the ring finger of her left hand.

No diamond ring.

"What a cozy little house," Gina said, giving the woman a cheerful smile.

"Billy painted it last spring. We have to keep up appearances, you know, living near the Historic District. I bought it before the prices went through the roof. All these houses were a mess before the Historical Society spruced them up. I couldn't afford to buy it now."

"Are there more rooms upstairs?"

"Yes, but we don't use them. It's too expensive to heat in the winter. I sleep in here on the daybed. Billy's room is downstairs in the basement."

Gina ostentatiously scribbled notes on her steno pad. "When did you say you bought the house?"

"Nineteen years ago." Mrs. Kay heaved a sigh. "A year after I had my accident."

"How awful! What happened?"

"You don't want to hear about that, you came to talk about the house." Gazing at her, her pale-blue eyes intent.

"I do, but a house is only a house. I like to write about the people who live in them."

"Oh. Well, I was in a bad car accident. Back then we lived in Lexington, Kentucky. My husband and my oldest boy were killed. Now it's just Billy and me. I used the insurance to buy the house."

"Is that where you're from? Kentucky?"

"No, I grew up in Atlantic City. Where they hold the Miss America Pageant?" She smoothed her hair and soft waves fell around her narrow face. "In high school everybody said I should enter the Miss Atlantic City contest. But you have to do a talent routine." Her lips pinched in a line.

Given her sour expression, Gina decided not to pursue that angle. "How did you meet your husband?"

Mrs. Kay's lips softened and the lines around her mouth smoothed out. "Silas was a salesman for a big liquor distributor. He had all the Atlantic City casino accounts. Silas was so handsome, a real go-getter. I quit high school to marry him." She stared into space. "We eloped to Kentucky. Then John was born."

Gina nodded, reading between the lines. Fast-talking liquor salesman sweeps working girl off her feet and soon there's a shotgun wedding.

"I had quite a life back then. We'd go dancing. Silas loved going to clubs. And he adored John." Her thin lips pursed. "Then *Billy* came along."

"Is that Billy?" Gina asked, gesturing at a framed photograph on a table, a handsome, dark-haired teenager smiling into the camera.

"Lord, no, that's *John!*" Mrs. Kay beamed. "Isn't he handsome? John took after his father. Billy was different." Her smile faded. "Silas said he didn't see how—" She looked away and scratched her nose. "What magazine did you say this was for?"

"*Boston Magazine*," Gina said, jotting notes in her steno pad: *Father, Silas, liquor sales. Brother, John.* She wondered if any of this would help Franco.

"I did another interview once. A newspaper reporter came to see me after Billy—" Her lips tightened. "Anyway, that's how we got the van. Billy drives me to church in it every Sunday. Are you a Christian?"

She glanced at the religious statues and pictures. She didn't want to listen to any religious rants. "It must have been a terrible accident. How did it happen?"

"We were going to a Little League game. John was the star pitcher. He was riding in front with his dad. Billy and I were in back. We were late so Silas was driving fast. The insurance company said he'd been drinking."

Gina felt a rush of compassion as Mrs. Kay stared into space, a bleak expression on her gaunt face.

"The good Lord spared me, but I almost bled to death. My leg was bleeding something awful. And Billy hurt his head real bad."

"Do you have a picture of him?" Gina asked.

"Billy? No." Mrs. Kay smiled at her. "Let's have a cup tea, shall we?"

"Thank you. That would be lovely." Gina followed her down a short hall. *Squeak, squeak* went the wheelchair. At the far end, Mrs. Kay pointed at a wide door. "That's the bathroom. The door to the left goes downstairs to Billy's room."

"Can I see it?" Mrs. Kay couldn't go downstairs, but she could. If she got into Billy's room, maybe she'd find Vicky's ring, or something else to give Franco what he needed for the search warrant.

"No, Billy keeps it locked. He never lets anyone in his room. Come in the kitchen and I'll put some water on for tea."

Gina wanted to scream in frustration. She made a mental note to tell Franco about Billy's room, a *locked* room in the basement. Creepy.

Opposite the door to the basement, an archway opened onto a small kitchen with worn gray linoleum. The exterior of the house looked spiffy, but the interior bordered on squalid: a clunky old refrigerator on one side of the sink, an ancient gas stove on the other. A steaming teakettle sat on the stove. Along one wall, a chrome kitchen chair with a ripped yellow-plastic seat stood under a cheap card table.

"Too bad Billy's not here," Mrs. Kay said. "Maybe he'll come home for lunch and you can meet him."

Her breath caught in her throat. Jesus! Did he come home for lunch? Suddenly the little cottage seemed claustrophobic, not cozy. She didn't want to meet Billy. What if he was the Jackpot Killer?

"I always tell Billy I'll fix a nice lunch for him, but he says it's too much trouble." Mrs. Kay put teabags into two cups and poured hot water over them. "But I cook us a nutritious hot meal every night."

"I'm sure you do." Gina carried the teacups to the card table, sat on the chair with the torn seat and stirred her tea, wishing it were coffee, wishing she could smoke.

Wishing she could get what she needed and get the hell out of here.

Mrs. Kay wheeled herself to the table and set paper napkins beside the teacups. She pulled up the sleeve of her jacket and scratched her forearm. A dainty scarab bracelet hung from her bony wrist. It looked expensive, Gina thought, out of place, considering the shabby furnishings.

"That's a beautiful bracelet, Mrs. Kay."

"Thank you." She held out her arm to show it off the bracelet: tiny oval scarabs in a delicate gold setting, amber stones alternating with green ones. "Billy gave it to me."

Her heart sped up. That might be a clue. According to Franco, the Jackpot Killer had taken jewelry from some of his victims. "When was that?"

"A couple of months ago. For my birthday. Why?"

A rush of adrenaline upped her heart rate. "Did he say where he got it?"

Mrs. Kay gazed at her silently. "No. Billy can be thoughtful sometimes."

Did he ever give you a diamond ring? Gina wanted to ask. But she didn't dare. A murder suspect lived here, and she was getting weird vibes. Scary vibes.

Casting about for something to say, she gestured at the calendar on the wall beside her. It had an excellent reproduction of a Matisse goldfish painting. "I like your calendar. Matisse is my favorite painter."

"That's Billy's calendar. He's crazy about goldfish. He's got some in his room downstairs." Mrs. Kay smirked. "His *girls*, he calls them. He gives them silly names. Tessa. Lulu. Florence. I could have sworn he named one of them Victoria, but he said he didn't."

An icy chill skittered down her spine. Victoria?

She said nothing and concentrated on the names, committing them to memory: Tessa. Lulu. Florence. And Victoria.

"Didn't you say you're from Boston? Where that girl got murdered? The girl that won the lottery?" Mrs. Kay shook her head. "Gamblers want money but they don't want to work for it."

"Vicky didn't win the lottery."

"Yes she did. It said so on the news. I saw it on TV."

Why was Mrs. Kay so interested in Vicky's murder? Gina wondered.

"Well, if she didn't win it, who did?"

"A friend of hers."

Mrs. Kay's teacup clattered into the saucer. "That Pops conductor?"

"Yes."

"How do you know?" Fixing her with those intimidating pale-blue eyes.

"He's a friend of mine."

"Then he didn't—" Mrs. Kay sipped her tea, avoiding Gina's eyes.

Gina resisted an urge to look behind her. Was Billy downstairs in his room? No. She was imagining things. Franco said he worked during the week, and there was no van outside.

The doorbell rang, a loud clang that sent her heart racing.

"Now who could that be?" said Mrs. Kay. "Help me open the door."

Reluctantly, Gina followed her down the gloomy hall, took a deep breath and opened the door. A husky UPS man in a tan uniform smiled at her and said, "Package for William Karapitulik."

"What is it?" Mrs. Kay said in a querulous voice.

Hefting a shoebox-sized package in a plain brown wrapper, he said, "Beats me. I need you to sign for it." He handed the package to Mrs. Kay.

"Goodness, it's heavy." Mrs. Kay set it on her lap and signed the slip.

"Have a nice day," the driver said, and hurried down the front steps.

"Could you put this in the living room?" Mrs. Kay said, thrusting the package at her.

Surprised at how heavy it was, she took the package in the living room, set it on the TV tray beside the wingchair with the frayed brown upholstery and studied the return address. Walker's Sporting Goods. Dallas, Texas.

Sporting goods. Frightening possibilities flooded her mind. She had no clue where Vicky's ring was, and everything Mrs. Kay had told her might be useless, but right now she didn't care. She had to get out of this creepy house.

She returned to the hall. "I've got to be going, Mrs. Kay. Thank you for talking with me."

"Oh, that's all right. I don't get much company. Maybe we can talk again sometime. Could I have your card? In case I forgot to tell you something?"

She didn't want to leave her card, but she didn't want to arouse the woman's suspicions. Besides, what if Billy *was* the killer? Mrs. Kay was no Miss Congeniality, but she was in a wheelchair. Helpless.

Gina took out her business card and gave it to her. "If you think of something, give me a call."

Mrs. Kay studied the card, then looked at her. Her pale blue eyes had a faraway look in them. "Yes," she said slowly. "I will."

CHAPTER 30

––

Suffolk County Criminal Court — 2:10 p.m.

From the witness stand, Frank stared at the defendant, but the scumbag wouldn't look at him. Dwayne "Top Dawg" Davis had on a suit and a tie today. He'd put on a few pounds since Frank had last seen him. Thanks to the code of the street—no snitching, don't talk to cops, don't testify in court—Davis had avoided justice for five years.

Now, after an endless series of pre-trial motions and postponements, Davis was on trial for the murder of Luciana Martinez.

Frank's goal was simple: Put Dwayne Davis away for life.

This morning, prior to his testimony, the prosecutor, DA Kevin Turley, had asked him about his experience as a Boston PD homicide detective. To demonstrate his sensitivity to racial issues, Turley noted the award he'd received for his work with African-American boys. His testimony about apprehending Davis had gone well, but at that point the defense team asked for a lunch recess, no doubt hoping the jury would forget Frank's damning testimony. The judge had granted the request.

Frank had eaten a turkey sandwich, ruminating about the case. Luciana's mother, Elena Martinez, had custody of Luciana's daughter. Last night, he'd gone to see them. Every day on the job he saw despair on the faces of homeless people, captured criminals, anguished parents of dead children. But never had he seen the look of despair he'd seen on Elena's face last night.

Tia-Maria was seven now, brain damaged by the slug that remained in her head. Small for her age and plump, she sat on the living room rug, her eyes dull and unfocused, her movements spastic, eating a chocolate-chip cookie. Elena, a thin woman with a careworn face, thanked him for coming and said, "I hope you put that piece of scum in jail forever, what he did to my daughter. I do what I can for Tia-Maria, but she don't care about nothing, just the cookies."

"I'll do my best," he'd said, and left, knowing Elena was never going to have a carefree day.

Now, Attorney Rockland Wallace, a slender black man with graying hair and a grim expression, rose from the defense table and strolled past the jurors: five black females, four Hispanic females, and three Hispanic males.

Wallace approached the witness stand. "Detective Renzi, when you arrived at the murder scene on the evening of July 21, 1995, did you know that Luciana Martinez was a drug dealer?"

"Objection!" DA Turley said. "Calls for speculation from the witness."

"Sustained," said the judge, a sharp-featured woman with long dark hair, peering at Wallace over the top of her granny glasses.

"I'll rephrase. Were you given information about Luciana Martinez's drug related activities?"

Frank waited in case Turley wanted to object. When no objection came, he said, "I received a private investigator's report stating that on one occasion in 1995 Luciana Martinez was observed in what appeared to be a transaction involving drugs."

Wallace jerked his head affirmatively as though he'd hit a homerun. "Now, you stated that on the night you arrested Mr. Davis, he behaved in a suspicious manner. What attracted your attention?"

"I flagged down his car, but he failed to stop. When I followed the car, he jumped out and ran away."

"At that time did you draw your service weapon?"

"No, I did not."

Wallace put on a skeptical look. "This was in the Mission Hill Housing Project, correct?"

"Yes."

"What time was it?"

"Approximately nine-fifteen at night."

"At that time it was dark, correct?"

"It was dark, but the street lights were on."

"How did you know it was Mr. Davis?"

Frank thought about Tia-Maria, seven years old and motherless, because when her mother saw Davis, she had shielded Tia-Maria with her body, absorbing six lethal slugs, one of which pierced Tia-Maria's brain.

"When I saw him drive by in his Toyota Camry, I recognized him. He was wearing a purple hoodie and he gave me the finger."

Wallace frowned. "Was Mr. Davis known to you at that time?"

"Yes. I had previously arrested him for assaulting—"

"Just answer the question," Wallace said. "Don't embellish."

"Yes, I knew Mr. Davis."

"Many young men wear hoodies, Detective Renzi. How could you be certain it was Mr. Davis?"

"Two weeks prior, he was wearing the same purple hoodie when I arrested him for assault and battery with a dangerous weapon." Spitting it out fast before Wallace could stop him.

Wallace glowered at him. "After Mr. Davis got out of the Toyota Camry, what did you do?"

"I yelled for him to stop, but he didn't, so I chased him. After he ran approximately twenty yards, he pulled out a gun and shot at me."

A long-suffering expression appeared on Wallace's face. "Did you fire back at him?"

"No, I did not. He tripped over something, fell down on the sidewalk and dropped his weapon."

"Detective, isn't it true that as Mr. Davis lay defenseless on the ground you struck him in the face?"

He bit back an angry response. Be calm. Stay cool. "At no time did I strike Mr. Davis. When I reached him, his forehead was bleeding from a superficial cut where his head hit the concrete when he fell."

"Did you render first aid to my client, Detective Renzi?"

Hell, no, I wanted to beat the shit out of him, Frank thought but didn't say.

"After I secured Mr. Davis's weapon, I searched him and found drug paraphernalia and a large amount of cash in his pockets. I cuffed him and called for a patrol wagon and medical assistance."

He locked eyes with Attorney Wallace. "The EMTs arrived and rendered first aid to Mr. Davis."

———

Sandwich — 6:30 p.m.

He forked up a bite of meatloaf, rolled the mushy glop around his mouth and swallowed. His mother was watching him. Aware of her laser-beam stare, he fixed his eyes on his plate.

He would not look at her.

"Do you like it? I got the recipe out of a magazine at the doctor's office. *Family Circle* had an article about thrifty meals. Bread crumbs make the meat go further."

That's what it tasted like, bread soaked in salt water.

"It's nice, Mom. Tasty."

He went to the refrigerator and took out a carton of skimmed milk. He hated skimmed milk. He poured some into a glass and returned to the table.

"What did you do today?" She bit into a celery stick and chewed rapidly. *Click, click, click* went her teeth.

"The usual. Repairs, a few installations." He ate some boiled potato and waited for her to make him tell her *exactly* how many repairs, *exactly* when he had lunch—

"I talked to a reporter today."

He put his hands in his lap, scratching furiously. "A reporter? Why?"

"For an article about architecture," she said, smirking at him.

"Why? We're not in the Historic District."

"She liked the way you painted the house. She liked your calendar, too. We had a cup of tea, and she was admiring it. I told her about your goldfish."

A sharp pain burst inside his head like a cloud of fireworks, brilliant red and yellow pain. "Did she go downstairs?"

"No. I told her your room was locked."

"How long was she here?"

His mother smiled. "We had a nice chat. I told her about the accident. Then we got talking about that murder up in Boston. She said the girl that got murdered didn't even *win* the lottery."

He clenched his fists. "Yes she did. It was on TV."

"No. She said that man won. The conductor. Maybe he didn't kill her after all."

He took his plate to the counter and scraped the entire plateful into the garbage.

"Billy, it's rude to leave the table when I'm talking."

He stood at the sink, the fireworks pounding his head. The scab on his thumb was bleeding. He ran the cold water, rinsed off the blood, returned to the table and sat down. And hid his hands in his lap.

"How does this reporter know the conductor won?"

"He's a friend of hers." Watching him with her watery blue eyes.

"What's her name?"

His mother's gaze shifted away. "I forget. She was pretty. Short dark hair and slim legs. She liked the bracelet you gave me for my birthday."

He stared at her wrist. Florence's bracelet. She'd told some reporter about Florence's bracelet? How could she?

Abruptly, he rose from the table and ran downstairs.

Why did his mother always have to ruin everything? The conductor won the lottery? No! It had to be a mistake. Victoria won. Lucky Victoria.

What was a reporter doing *here* at *his* house? Noticing things.

The bracelet. Did the cops know about the bracelet?

Seething with anger, he went in his room. Pain pounded his temples as he watched his girls swim around the fish tank, flicking their filmy orange-red fins. Tessa and Florence and Ruthie. And Judy.

He plunged his hand in the tank, captured Tessa, flung her on the floor and stomped her. Lulu was next. Lucky Lulu, trying to hide at the bottom of the tank, but she couldn't. None of them could. He grabbed Lulu, squeezed hard and flung her on the floor beside Tessa.

Florence and Ruthie cowered at the bottom of the tank. And Judy.

He would never hurt Judy.

201

Beautiful Judy with her glorious voice. His best girl.

He grabbed Florence in one hand, Ruthie in the other, squeezed hard and dropped them on the floor.

Now Judy was alone. Lonely. They were so much alike.

Judy had suffered, too. Her father died, and her mother was mean. Her mother made her take diet pills when she was just a little girl.

He opened his desk drawer and took out Victoria's diamond ring and the answering machine tape. He put the tape in his boom box, re-wound it and pressed play.

"Hi, luv, it's Nigel. I'm at the airport—" There was a beep, then silence.

Nigel Heath. The conductor. *The man who hit the jackpot.*

He forwarded the tape and hit play. "Hi, Vicky, it's Gina Bevilaqua. Hope you're feeling better. You said to call you next week so—" He hit Stop and forwarded to the next message.

And heard his own voice. "Victoria? This is—"

He advanced the tape again and hit Play. "Hi, luv, are you there? It's Nigel. I'm 'round the corner at the grocery shop, thought I'd call to see if you needed anything. Be there in half a mo."

Interrupting him. Ruining his triumph. Preventing him from leaving his autograph. That's why the cops thought Nigel killed Victoria.

But the reporter had told his mother that Nigel won the lottery.

How did she know? Because he was a friend of hers.

He powered up his computer, opened his Victoria file, scrolled down to the end and typed: *Nigel Heath = real winner.* Then he typed: *Reporter?*

He saved the file and closed it. His head throbbed with a dull ache. He had to find out who the reporter was. How could his mother talk to a reporter and not get her name? Why did she come to *his* house? Could his mother have called her? No. His mother didn't suspect.

He picked up Victoria's diamond ring and shut his eyes, savoring the memory, the moment when he'd seen it on her hand. Her limp, dead hand. Victoria had fought him but she couldn't win. He had BEATEN HER.

But *Nigel Heath* was the lucky winner, and he was still alive. The cops thought Nigel killed Victoria. There was only one way to fix that.

He'd never killed a man. Men were dangerous. Powerful, like his father.

But now he had a weapon. He dragged the Wagner's Sporting Goods box out from under his bed. If he shot the conductor, there would be blood.

He would never forget the blood gushing over his face and his neck. Years ago, but it felt like yesterday.

Men were powerful, but now that he had a gun that wouldn't stop him.

He would find the conductor and shoot him. Then Lucky Nigel would be DEAD. Then the cops would know who killed Victoria.

Then everyone would know.

Maybe that would make his mother's mouth be still.

JACKPOT

———

Dorchester — 7:35 p.m.

Frank dumped the remnants of his take-out BBQ chicken in the trash bin outside his room, went back inside and lay on the bed. Testifying in court today had taken its toll. He had a massive headache. Man, he had to start getting some sleep.

His cell phone rang. He grabbed it, checked the ID and smiled.

When he answered, Gina said, "Franco, I've got great news! I talked to Mrs. Karapitulik. Billy's mother."

"You what?? Jesus! Why?"

"You said you needed something to get a search warrant. I thought I might be able to find Vicky's ring."

"Where are you now?"

"At the beach house."

He breathed a sigh of relief. At least she was safe. Gina had brass balls, but what she'd done was foolhardy.

"Tell me what happened," he said tersely. "I take it Billy wasn't there?"

"No. He was working. I told his mother I was writing an article on Victorian architecture."

"Did you see Vicky's ring?"

"No, but the place was creepy. Billy's room is in the basement. I asked his mother if I could see it, but she said he keeps it locked."

"What do you mean, creepy?"

"Well, for one thing Billy keeps goldfish in his room. His mother said he gives them women's names. Tessa and Lulu and Florence."

The hairs on his neck stood up. That confirmed what the waitress said.

"Not only that, his mother said he named one goldfish Victoria, but later he denied it."

A surge of adrenaline zinged his veins. "What else?"

"She was in a bad car accident years ago in Lexington, Kentucky. Her husband and their older son were killed. The father's name was Silas. He was a liquor salesman. The older son's name was John. She said Billy hurt his head and one of her legs was mangled. They had to amputate. I felt sorry for her."

He jotted notes in his memo pad. Accident: Lexington, Kentucky. Father's name, Silas, a liquor salesman. Was that what the J&B nips were about? He felt like he was missing something, but he'd worry about that later.

"Anything else?"

"The house was a mess, peeling wallpaper, ancient appliances, junky furniture. Billy's mother had on this chintzy pants suit, but the weird thing was, she was wearing this expensive-looking bracelet."

It sucked the breath out of him. "What did it look like?"

203

"It was a really nice scarab bracelet."

"Jesus, that's it! He stole a scarab bracelet from one of the earlier victims. Gina, this is great, but you took an incredible risk."

"Franco, stop worrying. I'm fine. Can you get the search warrant now?"

He wanted to kiss her for getting the information, but if something had happened to her, he couldn't imagine how guilty he'd feel.

"Gina," he said sternly, "what you did was very dangerous. Don't you ever pull a stunt like that again."

After a long silence Gina said, "Well, it was kind of scary, but it's worth it if you can prove Nigel's innocent. How soon can you arrest this creep?"

If her information was accurate, Karapitulik was probably the Jackpot Killer, but arresting him wouldn't be quick and easy. Hank Flynn had to okay the search warrant application, and he'd go ballistic when he found out a civilian had been snooping for information at a murder suspect's house. On the other hand, Hank was as anxious as Frank was to nail the Jackpot Killer.

"First I have to get a search warrant. That could take a day or so."

"Why?"

"I'll try and get it tomorrow, but it's up to the judge."

"Okay," Gina said, clearly disappointed. "How'd it go in court today?"

"Very well. I'm pretty sure they'll convict the bastard and put him away." He glanced at his watch. "Gotta go, Gina. I want to call my FBI contact and give him the information."

He clicked off, called Ross Dunn and relayed the information Gina had given him.

"Great," Ross said. "The names will help. I'll tell my assistant to focus on accidents in Lexington, Kentucky. Let me know what happens with the search warrant."

"I will. How's it going with your suspects?"

"I eliminated the ones in New York," Ross said. "I still like the New Jersey librarian, but if your information on Billy Karapitulik is accurate, he might be our Jackpot Killer. "

"As soon as I get the search warrant," Frank said, "I'll go to his house. Hopefully, tomorrow."

—

CHAPTER 31

Wednesday, May 31 — Bourne, MA

He put on the earmuffs, picked up the gun and stared at the target. His heart was beating so hard he could hear the blood pounding in his ears. Blood. If he shot someone, there would be blood. Just thinking about it made his stomach feel queasy.

An hour ago he'd managed to leave without waking his mother and slip out the front door into the inky darkness. When he got to the shooting range, the sun was a faint glow on the horizon. The man behind the counter looked like a giant Sequoia. A sleeveless T-shirt exposed multi-colored tattoos on his biceps, and his armpits gave off a musky odor.

"You're early, got the whole place to yourself." He took out a pair of earmuffs and adjusted the sliding band on the top. "Little guy like you, we better make sure they fit."

Making fun of him, because of his size.

But no one else was here, no one to make fun of him if he missed. He stared at the Mark II with the dull-blue steel finish and the seven-round magazine. Rugged and reliable. His hands were shaking. There were scabs on his knuckles where he'd scratched the eczema. But no blood.

He looked at the target, willing himself to shoot. His hands were sweaty, slippery on the gun.

The man at the counter had said to squeeze the trigger gently.

He closed his eyes and visualized the lucky winner. Nigel Heath.

He opened his eyes and squeezed the trigger. Gently.

BAM! Even with the earmuffs, the noise hurt his ears. He squinted at the target, ten yards away.

"Start with it close," the man had said. "You'll get the hang of it."

But he hadn't. He'd missed the target completely.

An acrid odor burned his nose and throat, making him gag.

SUSAN FLEET

He clamped his hand over his mouth so he wouldn't puke, and sucked in air through his nostrils. He had to do better.

He raised the gun. Aimed. Fired.

The sound reverberated in his head. Dull pain pulsed his temples. After the accident, the doctors had said the pain would go away, but it hadn't.

He looked at the target and felt a surge of excitement. He'd hit it!

Methodically, he emptied the gun at the target.

The noise made the pain worse, mouth-mother pain beating his head, hearing her voice say, "Silas, you're going too fast! Slow down!"

"Don't tell me how to drive!" His father's loud voice, scaring him.

"Billy, stop crying! Judy, will you shut him up? He's such a little cunt-sissy."

"Watch your mouth, Silas."

"Why can't he be a tough guy like John? Gonna pitch a helluva game tonight, right John-boy?" His father turned and saw the tears running down his cheeks. "Jesus! Look at the little brat! That's what he is, Judy. A sniveling little *brat. Your* little brat, not mine!"

"Don't say that!"

"Well, he is. Ain't no son of mine! You and your flirty ways."

"Liar!"

"It's true! You flirt with every Tom, Dick and Harry—"

"I do not. Don't say that!"

"Stop whining, Judy. You sound just like your little brat. You make me sick, both of you!"

"I'm sorry I ever had him! Oh my God! Silas, watch out for that truck!"

And then the dump truck hit them. His head slammed against the door and he wet his pants. His mother's blood gushed over him, spilling over his face into his eyes and nose. He tried to wipe it off, but the blood got on his hands. Stinking. Slimy. Disgusting. He tried to push her away, but he couldn't. He was weak. His father was strong. *Ain't no son of mine. Your little brat, not mine!*

Now his father was dead. But his mother wasn't. *I'm sorry I ever had him!*

He ejected the empty clip and inserted the spare, his heart pounding, out of control, just like their car had spun out of control and he wet his pants and his mother's blood spurted over his face.

Blood. Stinking. Slimy. Disgusting. Blood.

If only he could forget the BLOOD.

He was glad his father was dead.

Soon his lucky winner would be dead, too.

Everyone thought Nigel Heath killed Victoria, but he'd show them.

He raised his rugged, reliable gun and fired.

Now he could kill and kill and kill, and no one could stop him.

———

206

10:15 p.m. — Squantum

Gina sank onto the futon in her beach house. On her stereo, Chet Baker was singing "My Funny Valentine," a sad song that matched her mood. She opened a fresh pack of cigarettes. Already the ashtray on the coffee table held four butts. She was smoking too much, but dammit, she was sick of waiting.

Why couldn't Franco hurry up and get the search warrant? Earlier he'd called and said he hoped to get it tomorrow. The cops were convinced Nigel killed Vicky. She was positive he hadn't, and now Franco agreed with her. But how long would it take to arrest the Jackpot Killer? How could she get what she needed to write a book if Nigel was in jail?

She hadn't been back to her house in Westwood since last Wednesday. Orchid kept urging her to leave Ryan. Fine, but she needed money. They had joint bank accounts. In theory, half the money was hers, but if she withdrew her share, Ryan would go ballistic. Orchid was in Arizona at a trade show.

Gina smiled, imagining Orchid's reaction to her Sandwich adventure. She'd be green with envy. When Orchid got back from the trade show, she'd take her out for a drink and give her the gory details.

Her cell phone rang. Thinking it was Franco, she punched on.

"Gina? Nigel here. I hate to bother you, but you're the only one I can talk to."

Not Franco, but Nigel was almost as good. He'd just admitted that she was his only confidant, and she wanted to make sure it stayed that way.

"No problem, Nigel. What's up?"

"More bad news. The bloody hotel's pestering me for payment."

"Can't you put it on your credit card?"

"A bit overloaded there, I'm afraid. My agent finally sent me a check for the Iowa gig, but it doesn't amount to much, nowhere near what I need. And that's not the worst of it. That Mulligan bloke had another go at me today. My lawyer thinks they might arrest me tomorrow."

"Jesus! How can they?" She gnawed her lip. Should she tell him about Billy? No. She'd promised Franco she wouldn't. "Nigel, if you can hang in there for a couple of days—"

"They'll lock me up and throw away the key."

His flat tone made her uneasy. "What does your lawyer say?"

"He wants his bloody retainer, but I haven't got it! All these legal blokes care about is money. If I don't pay him, I'm done for. The cops think I killed Vicky. I'll rot in prison for the rest of my life."

Gina massaged her forehead. Her life had turned into an endless tunnel of stress. Franco was living in a motel in Dorchester, and she was living at her beach house. Soon or later the shit would hit the fan with Ryan. Lord knows what would happen then.

"I'll never play a piano again. Never conduct another concert."

"Nigel, don't think like that. You have to stay positive."

"The cops will put me in jail forever. I'd be better off dead."

Her heart jolted. Better off dead? Was this a desperate cry for help?

"Nigel, don't say that."

"Why not? It's true. Save the bastards the trouble."

His dull monotone sent off alarm bells. He sounded suicidal. After her high school friend committed suicide, she'd done some research on the topic. Most of the studies said anyone with a family member who'd committed suicide was more likely to do it themselves. For heavy drinkers, the statistics were worse, and Nigel was drinking up a storm.

"Nigel, I want you to come and stay at my beach house."

"No. You'd get in trouble and it would be my fault."

"I'll pick you up at the hotel."

"No. I've caused enough trouble already. Look what happened to Vicky."

"You have to stop thinking like that. I want you to stay at my beach house until things get sorted out. I'll come to the hotel right now and sneak you out through the parking garage in my car."

A long silence. A heavy sigh. "Well, I s'pose we could give it a go. At least I could play your piano. That would be a comfort."

"It's settled then. I'll pick you up in half an hour."

"Bit late, isn't it? You must be tired. Let's wait till morning."

She assessed his tone. He still sounded despondent, but at least he wasn't talking about being better off dead. Suddenly she felt utterly weary.

"Okay, but only if you promise not to do anything rash tonight. If you did, I'd feel terribly guilty. And you know what that's like."

After a moment, Nigel said, "Yes, I do. What time will you pick me up tomorrow?"

"Early. Meet me at six o'clock on the second level of the garage near the elevator."

"Thank you, Gina. You're a wonderful friend. I'll make this up to you someday, I promise."

She replaced the receiver and massaged her eyes.

What the hell had she gotten herself into?

She'd just invited Nigel Heath, the man the cops were about to arrest for the murder of Vicky Stavropoulos, to stay at her beach house.

She had no idea how soon Franco would arrest the killer.

Billy Karapitulik. The weirdo who named the goldfish in his locked basement room after the women he murdered.

CHAPTER 32

Thursday, June 1

Sleep-deprived and squinty-eyed, Gina drove down Huntington Avenue and passed New England Conservatory at 5:50. Ahead of her, the rising sun cast a rosy-red glow over the glass facade of the John Hancock Tower. Traffic was sparse at this hour, but five minutes later when she got to the Back Bay Inn three television crews and several reporters stood outside.

Fortunately they were focused on the hotel entrance, not the street. She sped past them and entered the parking garage. How would she sneak Nigel out past those sharp-eyed reporters?

She stopped at the ticket dispenser, took a ticket, continued up to the second level and parked in a space near the elevator. She checked her watch. 6:02. *Nigel, please don't keep me waiting.*

A minute later he stepped out of the elevator, dressed in a white shirt and navy slacks, a duffel bag slung over his shoulder. His face lit up in a smile when she got out of the car. His smile faded when she said, "There's a mob of reporters out front. You'll have to hide in the trunk."

But when she opened the trunk, a carton of office supplies and an emergency repair kit filled most of the space.

"Hurry," she said urgently. "Put the carton in the back seat!"

Alert for the sound of approaching vehicles, she shoved the repair kit to one side. Fortunately, no cars passed them. She helped Nigel get in the trunk.

"Good thing I'm not claustrophobic. How long must I stay in here?"

"Fifteen minutes or so, depending on traffic. Will you have enough air?"

"Close the lid and we'll see."

She shut the lid and wiped sweat off her forehead. As a crime reporter she'd had her share of adventures, but nothing like this. Could she really smuggle a murder suspect out of his hotel in the trunk of her car?

She put her mouth close to the lid and said, "Are you okay?"

"Yes," came the faint reply.

She jumped in the car, drove down to the toll booth and paid the attendant. What if a reporter recognized her distinctive red Mazda? She sank low in the seat and averted her face as she drove past the hotel entrance, her hands sweaty on the wheel.

A minute later she eyed the rearview. No one was following her, but another problem loomed. Thelma, the woman who lived across the street from her beach house, watched television day and night, especially the news.

If Thelma saw Nigel, she would recognize him immediately.

Fifteen minutes later Nigel banged on the trunk, asking to get out. By then they were only a mile from her beach house. She found a restaurant that was closed for repairs, parked out back and opened the trunk.

"Bit cramped in here," Nigel said.

"Sorry. It was the only way I could sneak you past the reporters."

Blinking in the sun, he spotted the restaurant sign. "Can we have a spot of breakfast? It's been ages since I've had a meal outside the hotel."

He seemed rather cheerful for a man who'd claimed he'd be better off dead last night. Then again, she wasn't the one who'd been cooped up in a hotel for two weeks.

"Not now," she said. "Someone might recognize you. Stay in the trunk. In five minutes we'll be at my beach house. When we get there, you need to wear sunglasses. I don't want my neighbor to recognize you." She shut the trunk and got back in the car.

At 6:35 she pulled into the driveway alongside her beach house, thankful that she'd left the garage door open. She drove into the garage and got out, but before she could close the garage door, a voice called, "Good morning, Gina! Goodness, you're out early. Why are you coming home at this hour?"

Her heart sank. Shading her eyes against the dazzling sunlight, she looked across the street. Thelma waved to her from a second-floor window, dressed in a blue terrycloth robe, her snow-white hair neatly combed. Thelma kept an eagle eye on the neighborhood, a plus ordinarily, but not today.

"Want coffee?" Thelma called. "I just made a pot."

"Thanks, Thelma, but I can't. I've got things to do."

"I've got blueberry coffee cake," Thelma wheedled.

Thelma loved having company. "Not right now," Gina said firmly. "I have to get back to work."

Clearly disappointed, Thelma said, "All right. I guess I'll go do my laundry."

Too bad her garage didn't have a secret way to get into the house, Gina thought. A hidden staircase in the pantry led to a closet in her second-floor bedroom. In 1878 when the sea captain had built the house, fishing was hazardous. Wives watched for their husband's ships from porches on the upper floors. Some never returned, hence the term *widow's walk*. As a child, she loved climbing the secret staircase. She'd spent hours on the widow's walk, staring through her grandfather's binoculars. But that was years ago.

Now she had to smuggle a murder suspect into her house. She closed the garage door and let Nigel out of the trunk. She gave him the pair of oversized sunglasses she used at the beach and led him to the door that faced her cottage. "I don't want the woman across the street to see you. Wait here till I wave you in."

Without a word, Nigel put on the sunglasses. He seemed happy to have her in charge, a lot happier than she was. But she had to think positive and keep her eyes on the prize—a lucrative book contract. Franco would get the search warrant for Billy's house, find enough incriminating evidence to arrest him, and Nigel would be in the clear.

She unlocked the side door, checked to make sure Thelma wasn't watching and waved to Nigel. In three long strides he was inside her kitchen.

He took off her sunglasses, put them on the counter and set his duffle bag on the floor. "Good to get out of that trunk," he said.

"I'm sure it is. Let's get you settled."

She took him upstairs to a small bedroom with twin beds. "You can use this room. There's no TV set but you can watch the one in the living room."

"Forget the telly. Nothing but bad news there." He set his duffel on one bed. "You've no idea what a relief it is to get out of that bloody hotel. You're a life saver, Gina. I'll make it up to you someday, I promise."

Someday she would hold him to the promise and ask him to give her some juicy material for her book. But now was not the time to do it.

"There's no bathroom up here, just the one downstairs, but it has a shower. Wait here while I get you some towels."

She went to her bedroom, opened the bottom drawer of her bureau, took out a set of towels and took them back to Nigel's room. He gave her a smile, but the smile seemed forced and his sky-blue eyes were bloodshot. He looked like he hadn't slept in weeks.

When they went down to the living room, Nigel went straight to the piano, sat down and riffled the keys.

"Maybe you shouldn't," Gina said. "My neighbor."

"Right. Sorry. I forgot." Crestfallen, he sat on the futon, took a magazine off her coffee table and thumbed through it. He looked so forlorn she almost told him to go ahead and play, but she was afraid Thelma might hear him.

She checked the time. 7:15. Later than she had planned. By the time she got to the Expressway, traffic headed into Boston would be stop and go. She was going to be late for work. Maybe she'd wait until rush hour was over.

"Would you like coffee, Nigel? It'll just take a minute to brew a pot."

"Love a cup." Nigel rose from the futon and pointed to a Turner reproduction on the wall. A painting of an early nineteenth-century British warship, it featured Turner's trademark atmospherics: a slice of blue sky, mist rising from the water, a glowing orange sun.

"That's one of my favorite Turner paintings," he said. "When I was a kid, Mum used to take me 'round to all the London art galleries."

She filed the tidbit away for her book and went in the kitchen. Nigel sat at the table while she ground the coffee beans. Once the coffee was brewing, she said, "Excuse me, but I've got to check my messages."

"Of course. Don't let me upset your routine. Sorry to be such a bother."

"You're not a bother, Nigel. Wait here. I'll be right back."

She went in the living room and checked her cell phone. One missed call, but no message. Damn! Had Franco called her?

———

"This woman went there by herself?" Hank said, his blue eyes flinty.

Frank squirmed in the chair beside his boss's desk. This was going to be a tough sell. And Hank hated early morning meetings. "The suspect works during the week. She wasn't in any danger." Not true, of course. Billy could have come home from work early. Christ, anything could have happened.

Hank said nothing, expressionless. Frank figured he had maybe thirty seconds to make his case. "His mother was wearing a scarab bracelet. I'm almost certain it's the one he stole from the Vermont victim. That gives us probable cause for a search warrant."

"Frank, if this ever goes to trial, a good defense lawyer will nail us for an illegal search and say this reporter was acting as your surrogate."

"But she wasn't. I didn't ask her to go there. She did it on her own."

"How'd she get the name?"

He had no answer for that one. When in doubt, change the subject. "The suspect works for the cable company. I think that's how he gets the women to let him in. The daughter of the Rhode Island winner told me her mother said her television was screwed up the morning of the murder."

Hank's face remained stony.

"His father was a liquor salesman and his brother's name was John. J&B, get it? John and Billy." The realization had hit him as he lay in bed, unable to sleep after Gina told him she'd gone to Billy's house. "Nigel Heath swears he gave Vicky a diamond ring, but Gerry didn't find it in her apartment. I think the Jackpot Killer took it. The hype about Nigel being Vicky's killer pissed him off, so he killed the woman in Nashua."

"Maybe," Hank said grudgingly. His telephone rang. Hank answered and listened for several seconds, stone-faced. Frank could hear someone on the other end, yelling. After a moment, Hank said, "What time was this?" After a long silence, Hank said, "Okay, thanks for letting me know."

Hank ended the call and said, "Gerry Mulligan. He got a judge to issue an arrest warrant for Nigel Heath, but when Gerry and his troops went to his hotel this morning, Nigel was gone. The desk clerk said Nigel didn't order his usual room-service breakfast. Gerry got the manager to let him into the room. Nobody home, over and out." Hank smiled tightly. "Needless to say, Gerry is bullshit."

"How did he sneak out of the hotel with all those reporters around?"

"That's what Gerry wants to know." Hank tapped his pen on his desk. "He's pissed that you didn't tell him about the Jackpot Killer, too. What else did this reporter get?"

"The suspect keeps goldfish. His mother said he gives them women's names. Florence, like the victim in Chatham. Tessa, the Rhode Island victim. She said he named one goldfish Victoria, but later he denied it."

Hank let out a low whistle. "You think the mother suspects?"

"I don't know."

"Can this reporter I.D. the bracelet?"

"I've got jeweler's pictures from the victim's son. It's custom made and the setting is unique. If she can identify the bracelet, can we go for a search warrant?"

"Okay," Hank said. "But make sure she's positive. She might have to testify in court."

"I will." Frank left and hurried back to his office. He'd already done the paperwork for the search warrant. Now all he had to do was get Gina to identify the bracelet. He sat at his desk, about to call Gina, when his cell phone rang. He checked the ID and his heart did a cartwheel inside his chest.

He punched on. "Hi, Maureen, great to hear from you."

"Hi, Dad. Sorry I didn't return your calls. Grampa Sal called me last night and we talked for a while. You know, about the divorce. He said I should call you."

"I'm glad you did. I know it was a shock, Maureen. I don't blame you for being upset."

"Well, I am upset, but I miss talking to you. Grampa Sal said I shouldn't make harsh judgments. He said I didn't have enough experience, you know? Because I've never been married."

A warm glow filled his chest. *Thank you, Dad.*

"Maureen, your mother and I both love you very much. A divorce isn't going to change that."

"I love you, too, Dad."

A great weight lifted off his shoulders. "I'm about to wrap up a case. As soon as I do, I'll fly to Baltimore for the weekend so we can talk, okay?"

"Sounds great, Dad. Just call and let me know when you'll be here."

———

When Gina returned to the kitchen, Nigel stood at the counter, pouring coffee into two mugs. He brought them to the kitchen table, sat down, and said, "Mind if I smoke?"

"Go ahead. I've been smoking a lot myself lately." Too much, she thought as she opened the kitchen window. She joined him at the table and took a pack of cigarettes out of her purse. "Must be the stress."

"I know what you mean." His shoulders sagged and he rubbed his eyes. He looked exhausted, his face drawn and pale, droopy bags under his eyes.

Her cell phone rang. "I'll take it in the living room," she said.

When she answered, Franco said, "Where've you been? I called you earlier."

Speaking softly so Nigel wouldn't hear, she said, "Did you get the search warrant?"

"Not yet. Hank will only okay it if you can identify the bracelet. It's a custom job so I've got jeweler's pictures to show you. I can bring them over to the *Herald* in half an hour."

"No," she said quickly, "don't do that. I'm at the beach house. There was, uh, there's a plumbing problem so I had to call someone to fix it."

"You want me to come there?"

No, no, no! She gripped the phone. Franco was already pissed at her for going to Billy's house. He'd flip out if he found out Nigel was staying here.

"No, don't bring them here. I'll be in town in an hour. Let's meet at that coffee shop near the *Herald* where we go sometimes."

"Okay. See you there," Franco said, and hung up.

Her spirits soared. If she identified the bracelet, Franco could go to Sandwich and arrest Billy.

When she returned to the kitchen, Nigel said, "Must be good news. You look happy."

She was dying to tell him about Billy, but she didn't dare, walking a tightrope now, hiding things from Nigel, hiding things from Franco. Not to mention hiding the Gina-Franco affair from Ryan.

"I just need to take care of some business." She sat down at the table and lit a cigarette.

"Bloody nuisance, business. My father expected me to be the next Van Cliburn, but I wasn't and he never forgave me for it. After Mum's funeral, we never spoke again. Six months later he was dead." Nigel gazed at her. His eyes were very blue and very sad. "You don't say much about your husband. Bit of a cock-up there?"

A cock-up? More like a Force-5 tornado. "Sort of. But life goes on."

"That must be difficult. Do you have family to lean on?"

"No. My parents are dead and my brothers have their own problems."

"You loved him once, didn't you? In the beginning, I mean."

Without warning, her eyes filled with tears. Did she love Ryan in the beginning? She couldn't remember. Strange. Maybe she'd been mesmerized by the big Italian wedding her mother was planning. Maybe she'd been in love with the idea of Ryan, his persuasive charm and his constant attention. Maybe she'd been too young and stupid to get married in the first place.

"Now you're in love with Detective Renzi," Nigel said. "But he's married, too, isn't he?"

"Yes." Abruptly, she put out her cigarette and stood.

Nigel was beginning to get on her nerves. If she came back here tonight after work, she'd have to listen to more of his depressing stories.

Sooner or later she'd have to, if she wanted to write a book.

But tonight she'd rather be with Franco.

CHAPTER 33

—

Boston — 10:35 a.m.

Rushing and out of breath, Gina yanked open the door of the coffee shop. Predictably, there'd been an accident on the northbound Expressway, just a fender-bender, but it had snarled traffic for miles.

The coffee shop was small because most people got takeout. There were only two booths. Franco was sitting in one of them.

"Been waiting long?" she said as she slid into the booth beside him.

"A couple of minutes." He sipped his coffee and cocked an eyebrow. "Everything okay? You look frazzled."

"Traffic-jam on the Expressway," she said, flashing him a smile. "Have you got the pictures?"

"Yes," he said, tapping a finger on a manila envelope. "Want coffee?"

"No, thanks. I had some earlier. Show me the pictures."

He opened the envelope and took out two black-and-white photographs.

Visualizing the scarab bracelet she'd seen on Mrs. Kay's bony wrist, Gina studied them. The photographs had been taken from different angles, but the bracelet's delicate filigreed setting was distinctive.

"That's it. The exact same setting. I'm positive."

"Okay, but these are black-and-whites. Do you remember what color the stones were?"

"As I recall the scarabs were green and amber."

Franco smiled. "I was hoping you'd say that. Her son said those were her favorite colors, so he had the jeweler use green and amber stones." He squeezed her arm. "This is great, Gina. Just what I need."

"How soon will you be able to get into Billy's house?"

"Tomorrow, I hope. I'll call you tonight if we get the warrant."

She traced a finger down his forearm. "Call me? Why can't I stay at the Dorchester Palace tonight?"

216

He put his arm around her shoulder and pulled her close. "Sounds good to me, but I might have to work late. We've got a complication."

Her heart sank. She didn't need any more complications. "What?"

"Gerry Mulligan went to Nigel's hotel with an arrest warrant this morning, but he wasn't there."

Shocked, she stared him. Just as Nigel had predicted, the cops were going to arrest him for Vicky's murder. If she told Franco she was the one who helped Nigel escape, he'd be furious. Which meant she'd better act like she was furious at Gerry Mulligan. The best defense is a good offense. That's what Ryan said, and Ryan should know. He was a master at it.

"Gerry's going to *arrest* him?" she said indignantly. "How can he? What's he got for evidence?"

"Calm down, Gina." Franco tilted his head, reminding her that others were in the coffee shop. "I don't know what Gerry put on the arrest warrant. I haven't talked to him in awhile. He's pissed at me for not telling him about the Jackpot Killer. While I was in Hank's office today, asking him about the search warrant, Gerry called Hank and told him Nigel was missing. Nobody knows where he is. Gerry put out a BOLO on him."

Franco gave her a speculative look, one she knew well. He suspected something. Time for a diversion. "If you get the warrant, why can't you arrest Billy today?" Anything to shift the focus away from Nigel.

"Gina, you gave me good information, but I'm not sure what I'll find in the house. Besides, I need to set things up with the Sandwich police before I execute the warrant. Best case, that'll happen tomorrow."

She felt guilty about not telling him Nigel was at her beach house. But if Franco got what he needed tomorrow, it wouldn't matter. After he arrested Billy, she'd tell him about smuggling Nigel out of the hotel and they'd have a good laugh about it. But that hinged on capturing Billy, and if Billy really was the Jackpot Killer, he was dangerous.

"Be careful when you go to Billy's house," she said. "Did I tell you that UPS delivered a package while I was there?"

"No," Franco said sharply. "What was in it?"

"I'm not sure, but it was from a sporting goods store in Texas."

"You think it could have been a gun?"

"Maybe. The package was heavy. I'm worried about Billy's mother."

"Do you think she suspects him?"

"I don't know," she said, recalling the odd look in Mrs. Kay's eyes when she'd given the woman her business card.

Franco checked his watch. "Gotta go, Gina. The sooner I take the search warrant application to a judge, the sooner I'll get it."

She walked out of the coffee shop with him and they separated. Now that she'd identified the bracelet, Franco seemed certain he would be able to get the search warrant, but as she walked back to her office she felt uneasy.

If they didn't arrest Billy tomorrow, how long would Nigel have to hide out at her beach house? Grieving for Vicky. Obsessing over family baggage. Fodder for her book, but she had troubles of her own.

Still, tonight she'd be with Franco. When he got the search warrant, they'd have a glass of wine and celebrate. Tomorrow, Franco would go to Sandwich and arrest Billy, and everything would be fine.

Well, fine for Nigel, but not for her. Tomorrow was Friday. Ryan would fly back from Austin and come home to an empty house. Ryan was no dummy. He'd probably figure she was at the beach house. If he decided to confront her and found Nigel at the beach house, there'd be hell to pay.

———

Sandwich — 6:15 p.m.

"How do you like the fish, Billy?"

He stared at the glop on his plate. Mushy canned peas, fish with slimy gray skin. The stuffing she'd made to go with it was so dry and salty it stuck to the roof of his mouth. He could feel her watching him, waiting for him to say it was wonderful.

"Mom, why can't we ever have something simple? Hamburgers or barbequed chicken, something like that?"

"We can't afford it. Why can't you find a job that pays better?" She picked up a carrot stick and crunched it. Mouth moving, teeth clicking.

"If you didn't give so much money to the church—"

"Billy! The church is my *salvation*! And yours. You should get down on your knees every day and thank the Lord for saving you. And your mother." Pale-blue eyes boring into him. Lips pinched in a line.

He rose from the table, took his plate to the counter and scraped the stinking mess into the garbage. The room was quiet.

So quiet he could hear the wall clock ticking.

Almost quiet enough to hear his heart beating. Beating. BEATING.

He took out a loaf of Wonder Bread, opened a cupboard and took out a jar of Jif peanut butter, the crunchy kind. "Where's the grape jelly, Mom?"

"I didn't buy any. All that sugar rots your teeth. You'll thank me when you're older."

He refused to look at her. He would *not* look at her mouth moving.

He made himself a peanut butter sandwich, sat down at the table and took a big bite. She wasn't eating. She was watching him. He felt her eyes bore into him, but he still wouldn't look at her.

Mouth moving. Making pain in the head. Throbbing.

Blood beating. Boiling blood. BLOOD.

He thought about the gun. And his new skill.

"Did you fold the laundry?"

He chewed methodically, savoring his peanut butter sandwich. "Yes, Mom."

"Good. There's a program on TV tonight about gambling. I want you to watch it."

Gambling. He put his hands in his lap and scratched. When he looked down, his knuckles were bloody. BLOOD.

"I can't, Mom. I have to go out."

Her pale blue eyes bored into him. "What for?"

"I have to go somewhere."

"What do you mean? Where are you going?" Her eyes were relentless. Cold. Blue. Dead.

His heart fluttered like a moth at a hundred-watt bulb, faster and faster, fluttering wildly. Beating his chest.

Pounding his blood. Into his head. Making it hurt. Hurting. Him.

"I have to go to Boston." He dug his nails into the palms of his hands and looked at her. Looked at her cold dead blue eyes.

"What for?"

"I have to take care of something."

"You do not! Don't lie to me! You're not going *anywhere*. I *forbid* it! You're staying right here with me."

He got up and backed away from the table.

Away from his mother. Away from her eyes.

"Don't you *dare* leave while I'm speaking to you!"

Mouth-making pain in his head. He forced himself to look at her cold, hard blue eyes. For an instant he saw the briefest flicker of—

What was it? He'd seen that look before in Tessa's eyes. And Lulu's.

A tiny flicker of fear.

He ran downstairs, unlocked the door to his room and went inside.

Blood boiling. BLOOD. Heart beating. BEATING.

He went to the fish tank and stared at Judy. Now she was all alone. He plunged his hand into the tank and captured her, felt her fins flap against his hand. But she couldn't escape. He squeezed her hard, as hard as he could.

Then he dropped her on the floor and shut his eyes and the glorious ache surged into his groin.

He undid his fly, breathing in ragged gasps, stroking until the final exquisite shudder came.

He opened his eyes and stared at the orange mess on the floor.

Judy. Dead.

He took out his tool box and opened it.

Beating. His heart was beating. But slower now.

BEATING.

He opened his toolbox and took out the wrench.

CHAPTER 34

He sat down at Gina's piano and played a three-octave E-minor arpeggio. E-minor to go with his melancholy mood. His fingers wandered over the keys and launched unbidden into "Stardust."

Improvising on the familiar melody, he let his mind wander. Hollywood. A smoky cafe. Appreciative patrons. The sound of clinking glasses.

He eyed the amber liquid in the glass that stood on the corner of the piano. Vamping chords with his left hand, he picked up the glass with his right and took a long pull of Dewars. Straight. No ice.

His fingers feathered the keys and slithered into "Laura."

"Vicky," he said.

Speaking her name aloud brought a rush of memories. Her beautiful brown eyes. Her mischievous smile. Her wicked sense of humor. How he loved her sense of humor. Her bubbly laugh echoed in his mind.

He never should have bought those Megabucks tickets.

With merciless precision his fingers struck the keys.

He never should have given Vicky the winning ticket. Never should have asked her to claim the money. If he hadn't, she'd still be alive.

It was all his fault.

Forearms flailing, he pounded the keys. The sound crescendoed to a mighty clamor that thundered through the house. Moments later another sound penetrated the din.

Abruptly, he jerked his hands off the keyboard. The phone was ringing.

Should he answer it? No, before she left this morning Gina had turned on her answer-phone.

The ringing stopped. The machine clicked and whirred. Then, silence.

He gulped some Dewars and glanced at his watch. Almost 9:30. He should eat something. Gina had told him to help himself to whatever was in the fridge, but he wasn't hungry. He lit a Winston, set it in the ashtray and riffled the keys aimlessly, searching for a melody. But nothing came to him.

He felt utterly drained, numb with grief.

How could he go on living without Vicky?

He took the empty glass into the kitchen, sat down at the table, poured more scotch into the glass and massaged his eyes. Sooner or later the cops would find out he'd gone missing. And then what?

What in bloody hell was he going to do? How would it all end?

He took a coin out of his pocket.

Heads: it would work out. Tails: belly up.

He flipped the coin and slammed it down on the table. Tails.

He flipped the coin again. Tails.

Bollocks! He couldn't win!

The phone rang.

Now who was calling? P'rhaps it was Gina's husband. She hadn't said much about him, but he got the feeling her marriage was in trouble. He went in the living room and stood by the futon, staring at the phone.

It stopped ringing. The machine clicked and whirred.

Was someone speaking on it now? Gina had turned down the volume so he wouldn't be disturbed. *Don't answer the phone*, she'd said. *Let the machine get it.*

Maybe she was afraid her husband would call her. If her marriage was in trouble, it wouldn't do to have a man answer.

He went back in the kitchen, sat at the table and gulped some scotch.

His life was in the toilet. A monstrous feeling of dread overwhelmed him. Would he *ever* get out of this bleeding mess?

He fingered the coin. Tails: he would. Heads: not.

He flipped the coin. Caught it. Slammed it down.

Heads.

Bloody hell! He couldn't win! He was a loser. He'd *always* been a loser.

He poured more scotch into the glass.

––––

Thelma Delaney stood by the phone in her kitchen, trying to decide what to do. Gina had given her an emergency number in case something happened to the house while she was away. Orchid's number. She'd only met Orchid once. What a strange girl! Why on earth did she dye her hair purple?

But she was nice enough. Friendly. Gina's best friend. Should she call the girl? She was probably fussing over nothing. It was hot tonight so she'd opened all her windows, hoping to catch a breeze. That's when she heard all that loud music. But when she called Gina's number, all she got was the machine and Gina's voice saying, "Please leave a message."

When she called again, she got the same message. That worried her.

She went to her front window and looked across the street. It was pitch dark outside. She couldn't see Gina's car, but maybe it was in the garage. And maybe it wasn't. If Gina was there, why didn't she answer the phone?

And if she wasn't, who was pounding on Gina's piano?

She picked up the phone and dialed.

After three rings a voice said, "Orchid's Pots, Orchid speaking."

"Orchid? It's Thelma Delaney, Gina's neighbor?"

"Oh hi, Thelma. How ya doing?"

"I'm fine, but . . . " Thelma sighed. "Well, I was wondering if you talked to Gina today."

"Nope. I've been in Phoenix all week. Why? Is something wrong?"

"I'm not sure. Awhile ago I heard someone playing Gina's piano."

"So? Gina plinks away at it sometimes."

"I know, but this was different. Loud and sort of jazzy, you know? I don't want to seem like a busybody, but I called and Gina didn't answer."

"Maybe she's in the shower or something."

"That's what I thought, but I waited twenty minutes and called again and *still* got her answering machine. Do you think I should go knock on her door?"

"No, don't do that," Orchid said emphatically. "She could be, uhmmm, she could be *involved* in something, you know?"

Thelma smiled. These young ones thought she was an old fuddy-duddy, but she'd had her share of romances. "Yes, Orchid, I know. But it's just that, well, the music was really loud. And jazzy."

"Maybe her husband is there."

Orchid didn't sound too enthusiastic about that. In fact, she really didn't sound like she thought Gina's husband was there. "Maybe you're right," Thelma said, "Maybe they had the stereo on. Ryan's a nice young man. They had a spat a couple of weeks ago, didn't they?"

"What makes you think that?" Orchid said sharply.

"I don't know. Gina seemed a bit down when I talked to her last week."

Orchid chuckled. "Gina's the creative type. That can make for a volatile love life."

"Goodness, I guess I've made a tempest out of a teapot, haven't I? Sorry to bother you."

"No problem, Thelma. Call anytime."

She replaced the phone. There. She felt better.

She worried about Gina sometimes, a lovely girl like that, at odds with her husband. Ryan was a fine young man. Handsome, too.

Thelma poured herself a glass of wine, went in her living room and turned on the TV.

His heart thrummed with excitement as he crept upstairs and slipped into the kitchen. He heard voices on the television set in the living room. He crept to the doorway.

Seated in the wheelchair with her back to him, his mother was watching television in her bathrobe. She hadn't put her hair up in rollers yet. Stringy blonde hair drooped down to her shoulders.

He crept forward, silently inching toward her.

Suddenly, she turned. Eyes wide. Staring. At him.

"Billy! What are you doing?"

Mouth-moving pain in his head.

He swung the wrench.

"Stop!" she shrieked, raising her hands to ward him off.

But she couldn't.

He studied her mouth, her incessantly yapping mouth, making pain in his head. He raised the wrench and smashed it against her teeth. When she opened her mouth to scream, blood spurted out, but no sound.

Again he hit her. Beating. Beating. BEATING!

She groped at the wheels of her wheelchair with both hands, trying to get away.

NO! He couldn't let her escape! He swung the wrench again, beating her mouth and her cold, dead blue eyes.

Her face turned to BLOOD. Sickening. Spurting. Stinking.

Dark red blood gushing everywhere.

She slid out of the wheelchair and slumped to the floor, moaning. Blood matted her hair, dripping onto the rug. In a frenzy, he pounded her face with the wrench. Mouth-moving mother-pain in his head.

At last he stopped, gasping for breath, staring at her. Still.

Mouth still. Mother still. STILL.

His breathing slowed and a shudder ran through his body, as if his own heart had stopped beating.

But then her hand moved. Fluttered to her blood-soaked bathrobe. Hand moving. Slowly. Inching toward the pocket of her bathrobe. Almost.

He slammed the wrench down on her hand. Heard the bones crunch like snapping sticks. Now her hand was still.

What was in the pocket?

He tried to reach it, but her arm was in the way.

He mustn't touch her. Not touch. No.

Grasping the sleeve of her bathrobe between his thumb and forefinger, he lifted her arm away from the pocket. Reached inside. Pulled out a small rectangular piece of paper.

A business card.

He stared at it. Gina Bevilaqua, *Boston Herald* reporter.

Gina Bevilaqua. The woman who'd left the message on Victoria's answering machine.

The reporter who'd come here to interview his mother. The woman who knew the conductor. Nigel Heath. The lucky lottery winner.

The man who had ruined his Victoria victory.
The police thought *Nigel Heath* killed Victoria. Victory-Victoria.
VICTORY was near.
He studied his mother, lying on the floor.
Quiet and still. Face bloody. Eyes shut. Dead eyes.
Not watching.
Not anymore.
He went in the kitchen and washed the blood off his hands.
His clothes stank of blood and sweat. Disgusting.

He went down to his room and took the gun out of the Wagner's Sporting Goods box, feeling the weight and the power, remembering how he'd hit the target at the shooting range. He wrapped the bloody wrench in a towel and put it in his toolbox. Then he took Victoria's diamond ring out of his desk drawer and put it in the top tray of his toolbox.

He studied the business card and felt a delicious thrill of anticipation.
Gina Bevilaqua. Friend of Nigel Heath.
The lucky lottery winner.
But not anymore. Nigel Heath's luck had run out.
All he had to do was find him.

CHAPTER 35

Friday, June 2 — Sandwich

The two-story cottage looked like a picture-postcard, morning sun falling on the bright-blue clapboards and fresh white trim. But inside, Frank knew, was a locked basement room. Billy's room. What dark secrets did it hold?

Earlier he had called the National Cable Company office and asked the manager if Billy was working today. Bad news. Billy had called in. His van wasn't parked outside the house, but that didn't mean he wasn't here.

And what about the Wagner Sporting Goods package? Gina had said it was heavy. If Billy wanted to lift weights, he wouldn't order dumbbells through the mail, he'd buy them at Wal-Mart. It had to be a gun.

Frank wished he had a bigger team to execute the search warrant. What he had was Chief Duggan, a gray-haired man in his sixties, and Officer Pell, another Sandwich policeman, standing with him at the front door. Last week, Duggan had seemed skeptical that a serial killer was living in his sleepy little town. Now that Frank had a search warrant, he was taking it seriously. Still, Frank wondered how long it had been since Duggan had drawn his service weapon. But Officer Pell, a strapping young redhead with a sunburned face, had a determined look in his eyes.

For the third time, Frank pressed the doorbell.

Faint chimes echoed inside the house.

A frown grooved Duggan's forehead. "All the blinds are closed," he muttered. "That's odd. Mrs. Kay should be up by now. She hardly ever goes out, except on Sunday."

Frank said to Pell, "Get the battering ram. We're going in. Chief, I need you to cover the back door, but be careful. Billy may be armed."

Duggan went down the steps and disappeared around the side of the house. Pell ran to his squad car and came back lugging a three-foot piece of steel with two handles. Pell looked at him and Frank nodded.

Pell hit the door with the ram once, twice, three times.

The wood shattered and the door buckled.

Frank went in low and fast, yelling, "Police! Freeze!"

Then the stench of death hit his nostrils.

He looked in the room to the right of the door. Beside an overturned wheelchair, a woman's body lay in a pool of congealed blood, one leg splayed to one side. Blood spatter on the walls, the television screen, the rug, and the woman's bathrobe. Billy's mother, Frank assumed, her face beaten to a pulp.

"Jesus!" Pell said, staring at the carnage. "What a bloodbath!"

"Rage," Frank muttered, eyeing the bloody footprints on the runner in the hall.

The house was silent and still. Was Billy still here? The battering ram had made a helluva racket, and when Frank went inside, he'd yelled: *Police. Freeze.*

Was Billy lying in wait for them with a gun?

Frank signaled Pell to be quiet. Weapons drawn, they advanced down the hall to a wide door at the end.

To the right, an archway opened onto a small kitchen. No one was in there, but Chief Duggan stood at the rear door, motioning to him through the window in the upper half. Frank went to the door, opened it, and whispered, "Bad scene. The mother's dead in the living room."

"Mother of God," Duggan muttered.

Frank shushed him and whispered, "The killer may still be in the house."

They joined Officer Pell in the hallway outside the wide door.

Duggan positioned himself on one side, Pell on the other, and Frank burst inside. A bathroom, empty, no blood visible, nowhere to hide, just an old-fashioned claw-footed tub with handicap bars, a sink and a toilet.

According to Gina, the door opposite the kitchen led to Billy's locked basement room. Frank pointed to the door and whispered, "Billy's room is downstairs." He turned the doorknob and pulled.

The door creaked open, revealing a dark stairway.

"Light switch," Duggan breathed, pointing.

Frank flipped the switch. A bare bulb at the top and another at the bottom illuminated a flight of wooden stairs. Was Billy in his room? Frank waited a moment, heart pounding, hands sweaty on his Sig. No activity below him, no shots, no screams, just a musty odor, and the sound of ragged breathing, Duggan's, Pell's and his own.

With his Sig Sauer extended, Frank eased down the steps one at a time, aware that Duggan and Pell were following. At the foot of the stairs he stopped and listened. Silence. Here the musty odor was stronger.

To his left, a rickety wooden table held a plastic laundry basket and laundry detergent, beyond the table, a fake Christmas tree and boxes of decorations. Under the stairs, plastic shelves held overflow from the kitchen pantry: boxes of cereal, crackers, dry pasta, cans of soup. To his right, a door stood ajar. Dim light emanated from the room. Billy's room.

"Cover me," Frank mouthed to Pell and Duggan.

He slammed open the door and sprang into the room. No one there.

"Clear," he said, and flicked on the overhead light.

Bloody clothes were strewn over a narrow bed. Beside the bed, a fluorescent light shone down on a rectangular fish tank. A mangled orange goldfish lay on the tile floor. Frank read the nametags on the fish tank and felt both revulsion and validation. Lulu. Tessa. Lilly. Betty. Rosie. Florence. Victoria. Ruthie. With slight variations, the names of eight murdered lottery winners. No doubt about it. Billy was the Jackpot Killer.

But another nametag was pasted to the tank: Judy. Who was Judy? Another lottery winner? According to Ross Dunn, Judy Garland was one of the featured women at the Poughkeepsie conference. Then Frank remembered Mrs. Karapitulik's first name. Judith. Billy had killed her, too.

Pell and Duggan entered the room.

"Jesus," Pell said, "look at the blood on those clothes."

"Gotta be Billy's," Duggan muttered as he pulled on latex gloves. "What's with the goldfish, I wonder?"

"He names them after his victims," Frank said.

"Check *this* out." Kneeling beside the bed, Duggan held out a magazine in his gloved hand. "Billy's a Judy Garland freak. She's on half the covers."

Frank put on a pair of latex gloves and took the magazine. It was dated December, 1964. A tag on the front said BOURNE CITY LIBRARY. The librarian was right. Billy had stolen it.

"I better get a forensic team over here," Duggan said, "so we keep control of the scene." He shook his head. "I can't believe Billy beat his mother to death. I wonder where he is."

"I don't know," Frank snapped, "but we need to find him. Put out a BOLO on his van. Alert every patrol car on the Cape. You got any idea where he might go?"

Duggan grimaced. "Not a one."

Frank gestured at the computer on the desk beside the fish tank. "Maybe the computer will tell us."

———

Nigel poured coffee beans into the grinder and pressed the button. The noise rattled through his head like a fortissimo drum roll. Bloody hell, what a hangover! He eyed the nearly-empty bottle of Dewars on the counter. Should he have a pick-me-up? P'rhaps not. He'd had a skinful last night.

The phone rang. Who the bloody hell kept calling?

He'd finally fallen asleep at 4:00 a.m., but the phone had woken him at 8:00. He'd tried to doze, but five minutes later the phone rang again.

Now it was 9:30 and the bloody phone was ringing yet again.

Mercifully, after four rings, it stopped.

He parted the window curtain above the kitchen sink. Bright sunlight bounced off the water and hit his eyes, sending stabbing pains into his head. He poured the coffee grounds into a filter, filled the machine with water and sat down at the table. He was feeling a bit peckish, hadn't eaten anything since yesterday noon.

The memory of his last breakfast with Vicky flashed in his mind. The blueberry scones she'd bought him. Lovely scones. Lovely Vicky.

The sweetest girl in the world.

Tears filled his eyes. How would he live without her?

He massaged his temples, but it didn't ease the pain, the mother of all headaches.

What would happen when his solicitor found out he'd flown the coop?

Merrill Carr was a bloody hypocrite, talking tough to the detectives, then turning on him. Demanding his retainer. Telling him to ante up or he'd land in jail. And the bloody detective was worse. Gerry Mulligan.

The bastard was probably looking for him right now.

The doorbell chimed. His heart shot into his throat.

Good Christ, the coppers were here to haul him in!

———

Dorchester

Gina stood with a group of reporters outside a rundown three-decker. Smelly trash barrels beside the front steps gave off a putrid odor. A dozen police vehicles were parked along the narrow side street. Two hours ago a man had broken into the second-floor apartment and attacked his estranged wife. Neighbors heard her screams and called 9-1-1. When the cops arrived, the man had shot himself.

Now it was 9:30. The woman was dead, and the cops were still inside processing the scene. Like the other three-deckers along the street, this one had a flat roof, a vertical stack of bay windows on one side, and front porches on each floor. Nearby residents had gathered on the opposite sidewalk, talking among themselves.

Gina was in a great mood, but trying not to show it. Considering what happened to the woman, that would be disrespectful. Last night she'd stayed with Franco at his motel. The judge had signed the application for the warrant to search Billy's house, and they had a mini-celebration, take-out pepperoni pizza accompanied by Chianti. She'd been sorely tempted to tell Franco that Nigel was staying at her beach house, but she hadn't.

Why jump the gun? If Franco arrested Billy today, the police might drop the murder charge against Nigel.

"Hey Gina," said a *Boston Globe* reporter, finger-combing his bushy brown hair. "About time you did a series on domestic violence." Gesturing at the house, he said, "Here's your hook."

"I might," she said. "Too many of these guys get pissed off at their wives and kill them."

A chill skittered down her spine. What would Ryan do when he came home to an empty house at four o'clock? Ryan had an explosive temper, and he could be unpredictable. What if he went to the beach house to see if she was there?

Unwilling to think about it, she left the group of reporters and went over to a cluster of women on the opposite sidewalk. A middle-aged white woman with a pinched look on her face stood to one side by herself. "Excuse me," Gina said to her. "Did you know the woman that was murdered?"

"Knew her well enough to know she had big problems with that asshole." The woman's mouth quirked in disdain. "Before she threw him out, I'd hear them fighting all the time."

"Just yelling? Or did he hit her?"

"A lotta yelling and screaming. Gave her a black eye once."

"Could I have your name?" Gina said. "So I can quote you? I write for the *Herald*."

"Jesus, no! I'm hiding from my ex-boyfriend. He finds out I'm living in Dorchester, he'll track me down and hurt me!"

Gina touched the woman's arm. "Okay. I'm sorry for your trouble."

She spotted two police officers leaving the three-decker and ran back to join the other reporters. Both officers appeared shaken: faces drawn, lips set in grim lines, eyes squinty. As the TV crews filmed them for the noon news, reporters yelled questions. But the officers gave them a curt *No Comment* and headed for their squad cars. She recognized one officer and ran after him.

"Tom! Gina Bevilaqua! You got anything for me?" Three years ago when Tom was working homicides in the Mission Hill area, he'd given her some choice quotes.

"Hi, Gina," he said, and kept moving.

Running to keep up, she said, "What's it like in there?"

He reached his squad car and opened the door. "Ugly. He must have stabbed her thirty times, mostly in the face and chest. She didn't have a chance. The guy weighed two hundred pounds. Then he put a gun under his chin and blew off the top of his head. Blood everywhere."

"Can you give me a name?"

"Negative. Not until we notify the next of kin." Tom swung into the driver's seat, looked up at her and winked. "Now I'm gonna go get me a Big Mac with lotsa ketchup. Wanna come?"

She laughed. "Tom, you are so baaad."

"Good to see you, Gina. What I said is off the record."

She gave him a thumbs up. "Thanks, Tom. No names, I promise."

She got in her Mazda, scribbled notes in her steno pad, sat for a moment to compose the lead and called the *Herald* copy desk. She dictated her story, including the details she'd obtained from "a source close to the investigation."

Within the hour, her story would go up on the *Herald* website as a Breaking News Item. She checked the time. 9:55. Franco had to have gotten into Billy's house by now. When they'd left his motel at 7:30, he was driving directly to Sandwich. On her way to work she'd caught the domestic violence call on her police scanner and had driven straight to the scene.

Why hadn't Franco called? Another chill prickled her neck. She hadn't forgotten the odd look in Mrs. Kay's eyes when she asked for her card. Or the Wagner's Sporting Goods package. What if Billy had a gun?

What if he shot Franco?

If anything happened to Franco, she didn't know what she would do.

She tried to think positive. Maybe he had found enough incriminating evidence to arrest Billy. Maybe he was with the Sandwich police right now, taking Billy into custody. She pulled away from the curb, drove two blocks, turned onto the main road and stopped at a traffic light.

Given Nigel's need to talk, she was surprised he hadn't called her. Last night on the news, Gerry had issued a statement about the arrest warrant and his inability to locate Nigel Heath. Yesterday Nigel had said he didn't want to watch television, so maybe he hadn't seen it.

But maybe he had. She didn't want to talk to him while she was driving, didn't want to talk to her editor, either. She took her cell out of her purse and shut it off. If Franco called, he would leave a message.

When the light changed, she entered a rotary and took the entrance to the Expressway headed south. Now that she'd filed her murder-suicide story, why rush back to the office?

It would take fifteen minutes to get to her beach house. By then Franco would probably have called her with the good news about Billy.

When she got to the house, she could tell Nigel and put his mind at ease.

—

CHAPTER 36

The doorbell chimed again.

The sound sent pain rocketing into his head. Bloody hell, how could he talk to the cops when he had a vicious hangover? His mouth was dry as toast, his stomach was queasy, and his head was fuzzy.

He went in the living room and crept to the front window. Dreading what he would see, he parted the curtain and let out a sigh of relief.

A stocky bloke with a thatch of blond hair stood outside the door, holding a toolbox. He had on a blue uniform shirt, but not the sort the police officers wore, no gun strapped to his belt.

Who was he? Gina's husband? Bit short for her, if he was. Young, too.

The bell chimed insistently.

A sense of foreboding made him hesitate.

Gina hadn't said she was expecting any visitors. Trying to quell his trepidation, he cautiously approached the door. Should he open it?

The doorbell clanged again.

He took a deep breath and opened the door. "Help you?" he said.

The man smiled at him, looked like a cherub with his round face and chubby pink cheeks.

"I'm the cable man. I'm here to repair the cable box." Maintaining his smile, the man stared up at him.

There was something unnerving about his implacable gaze. Was that a hint of recognition in those blue eyes?

Bloody hell, did the bloke know he was hiding from the cops? Lord knows his picture had been all over the telly for the last two weeks.

"D'you have some identification?"

The man's eyes flickered and his smile disappeared. He pointed to the pocket of his uniform shirt and said, "My customers know me."

Nigel studied the name on the pocket. John. He hesitated, undecided.

He didn't want to let anyone in the house, but he didn't want to interfere with Gina's cable repair. She hadn't mentioned it, but maybe she'd forgotten.

He opened the screen door, let the man into the living room and shut the door. "What's wrong with the telly?" he said.

The man didn't answer, just walked past Gina's piano and set his toolbox down on the rug in front of the telly.

What was wrong with the bloke? Why didn't he answer?

The man knelt down, opened the toolbox, took something out and rose to his feet. It looked like a gun.

Bloody hell, it *was* a gun!

His heart thumped his ribs. He let out a nervous laugh. "I say, old boy, you're full of surprises. That's quite a little pop gun you've got there."

"Don't call me little!" The man's eyes hardened into blue agates. "That's what you *always* said. Be a big boy like John, you said."

What in bloody hell was he talking about? "Look here, I think you've made a mistake—"

"I don't make mistakes. Sit down over there." Holding the gun with his right hand, the man wiped sweat off his forehead with his left. Ugly scabs disfigured his hands. Did the bloke have some kind of illness?

And why was he pointing that gun at him?

Nigel carefully lowered himself onto the futon and sat very still.

"Where's Gina Bevilaqua?"

"She's not here. She had to go—" Wait. Don't tell him anything.

How did he know Gina? Who *was* this lunatic?

The phone rang.

"Don't answer it!" the lunatic screamed.

The ringing telephone seemed to send him into a frenzy, pacing back and forth, agitated, aiming the gun at him. "Sit there and don't move."

"Not to worry," he said, to humor him. "The machine is on."

For some reason that reminded him of the answer-phone in Vicky's living room. His beloved Vicky. But he couldn't think about that now, not while this lunatic was aiming a gun on him.

And who the bloody hell kept calling? Was it Gina? Her husband? *Who?*

Keeping the gun trained on him, the lunatic backed up until he reached his toolbox. Then he bent down and took out a long-handled wrench. What the hell was the bastard up to?

Then he saw the stains on the wrench.

Ugly brown stains that looked like blood.

"Look here, be a good chap and tell me what you want. I haven't much money, but you can take—"

"You've got plenty of money!"

"I don't!" Bloody Christ, who was this lunatic?

"Yes you do. Don't lie to me!" His blue eyes blazed with fury. "*You* won the lottery, not Victoria." The man lowered his left hand, the hand with the wrench, and scratched it. Then he paced the room, the gun in one hand, the wrench in the other, staring at him, his eyes glittering with malice.

"You tried to fool me, but you can't."

Nigel sat very still, thoughts flitting through his mind like furry gray bats. Was this some friend of Vicky's who wanted to punish him?

"Look here," he said, "I gave the ticket to Vicky—"

"*Victoria*." The man smiled, an evil smile, frightening to behold. "You tried to trick me, but you couldn't. I know you won the lottery. That's why I have to *kill you*."

Kill you. Nigel flinched. This lunatic was going to kill him.

The lunatic marched to his toolbox, took out a small white envelope and came back, standing five feet away now. Close enough for Nigel to smell his rank body odor. Then he took something out of the envelope.

"See this?" he said, and smiled his evil lunatic-smile.

Nigel stared in disbelief. Bloody hell, *Vicky's diamond ring!*

He felt like a giant hand had crushed him. His throat heaved in a convulsive swallow. He tried to take a breath but couldn't, lungs constricted, heart pounding. Bloody hell, was he having a heart attack?

"You?" he gasped, his heart raging in his chest. "*You* killed Vicky??"

It was too monstrous to comprehend.

"Why? Why did you have to kill Vicky? She never did anything to you. She was a dear sweet—"

"I thought *she* won the lottery. Winners are lucky. Lucky winners get punished." The lunatic smiled. Droplets of blood oozed from the cracked skin on the knuckles of his right hand, the hand with the gun. "John was a winner, too, and he got punished. He got exactly what he deserved."

Frozen with fear, mesmerized by the crazed look in the man's eyes, Nigel took shallow breaths, his calming pre-concert routine. But this was infinitely more terrifying than playing a piano solo.

"You tried to make me think Victoria won, but she didn't. *You* won, and you're going to pay."

"I've already paid," Nigel moaned. "Vicky's dead."

Overcome with despair, he buried his face in his hands. It was his fault. He *deserved* to die. He'd let his mother down, let his father down, too. He was a loser. A failed soloist. A wretched gambler. Bloody Christ, he'd won twelve million dollars and he was *still* a loser. Vicky was dead. Murdered.

He raised his head and looked at the blond man with the round face and the glittering blue eyes.

The bastard was right. It was his fault Vicky was dead and he wanted to die, too. What did he have to live for?

———

"Ross!" Frank said into his cell phone. "I'm at the Sandwich suspect's house with two local police officers. Billy Karapitulik murdered his mother."

"Jesus, when?" Ross said.

"Last night or early this morning, hard to tell. No sign of the suspect."

"Gotta be our guy. I'll hop on a plane and get there as soon as I can. Any idea where he is?"

Frank glanced at Chief Duggan, who was listening to his end of the conversation. Officer Pell was upstairs, securing the scene. "No. The police chief put out a BOLO on Billy's vehicle. He's got a computer, but it's password protected. If I can get into it, maybe I can figure out what he'll do next. Are there any FBI agents nearby that could hack into it?"

"Closest office is in Boston," Ross said, "might take awhile to get there. I'm no computer whiz, but try this. Type in "administrator" for the username. Don't enter a password, just hit Enter. That might do it."

Frank did what Ross said, hit Enter and held his breath.

The computer whirred and the Windows desktop appeared.

"Ross," he said, "I'm in. Hold on."

Chief Duggan came over and stood behind him. "What have you got?"

Frank clicked the Libraries icon, then Documents, and saw three folders: one labeled RESUMES, one labeled JUDY, another labeled WINNERS. He clicked on the WINNERS folder and studied the files.

Behind him, Duggan said, "Looks like the file names are in code."

"Right," Frank said, "but the numbers might be dates."

"What's going on?" Ross said impatiently, clearly frustrated that he was miles away and out of the loop.

"I'm opening the first file," Frank told him. "F-dash-4-dash-25." He waited until the Word document opened. "It's the Chatham victim. Florence, murdered April 25. The files are coded."

"What about the Nashua lotto winner?" Ross asked. "Ruth Bennett."

He scrolled down to a file labeled R-5-23 and opened it.

"Got it, Ross. Ruth Bennett, murdered May 23rd. Hold on a second while I see if there's a file that starts with V for Vicky." He hit the scroll bar and saw V-5-15.

"Got it. Vicky was murdered May 15th." He clicked on the file.

A Word document opened: *Victoria Stavropoulos. $12 million. Megabucks. Boston, MA.*

Duggan let out a low whistle. "Unbelievable. He kept a file on all of his victims."

Frank scanned the document and his heart sank. *Nigel Heath = real winner.* The next line made his stomach turn over. *Reporter.*

Jesus! Did Billy's mother tell him about Gina?

"Ross! Billy found out Nigel Heath bought the winning ticket. He might go after him next. I need to warn Nigel and the reporter that talked to Billy's mother."

"Do it and call me back," Ross said. "I'm heading for the airport."

Frank ended the call and wiped sweat off his forehead, planning his moves. If he didn't hurry, Nigel might die. No sense calling his hotel. Nigel wasn't there. No sense calling Gerry Mulligan, either. Mulligan had no clue where Nigel was. But Gina might.

He dialed her cell phone and waited, willing her to answer. After four rings her voicemail came on: "Sorry I can't take your call right now. Please leave—"

He clicked off, punched in the number for the *Herald*, then Gina's extension and waited, his palms sweaty on the phone. He got her voicemail and hung up. Where the hell was she?

He redialed the main number for the *Herald* and waited through five rings, fists clenched.

Finally a woman's voice said, "*Boston Herald*, how may I assist you?"

"This is Detective Renzi, Boston PD. I need to speak to Gina Bevilaqua immediately. I just called her extension and got her voicemail. Can I speak to her editor?"

"Certainly, sir. She might be covering that murder-suicide in Dorchester. Hold on."

Frazzled, he glanced at Chief Duggan, who had resumed bagging and tagging the magazines he'd found under Billy's bed.

After an eternity, a voice said, "Dirk Marshal, Metro editor."

"This is Detective Frank Renzi, Boston PD. I need to talk to Gina Bevilaqua ASAP. Do you know where she is?"

"She was covering a murder-suicide in Dorchester this morning, called the copy desk awhile ago and filed her story. She should be back soon."

"Okay, thanks." Cursing silently, he clicked off.

Gina had already called in the murder-suicide story. Why wasn't she back in her office? He wiped sweaty hands on his pants, considering possibilities. She decided to eat lunch before she went back to the office. She was at her house in Westwood. Neither possibility seemed plausible.

His gut was telling him that Nigel was at her beach house. He jumped up and headed for the stairs. "Chief, I think Billy might be headed into Boston, looking for Nigel Heath. Alert your patrols."

He raced upstairs, jumped in his squad car and cranked the engine. Before he peeled out, he punched in the number for Gina's landline at the beach house, but after four rings, he got her voicemail.

Damn! If Nigel was there, why the hell didn't he answer? If Billy found him, he'd kill him. Then a more devastating possibility rocked him.

What if Gina was already at the beach house?

———

Gina lowered the car window, inhaled the salt sea air and stifled a yawn. She wanted to sleep for a week. Yesterday she'd crawled out of bed at 4:30 and, despite her fears, smuggled Nigel out of his hotel. Good thing. Scant hours later, Gerry Mulligan had gone there to arrest him. But Franco now believed the Jackpot Killer had murdered Vicky, not Nigel. Not only that, Franco seemed certain Billy was the Jackpot Killer.

She smiled, imagining the celebration they would have once Franco arrested Billy. They'd go out for drinks and dinner. After Franco told her about capturing Billy, she'd tell him about smuggling Nigel out of the hotel in the trunk of her car. Franco was sure to get a laugh out of it.

Squinting against the glare of the sun, she pulled into her driveway, parked in front of the garage and studied the house. All the curtains were closed. Good. Nigel had heeded her warning to stay out of sight.

She stifled another yawn. More than anything in the world, she wanted to sneak up the secret staircase to her bedroom and take a powernap. But Nigel was here, and he would want to talk.

When she got out of the car, an ocean breeze ruffled her hair. She glanced across the street. No sign of Thelma, thank goodness, but the sun was merciless, beating down on the driveway. She decided to put the car in the garage so that it wouldn't be a blast furnace when she drove back to work.

———

Unable to control his excitement, Billy paced the room, gleefully watching his lucky winner. Nigel Heath sat on the futon, slumped forward, his face in his hands. His lucky winner was beaten. BEATEN. Victory was near. The thought exhilarated him, made his whole body tremble. Soon the cops would know who killed Victoria and so would everyone else.

He looked at the gun, remembering the loud bang it had made at the shooting range. But that wasn't the worst part.

When he shot his lucky winner there would be blood.

If only he didn't have to look at the blood.

He pictured the blood gushing from his mother's mouth. Mouth-mother making pain—

He heard a sound and cocked his head, listening.

Nigel raised his head, his face twisted in a look of . . . what? Fear?

No. Not fear. His lucky winner's face was frozen in a look of horror.

More sounds, coming from the kitchen. The back door.

Someone was coming!

His heart jolted. Was it the police?

Then he thought, *No. Gina Bevilaqua.*

The woman whose name was on the cable television account.

236

The woman who owned the house.

The reporter who'd come to his house asking questions.

Friend of Nigel Heath.

He stepped closer to Nigel, close enough to see beads of sweat on his lucky winner's face.

Close enough to touch his head with the gun.

"Be quiet," he hissed, "or I will KILL you!"

He heard a door open, then footsteps.

His heart beat a frenzy of excitement.

Beating. BEATING.

CHAPTER 37

She unlocked the door and stepped into the kitchen. "Nigel?" she called.

No answer. Puzzled, she went to the doorway of the living room.

Seated on the futon, Nigel looked at her, eyes bloodshot, his face ashen. Standing beside him, a short blond man held a gun to his head.

She felt like she'd been kicked in the stomach. She clamped a hand over her mouth to keep from screaming.

The room was utterly still.

"Sit over there beside Nigel," the man said.

Fear blossomed inside her like a mushroom cloud. She stood there, panic-stricken, unable to move.

"Do what I tell you!" the man screamed.

She stared at him, trying to make sense of what was happening. Then it dawned on her. The man with the gun was Billy. But how could it be? Franco was supposed to arrest him today. Her heart slammed her chest.

Did Billy shoot Franco? Tears flooded her eyes, blurring her vision.

What if Franco was dead? The thought crushed her.

The shrill sound of the telephone made her jerk convulsively.

"Don't answer it!" Billy screamed, wild-eyed, waving the gun.

"Look here," Nigel said, "she got several phone calls last night and several more this morning. Why not be a good chap and let her answer it?"

Phone calls last night? Who had called her? Not Franco. She'd been with him at his motel. But forget phone calls. What about the gun? It looked like some kind of semi-automatic, dull-black and deadly-looking.

And Billy's finger was on the trigger.

The phone kept ringing, a piercing sound that filled the room.

Was it Franco? Maybe he wasn't dead. But why would he call the landline at her beach house? He didn't know Nigel was here.

She had no idea what had happened in Sandwich, but one thing was clear. Now Billy was here, and he had a gun.

Chills radiated through her body. She tried to calm herself. The phone was on the end table beside the futon. Maybe it *was* Franco calling. Maybe she could grab the phone and warn him.

She edged forward, inching closer to the futon.

Billy's face contorted with fury. "Don't answer it!" he screamed, gesturing with the gun, his eyes glittering like blue agates. "Sit beside Nigel."

Nigel shook his head, warning her not to. He was right. If she did, they'd be sitting together like ducks in a shooting gallery. Easy targets for Billy.

She edged away from the futon, inching toward the staircase to her right.

The phone stopped ringing.

Her answering machine clicked and whirred. Silence.

Tears blurred her vision. It didn't matter who called. No one could help them now. The room was so quiet she could almost hear her heart beating against her ribs. She looked at the man with the gun.

"Billy," she whispered.

He smiled, an evil smile, cruel and vindictive. "My mother told you about me, right?"

Gripping her leather purse with both hands, she shrank back, too terrified to speak.

"I know you talked to her. She told me you were there."

"Where?" Nigel sat up straighter on the futon, staring at her intently.

"Billy lives in Sandwich," Gina said. "With his mother." She took a deep shuddering breath. "How's your mother, Billy? Is your mother all right?"

He bared his teeth, a grotesque imitation of a smile, his blue eyes cold as death. "My mother's fine. Fine and dandy."

"Billy," Nigel said, "be a good chap and put the gun down so we can—"

"Shut up!" Billy turned and aimed the gun at Nigel's head. "Why did you always make fun of me? What kind of a father are you?"

Nigel frowned. "Look here, I'm not your father—"

"*Don't say that!*" Billy's face turned crimson. His hands trembled as he stepped closer to Nigel. Now the gun was inches away from Nigel's head.

Her heart was a sledgehammer beating her chest. If she didn't do something, Billy would shoot Nigel.

Her purse. She'd throw it at him. Wait. Her cell phone was in it. While Billy concentrated on Nigel, she slipped her hand into her purse, eased out her cell phone and held it behind her back.

"Nigel," she said. "Billy killed Vicky."

"No," Nigel said in a low voice. "He didn't kill Vicky. I'm the one that killed her."

Billy's face contorted in rage. "*You did not!* I killed Victoria! She tried to stop me but she couldn't. No one can stop me! The cops think *you* killed Victoria, but I'm going fix that. I'm going to kill you. Then those stupid cops will know who's got the power."

Rivulets of sweat ran down Billy's forehead and his flaming red cheeks. He turned to her and smiled, a smile more terrifying than his wild rant. "I'm going to fix you, too."

Her legs turned to jelly. He was going to kill them. She gripped the cell phone in her sweaty hand. Could she dial 9-1-1? Would anyone get here in time to save them? If Billy realized she had a cell phone, he might shoot her. And then she remembered. After she left the Dorchester murder scene, she'd shut off her cell phone. Damn!

She felt for the On-button with her finger, but kept her eyes on Billy. Now he was backing away from Nigel. He stopped at a toolbox on the floor near her television set. She hadn't noticed the toolbox before. She'd been too focused on Nigel and Billy. And the gun.

Billy reached into the toolbox and took out two nip bottles of J&B.

She recoiled in horror.

"No," she whispered.

———

Frantic with worry, Frank raced up Route 3 toward Quincy, lights flashing, siren wailing. Gripping the wheel in his left hand, he dialed 9-1-1.

"Duxbury police, what is your emergency?" said a woman's voice.

"This is Detective Frank Renzi, Boston PD. I need to talk to the Quincy police ASAP. It's an emergency. There's a hostage situation at a beach house in Squantum. Can you patch me through?"

"Right away, sir. One moment."

Willing her to hurry, he whipped around a black SUV and accelerated to ninety, whizzing past slower-moving vehicles.

"Quincy police, what is your emergency?" the dispatcher said.

"Detective Frank Renzi, Boston PD. I just executed a search warrant at a murder suspect's house in Sandwich. We found his mother dead. The suspect killed her. The Sandwich police chief will verify this. The suspect wasn't there. We believe he's going to a beach-front cottage in Squantum."

"I'll send an officer right away. Do you know the address?"

Frank gave her the address and said, "The suspect is armed and you may not have much time. We don't know how long ago he left the house in Sandwich. Call Chief Duggan, he'll give you the make and model of the suspect's vehicle."

"Yes, sir, Detective Renzi. I'll alert Captain Abbott right away."

Frank stomped the accelerator. The needle on the speedometer hit one hundred, trees along the roadside whipping past in blurred images.

Moments later he passed a sign: QUINCY, 30 MILES

He'd be there in fifteen minutes. But that might not be soon enough.

———

Gina thought her heart would stop. J&B nips. She knew what that meant. The Jackpot Killer planted them on the lottery winners he murdered. Her stomach clenched, a painful knot.

Billy set the two J&B nips on the coffee table in front of the futon and looked at her, a terrifying image: hair matted with sweat, cheeks mottled red, a crazed look in his eyes. Worst of all, his hands gripped the gun.

"Don't," she whispered.

Smiling his terrible smile, Billy said, "I'm going to make sure the cops know who killed Victoria."

She looked at Nigel, but Nigel wasn't looking at her.

Leaning forward on the futon, Nigel was staring at Billy. Anger had transformed Nigel's usual genial expression. Now his face bore a look of fury: jaw clenched, lips thinned in a line, eyes cold with anger.

"Run, Vicky! Run away!" Nigel yelled. Then he leaped off the futon and lunged at Billy.

"Nigel!" she screamed.

The gun went off, a deafening roar.

Too terrified to move, she watched Nigel grapple with Billy, both of them grunting as they lay tangled together on the floor, flailing at each other, fighting for control of the gun.

Nigel's face contorted and blood spurted from his mouth. But his eyes remained fixed on Billy.

She heard a shrill sound, someone screaming, and realized it was her.

Nigel slammed his fist against Billy's head, rolled on top of him and wrapped his hands around the gun. Bright red blood gushed from his mouth.

"Get off me!" Billy screamed. "You're bleeding all over me!"

She had to do something. Call for help! She tried to open her cell, but her hands were shaking, slick with sweat.

Now Billy's hands were on Nigel's hands, clamped around the gun.

Another shot sounded.

Nigel's head jerked back. Blood spurted from his neck.

"Vicky," he moaned.

"Get off me!" Billy screamed.

Horror-stricken, she watched him try to push Nigel away. But Nigel was too heavy, slumped on top of him. Seconds later Billy squirmed out from under Nigel's lifeless body, his face streaked with Nigel's blood.

Holding the gun in his right hand, he swiped at the blood with his left.

Gasping for breath, he struggled to his knees and looked at her. His blood-streaked face looked like some hideous character in a horror film, but the look in his eyes was worse, crazed with rage and hate.

He was going to kill her! She had to get away!

But Billy stood between her and the front door, and she didn't dare turn her back to run in the kitchen.

Clutching her cell phone in one hand, she threw her leather purse at him, whirled and bolted up the stairs.

"Stop," he screamed. Then he shot at her.

The gunshot was loud, terrifying, but the shot went wide and missed her, slamming into the wall below her.

Panting, she reached the second-floor landing and bolted down the dark hallway. Her bedroom was at the far end. If she could just make it to her bedroom . . .

She heard sounds behind her. Billy's footsteps on the stairs.

Driven by desperation, she sprinted to her bedroom, went inside and shut the door. But she couldn't lock it. None of the bedroom doors had locks. She ran to the window beside her bed. Should she climb out the window onto the widow's walk? Then she'd be trapped.

If he came to the window with the gun, she'd have to jump. Even if she didn't break her leg, he could still shoot her.

"I'll kill you!" Billy's distant voice, shrill with rage and hate.

Her heart jackknifed into her throat. She was trapped.

She couldn't breath, couldn't think.

Frantic, she yanked open the closet door, shoved aside three pairs of slacks and plunged inside. Gasping for air, lightheaded and woozy, she tried to catch her breath but couldn't, her heart racing out of control.

The hidden stairway to the pantry was her only refuge. She gripped the small black knob on the plywood door with one hand and yanked.

The door didn't budge. Damn! It had been years since anyone used it.

"Where are you? I know you're up here!" Billy's voice. Closer.

Half-sobbing, she grabbed the small knob in her sweaty fingers and yanked again. Again, it didn't budge.

She jammed her cell into the waistband of her pants, took the knob in both hands yanked again. The plywood door creaked open. Musty air seeped into the closet from a dark narrow stairway.

"I'll find you, and when I do, you'll be sorry."

She redistributed her slacks on the clothes rod and hurriedly pulled the closet door shut. Her body trembled, rocked with icy chills. She squeezed through the narrow opening onto the hidden staircase. Crept down one step, then another, and pushed the plywood door shut.

The darkness was complete. Silence, except for her ragged breathing. She was panting as though she'd just run a mile in record time. Hugging herself, she took a series of short breaths, inhaling the musty air.

Ugly images flooded her mind. Nigel. Blood gushing from his mouth.

Her eyes brimmed with tears. If she didn't call for help, Nigel would die.

And if Billy found her, she would die too.

"You can't escape. I'm going to kill you." Billy's faint voice filtered through the closet door into the hidden stairway.

She opened her cell, about to dial 9-1-1, when the phone rang. Within the enclosed space, the sound was so loud it scared her. She punched on to silence it.

"Help," she whispered.

"Gina? Is that you? Where are you?"

Franco's voice. The most beautiful sound she'd ever heard in her life. Franco wasn't dead, he was alive!

"Beach house," she whispered. "Billy shot Nigel. Now he's after me."

"Where are you? Are you safe?"

"Hidden stairway," she breathed, hoping Franco would remember. She'd showed it to him once, but that was years ago.

"Gina, the Quincy cops are on their way, and I'll be there soon. I'm on Route 3. I need to hang up so I can get a SWAT team over there."

"Send help for Nigel," she whispered.

"I will. Set your phone to vibrate. Call you back after I talk to the cops."

"Hurry," she whispered.

CHAPTER 38

Sweating and out of breath, one hand clamped on the gun, the other gripping the wrench, he stood at the top of the stairs, listening.

In the silence he felt his heart beating inside his chest. BEATING.

"I know you're up here," he screamed. "You can't escape. I'm going to get you."

This part of the hall was dark, but at the far end, sunlight spilled through a small round window onto the wood floor. He took a step forward. Stopped when the floorboard creaked under his foot. Quiet. He had to be quiet and sneak up on her. As his eyes adjusted to the gloom he saw three doors along the hall ahead of him, two on the left, one at the far end on the right.

But no reporter. Where was she?

Two quick silent steps got him to the first room on the left. The door was open. He tiptoed inside, blinking at the sunlight streaming in the window. The window was shut and the room was hot and stuffy. Sweat dripped down his face. Sweat and blood. Nigel Heath's blood. His lucky winner.

This appeared to be a child's room, decorated with cutesy nautical posters. To his left, a set of bunk beds stood against the wall, with navy-blue bedspreads tucked over them. He got down on his knees and looked under the lower bunk. She wasn't there. He went to the closet and opened the door. No clothes, just wire hangers bunched together along a wooden dowel.

At the foot of the bunk beds was a wooden toy box, its lid open. Inside, a red-and-white beach ball sat on top of a red plastic beach pail. When he was a kid living in Kentucky, he never got to go to the beach. His father made him play baseball and soccer. John excelled at both sports.

Big brother John was always the star. On weekends his father would take them to the soccer field. To practice, his father said. A lie.

His father did it to humiliate him.

He stared at the red-and-white beach ball, hearing his father say, "Okay, you little runt. Let's see you get the ball." When his father threw the ball, he ran after it as fast as he could, ran so hard he thought his heart would burst. But John could run faster. He'd race past him, smirking, and yell, "The little runt loses again." Laughing at him when he cried.

He stared at the beach ball, the rage a living thing inside him.

He set the gun on the lower bunk bed and gripped the wrench with both hands. Felt his heart beating. BEATING.

He raised the wrench over his head and slammed it down on the beach ball with all his might. BLAM!

The ball popped and crumpled into a red-and-white piece of plastic.

When he found the reporter, he'd bash her head, too, and watch it explode. But then there would be blood.

He could still see the blood on his mother's face, and Nigel's, gushing onto his face as they fought for the gun. But he had beaten him, and now his lucky winner was dead. He slid the wrench into the pocket of his overalls, picked up the gun and returned to the hall.

Holding the gun in both hands the way the cops did on TV, he extended his arms and advanced down the hall. The second door on the left was open, too. His heart beat faster. Was she in there?

Gina Bevilaqua. Nigel's friend. The reporter who'd come to his house. The one who told his mother that Nigel was the lucky winner, not Victoria.

But today Nigel's luck had run out.

So had his mother's. He'd beaten both of them.

When he found the reporter, he'd beat her, too.

His heart thrummed in anticipation as he tiptoed into the room and looked around. Where was she?

This room was hot and stuffy, too. The only window was closed. Pale yellow bedspreads covered two single beds. A maple bureau stood between them. A duffle bag sat on the floor beside the bureau. Holding the gun in one hand, he got down on his knees and looked under both beds.

Nothing but dust balls.

He studied the door on the opposite wall, another closet, probably. Maybe she was in there. He tiptoed to the door and whipped it open.

It was a closet, but the reporter wasn't in there, just two polo shirts and a pair of trousers draped on wire hangers. Men's shirts and trousers.

He smiled. The reporter must be hiding in the room across the hall. She couldn't escape him now. He was going to find her and make her pay.

His heart beat faster, pounding his chest. Beating. BEATING.

―――

Three steps down from the plywood door inside her clothes closet, Gina sat hunched over on a stair. She felt sick to her stomach, breathing in shallow gasps, clutching her cell phone, her lifeline to Franco, agonizing over her decision to run upstairs, remembering Nigel's words. *"Run, Vicky. Run away!"*

Lost in his own private hell, Nigel had called her Vicky by mistake.

Tears flooded her eyes. Maybe it wasn't a mistake.

Thank you Gina. Someday I'll make it up to you. Nigel, thanking her yesterday for hiding him at her house.

Nigel had attacked Billy so she could escape. Nigel was convinced that he had caused Vicky's death, guilt-ridden because he'd asked her to claim the Megabucks prize. Maybe this was Nigel's way of redeeming himself. He didn't want another woman's murder on his hands.

Her stomach cramped. Was Nigel dead, or alive?

After Billy shot him blood had gushed out of Nigel's mouth.

Franco had said he would send an ambulance. If the medics got here soon, maybe they could save him.

A loud popping sound startled her. It didn't sound like a gunshot.

What was it? It had to be Billy.

Shivering in the darkness, she held her breath and listened.

Another sound, louder and closer. Was Billy in her bedroom?

Please don't look in the closet. If Billy looked in the closet, he might notice the plywood door to the hidden staircase.

If he opened the plywood door, he would see her and kill her.

She eased the cell phone—her lifeline to Franco—into her pocket. Bracing both hands on the staircase, she inched down one step, then another.

Please, Franco. Call me back and tell me you're here.

———

Billy stood outside the door at the end of the hall. Unlike the other two, this door was closed. For some reason, it reminded him of that stupid game show his mother always watched. *Let's Make a Deal.*

What's behind Door Number Three?

He smiled. The reporter. She had to be in there.

Now he would find her and make her wish she'd never been born.

Holding the gun in his right hand, he opened the door with his left and tiptoed inside. The first thing he saw was a rose-colored brocade suitcase, the kind a woman would buy, standing upright beside a double bed.

It had to be hers. His heart thrummed his chest. He had her now.

The bed was neatly made, draped with a maroon comforter.

Was she under the bed, quaking in terror, like a cornered mouse?

Bright sunlight poured through two tall windows on either side of the bed and two smaller windows on the opposite wall. The glare hurt his eyes, sent pains rocketing into his head. No curtains or shades on the windows, and all of them were closed. No wonder the room was sweltering.

In one swift motion, he whipped the maroon comforter up onto the bed, got down on his knees and looked. She wasn't there.

Where could she be? She couldn't have slipped past him in the hallway. He would have heard her.

"Gee-na," he called. "Where are you?"

Squinting against the glare of the sun, he went to the window to the left of the bed. Outside the window was a narrow porch with a low white railing. Beyond the railing he could see the ocean, calm and green. Inviting. But he wasn't planning on going for a swim.

He was going to find Gina Bevilaqua, the reporter who'd come to his house, uninvited, and planted ideas in his mother's head. When he found her, he'd beat her, too. BEAT her to death.

A fierce ache pounded his temples. The key to revenge was patience. It might take a lifetime, but if you had enough patience—and he did—you could even the score. All his life people had mocked him, the kids in school, his teachers, his bosses. After a while he got used to their insults, but he stored them away in his memory, fueling his fury.

Every day he took the crap they dished out and smiled at them. Every night, he lay awake in bed, thinking about ways to punish them.

Some had already paid for their cruelty. Look what happened to John. Ever since he could remember, he'd hated his brother. John had dark hair and dark eyes like his father. John excelled at everything, schoolwork, sports, you name it. That's why Father loved him. He hated his father, too, always mocking him, saying he was weak and little. A sissy.

But Father had mocked him once too often.

His heart fluttered in his chest. That was Father's downfall, and John's. Both of them had died in the accident. He was glad.

He hated John and he hated his father.

Most of all, he hated his mother. Always gloating at his failures.

Mouth always moving, making pain in his head.

A certain wily intelligence lurked behind her narrow pinched face, an ever-present danger that warranted extreme caution. Like a downed electrical wire, sparking as it lay on the ground, vicious words spewed from her mouth incessantly, killing him with a thousand cuts. But when she grew quiet, it was worse. That's when he feared her the most. Her stillness was a deadly force.

When that happened he wouldn't look at her. If she saw fear in his eyes, it might trigger the fury within her, bubbling under the surface. Then she would set upon him with her taunts, humiliating him.

But not anymore. He'd seen to that.

A loud sound captured his attention. It sounded like a car door. No, several car doors, slamming shut one after another.

He went to a window on the opposite wall and looked out.

His heart spasmed in fear, skyrocketing into his throat.

An army of cops clustered around a half-dozen police cars, some in uniform, others not. Most wore pale-green fluorescent vests and sturdy shoes and wide belts with extra ammo and other police gear. Some brandished handguns. Others carried rifles.

But so what?

If they thought they were going to stop him from killing the reporter, they were wrong. Dead wrong.

He moved away from the window, felt the mouth-mother pain in his head. Already he could imagine the spiteful things they were saying about him, relishing his humiliation now that they had him cornered.

But he'd show them.

The reporter was inside the house and he was going to find her.

When he did, he would kill her. The cops had no way to stop him.

———

Frank whipped around the corner onto Gina's street and breathed a sigh of relief. The Quincy police had blocked off the street with sawhorses. An ambulance stood inside the barrier, its motor idling. Beyond it, police officers stood outside a half-dozen police vehicles parked in front of Gina's house. Residents of nearby homes stood outside on their porches. No television crews yet, for which he was profoundly grateful.

But Nigel was wounded, and Billy was hunting for Gina.

And if Billy found her, he'd kill her.

Frank pulled around the sawhorses and parked behind the ambulance, trying to visualize Gina's bedroom closet. Inside the closet was a hinged plywood door with a small knob. A thin piece of plywood keeping her safe.

For the moment, anyway.

Years ago when Gina showed it to him, she'd said, "When I was a little kid, five or six years old, I thought it was the coolest thing. Go in the pantry, climb a dark narrow staircase and come out in the bedroom closet."

Now she was sitting on those stairs, terrified, hiding from a demented killer with a gun.

He dialed her cell. The instant she clicked on he said, "Gina, I'm outside the house now. Stay calm. We're going to get you out. Can you tell where Billy is? Have you heard any sounds in the last few minutes?"

"Yes," she whispered. "A loud bang."

He gripped the phone. "Nearby? In the your bedroom?"

"No. But that was awhile ago."

"Okay. Stay on the line while I talk to the cops. Don't hang up."

"Thanks, Franco."

His throat thickened. Gina, thanking him, in the midst of her terror.

"Hang in there. I'm going to get you out, I promise."

He left the car and ran toward the police vehicles in front of Gina's house. A lanky older man in plain clothes holding a bullhorn met him halfway. "Renzi? Detective Captain John Abbott."

"Thanks for getting here so fast," Frank said.

"Right," Abbot said, "but fifteen minutes ago, when I was on my way here, a woman called 9-1-1 and said she heard shots fired at this location."

"I just talked to the woman who owns the house. She said the suspect shot a man. Now he's after her."

"Where's the woman?"

"Hiding. I just talked to her on her cell and told her the police are here."

"Try and keep her on the line. She might help us pinpoint his location."

And Billy might kill her if he hears her talking. "We need to get her out fast. This guy's a killer."

"Are you still in contact with her?"

"Yes." Frank held up his cell phone. "She's okay for now, but I don't know how long."

"Where is she?"

"There's a hidden staircase in the kitchen pantry that goes up to a second floor bedroom with a widow's walk. That's how we're going to get her out. I know the layout of the house. You got any spare body armor?"

"I've got a Kevlar vest in my trunk. Why?"

"I want to climb up to the widow's walk and bring her out the back window. But we need a ladder."

Abbott frowned. "What if the subject sees you?"

"I need you to distract him. Talk to him on the bullhorn. Keep him focused on the front of the house."

"I'll try, but I don't know if it'll work."

"Make it work," Frank snapped.

Abbott looked at him, taken aback. "You know this woman personally?"

"Yes. Gina Bevilaqua. She writes for the *Herald*. She's gutsy, but she's not safe in that staircase. If he goes in her bedroom closet and sees the hidden door, she's dead. He already shot the man that was staying here, and he beat his mother to a pulp last night at his house in Sandwich."

"Any idea what kind of weapon he's got? Or how much ammo?"

"We found a box in his room for a Mark IV semi-automatic, no telling how much ammo he's got."

"What about the injured man?"

"I don't know where he is or anything about his condition." Frank didn't want to tell Abbott it was Nigel Heath. That would only cause a delay, and he had no time to waste. He had to get Gina out now.

"Gina said Billy shot him. Billy Karapitulik, the suspect. She can only whisper a few words at a time. If she talks any louder, he'll hear her. I figure shots were fired downstairs and she ran upstairs to get away. We need to move fast. Get me the vest. While I'm suiting up, have your officers put a stepladder up to the widow's walk at the rear of the house. Hurry!"

CHAPTER 39

--

He stood beside the front door and peeked out the window at the cops.

Ten minutes ago one of them had yelled at him with a bullhorn.

"Billy, you're surrounded. Put down your weapon and come out of the house with your hands behind your head."

Giving him orders. Like his mother. Making pain in his head

When that happened, he had been upstairs in the reporter's bedroom. Fury jolted him into action. Squinting down the barrel of the Mark IV, he lined the man up in the sights, a tall man with silvery-gray hair.

But he didn't dare shoot. He'd already wasted two bullets, and he didn't want to waste any more, not until he found the reporter. After he killed her, he would use the remaining bullets to kill some cops. Then he had decided to come downstairs to get a better look at the cop that was ordering him around.

Now there were more police officers, milling around like hornets swarming a hive. An ambulance was parked beyond the line of police cars.

He smiled. Who did they think they were going to save?

The conductor? Fat chance. The reporter? Not if he could help it.

He left the window and walked past Nigel Heath. His lucky winner lay on the floor, eyes staring at nothing. The stench was horrible. He didn't want to look at the blood, but he couldn't avoid it.

Fearing he'd puke, he hurried to the stairway, crept upstairs and stood in the hallway, listening. All quiet up here.

He advanced down the hall, holding the gun in front of him chest high, and stopped at the reporter's bedroom. He'd left the door open. Not that he thought she'd come out from wherever she was hiding.

She was too scared to do that. She knew he had a gun.

He tiptoed into the bedroom. Where could she be?

He'd already looked under the bed. Maybe she was hiding in the closet.

His heart thrummed with excitement as he approached the closet.

But as he reached for the door knob, a telephone rang, not a cell phone, the one downstairs on the table beside the futon.

The shrill sound shot through him, making mouth-mother pain in his head. Who was calling? The cops?

———

It took ten endless minutes to find a stepladder and put it in place. Frank used the time to strap on the Kevlar vest. When he finished, he got on his cell and told Gina he'd get her out soon. Detective Abbott was following the plan, calling to Billy on the bullhorn every minute or so to focus his attention on the front of the house, not the back.

Abbott came to the corner of the cottage. Frank trotted over to him and said, "We're set, but I need a diversion after I go up the ladder. When I'm in position, I'll have one of your officers give you a high sign. Then I need you to distract him."

Abbott gave him a dubious look. "Yeah? How do I do that? Offer to get him a Big Mac?"

"No. I want you to fuck with his head. Call the number I gave you. It's the landline to the house. The phone is hooked up to an answering machine so you'll get voicemail after three or four rings. Don't leave a message. Hang up and get on the bullhorn and tell him his mother wants to talk to him."

Abbott's eyes widened. "I thought you said he killed her."

"He did, and believe me, it was brutal. But distraction is the name of the game. It will get him thinking, might cause him to make a mistake. I'm heading out now. Give me a minute."

He trotted along the side of Gina's cottage and stopped at the corner.

The back side of the two-story house overlooked the ocean. A brisk sea breeze hit his face, but it didn't cool him off. He was drenched in sweat, droplets running down his nose. He focused his mind and got into a zone.

Get Gina out of there and capture Billy.

———

Billy stood in the bedroom doorway, counting the rings, willing the sound to stop. After four rings, the phone went silent. He went back in the bedroom and reached for the doorknob, about to open the closet door.

The telephone started ringing again. The strident sound grated on his ears, just like his mother's nagging voice, questioning him, belittling him. Forbidding him to leave the house.

But not anymore.

Flushed with anger, he turned away from the closet and went to the front window that overlooked the street.

Now the cop with the silvery-gray hair raised the bullhorn. "Billy. Please answer the phone. Your mother wants to talk to you."

He reeled back as though he'd been shot. His mother?

His MOTHER wanted to talk to him? Mouth-mother pain in his head.

"Stop!" he screamed.

"Billy! Answer the phone. Your mother wants to talk to you." The voice on the bullhorn.

He ran out of the bedroom and raced downstairs. The telephone was louder down here, a shrill insistent sound that penetrated his head.

Warily, he moved closer to the futon and stared at the telephone.

His mother wanted to talk to him? How could she?

Last night he'd beaten her head to a pulp.

Or had he only imagined it?

Just like the thousands of times he had imagined it . . .

———

Weighed down by the four-pound Kevlar vest, Frank scrambled up the ladder, sweating from the heat buildup inside the insulated vest. Jammed into the waistband of his pants underneath his shirt, his Sig Sauer was a reassuring presence.

He swung one leg over the railing of the widow's walk, then the other.

A faint voice came from the front of the house, Abbott yelling to Billy with the bullhorn.

He gave the two officers holding the ladder a thumbs up and studied the fifteen-foot portion of the cottage that bordered the widow's walk. Two tall windows to his left, a small round window to his right.

Three long strides got him to the smaller window. He peered through it and saw a long hallway. But nobody with a gun.

The two larger windows opened onto Gina's bedroom. He crept to the closest one, risked a quick peek inside and saw no one.

Then he heard a telephone ring. Excellent. Abbott was calling Gina's landline, then messing with Billy's head with the bullhorn.

The bedroom window was double hung, six small panes of glass above the sash, six more below it. He put his palms on the sash and shoved. The window didn't budge. Then he noticed the half-moon metal device in the center of the sash. Damn! The window was locked.

He went to the railing and motioned to the two cops.

In a soft voice, he said, "Window's locked. Throw me your shirt. I need to break one of the panes."

Without hesitation, one officer stripped off his shirt, exposing his Kevlar vest, wadded up the shirt and threw it up to him. He caught it and returned to the window.

If Billy heard breaking glass, would he rush upstairs?

Frank wrapped the shirt around his fist and waited.

The instant he heard the telephone ring, he punched the pane of glass above the lock with his fist.

The glass broke into large pieces that fell into the room. He reached through the opening, released the lock, put both hands on the sash and pushed. To his relief, the bottom half of the window opened. He tossed the cop's shirt over the railing and climbed into the bedroom.

Now the sound of the telephone was louder.

He heard a voice scream: "Shut up!" Billy's voice, downstairs.

Moving quickly, he went to Gina's closet and opened the door. Several shirts and three pairs of pants hung from a wooden dowel. He shoved them aside and saw the plywood door. He tapped it once and said softly, "Gina, it's me." He yanked on the knob and the plywood door opened.

"Franco." A soft whisper.

But he couldn't see her. The stairway was dark as pitch.

"Get up here," he whispered. "Hurry!"

He heard sounds, and then she was in his arms, moaning, her body shaking like trees in a hurricane.

"Come with me," he whispered, "but be quiet. You need to go out the window."

She gripped his hand. Her hand felt cold and clammy. He led her out of the darkened closet. In the sunlight, her face looked ashen, beaded with sweat. Downstairs, the telephone rang again. Gina flinched.

"Shh," he said, and gestured at the open window. "There's a ladder propped up to the widow's walk. Two cops are there. They'll help you down."

She gazed at him, eyes wide, terror-filled eyes.

He helped her out the window and pointed to the ladder.

"Go," he whispered.

She grabbed his arm. "What about you?"

"Go," he said urgently. "Now."

He waited until she swung her legs over the railing and got on the ladder. Then he returned to the closet. The plywood door to the secret staircase was still open. He shut the bedroom closet door, slipped into the dark narrow staircase and pulled the plywood door closed behind him.

Inky darkness and a musty odor enveloped him.

He inched down the staircase one step at a time, willing Abbott to keep calling Gina's landline.

Distracting Billy was a crucial part of his plan.

The door in the closet was hidden, but the door at the bottom of the stairs in the kitchen pantry wasn't.

CHAPTER 40

He stared at the telephone. Now it was silent, but that didn't fool him.

Sometimes his mother was silent too, watching him, planning her next attack. He knew the phone would ring again. Then the cop with the bullhorn would yell at him. He mopped sweat off his forehead with his shirtsleeve, trying to ignore the stench. Nigel's stench.

He didn't want to look at him. If he saw the blood, he might puke.

Then, as he knew it would, the telephone rang, sending mouth-mother pain into his head. Fury boiled into his throat.

"Shut up!" he screamed. "Shut up, shut up, shut up! Leave me alone!"

Another ring. A third and a fourth. Then, silence.

The answering machine clicked and whirred.

He stared at the machine. It looked a lot like the machine in Victoria's apartment. Nigel, the lucky winner, calling her, leaving a message, saying he'd be there soon. Interrupting his glorious triumph.

Just like the cops. Interrupting his plan, distracting him.

He had to find the reporter.

But his bladder felt dangerously full, a nagging ache low in his gut. Where was the bathroom? His throat was dry and scratchy, too. He wanted a drink of water, but if he went in the kitchen he would have to pass Nigel's body. And the blood.

"Billy."

He flinched. The man with the bullhorn. The phone began to ring.

He stared at it, counting the rings. One. Two. Three.

"Answer the phone, Billy. Your mother wants to talk to you."

"Liar!" he screamed. "Liar, liar, liar! My mother is dead!"

His heart pounded, making his blood surge, the merciless mouth-mother pain ripping into his head.

"I'll fix you," he muttered.

Steeling himself, he turned and sidled past Nigel's body.

254

Don't look at the blood. Don't look. Don't.

He squeezed his eyes to slits and focused on the toolbox on the floor in front of the television set. Holding the gun in one hand, he took a claw hammer out of the toolbox. It felt good in his hand, heavy and powerful.

Rugged and reliable, like his Mark IV. But when he turned, he saw the dark red clumps of clotted blood under Nigel's head. Disgusting. Gritting his teeth, he edged past it. The stench was nauseating, worse than a gas station restroom that hadn't been cleaned in a month, stinking of piss and shit.

That didn't deter him from his goal. With single-minded purpose, he put the gun down on the futon, wiped sweat off his face and stared at the telephone, waiting for it to ring.

"This time I'll fix you," he muttered.

Seconds later the shrill sound erupted, mouth-mother-pain attacking his head. Grasping the claw hammer in both hands, he swung it at the telephone.

The black plastic receiver broke in half. Still he pounded, harder and harder, pounding the evil machine with all his might. The telephone shattered and pieces of black plastic scattered over the floor.

The evil sound stopped.

He dropped the hammer on the futon beside the Mark IV and massaged his temples. Mouth-mother-pain in his head. Would the pain never stop?

"Billy," said a deep voice.

Startled, he grabbed the Mark IV. That wasn't the man on the bullhorn outside. That was different voice. Closer. Behind him.

He whirled and looked, but saw no one.

"Billy, I need you to put down your weapon and—"

"Shut up!" he screamed. "Stop giving me orders!"

"I understand how frightened you must be—"

"I am not! I've got a gun."

"Billy, I just want to talk. My name is Frank. Let's just relax for a minute and talk."

He felt a sudden desperate urge to pee. Moaning softly, he squeezed his thighs together. If he wet his pants, it would be a total humiliation.

Where was the man? The cop named Frank. The man didn't say he was a cop, but that didn't fool him. The man thought he was stupid. He couldn't see him, but he sensed his presence. How did the cop get into the house?

Cops were killers. Was this cop going to kill him?

His heart pounded. He felt like a rabbit cornered by a wolf, abuzz with fear, clammy with sweat. This must be how the rabbit felt right before the wolf's teeth tore him apart.

He realized he was holding his breath and sucked in air, filling his lungs. That made him feel better.

Why be afraid of the cop? There were still bullets in his Mark IV.

"Why should I talk to you?"

"Let's make a deal, Billy. Put down the gun, and I'll come in the living room so we can talk."

"You think I'm stupid? You're a cop. I bet you've got a gun, too." He stared at the archway that led to the kitchen. If the cop took one step through that doorway, he'd shoot him.

"I don't think you're stupid, Billy. I think you're very smart."

"Liar. You don't even know me."

"Yes, I do. I've been following your activities. You killed a lot of lottery winners, didn't you?"

"Yes. And no one could stop me."

"How many did you kill?"

He frowned. Was this a trick?

"I don't remember. A lot."

"It started in Poughkeepsie, right? With Lulu?"

That surprised him. Maybe the cop *did* know about him. Lulu was his first lucky winner. Maybe the cop was telling the truth. It sounded like he admired his skill. "Lulu was my first," he said. "Lucky Lulu."

"And seven more, right?"

He glanced at the body lying on the floor in a puddle of blood.

"Wrong. You forgot Nigel. He was the real winner. That's what the reporter said." He stopped. The reporter. The incessantly-ringing telephone and the cop with the bullhorn had made him forget about her. He glanced at the staircase. Should he run upstairs now and kill her? No. If he turned his back on the cop, the cop might shoot him.

"What do you want, Billy? Are you hungry? I can get you some food if you want."

"Shut up. You're giving me a headache." Mouth-mother pain, pounding his head.

"Tell me what you want, Billy."

"I want you to go away and leave me alone."

———

Frank mopped sweat off his brow with his shirtsleeve. This was going nowhere fast. He was relieved that Gina was safe, and Abbott had done his part, distracting Billy. But now that Frank had managed to get downstairs and draw Billy's attention by naming one of his victims, all the scumbag wanted to do was brag about how many innocent people he'd slaughtered.

A kaleidoscope of images played in his mind. Photographs of Billy's victims. The achingly-sad publicity shot of Vicky holding her clarinet, smiling. Her father's anguished expression and his angry words: *I want you to get the putz that did this to my Victoria.*

Vicky's father wanted justice and so did Frank. As it had countless times since Vicky's wake, anger rose up inside him, a palpable rage that clogged his throat and made his blood boil. Vicky deserved justice, and so did all the other victims this egomaniac had murdered. He had no idea what had driven Billy to kill, and he didn't care.

He glanced out the kitchen window. The sun was going down, an orange-red sphere low in the sky. Soon it would be dark, and darkness would bring nothing but problems. He had to take the Jackpot Killer down now, and the only way to do that was to establish some kind of rapport with him.

That's what negotiations were about, personal relationships.

Forget your contempt for the suspect. Empathize with him. Figure out what he wants. Flatter him. Exploit his weaknesses. Show him he's not alone. Somebody cares about him. A moment ago when he'd asked Billy what he wanted, Billy had said: *Go away and leave me alone.*

"Billy," he said, "I don't want to leave you by yourself in here. I'd worry about you."

No response from the living room. "Tell me how you found Nigel. That was very clever. How did you do it?"

"Ha. That was easy. The reporter gave her business card to my mother."

Jesus! Gina hadn't told him she'd given her card to Mrs. Karapitulik.

Frank sucked in air, a deep breath down to his diaphragm. It brought the odor of death to his nostrils.

Nigel Heath, dead in the living room.

"On the card, it said she worked for the *Herald*, so I figured she lived near Boston. I checked to see if she had cable and found this address."

Frank gritted his teeth. The deadly trails we leave behind. Cable television connections that allowed a demented cable worker to access his victims' homes.

"How did you know Nigel was here?"

"Where else would he be? My mother said he was her friend."

That answered one question, but it didn't solve his problem. Billy didn't seem interested in giving up his gun or surrendering.

What would work? A threat? A promise?

Suddenly it dawned on him. He knew exactly what Billy wanted. Billy wanted to be admired. In his mind, killing all those lottery winners was an accomplishment. Billy wanted an audience.

"How about if I get a television crew to come to the house and tape an interview with you?"

Silence. Then, "You could do that?"

"Sure, but you'd have to give me your gun first. They'd never agree to come in here and interview a man with a gun."

"Bullshit. You're trying to trick me. You just want me to give up my gun."

So much for that idea, Frank thought. His body trembled, overwhelmed with fatigue. He was fresh out of patience. This had to end, now.

"Here's the deal, Billy. The house is surrounded. You can stay here as long as you want, but you can't escape. Bottom line, this house is your prison. I'm coming in the living room. You better not shoot, Billy, because right now, I'm the only friend you've got."

No response from Billy. A jolt of adrenaline upped his heart rate. Now or never. Time to step into the danger zone. The Kevlar vest would protect his torso, but not his head or his legs.   —

He gripped the Sig with both hands, set his forefinger on the trigger and edged to the archway. No sudden moves.

He eased into the archway and braced himself.

No shots, no sounds, just silence.

A red-faced man with blood-spattered cheeks stood in front of Gina's futon. A short dumpy man, holding a black semi-automatic in his hands.

Frank had expected an innocent-looking man, a man able to convince unsuspecting women to let him into their homes. Part of it was true. Billy had a round chubby face and average features, but his wide blue eyes projected a mix of cruelty and malevolence. Directed at him.

Crouched in the doorway, Frank glanced at Nigel Heath. Ten feet away, the conductor lay on the floor, his head resting in a pool of congealed blood. Another victim of this demented egomaniac.

Anger bubbled into his throat, but he fought it down.

Stay cool and focus on the killer.

"I bet you remember the names of all those lottery winners you killed, don't you, Billy?"

"Yes."

"You kill someone, you never forget them, right?" Frank said, gripping his weapon, alert for the slightest motion, the tiniest indication that Billy was going to shoot.

"That's right. My lucky winners. I remember every one of them."

Right, you sick-O. You named your goldfish after them.

"What about your mother? Was she a lucky winner?"

"Shut up! Don't talk to me about my mother!"

"Why did you kill her?"

"All the suffering she caused? I made her pay!" A vicious snarl.

"Whose suffering?"

"Mine!" Billy was breathing hard, his cheeks mottled a deep red, his face twisted in a vindictive mask.

"What kind of suffering?"

Billy said nothing, glaring at him, still as a statue, both hands clenched on the gun.

Frank tried to work up some sympathy for him. Maybe he'd been jilted by a girl as a teenager. Maybe someone made fun of him because he was short and had a boyish face with chubby red cheeks. His mother, maybe.

Or his father. Or his brother. J&B. John and Billy.

"What about your father? Did he make you suffer?"

"Shut up! My father's dead!"

"Maybe it was your brother. But he died in the car accident, didn't he?"

"Yes, and I'm glad! He deserved it."

"So that left your mother, right?"

"Stop bugging me about my mother. She got what was coming to her!"

"You can't bring yourself to say her name, can you?"

"Shut up shut up shut up!"

"Her name was Judy, right?"

"Don't talk about Judy!"

He had an instant flashback to the mangled goldfish on the floor in Billy's basement room. The mother seemed to be a sore point. If he provoked him, Billy might make a mistake.

"Which Judy?" Frank said. "Judy Garland? Or your mother?"

Billy pulled the trigger.

The slug hit him square in the chest.

The Kevlar vest absorbed part of the impact. Even so, the slug knocked him backwards onto the floor, punching his chest, ripping the air from his lungs. He rolled away and scrambled under Gina's piano.

Billy shot at him again. Bam, bam, bam.

Even after his ammo ran out, Billy kept shooting, the firing pin clicking on an empty chamber.

Frank squirmed out from under the piano, struggled to his feet and advanced on Billy.

"Leave me alone!" Billy screamed, and threw the Mark IV at him.

He ducked and the gun clattered to the floor near one leg of the piano.

"I hate you!" Billy's face turned crimson. "You never loved me! You only loved John. You said I wasn't even your son."

Who said that? Frank wondered. Billy's father?

But he had no time to analyze it.

With a scream of rage, Billy lowered his head and charged at him.

He braced himself, whacked the side of Billy's head with his Sig, and they fell to the floor.

Yelling and screaming, Billy squirmed away, but Frank caught him.

Billy kicked out with one foot, slamming it into Frank's chest.

He grabbed Billy's ankles, jerked hard and rolled him onto his back.

"I hate you!" Billy screamed, his face contorted in rage.

Frank sat on his mid-section and pinned his arms against his sides with his knees. Breathing hard, sweating profusely, he tried to catch his breath. Sweat ran down his nose and dripped onto Billy's face.

"Get off me!" Billy screamed, beating at his chest with his fists.

SUSAN FLEET

Frank heard voices outside the front door. Abbott and his troops were following the plan: If you hear shots, break through the front door. Which didn't leave him much time. He stuck the Sig in his waistband, grabbed Billy's hands, squeezed hard and saw the pain register in Billy's eyes.

"Stop," Billy whimpered.

Billy thought this was as bad as it was going to get. It wasn't.

Frank squeezed harder.

"Stop hurting me. I didn't do anything to you."

Frank thought about Vicky, a talented clarinetist with a brilliant career ahead of her, thought about the pain and anguish her death had caused her family, not to mention her lover, Nigel Heath. It took all the restraint he could muster not to punch Billy in the face.

He stared into Billy's eyes and squeezed his hands as hard as he could.

"Shut up you worthless piece of shit. The women you murdered didn't deserve to die. You're a coward. You didn't even have the guts to look them in the face, had to put a bag over their head. Those women had friends and family, people who loved them. If it weren't for you, they'd still be alive."

Then the front door shattered and the cops burst inside and it was bedlam, footsteps pounding the floor, voices screaming: *Drop your weapon!*

A moment later Abbott put a hand on his arm.

"It's okay, Frank. You can let him up. We got him."

Frank let go of Billy, rose to his feet and felt an enormous weight come off his shoulders.

At last it was over. Billy was going to jail.

Never again would the Jackpot Killer kill another innocent person.

CHAPTER 41

Hunched over in the police cruiser, reliving the horror, Gina shivered uncontrollably, unable to rid her mind of the hideous images. The hatred in Billy's eyes. The gun in his hands. The blood gushing from Nigel's mouth.

Now she was safe, but Franco wasn't.

He was inside her house with Billy. And Nigel. Poor Nigel.

Was he alive? It seemed like an eternity had passed since Billy shot him.

After the police officer helped her down the ladder, he had asked if she needed medical attention. She said she didn't, but a seriously-wounded man was still in the house. The officer told her the emergency workers couldn't go inside until the gunman was disarmed. Then he'd brought her to Franco's squad car.

Endless minutes crawled by, like cars inching past a wreck on the Expressway. She wanted to scream, wanted to tell the policemen to hurry up and break into her house. But her legs felt like jelly, every muscle in her body quivering with exhaustion. Most of all, she wanted Franco to be safe.

Her body felt weird, hot and cold at the same time. It was hot outside, hotter still in the squad car, but she felt like a giant bag of ice was inside her, freezing her in place. She stared at her front door, willing it to open.

More than anything in the world she wanted to see Franco walk out that door, safe and sound.

There had to be a dozen policemen clustered around the cruisers in front of her house. Why didn't they go in and help him?

Then she heard a gunshot.

A chill ran down her neck and her throat closed up.

More shots, one after another.

"No," she whispered.

Billy was shooting at Franco. She'd seen the fury in his eyes. He was insane, full of rage and hate.

Now, led by a tall gray-haired man in civilian clothes, eight policemen were running to her front door, their weapons drawn. One officer carried a battering ram. Gina clenched her fists, watching him ram the device against the door—bam, bam, bam—the sound clearly audible through the open car window.

Damn it to hell! What was taking them so long?

At last the door gave way and the policemen burst into her house.

Eyes fixed on the door, she held her breath.

Her vision blurred and she realized she was crying. But it felt like someone else was crying, a strange out-of-body sensation, as though she were on a faraway planet, watching herself from a great distance.

One agonizing minute passed. Then another.

Her heart pounded. She could hardly breathe. *Please let Franco be all right.*

Two policemen muscled Billy through the front door, his hands cuffed behind him, and led him to a police van.

But where was Franco?

Was he lying on the floor in a puddle of blood like Nigel?

Her throat closed up. She clenched her fists, staring at the door, willing him to appear.

More minutes ticked by, an eternity of increments, each one more painful than the last.

Where was Franco?

At long last, when she'd almost given up hope, he came out the door, carrying his shirt in his hand. Her heart surged. Franco was alive!

He stripped off the bulky gray vest he was wearing and gave it to a police officer. Then he saw her and ran toward the squad car.

Tears of relief spilled from her eyes and ran down her cheeks.

———

Frank jumped in his squad car and looked at Gina. Tears were running down her cheeks. "Hey," he said.

He pulled her to him and wrapped his arms around her. Her body was shaking, as though she had chills from the flu.

"Franco," she gasped, her breath warm against his neck. "When I heard all those gunshots, I thought Billy shot you."

Frank stroked her cheek. "He did, but the slug hit the Kevlar vest. See?" He showed her the hole in his shirt. "Then I dived under your piano. He kept shooting until he was out of ammo, but he didn't hit anything."

She wiped away the tears, gazing at him with her dark eyes. "If he killed you, I don't know what I would have done."

"But he didn't. And now he's going away for a long time. Justice for Vicky and all the other victims."

"What about Nigel?"

He hesitated. He was certain Nigel was dead, but he didn't want to tell her. "He didn't look good."

"He saved my life," Gina said in a shaky voice.

"Don't think about it," he whispered, stroking her cheek. "We can talk about it later."

She looked at him. Her eyes had that thousand-yard stare, the look he'd seen in the eyes of other victims of violent crimes.

"Billy was acting crazy," she said, "walking around, ranting, waving the gun at us. Nigel was sitting on the futon. I was standing near the stairs. All of a sudden Nigel yelled: *Run, Vicky, run away.* Then he jumped up and tackled Billy and the gun went off and they fell on the floor. It was horrible."

Frank listened to the torrent of words, rubbing her back, knowing she had to get it out.

"It happened so fast. Nigel was bleeding, blood gushing from his mouth. I knew he was hurt. I took out my cell phone to call 9-1-1, but Billy and Nigel were on the floor, fighting for the gun. When Nigel tried to get the gun away from Billy, the gun went off again and then—" She swallowed hard.

"You don't have to talk about it now. We can talk later when you're feeling better."

"No. I have to explain about Nigel." Gina looked at him, her eyes brimming with tears. "I'm sorry I didn't tell you he was here. But when he called me Wednesday night, he sounded desperate. Suicidal, like his mother. I was afraid he might kill himself. The next morning I snuck him out of the hotel and brought him to the beach house. I only wanted to help, but now he's dead." Tears spilled over and ran down her cheeks.

Aching for her, he kissed her cheek. "Don't second-guess yourself, Gina. You did what you thought was right. People do what they do."

"I know, but I should have told you."

Frank smiled. "Yeah, well, I suspected it might be you that smuggled him out of the hotel. Gerry Mulligan was furious when he went there and Nigel was gone."

"But if Gerry had arrested him, Nigel would have been in jail and—"

"Gina, stop. You did what you could. Maybe Nigel wanted to be with Vicky. Maybe he didn't want to live without her."

She sucked in a big breath and let it out. "I can still see the haunted look in his eyes. He felt so guilty about Vicky. Nigel jumped Billy and that saved my life. After Billy shot him again, I heard him say: *Vicky.*"

"He was brave to do what he did, going after a maniac with a gun. But in the end his thoughts were with the woman he loved." Frank took a crumpled pack of cigarettes out of his glove compartment.

In a crisis, never give up your favorite crutch.

He rolled down his window, lit two cigarettes, and gave one to Gina. Anything to make her feel better. Would he ever see her smile again?

She took a drag and exhaled, a heavy sigh. "What about Billy's mother?"

Telling her about Billy's mother would be another devastating blow. But she'd find out soon enough. This would be a huge story. Tonight it would be all over the news.

"Billy killed her."

Gina's face crumpled. "Why? Why would he kill his own mother? And all those other women?"

Frank visualized the horrific scene at Billy's house. "Only Billy knows for sure. But it's clear that he hated his mother. Maybe that's why he killed older women who won the lottery. Maybe they were stand-ins for his mother. Maybe he was working up the guts to kill his mother all along."

Gina puffed her cigarette and blew smoke out the window, staring off into the distance.

"Try not to think about it," he said, and threw his butt out the window. His mouth tasted awful, dry as sawdust. He wanted to drink a gallon of water, followed by a large bottle of beer.

A cell phone rang. He checked, but it wasn't his. Gina took hers out and checked the ID. Her shoulder slumped. "Sorry, Franco, I need to take this." She clicked on and said, "Hello."

Frank watched noxious emotions ripple over her face: distress, anxiety, then fear. Whoever was calling wasn't someone she wanted to talk to.

She stayed silent for awhile. At last she said, "Ryan, this is not a good time to talk."

Her husband. Maybe he should leave and give her some privacy.

But then he heard Ryan's voice, loud and strident, indistinct sounds, not individual words. Frank clenched his fists.

Gina didn't need more hassles right now. A tear ran down her cheek.

That tore him up. He reached over and gently took the cell phone out of her hand. When he held it to his ear, he heard a voice yell: ". . . told you to start acting like a wife, but you're too wrapped up in your stupid job to pay any attention to me. I don't know why I married you. I invite you to go away for a weekend and you blow me off. Today I came home to an empty house. Again. You're screwing that Pops conductor, aren't you? When I find out where you are, I'm going to come over and slap the shit out of you."

"Are you done?" Frank said.

Silence on the other end. Then, "Who's this?"

"Never mind who's this. Your wife just went through a traumatic experience. She's in no shape to listen to the crap you're dishing out."

"Who are you? What gives you the right to tell me how I should talk to my wife?"

A haze of anger blurred his vision. "You married a terrific woman, Ryan, and you blew it. You don't deserve her. She's is a great reporter, intelligent and gutsy, and she cares about people. All you care about is yourself. If I ever hear you threaten to slap her again, you will regret it. Understand?"

Silence on the other end.

"Tell me you understand, asshole, or I'll come over to that fancy house in Westwood and rip your fucking balls off."

Silence. Then a click. He looked at Gina.

She shook her head, not laughing but close. Moments ago her dark eyes had looked lifeless. Now there was a spark in them.

"Gee, Franco, why not tell him what you *really* think?"

"I meant it," he said, and closed her cell phone. His hands were shaking.

Gina reached over and touched his face. "Thanks, Franco. I can't handle another crisis right now."

He took her hands in his. They were ice cold and clammy with sweat. "Exactly right. You don't need an abusive husband yelling at you. I think you better stay with me tonight."

When she looked at him, her eyes had that familiar spark. "That's the best idea I've heard all day."

"But the Quincy police are going to want to get a statement from you."

The spark left her eyes and her shoulders slumped. "Now?"

"Maybe I can stall them off. Wait here."

Gina reached for her cell phone, but he put it in his pocket. "We're going to get you a new cell with a new number so your asshole husband can't call you. Be back in a second."

He left the car and hurried toward Abbott's police van, marshalling his arguments. He'd just handed Abbott a helluva coup. The lead officer in a hostage situation, collaring a serial killer? Abbot's name would be all over the news, local, national, the works. He figured Abbott owed him a favor.

Abbott saw him coming and got out of the van. "I had my officers take the subject to headquarters. As soon as I wrap things up here, I'll interview him. Want to sit in on it?"

"Yes, but here's the thing. I know you need statements from me and Gina Bevilaqua, but she's very shaken up. Any way we can postpone that?"

Abbott frowned. "Frank, you're a detective. You know it's best to nail things down as soon as possible after an incident like this." Abbott checked his watch. "Man, it's after four. Where did the day go?"

"I don't know. Gina hasn't eaten since breakfast. How about if I bring her to the station in a couple of hours? Six o'clock, say?"

Abbott's mouth quirked. "Okay. But no later."

Frank trotted back to his squad car and got in. "I bought us a couple of hours, told Abbott we'd come to the Quincy police station at six."

"That's good," she said. But her voice was listless, and her eyes had that thousand-yard stare again.

He pulled her close. Her body was shaking again. Maybe she was going into shock. Maybe he should take her to a hospital. Then he thought: Gina doesn't need a hospital. She needs to know someone loves her.

Frank cranked the car and drove past the police vehicles lined up along the street. As he turned onto the main road, a black crime scene van passed them, heading toward Gina's beach house. The crime scene would keep them busy for hours, maybe until midnight.

"Where are we going?" Gina asked, her voice listless.

He almost said, home, thinking of his house in Milton, but he no longer lived there. Evelyn did. A month ago he used to dread going home every night. Now he was living in a crummy motel room, but strangely, that didn't seem to matter. He'd be with Gina, the woman he loved.

"To my Dorchester Palace," Frank said, deadpan. "We'll skip the Chianti and caviar, take a hot shower, get under the covers and cuddle."

She smiled at him, the first smile he'd seen on her face all day.

"That sounds perfect."

####

Wish there were more? There is!

Keep reading for an excerpt of *Natalie's Art*

Susan says . . .

If you'd like an email alert when my next book comes out, sign up at
http://eepurl.com/ExkX9 I'll never use your email for anything else.
If you enjoyed *Jackpot*, I would very much appreciate an honest review on
Goodreads and/or whatever Amazon site you purchased it. Thank you!

ABOUT THE AUTHOR

In her travels, Susan Fleet has worn many hats: trumpeter, college professor,
music historian and award-winning author, to name a few. The Premier Book
Awards named her first novel, *Absolution*, Best Mystery-Suspense-Thriller of
2009. She now divides her time between Boston and New Orleans, the
settings for her crime thrillers. See more at http://www.susanfleet.com Send
her an email, she would love to hear from you!

More crime novels by Susan Fleet

Absolution http://bookShow.me/B003MNH7JY
Diva http://bookShow.me/B0056ASYCU
Natalie's Revenge http://bookShow.me/B009EAWCDK

Non-fiction ebooks by Susan Fleet

Women Who Dared: Trailblazing 20th Century Musicians
Violinist Maud Powell and Trumpeter Edna White
http://www.susanfleet.com/women_who_dared-vol1.html

Dark Deeds: Serial killers, stalkers and domestic homicides
http://bookShow.me/B00CLS62D8

See Susan's true crime blog:
http://darkdeeds.susanfleet.com/index.html#.UhUfUj-YFaI

ACKNOWLEDGMENTS

Creating my Frank Renzi novels has been a remarkable and richly rewarding experience, each in its own way. Because of my music career, Jackpot was a particular pleasure. As a young musician growing up in Massachusetts, I attended many Boston Pops concerts. Years later, I once played for legendary Pops conductor Arthur Fiedler, not with the Boston Pops, but as a freelancer, I worked with many musicians who did, which gave me an insider glimpse of the orchestra. However, the Jackpot characters who play with the Pops are entirely fictional.

Compulsive gambling is a serious problem. For those interested in pursing the topic, I recommend these books: *Thinking Big: Education of a Gambler*, Sol Fox, 1985; *The Luck Business*, Robert Goodman, 1995; *Invisible Masters: Compulsions and the Fears That Drive Them*, George Weinberg, 1993; *Losing Your Shirt: Recovery for Compulsive Gamblers and Their Families*, 2nd ed. 2001

Much of my British lingo came from my longtime friend Richard Lister, a British trombone player and Monty Python enthusiast. Thanks to my British and Australian writer friends, Tom Bryson and Diana Hockley, for other suggestions. Thanks also to Massachusetts State Trooper Bruce O'Rourke for sharing his expertise on Massachusetts homicide cases and crime scene investigations. However, *Jackpot* is a work of fiction. Any errors or inaccuracies are mine alone.

Many thanks to Carolyn Wilkins for her helpful comments on early drafts. Thanks also to Tammy Gross, editor extraordinaire, who found and eliminated all those pesky little mistakes in the manuscript.

And finally, my heartfelt thanks to you, my readers! I would greatly appreciate an honest review of *Jackpot* on whatever site you purchased it. I love hear from readers. You can contact me via my website: www.susanfleet.com
To get an alert when my next book comes out, sign up for an email alert via Mailchimp.

And now, turn the page for a glimpse of
Susan Fleet's next exciting crime thriller, *Natalie's Art*

CHAPTER 1

April 2010   Oxford, UK   2:55 a.m.

"What should I do?" the security guard asked, gazing at her with frightened eyes.

She took out her weapon, a Beretta 92FS with an Evo 9 Suppressor attached to the barrel. The weapon she thought she would never have to use.

"No!" said the guard, raising his hands. "Please! I didn't know he was coming, I swear it! Sometimes he stops by without warning."

Maintaining a calm expression, one that belied her inner turmoil, she went to the security desk and studied the monitor that displayed video from the camera outside the employee entrance. The Security Director, a burly older man with a Van Dyke beard, stood outside the door. He did not appear to be armed. The security guard wasn't either. Brits were touchy about civilians carrying firearms.

She turned away from the security desk and pulled the balaclava down over her face. "Let him in," she said. "I'll hide in the closet in the anteroom."

A slight man with sandy hair and an acne-pitted face, the guard frowned. "Then what?"

She flicked the Beretta. "Hurry up. Unlock the closet."

Fumbling with his key ring, the guard preceded her into the anteroom, a six-foot-by-eight-foot area just inside the employee entrance. He stopped at a door on the left-hand wall and unlocked it.

"Do what you are being paid to do," she hissed. "Let him in. Act normal."

The guard nodded, frowning anxiously, and went to the entry door.

She stepped inside the closet and pulled the door toward her, leaving it open a crack. The closet was dark and smelly. The guards used it to store their clothes after they changed into their uniforms.

Now she couldn't see the guard. She hoped he was punching in the security code for the door so the alarm wouldn't sound when he opened it.

269

But what if he wasn't? Her stomach clenched. What if this was a set-up?

Then she heard the guard say, "Hello, sir. I wasn't expecting you tonight."

"Why would you?" said a gruff voice. "That's the point."

The words failed to reassure her. Shifting the Beretta to her left hand, she took a steel baton out of her knapsack and waited in the darkness, tense and alert. When the Security Director passed the closet, she opened the door, took one step forward and slammed the baton against the side of his head.

The man grunted and slumped to the tiled floor.

The guard's mouth fell open, but he said nothing, his expression horrified.

She stuck the baton in her knapsack. Held the Beretta in her right hand. Her shooting hand.

"What do we do now?" the guard asked in a shaky voice.

"Tie him up," she said curtly. "Use the twine. Put duct tape over his mouth. Hurry!"

The guard took a ball of twine off the security desk and knelt down beside the Security Director.

She checked the time. She'd been here almost thirty minutes. Much too long.

Her cell phone vibrated against her leg. She took it out, punched on and said, "Yes."

"What's going on?" said a gravely voice, a voice that sent chills down her spine.

She'd never met The Voice, but she knew he was nearby. Watching.

"The Security Director paid us an unexpected visit. I disabled him."

"Kill them," said The Voice.

Her heart sank. She only carried the Beretta on these jobs to intimidate the security guards in case they had any last minute reservations.

"Adam didn't know he was coming," she said. Adam was the guard's code name, not his real one.

The guard had bound the Security Director's wrists and ankles and was putting tape over his mouth. When she said his code name, the guard's head jerked up.

"Shoot them," said The Voice. "If you don't, you will die, too."

She had no doubt of it. "Got it," she said, and closed the phone.

The guard rose to his feet and backed away, staring at her eyes, the only part of her face not hidden by the balaclava.

"I didn't know he was coming. I didn't!"

"I believe you, but we have to make this look like you weren't involved, remember? Give me the twine, turn around and put your hands behind your back so I can bind your wrists."

As docile as a sheep, the guard gave her the twine, turned around and put his hands behind his back.

She shot him in the back of the head. The Beretta made a soft popping sound, and the guard fell to the floor. Blood spurted from his head.

A momentary flashback blindsided her. Shooting Tex in the back of the head near the golf course in New Orleans. Her throat tightened. She gritted her teeth, willing the memory away.

She had to get out of here, fast. But first she had to finish the job.

Rigid with tension and full of angst, she stood over the Security Director's lifeless form, curled on the floor, his eyes mercifully closed. She extended the Beretta, then lowered it to her side.

How could she kill this defenseless man?

Shoot them. If you don't, you will die, too.

Tears misted her eyes. Why did it always come down to this? Her life or someone else's?

Fighting down her revulsion, she shot the man in the head. Nauseated and sick at heart, she jammed the Beretta into the knapsack. She had no time for remorse or guilt feelings, she had to get out. Anxious to leave, she took a last look around. Certain she'd left no trace of herself, she grabbed the flat carton that held the Rembrandt, went to the employee entrance and tried to calm herself.

Her heart refused to cooperate, pounding her chest like a wild thing.

Where was The Voice? Somewhere near the museum, for sure. Not close enough to hear the gunshots, but close enough to see her when she left.

Her heart pounded as she opened the door and stepped into the darkness. The moon was hidden, the sky overcast with clouds. She closed the door, averted her face and strode past the security camera. Then she pulled off the balaclava, stuck it in her pocket and set off down the sidewalk with a purposeful stride.

Walk, don't run. Running attracted attention, and that was the last thing she wanted, not while she was carrying a painting worth several million dollars. The getaway car was two blocks away. The two-door Toyota Yaris was stolen. The license plate was also stolen, stripped from a different vehicle, one that wouldn't cause problems if by chance the police stopped her. She'd been given a cover story in case that happened.

Be prepared. Leave nothing to chance.

But the Security Director had foiled that part of the plan.

She came to an intersection and crossed the street. So far so good. Usually, she was afraid witnesses would see her, or the police. Not tonight.

Where was The Voice? *If you don't, you will die, too.*

Her stomach clenched. She rotated her head and stretched her neck. This allowed a quick glimpse of the brownstones that lined the street. Her neck prickled. Was The Voice inside one of the buildings, standing in an upper window with a Bushmaster, drawing a bead on her head?

She strode down the sidewalk, breathing in quick, shallow gasps, trying to reassure herself. The Voice wouldn't shoot her now, not while she had possession of the painting.

Gripping the carton, she walked faster. Get to the car and get inside. Then she'd be less of a target.

In the distance, she heard a car engine start somewhere behind her. Her heart jolted. She didn't dare turn and look. Moments later, she glimpsed the faint gleam of headlights behind her, closing fast, the car's engine roaring.

She broke into a dead run. In thirty seconds she reached the Yaris. The headlights came closer.

Forget hiding the Rembrandt in the trunk. Get in the car! With trembling hands, she unlocked the door, yanked it open and jumped inside. A black Mercedes passed her and flashed its lights. The Voice.

Filled with despair, she started the Yaris and pulled out of the space. Ahead of her, the street was deserted. No cars. No black Mercedes. But so what? Now they had a club to hold over her.

Stealing a painting was one thing. Murdering two people was another.

———

1:05 p.m. New Orleans

Riding shotgun with his partner, Homicide Detective Frank Renzi said, "What was he thinking? Steal a car and take the woman with him?"

A complication he didn't need right now, not with an intriguing Interpol message about some recent European art thefts awaiting him in his office.

"Gotta be a nutcase," said Detective Kenyon Miller, grimly focused on the road. "Either that or he's on something. Drive an old rattle-trap that fast? A tire blows, the car might roll over."

Hot, humid air whipped through the open window as their cruiser rocketed up Elysian Fields Avenue—lights but no sirens—in pursuit of the blue Chevy one block ahead of them, a beat-up Cavalier. The carjacker, a white male in his twenties, had held up a bank in the French Quarter, but the teller hit a silent alarm and a patrol car arrived, sirens screaming.

Ten minutes ago, Frank and Miller had been eating lunch two blocks away when their handsets erupted: *Carjacking in the Quarter, white male took off with the female driver, headed north on Elysian Fields.*

"I hear you," Frank said, "but the guy's a bank robber, not Albert Einstein."

"True. No telling what he'll do with the woman."

The Chevy hit the brakes and swerved right into the Gentilly Acres, a new housing development.

Frank got on his handset, identified himself and said, "Carjacker just drove into the Gentilly Acres subdivision. We're in pursuit. Get more squads over here."

Miller swung into Gentilly Acres. Fifty yards ahead of them, the Chevy's speed increased. Moments later one of the front tires blew.

The car careened over a curb, skidded and slammed into a big oak tree.

Miller slowed and stopped twenty yards behind it. Steam billowed out of the Cavalier's hood. The carjacker yanked the woman out of the car and ran, dragging her with him, his hand clamped around her arm.

"My baby!" the woman screamed in a thin, shrill voice.

"Shit," Miller said. "There's a baby in the car?"

Frank jumped out and yelled to Miller, "Stay with the child. I'll take Einstein."

He drew his Sig Sauer and ran after the carjacker. The woman, wearing a bright yellow dress, was fighting the man, dragging her feet to slow him down. They disappeared around the corner of a house.

The subdivision was still under construction, two-story homes along the street roughed-in but not ready for occupancy, no shingles on the exterior or the roof. Frank ran to the corner of the house and saw the carjacker drag the woman through an open door into the adjacent house. A white van stood beside it, THIBIDEAU ELECTRIC stenciled on the side.

He ran to the door, eased inside and stepped into what would someday be a kitchen. The smell of sawdust and fresh-cut wood filled his nostrils. The studs were up on the walls but no sheetrock so he could see into the next room. The carjacker, a scrawny guy in cutoff jeans and a white T-shirt, had the woman clamped to his chest. In his right hand, he held a butcher knife inches away from the woman's throat.

Red splotches stained his white T-shirt. Frank's heart jolted. Jesus, did he already cut her? Then he realized the splotches were from the dye-pack inserted into the money the man had taken at the bank.

"Let the girl go!" said a man's voice.

Two men stepped into Frank's field of vision, the electricians he assumed, white males in their thirties, one tall and wiry, the other short and stocky. The tall one had an electric drill in his hand, the short one held a staple gun, advancing on the carjacker and the woman.

Not good. A disastrous situation was about to get worse. Way worse.

"Get away or I'll cut her," the carjacker screamed, agitated, clenching the woman against his chest with his left forearm, holding the butcher knife in his right hand to her throat.

"Hold it," Frank said, stepping into the room. "Let's all take a deep breath and calm down."

The woman's eyes locked onto his. Her mouth opened but no sound came out. A young, light-skinned black woman, she was maybe five feet tall, couldn't weigh more than ninety pounds. She had a pretty face, looked a lot like Halle Berry, might have been even prettier except for the look of terror on her face.

Fifteen feet away from the carjacker, the electricians stopped and looked at Frank.

"Detective Frank Renzi," he said. "I'd show you my badge, but my hands are busy." Busy holding the Sig Sauer, carefully aimed at the floor, but poised to raise it should the need arise.

The carjacker's lips drew back in a snarl. "Don't come any closer or she's dead."

"No need to harm the lady," Frank said. "Stay calm and nobody gets hurt." To the electricians, he said, "Thank you for your assistance, gentlemen, but I think it would be best if you left." He tilted his head at the doorway behind him and gave them his don't-fuck-with-me look. "Now."

"Okay," said the taller electrician, frowning. "If you say so."

The electricians lowered their makeshift weapons, the drill and the staple gun, and left the area through the doorway Frank had used. He hoped they'd keep going and leave the house, but he didn't dare turn his head to look, didn't dare take his eyes off the carjacker.

"My baby," said the woman, her eyes fixed on Frank.

"Your child is in good hands. My partner's with your baby. He's got two kids of his own. What's your baby's name?"

"Bella. She's only sixteen months old!" the woman said, her voice rising in panic.

Frank gathered himself, got into a zone and focused on the carjacker. Barely out of his teens, the man grew more agitated, eyes darting this way and that, pinprick pupils, looked like he might be on crystal meth. Bad news. Oxy and heroin addicts tended to be laid back and sleepy, but crystal meth was a stimulant. Meth addicts were hyperactive and unpredictable, and often went for days without sleep. Dangerous.

"You're having a rough day, buddy," Frank said, edging closer but not too close, twenty feet away now. "The holdup didn't go the way you planned, then you stole a car with a woman and a baby inside."

"I didn't know the kid was there!"

"I'm sure you didn't. But we need to let the mom get back to her little girl. Give her a hug and make sure she's okay."

The woman nodded, her eyes brimming with tears.

Sirens sounded in the distance. About time, Frank thought.

"Hear the sirens?" he said. "More police will be here soon. Quit while you're ahead. Nobody got hurt. Let the woman go and put down the knife."

"No way!" The man clenched his forearm tighter around the woman.

Her eyes widened and she shook her head. "Please," she whispered.

Frank took a deep breath, assessing the situation, his hands frozen claws around the Sig Sauer. He didn't want to use it, but if push came to shove, he would.

The sirens whooped to a stop somewhere nearby.

The cavalry was here.

Frank locked eyes with the carjacker. "Listen carefully. The bank stickup went wrong and you stole a car. Neither of those things will put away for life, but then you took the woman. Now you're threatening her with a knife, a deadly weapon. That carries big penalties. Let's end this now. Nobody needs to get hurt. Let the woman go, put down the knife, and we'll all walk out of here safe and sound."

"No!" screamed the carjacker, his face contorted, holding the knife to the woman's throat.

Frank set his finger on the trigger and raised the Sig. "Touch her with that knife and you are dead."

"Go ahead! Shoot me!" The carjacker shoved the woman to the floor and charged at Frank, brandishing the knife, his movements uncoordinated, his eyes glassy.

Shoot him, or not? Split seconds to decide. A life or death decision.

At the last instant, Frank dodged the knife and slammed the Sig against the bridge of man's nose with all the force he could muster.

The carjacker dropped the knife and fell to the floor, clutching his bloody nose and screaming obscenities.

Frank kicked the knife away, and a half-dozen officers swarmed the room and subdued the carjacker.

The woman struggled to her knees. When Frank helped her to her feet, she leaned against him, sobbing as though her heart would break.

"You were very brave," he said. "You kept cool and stayed calm. Let's get you back to your little girl."

"Thank you," she said, wiping away tears. "I was afraid he was going to hurt Bella."

"But he didn't. You'll be fine." But not right way. For a while, months probably, she'd have nightmares, thinking about what might have happened.

He should know. It had been two years since Natalie Brixton shot him and he was still having flashbacks. Natalie Brixton, the woman with the distinctive stride.

The Interpol package on his desk included details about a series of European art heists. After the most recent one, a late-night robbery four months ago, someone had seen the thief leave the museum. The witness had told police he was certain it was a woman.

Because of her distinctive walk.

Manufactured by Amazon.ca
Bolton, ON

26504780R00155